KU-202-540

Unexpected Surprises:
Their
Surprise Gift

THERESE BEHARRIE

JENNIFER FAYE

EMILY FORBES

MILLS & BOON

First Published in Great Britain 2022
By Mills & Boon, an imprint of HarperCollins*Publishers,* Ltd
1 London Bridge Street, London, SE1 9GF

www.harpercollins.co.uk

HarperCollins*Publishers*
1st Floor, Watermarque Building,
Ringsend Road, Dublin 4, Ireland

UNEXPECTED SURPRISES: THEIR SURPRISE GIFT © 2022 Harlequin Enterprises ULC.

Tempted by the Billionaire Next Door © 2018 Therese Beharrie
Married for His Secret Heir © 2017 Jennifer F. Stroka
One Night That Changed Her Life © 2017 Emily Forbes

ISBN: 978-0-263-30465-7

MIX
Paper from
responsible sources
FSC
www.fsc.org
FSC™ C007454

This book is produced from independently certified FSC™ paper
to ensure responsible forest management.

For more information visit: www.harpercollins.co.uk/green

Printed and Bound in Spain using 100% Renewable electricity at
CPI Black Print, Barcelona

TEMPTED BY THE BILLIONAIRE NEXT DOOR

THERESE BEHARRIE

For Grant, my best friend.

And Jenny, for taking the squirming, questing and searching journey of friendship with me.

I can't imagine doing this without you.

CHAPTER ONE

JESSICA STEYN HADN'T deliberately sought out the half-naked man who'd entertained her over the last week. But she couldn't deny that watching him had fast become her new favourite hobby.

She watched as he bent over to pick up another stack of logs—watched as the muscles of his naked back rippled, the lightest sheen of sweat defining them even more—and conceded that it was *definitely* top-notch entertainment.

Guilt poked at her, but she ignored it. It wasn't *her* fault that he wasn't wearing a shirt. Nor was it her fault that he'd made a routine of cutting up the trees in his yard. Every day at noon he emerged from the house—wearing an old T-shirt that inevitably got tossed aside about five minutes into his task—and hacked the trunks he'd cut down the day before into logs. He then placed them in a pile, before carrying them over to an enclosed area where he'd set them down and start all over again.

So, ever since she'd noticed there *was* a routine, every day at noon she would settle in front of the window that overlooked his property to enjoy the show.

Thank goodness she'd discovered him, she thought as he gulped down a bottle of water. Water that dribbled over his chin, creating an enticing path down the column of his throat, between his pecs and the impressive ridges of his abs. Her heart rate immediately skyrocketed, and she thought that maybe *she* needed a glass of water, too.

He was a pretty decent distraction in an otherwise boring day. Now that her friend and boss, Anja, was away with her husband, Chet, on business, Jess's days were mostly free. Apart from watching Mr Sexy-Next-Door.

And, of course, thinking about the child she carried.

Before her mind could take that detour—about how this child made Jess feel as if her life was actually worth something for the first time—she thought about how annoyed she was with Anja for not telling her that there *was* a Mr Sexy-Next-Door.

She'd been helping Anja manage her yoga studio for almost two years now, and this was the first time Jess had seen him. Though, to be fair, it was also the first time Jess had stayed at Anja's house for longer than a few days. But she still expected Anja to tell her about the man. Perhaps not as her boss, but as her friend.

And definitely as her *best* friend.

But all thoughts of that vanished when the top log of the stack Mr Sexy had set down started to roll. He'd already turned away, so didn't see the snowball effect of that one log. Jess pushed out of her chair, a wordless cry of warning on her lips, but it was too late. The logs had rolled under his feet and she watched in horror as he fell to the ground, twisting his body so that he landed on his hip.

Before she knew it, she was out of the front door. She had to turn back when she realised she hadn't locked the house and, after she did, she ran as fast as her swollen body would allow to her temporary neighbour's house. She said a silent prayer of thanks when she found his gate open and then she was kneeling beside him, her hands running over the chest she'd admired only minutes before.

She ignored how the grooves of his muscles, his abs, felt beneath her hands and focused on identifying whether anything was broken. She realised that he'd turned over onto his back then, but it only made her pause for a second. Then her hands were on his ankles, his calves, but, before she could feel his thighs or hips, two large hands gripped her wrists.

'I'm not opposed to having a beautiful woman run her hands over me, but maybe we should leave that particular area for when we know each other better.'

Jess felt her face burn and quickly pulled back. But her balance was off and she landed on her butt. Her hand immediately went to her stomach, but she dropped it just as quickly. Not because his eyes had followed the gesture, and the way the interest there had cooled reminded her of the dismissive looks her parents had used to give her, but because she was fairly certain the baby was fine. She hadn't fallen very hard. Though she really had to remember that pregnancy had made her clumsy.

'I'm assuming that response means you didn't knock your head on the way down.' She debated not saying anything else, but she knew she would worry if she didn't ask. 'Are you okay?'

'Yeah, I guess so. Well, as okay as you can be when someone witnesses a couple of logs trip you.' He moved to push up to his forearms, but she crawled forward and set a hand on his chest, pushing him back down.

'You should stay still until we're sure you're really fine.'

'I *am* sure. I'm fine.'

Realising he was the stubborn sort, Jess pressed a hand against his hip and nodded when he winced. 'You're not fine. I'm calling an ambulance.'

Before she could move to her feet, he grabbed her wrist again. This time, she felt the heat of his hand on her arm. Felt the callused bumps at the base of his fingers rub against her skin. She wasn't sure why it sent a flush through her body, but she stilled and then gently pulled her arm out of his grip.

His expression didn't change, though something in his eyes flickered. 'I really am fine. I'll probably have a bruise on my hip tomorrow—and my ego will probably need to be resuscitated since it was murdered so cruelly—but I promise you, I'm fine.'

He sat up then, and she let him. 'Besides,' he continued with a smile that made the flush in her body go hotter, 'if I'm not fine, maybe you'll come to my rescue again.'

'Unlikely,' she replied, ignoring the way her lips wanted to curve at his words. 'I just happened to be looking out of my window when you fell.'

It sounded legitimate, she thought, and almost patted herself on the back when she saw he'd bought her excuse. Good thing, too. She wasn't sure how she could explain the real reason she'd seen him.

'I appreciate you wanting to help me. Are you a doctor?'

'No.'

'Nurse?'

She shook her head.

'So, you just ran over when you saw me fall without any medical skills whatsoever?'

'I was a lifeguard when I was a teenager.' A choice her parents had disapproved of heartily. Funny how they'd chosen to be interested in something so insignificant when they'd ignored everything else in her life. When they'd ignored *her*. 'I have first-aid experience, and falls were the first thing they taught us to deal with.'

'I stand corrected.' His smile was more genuine now, less cocky, and yet it had the same effect on her body.

Or maybe it was the fact that he still didn't have a shirt on, and she was being treated to her afternoon entertainment close-up.

She almost lifted a hand to check whether she was drooling.

'Well, now that I know you're okay I should probably be off.' She took a long time to get to her feet, and cursed silently when she saw how smoothly he did it.

'How can I repay you?'

She snorted. 'For what? Rushing over here and embarrassing us both?'

'Why would you be embarrassed?'

Good question. 'Because clearly you were fine and I panicked over nothing?'

'You panicked?'

She rolled her eyes. 'It was a hard fall, okay? I was worried.'

She couldn't tell what had changed on his face, but something had. And it made his already too perfect features seem even more appealing. 'So, I'm repaying you for being worried. It's not often that people care.'

'No, it isn't,' she agreed, feeling the words hit a little too close to home. 'But I don't need to be repaid. You're fine. Right?' He nodded. 'So, I'll be seeing you.'

She turned to leave and managed to get a few steps away from the gate before his voice called out, 'Which window?'

She turned back. 'What?'

'From which window did you see me fall?'

'That one.' She nodded to the window on the second level of the house next door, grateful that the chair she'd been sitting on—or the chips she'd been eating while watching him—wasn't visible.

'That's my sister's house.'

It took a moment for her mind to process the new information. 'Your sister?' she repeated. '*You're* Dylan?'

'Yeah,' he said, his forehead creasing. 'Who are you? And why are you staying in my sister's house?'

'I'm Jess. Jessica,' she added quickly. 'I'm staying at the house while Anja and Chet are away.'

His features tightened. 'Away where?'

'Sydney. They wanted to get Anja's new yoga studio up and running before the—' She caught herself before it was too late. She couldn't tell Dylan about the baby. Anja would kill her. And she didn't need to upset one of the few people who cared about her. 'Does she know you're here?'

'No.'

'Oh.'

There was a long stretch of silence before either of them spoke again. And then she asked, 'You've been back for at least a week. Why haven't you come over? Or tried to call her?'

He frowned. 'How do you know how long I've been back for?'

Jess felt her eyes widen, her cheeks heat, before she managed to reply with something other than *I've been watching you.* 'I heard the garbage truck pick up your bin earlier this week.' She held her breath and hoped he'd buy the somewhat lame excuse.

'And how do you know that I haven't tried to call her?'

'She…would have told me.'

He studied her. 'How exactly do you know Anja?'

Something about the way he asked it put her back up. 'I'm her PA.'

'She let her PA stay in her house?' There was barely a pause before he continued. 'She would tell her PA if her brother called her?'

Jess straightened. 'Yes. Your sister and I are also friends. Good friends.' She kept her hand from going to her stomach—to the proof of the bond that she and Anja shared—and forced herself to calm down when an inner voice questioned why she was responding so defensively. 'I didn't realise it was you when I came over.'

'But you knew I lived next door?'

'Yes,' she replied, but it got her thinking about why it hadn't occurred to her that Mr Sexy-Next-Door was actually Anja's brother. 'I knew you lived next door, but Anja didn't tell me *which* next door you lived in.'

'And you never asked?'

You're not exactly a topic of conversation either of us readily bring up. 'It didn't matter.'

'Because my sister doesn't talk about me?'

'Because you weren't here.'

Though both answers were true, it seemed as if Dylan cared more about the option she'd offered. Because when he'd given *his* option his face hadn't tightened the way it had after *she'd* spoken. Hurt hadn't flashed across his face, quickly followed by a blankness she couldn't help but feel was desperate.

'Why *are* you here?' she said after a moment, unable to help herself.

'I live here.' There was a beat of silence. 'This is my home.'

'It hasn't been,' she reminded him, still compelled by reasons she wasn't quite sure of. 'Not for the last two years.'

'No, it has been,' Dylan replied softly. 'But even the best of us run away from home sometimes, don't we?'

Her heart stalled, reminding her of the old car she'd seen just that morning, spluttering down the road in front of Anja's house. Why did it feel as if he was talking about *her*? *To* her? As if he instinctively knew that she'd turned her back on the place she'd once called home? As if he knew that she'd run from the parents who hadn't cared enough to even try to make her believe that they wanted her to stay?

'When are they coming back?' Dylan asked gruffly. Jess shook her head, ignoring the need to push for more answers. To find out why telling her he'd run from home had clearly upset him. It was none of her business.

'The end of the month.' Though Jess had a feeling it would be a lot sooner once she told Anja that Dylan had returned. 'How long *have* you been back?'

'You were right,' he replied. 'About a week.'

So he'd been chopping up wood since the day he'd returned, she thought, and forced away the sudden disappointment that came from knowing she'd no longer be able to watch him. How could she, knowing who he was?

Older brother of her best friend. Uncle to the child she carried.

'Do you know where I've been?'

'The UK?' He nodded. 'Yeah, Anja told me you've been away for…business.'

'Clearly that isn't all she told you,' he said with a self-deprecating smile.

'No.'

The smile dimmed. 'There's a lot you seem to know about me, Jessica, and yet I haven't even heard about you.'

'Does that surprise you?'

'No.' A fleeting shadow of pain darkened his features. 'But I'm back now.'

'So you are.'

'And I'd like to have my return start on the right foot.'

Something pulsed in the air between them, but Jess refused to acknowledge it. 'Yeah, okay. Go for it.'

He smiled at her, and this time it wasn't laden with emotion. It was an easy, natural smile she imagined he'd give when he saw an old friend, or during his favourite movie. But it sent an unnatural frisson through her body.

'You should have lunch with me.'

'No,' she said immediately.

'You have somewhere else to be?'

'No, but—'

'Then have lunch with me.'

'No, thank you,' she said more firmly, hoping none of the panic she felt was evident in her voice. 'You were... busy before I interrupted.'

'After what happened, I think I'm done for the day.'

'I really don't think I should—'

'Please.' His smile widened and she almost felt faint. 'I'd like to get to know the woman staying in my sister's house. The woman who's clearly a good friend of hers.' He paused. 'That's what I meant by having my return start on the right foot. If you and I are on good terms when Anja gets back...'

The seconds ticked by, and then Jess narrowed her eyes. 'You're *schmoozing* me!'

Surprise captured his features, and then he laughed. A loud, genuine laugh that started at those fantastic abs and went all the way up to his perfect hair. It was fascinating to watch. The even angles of his face were animated with joy, those chocolate-whisky eyes she only now noticed he shared with his sister alight with appreciation.

She'd never been much of a beard woman, but Dylan's stubble was dissuading her of that belief. She loved that his skin reminded her of oak—not too light, not too dark. And she *really* loved that he still didn't have a shirt on, so she could appreciate that colour over hard, defined muscle...

'If I told you I was, would that make you want to have lunch with me any less than you already do?' he asked, interrupting her hormone-driven thoughts.

'Probably.' She waited. 'So, are you?'

Now he chuckled. 'No.'

She tilted her head. Watched him. 'You're the CEO of an international engineering company. I'd imagine that requires some measure of intelligence.'

'You're saying I'm not intelligent?'

'Only if you expect me to believe that you're not trying to…charm me into having lunch with you.'

'Well, I *am* taking some time off from work. Perhaps that's why I'm off my game. Why I've made such an unforgivable mistake.'

'You're still doing it!'

He smiled. 'I can't help it.'

'Great. It'll make my refusal so much easier then.'

'No, wait,' he said, grabbing her wrist when she turned. He let go when she turned back. Her skin prickled. 'I'm sorry. It's just…easier to schmooze than to…earnestly ask you to have lunch with me.'

'Why do you want to have lunch with me so badly?'

'You're Anja's friend and…and I'd like to show her that I'm serious about coming back to fix things. That's why I'm here,' he told her softly. 'I want to fix what I broke when I left, and if you and I are on good terms…' He shrugged. 'I wasn't lying about that, Jess.'

As Jess studied him she felt herself soften. She hated that she did, but she couldn't ignore the emotion behind his words. The hope. She also couldn't ignore how much it spoke to her own desire. The deep, dark one that she would never have admitted aloud to anyone.

That some day her parents would show up for her, just like it seemed Dylan had for Anja. That some day they'd want to fix things with her just as badly as Dylan clearly wanted to with his sister.

It was a stupid hope, one her experiences growing up had taught her not to entertain. But still, it made her want to say yes to Dylan. That, and the desire to prevent the child she carried from growing up in the tension, the brokenness that currently existed in Anja's family. The same kind of tension and brokenness that Jess had grown up with.

Jess knew Anja was stubborn, and she wouldn't let the

brother who'd left her after their father had died just come strolling back into her life. Not when that brother had broken her heart by leaving. Not when he'd broken his promise to always be there for her.

'I don't know why you left, Dylan,' Jess said softly, 'or why you didn't come home for two years. That's probably none of my business…though what I'm about to ask you falls under that category, too. But…why haven't you come over to speak with Anja since you got back?'

It was such a long time before he answered that Jess was sure he wouldn't answer her at all. 'I didn't know whether she'd want to see me, and staying away, keeping my mind and body busy with menial tasks…they were all excuses to postpone the inevitably difficult conversation I would have to have with her.'

Surprised by his candour—and more than a little touched—Jess nodded. 'Okay.'

'Okay?'

'Okay,' she repeated. She waited a beat before she said, 'You better have enough food to feed a pregnant woman, Dylan.'

It took Dylan a moment to realise what he'd done. Another to process what he'd said. And even then he wasn't sure what he was doing. Inviting a woman he barely knew into his home? Offering to make her lunch? Sharing his intention of fixing things with Anja? Hoping that she'd be able to give him some insight into his sister?

It was crazy, but his craziness was dipped in desperation. Desperation because his sister hadn't spoken to him—not properly—in almost two years. Desperation because his plan to speak with her when he got home wasn't working.

Because every time he'd wanted to go over to her house to talk with her he'd remembered her face when he'd left.

He'd remembered how broken she'd looked, how her voice had cracked when she'd said goodbye.

How he'd left anyway.

And now, when he'd finally told himself he would go to see her *that night*, it turned out she wasn't even there.

He was disappointed, and perhaps that had been another reason for his invitation to Jess. But then the desperation, the craziness, the disappointment had landed him a meal with a beautiful woman, so was it really that bad?

Yes, an inner voice answered him. *Of course* it was. Because though the beautiful woman knew things about his sister that *he* didn't know—that he wanted to know—she was also pregnant. *Pregnant.* Which meant someone had got her pregnant. His eyes searched her hand for a ring, but they didn't find one.

It sent an absurd surge of hope through him, and he rolled his eyes as he led the way into his house. He bent down when he heard the scurry of paws against the wooden floor and fussed over his Labrador, Daisy, when she came bounding around the corner.

But she quickly lost interest in him and made her way to the woman he'd invited for lunch. Dylan watched as Jess's face lit up and she lowered—carefully, he saw—before rubbing his dog vigorously. It sent another surge through him, but this time it was warmth. A bubble of warmth that floated from his heart and settled in his belly.

A bubble that abruptly popped when he remembered that no wedding ring didn't mean that she was available.

And that a baby meant she *definitely* wasn't available.

'Daisy, back,' he snapped, the words coming out harsher than he'd intended because of his thoughts. The dog gave him a beseeching look but stepped back and sat, and Dylan offered a hand to help Jess up.

'Sorry about that. She gets a little excited around people.'

He sucked in his breath at the sizzle he felt coming

from her hand. Held his breath when the vanilla scent she wore settled in his nose. As soon as she was steady, he broke the contact.

'Don't worry. I love dogs.'

'Do you have any?'

Sadness dulled her eyes. 'No, my parents weren't really fans of pets when I was younger. Or children.' She laughed breathlessly, but he could tell that it was meant to cover up her mistake. She hadn't meant to tell him that.

Well, that makes two of us, he thought, remembering what he'd told her about coming home. And because of it he didn't address her slip. Instead, he approached it from a different angle.

'Why don't you have any now? Doesn't your husband want pets either?'

'No husband.' She shrugged. 'I'm just your typical unwed pregnant woman, I guess.'

She didn't look too bothered by it, which forced him to ignore the hope that stirred inside him again. 'Somehow I doubt that.'

'That I'm unwed and pregnant?'

'That you're typical.'

'You barcly know me, Dylan.'

Her eyes met his and it felt as if lightning flashed between them. The seconds ticked by, the current of energy between them grew more intense, but neither of them looked away. Eventually, he said, 'What are you in the mood to eat?'

A moment passed, and then he could see her force herself to relax. 'Do you have peanut butter?'

It was such a strange request that it broke the tension he still felt inside him. 'Yeah, I think so.' He narrowed his eyes. 'You want *peanut butter*? I'm pretty sure there's something more substantial in the fridge.'

'Peanut butter is plenty substantial,' she replied defensively. 'Especially if you serve it with those bananas over there.'

She nodded to the fruit bowl on his kitchen table, and he felt the smile on his face almost before he even knew it was there. 'Peanut butter and banana?'

'Peanut butter and banana,' she confirmed, and smiled. 'I tried to warn you about what you were getting into by inviting a pregnant woman for lunch.'

'Yeah, you did,' he answered, though he struggled for the words because her smile was so...*distracting*. As was her face—the smooth curves of its oval shape, the high cheekbones, those cinnamon eyes, the glossy olive of her skin, those generous lips...

Even her *hair* was distracting. The dark brown strands were clipped back into a messy style that he couldn't decide whether he liked. Mostly because it made him want to tidy it up. *No*, he corrected his thoughts immediately. Because it made him want to muss it up even *more*.

Her clothing was loose, hiding the curve of her stomach. That was why he hadn't noticed she was pregnant at first—though he'd discovered it pretty quickly, so he couldn't blame ignorance for the fact that he'd flirted with her.

But he didn't want to think about what he could blame flirting with her on, so he was glad when she spoke.

'Who looked after Daisy while you were away?'

'Actually, I got her in London and then brought her back with me.'

Daisy wagged her tail when he looked over at her and love filled his heart. She'd saved him from depression, from the loneliness of his grief and anger. From his guilt. And she'd needed him in a way that was more simple than he could ever remember being needed.

His experience of being needed by his mother and sister had always—*always*—been complicated. And he blamed himself. *He'd* been the one who'd chosen to look after their family when his father had abandoned them. When his father had decided that gambling was more important than the woman he'd married. Than his children...

Dylan had been the one to take care of the household when his father's abandonment had meant that they couldn't rely on their mother any more either. So yes, maybe after they'd found out the man had died, Dylan had wanted to leave it all behind. And yes, maybe finding out a few days before his father's funeral that his mother hadn't been the victim she'd pretended to be all those years ago had given him even more incentive to leave.

But he was back now. Because his sister hadn't lied to him, hadn't betrayed him. And it was time that he stopped acting as though she had.

'Daisy's English?' Jess asked, interrupting his thoughts. She snapped a finger and Daisy was at her side in an instant. 'I've never met an English dog before,' she said, cooing at his pet.

'I don't really think they have nationalities.'

'Really? Because Daisy gives off a distinct English vibe. Like she'd invite me for tea and scones every afternoon at three.'

He laughed. 'The English actually have their tea—' He broke off at her smirk, and the laugh turned into a smile. 'You don't care, do you?'

'Not unless I'm going to the UK, which is obviously not happening any time soon.'

'How far along are you?' he asked, and began to prepare their lunch. Since peanut butter and banana didn't seem quite as appealing to him, he decided on a chicken mayo sandwich for himself.

'Just over five months. Um, Dylan?' He glanced at her. 'I know the naked chef is a thing in the UK, but you not having a shirt on… Well, it's really distracting. Do you mind?'

CHAPTER TWO

His EYEBROWS ROSE, and then a grin curved his lips. 'I'm *distracting* you?'

'Yeah,' Jess said, and tilted her chin. 'Wouldn't you be distracted if I made your food half-naked? No, don't answer that,' she added quickly, when his grin turned naughty. 'It wasn't the right comparison.'

'Probably not, but I liked it.' He winked, and something flipped in her belly. She was fairly certain it wasn't the baby. 'I'll grab a T-shirt.'

He left the kitchen and finally air flowed easily through her lungs again. She hadn't noticed how hard it had been to breathe around him. But she knew it was a sure sign that she was digging a hole that she might not be able to get out of.

And it wasn't only because of how he made her feel. It was because Jess knew what Anja and Dylan's relationship was like. And because she knew how much he'd hurt her friend by leaving.

Anja hadn't even told Dylan that he was going to be an uncle. Or that his niece or nephew would be brought into the world by a surrogate. She hadn't told him about her miscarriage after years of fertility struggles, or how those struggles and that miscarriage had been the reason she'd decided to use a surrogate.

Or, Jess thought, about the fact that *she* was that surrogate.

Jess couldn't say she agreed with her friend's silence. But then, Jess didn't understand the dynamic between siblings since she didn't have any. Nor did she understand what it was like to be part of a real family unit, where hurt and betrayal resulted from a member of that unit doing something the others didn't approve of.

She could barely call her family a *family*, for heaven's sake, let alone a *unit*.

Anja was the closest thing Jess had to family, which was why she'd offered to be Anja and Chet's surrogate. It was also why she should have been calling Anja, telling her about Dylan's return instead of waiting for him to put a shirt on so that he could make her lunch.

Jess distracted herself by looking around. The open-plan living room and kitchen were filled with light from windows and doors that made up most of the rooms' external structure. From where she stood, she could see a sunroom where she would kill to spend a few hours in the afternoon sun, furnished in muted colours that told her Dylan had incredible style, or had hired someone who did.

The living room was just as stylish, though she wasn't a big fan of the darker finishes he'd chosen. She couldn't deny that it was striking against the cream-coloured walls and solid brick fireplace, but she preferred the warmth of the kitchen. With its light waterfall counter and space around the island, it was the type of room she'd always felt more comfortable in. Understated and tasteful. Despite the fact that she'd grown up in opulence. But more likely because of it.

Before she could go down that path, Dylan walked in wearing a blue T-shirt that did nothing to detract from his sexiness. She almost sighed when her heart did a quick tumble in her chest, and a voice in her head asked her to rethink agreeing to have lunch with him.

'Still hungry?' he asked and, despite the warning, Jess heard herself say, 'Yes, I am.'

She watched him go through the rhythms of making their lunch. Watched as he didn't so much as give her an indulgent smile as he chopped the bananas and plopped them in a bowl, adding a generous dollop of peanut butter as though he'd made the meal countless times before. He finished his sandwich almost as quickly and then offered her something to drink. Before she knew it, she was following him into the sunroom she'd admired earlier.

'You didn't have to go to all this effort,' she said when they sat.

'It wasn't really an effort.' He shrugged and took a big bite of his sandwich.

She followed by spooning banana and peanut butter together, and then lifted it to her mouth. When she'd swallowed, she looked up to see him watching her, a strange expression on his face. She wasn't sure why it made her feel flushed and, though she wanted to, she didn't think she'd be able to blame it on pregnancy hormones. It had her blurting out the first thing that came to mind.

'I quite liked the trees in your backyard before you cut them down.'

'I did, too. But their leaves were clogging the gutters and, with winter coming, I thought I'd do something about it. You know, make sure the gutters work when the rain comes and have wood for the fireplace.'

Dutifully, she said, 'The fireplace is wonderful. Your whole house is.'

His eyes scanned her face and she felt another flush of heat. 'Why don't I believe you, Jess?'

'I don't know,' she replied, and quickly ate another spoonful of peanut butter. She regretted it immediately when she noticed he was still watching her, and tried her best to act casually. When she'd swallowed, she reached for the bottle of water he'd offered her earlier and drank greedily.

'I don't really like the décor,' he continued as though there hadn't been any pause after her answer. 'But I'd already left before it was finished, so I wasn't really involved with the decision-making. Anja was, though, since we used the same guy for both our places, and I prefer hers.'

'I thought you hadn't been back since…since you left,' she finished lamely, though his expression told her he knew she'd meant to say *since your father died.*

'No, I haven't been back, but I saw pictures of both our places. I think Anja purposely gave the designer free rein to get back at me.'

'For what?'

'For leaving.' His eyes stayed on hers. 'Though you'd know more about that than I would.'

'Anja didn't tell me about the décor at all. I think it might have been before my time.'

'I wasn't talking about the décor.'

She forced herself to hold his gaze. 'I'm not sure what you're talking about.'

'About my sister's feelings about me leaving. You mentioned that she told you more than just the fact that I'd left for business.'

'Yes.'

'Care to share?' He gave her a smile that told her he was trying to charm her again.

'No.'

The smile faltered. 'I thought—'

'What?' she interrupted. 'That I'd tell you everything your sister told me?'

He lifted an arm. Rubbed the back of his neck. 'I

thought that since you were her friend, you must know… something.'

'The fact that I'm her friend means that I wouldn't tell you what I know.' Jess set down her bowl and perched on the edge of her chair. 'You didn't ask me over because you wanted the two of us to get along for Anja's sake. You asked me over so that I could tell you something that would help *you* get along with Anja.'

'And if I tell you you're right?'

'Then I'd say that it was lovely meeting you, Dylan, and wish you all the best for your return to Cape Town on my way out.'

He set his lunch down just as she had, and when he met her gaze his expression was a plea she felt hit her right in the chest. 'You must have known that was part of the reason I asked you over.'

She considered it. 'Maybe. But—'

But I wanted to believe that you wanted to get to know me.

She nearly laughed at herself. Clearly she hadn't learnt her lesson yet. People never wanted *her*.

'It seems like you want something from me that I'm not willing to give you. So it's probably best if I just leave.'

'No, Jess, don't.'

'Why not?'

'Because… I'm sorry.' He ran a hand through his hair. 'I've handled this poorly.'

'You're apologising way too much for someone who's only just met me,' she said softly. Coolly.

'So I'll be honest instead,' he replied, his voice tight. 'I wanted to know…what I was coming back to. The extent of the damage I caused by leaving.'

'I think you already do.'

He nodded. 'It would be nice to have some more… context.'

She shook her head and rose to her feet. 'I don't have context to give you. No,' she said when he opened his mouth to protest. 'Your context should come from Anja. Or your mother.'

His face darkened. 'I suppose I'll have to wait for Anja to get back then.'

Jess frowned. 'You don't have to. Your mother lives—'

'Thank you, Jess,' he interrupted, and stood with her. 'It's been lovely meeting you.'

Though Jess didn't understand his reaction, she knew that he was asking her to leave. She would have been offended if she wasn't so...curious. It was clear that Dylan had no intention of asking his mother about what had happened after he'd left. And the look on his face told her that there was a reason for that. A reason even Anja didn't know, or else Jess would know, too.

It was all very interesting, but Jess told herself it was none of her business. Again. She didn't know why she had to remind herself of that so often, so she murmured her thanks to Dylan and walked towards the door.

'Jess—' Dylan said from behind her.

'It's okay.' She opened the door and gave Daisy one last pat. 'You don't have to explain it to me. I get it.' She paused. 'It was lovely meeting you, too, Dylan. I hope your return to Cape Town is everything you hoped it would be.'

She walked out before he could reply.

Dylan stared at the door long after Jess had left, hoping that their interaction wasn't an omen for the rest of his return.

He knew the way things had spiralled between them was his fault. But he'd wanted to know what Jess knew. He told himself it was because it would give him an indication of what Anja knew. Of what his sister thought of him. But, deep down, he knew it was because he didn't want Jess to judge him based on the only thing he'd done in his life that had disappointed his sister.

Because he'd been disappointed, too, and he knew what it felt like. His entire life, his father had disappointed him. It was the best—or, rather, easiest—word to use to describe how Dylan felt about his father. About the man's gambling addiction. About his absence. And perhaps Dylan would have been able to put it all behind him after his father had died if he hadn't found out his mother had known about his father's problems before he or Anja had been born.

He and Anja had spent their entire childhood trying to comfort their mother after their father had left them. They'd no longer been children. Instead, their existence had been dedicated to keeping the woman who'd borne them from spiralling into a deep depression.

What had been the point of all that when his mother had known what she'd been getting into with his father?

When Dylan had found out, he couldn't bring himself to tell Anja. So he'd left, and tried to deal with the anger by himself, away from her. His anger at the secret his mother had kept from them. His anger about the inexplicable grief he felt at losing a man he'd barely known.

He couldn't get past the irony that by wanting to keep Anja from the same disappointment he'd felt in their parents, *he'd* disappointed her. More than that, he thought, remembering that expression on her face when he'd told her he was leaving again. He'd *abandoned* her.

Just like his father had abandoned them.

CHAPTER THREE

JESS WOKE UP to water dripping onto her face.

It took her a moment to realise that water was dripping on to her face, and more time to realise that that wasn't a *good* thing. She sat up and looked at the ceiling, only to see a long, slim strip of water dripping across the length of the room.

Her first thought was that she needed to close the water main, and that she'd figure out where the water was coming from once she had. But when she reached down to put her shoes on, she realised that she didn't actually know where the water main was.

It took her another few minutes to figure out that she needed to ask Dylan for help, and she sighed before slipping on the soft boots she wore as slippers.

The entire floor of the passage to the front door was wet, and Jess's heart beat heavily in her chest as she walked through the water. She locked the door and then rushed to Dylan's house, and waited impatiently for him to answer after she rang the bell.

Seconds later he opened the door, and Jess found herself staring into a bare chest. Again. Why didn't he have a shirt on? she thought, annoyance straightening her spine. Didn't he realise it was *autumn*? She tilted her head up, and only then saw that his hair was mussed from sleep. Which, she discovered, had the same effect on her as his bare chest.

She forced herself to focus on the reason she'd woken him. 'Do you know where the water main to Anja's house is?'

He frowned. 'Yeah, why?'

'No time. I'll explain after you shut it off.'

His eyes swept over her, and for the first time she realised that the only thing she'd done after waking up was put her slippers on. She must look a mess, she thought, wincing internally. But she wouldn't dwell on it now. Which was probably a good thing since a voice in her head reminded her that she'd woken with water on her face, which had probably made her look even worse.

Thankfully, he seemed to take her appearance as a sign of urgency and he walked past her, barely waiting for her to waddle after him before he was at the front of Anja's house, opening a concealed hatch and reaching inside. Then he was at her side again, offering her another view of his naked chest.

'You're going to catch a cold if you don't put a shirt on,' she said, crossing her arms when her comment reminded her that she didn't have much on either. She was more dressed than he was, but her oversized shirt and black pyjama pants were not exactly the items she'd have chosen had she known she was going to see anyone, let alone *him*.

Besides, she wasn't wearing a bra, and she knew her pregnancy boobs weren't going to politely refuse to be noticed, especially in the cold.

'If you keep telling me to put a shirt on, I'm going to think you have a problem with me being shirtless. And then I'd have to ask why you have problem with me being shirtless, and I'm guessing that's not a conversation you want to have.'

As if to prove his point, he ran a hand through his hair. His biceps bulged and her throat went dry.

'I'm only worried about your health,' she managed stiffly.

'Oh, I forgot. Because of your medical background, right?' He grinned and she almost—*almost*—smiled back. Instead, she pressed a hand on his hip and pressed gently, much like she had the day before. And, just like he had the day before, he winced.

She gave him a sweet smile. 'How's your hip feeling?'

'Oh, aren't you hilarious?'

'I'm not the one trying to be a comedian this morning.'

'I wouldn't have had to be anything besides asleep if you hadn't woken me up.' Now he ran a hand over the back of his neck, pushing his chest out ever so slightly. She swallowed. 'What time is it?'

'I…I don't know,' Jess replied as she realised she didn't. She winced. 'I'm sorry for waking you up. I just didn't know what to do…' She waited a beat. 'Thank you. For your help.'

He nodded. 'You have a burst pipe?'

'Your guess is as good as mine. All I know is that I woke up with water dripping onto my face.' She sighed. 'The house is a mess.'

It would be a logistical nightmare for her. Not because she would have to take care of getting it fixed, but because she wasn't only staying at Anja's house to house-sit. No, she had just bought her own place and was staying at Anja's until her new home could be made liveable. It was small, and the deposit had taken most of her savings, but it was her own. A fact that always, always brought her joy.

It reminded her that when she'd cut ties with her parents two years ago she had nothing except her university degree. It could have been enough, especially since her surname meant something in the finance industry she'd been trained for, but she hadn't wanted to rely on that. She wanted something of her *own*. Something that couldn't in any way be attributed to her rich, successful parents whose only concern had been their business.

Not the child they'd mistakenly conceived.

So she'd applied for a job she was wholly overqualified for, doing the day-to-day admin for a yoga studio. She updated and maintained Anja's website, managed bookings, dealt with queries, emails and, for the past year, helped Anja with the admin for opening her studio in Sydney. It had been a dream of Anja's as Chet was Australian and she'd wanted roots there just like Chet had in South Africa.

And the job had turned out to be a dream for Jess— the constant stream of things to do a welcome distraction from the past and the parents she'd walked away from.

For two years Jess hadn't spent any of the money she'd earned on anything besides the essentials. It meant that she was able to afford the small flat she'd bought, twenty minutes away from Chet and Anja's place. But that flat was a mess.

She couldn't begrudge it since its state was why she'd got it at such a good price, but it needed a lot of work before anyone could live there. Since Chet owned a construction company he'd offered to do the work for her, and had refused payment. And then Anja had found out Jess's lease was ending and her landlord was being difficult about letting her stay there on a month-to-month contract and had offered for Jess to stay at their place until her flat was habitable.

She knew they felt indebted to her. Especially since *she'd* refused to consider payment for carrying their child. But really, she saw them as family. As the only family she had. And family did things like that for one another. They cared, and helped, and sacrificed. Not because they wanted anything in return, but because they loved one another.

The concept was foreign to her parents, and that was part of the reason she hadn't spoken to them in two years. But it was okay. She'd found her place.

Except in the literal sense, since her place was currently flooded.

She sighed again. 'I should probably call Anja. Excuse me.'

'There's not much she can do from there.'

'Maybe not, but I still need to tell her before I start sorting it all out.'

'Sure,' he agreed. 'Or, if you give me a moment to put on a shirt, I can have a look and help you sort it out. So when you *do* call Anja you'll be calling her with answers, not just a problem.'

Relief swept through her first, and then came the niggling suspicion. Why was he offering to help her? What would he get from it?

'You're trying to get back on Anja's good side again, aren't you?'

'Isn't that why I do everything?' he replied dryly, making her wonder what he really meant. Dozens of options went through her head but, for the life of her, she couldn't focus on one of them. Realising it meant that she was tired, that she needed help, Jess nodded.

'I'd appreciate the help. Thanks.'

'I'll see you in a minute.'

She watched as he jogged back to his house, taking in the way his jeans rode low on his hips. It gave her the perfect view of a very fine butt, and a muscular back just asking her to run her hands over it.

Jess tried to ignore the way her body responded to the idea, but then she realised that Dylan wearing jeans to bed didn't make sense. If he didn't wear a shirt, he definitely wouldn't wear jeans. Which meant that he must have just thrown on the first thing that had been close by…and that he probably didn't wear any pants to bed either…

The image sent her thoughts down a dangerous road, and suddenly she couldn't stop imagining what Dylan would look like naked. Or what it would feel like to be in that bed with him, turning over during the night to run her hands over that delicious body of his. To snuggle closer and kiss him, to feel the way his body responded to hers. With him naked, there would be no barrier to what would happen next, and she'd be able to—

'Jess?' She jumped and felt her cheeks flush when she saw Dylan in front of her, completely clothed, with a puzzled look on his face. 'Are you okay?'

'Yeah, I'm fine. Ready to go inside?' She didn't wait for his answer and instead walked to the house.

Where had *that* come from? she thought. She wasn't the kind of girl who had fantasies about men she barely knew. Hell, she didn't have fantasies about men at all. She'd never been the type. She hadn't felt the need to date around and see where it would take her. She'd had two steady boyfriends in her life, and both relationships had only lasted about a year.

When her last relationship had ended, Jess had seen no point in trying again. Sure, it might have been because her life had completely changed shortly after the break-up. But she'd worked hard to rebuild it—by herself—for the last two years and she hadn't seen the point in having a man around while she did.

So perhaps the fantasy she'd just had about Dylan was the result of the nothingness she'd had in her life since she'd broken up with her last boyfriend. Or it could have been her over-excited pregnancy hormones. She would put it down to both, and refuse to acknowledge the third option.

That maybe she just *wanted* her best friend's brother.

She was almost relieved when she saw the puddles on the floor when she walked in. It gave her something else to think about. Something else to worry about.

'Wow,' he said from behind her.

'Yeah,' she replied, taking it all in. 'I'm not sure what happened.'

'It looks like it came from the second floor. I'll go take a look.'

While he was upstairs, Jess tried to do some damage control. She used towels to soak up the water on the floor, and wiped all the surfaces that had been affected. Fortunately, it seemed the water had only leaked in her bedroom, the kitchen and onto the passage that led to the front door, missing the carpeted lounge and its expensive furniture.

But she was still out of breath when Dylan returned.

'It looks like a geyser burst. A quick fix, though I'm not sure we can say the same for the ceiling. There's some water damage—' He broke off and frowned at her. 'Are you okay?'

'Yeah, fine.' She waved a hand. 'I'm just not used to not being able to do normal things like dry the floor.'

'Why don't you rest for a bit? I'll finish up here and make the necessary calls.'

'No, you don't have to.'

She stepped onto the towel in front of her to pick up the one just beyond it, but it slipped under her feet and she felt herself falling before she fully realised what was happening. A strong arm went around her waist and drew her up, and then Jess found herself staring into Dylan's eyes.

There was concern there, but she could also see the faint light of anger at her refusal. But seconds passed and neither of them looked away, and soon his eyes changed. The concern, the anger, faded and was slowly replaced by interest.

By attraction.

That was the word for it, she thought. And it was a dangerous thought since something instantly sprang inside her chest at the prospect, at the recognition of what had caused her fantasy about Dylan earlier. She swallowed as the attraction changed to desire, and more seconds passed as she realised that that change was because of whatever he saw in *her* eyes.

Because being reminded about the fantasy she'd had about him earlier had made her body go hot. Had made her tingle, ache. Now she was pressed against the chest she'd spent days admiring, her hands braced against it, and she could feel his heart thudding against her hand. She should move, she told herself.

But she couldn't bring herself to put distance between them. The only movement she wanted to act on was to press herself even closer against him. To feel his muscular body tight against her, and have him feel the softness of her body. Her belly would get in the way, but she could—

The thought stopped her imagination abruptly, and shame took the place of desire. How *could* she be thinking these things when she was *pregnant*? When she was carrying a member of Dylan's family?

There was no way she could entertain these fantasies. She couldn't think about Dylan in any way other than as Anja's brother, the uncle to the child she carried. Getting involved with him had no benefits. It would probably hurt her best friend. It might even hurt the baby.

And though she wasn't the biological mother, while she carried him or her, *she* was responsible for the baby. *The baby* was her most important priority, and she couldn't ignore that just because Dylan made her feel things she'd forgotten she could feel.

Her relationship with Anja was important to her. More important than anything else. She would *not* screw it up.

'Thanks,' she murmured, thoroughly doused of the heat of attraction. 'Why don't you get this cleared up and I'll make the calls? I have the information on my laptop.'

'It's not damaged?' he asked her quietly, taking a step away from her.

'It's in the lounge. The water didn't get there.'

'Okay then.'

With careful steps, Jess made her way to the lounge. There would be no repeat performance of the last ten minutes.

Not now, not ever.

CHAPTER FOUR

BY THE TIME Dylan was done clearing up, the plumber had arrived and confirmed his suspicions: the geyser *had* burst. While they liaised with the insurance company and arranged for it to be replaced and informed them of the other damage, Dylan watched Jess. She'd been acting strangely from the moment he'd answered the door that morning, and he couldn't quite figure out why.

Was it because of the way things had ended between them the day before? Maybe, he thought. But then he remembered the way things had crackled between them when he'd saved her from falling. The way his body had reacted to her body's proximity, and the shame he'd felt when she'd pulled away.

She was pregnant, for crying out loud. There was no circumstance in which that didn't make her off-limits. He needed to remember that, he thought, when his heart stuttered as his eyes rested on her.

But, damn it, there was just *something* about her that pulled him in. That made rational thought not matter, and made hope flair when it shouldn't. And it had nothing to do with her relationship with his sister.

He told himself to pull back, to control himself, and went over to talk with her.

'The insurance is sending out their own evaluators this afternoon,' she said, and he saw the fatigue in her eyes.

'Figured as much when we realised the plumber we called wasn't on their list of approved service providers.'

'I've told them what the plumber identified the problem as, and gave them the details of the geyser. I doubt they'll arrive with it—wouldn't want to waste their money in case it wasn't what we said—but it should be replaced by the end of the day.'

'And the ceiling?'

'They're sending someone out for that and the rest of the damage today, too.'

He nodded. 'I don't think the ceiling will be too much of an effort. Might just be a paint job. The rest will have to dry.'

'It'll probably take a good solid two days,' she replied. 'And the water will probably be off for today. The painting should be done tomorrow, but the fumes might keep me out for at least another day.' She bit her lip. 'It might end up being more than two days.' She rested a hand on her stomach, and the action did something strange to his insides.

'Do you have somewhere to go?' he asked, his thoughts making his words gruff.

'No,' she said softly.

'Where do you live when you're not living here?'

'I just bought a place that isn't ready for me to move in yet. And the lease of the one I rented before is up.' She sighed. 'Anja and Chet are letting me stay here until my flat's ready.'

He processed the information. 'What about the father of the baby?'

She hesitated. 'He isn't an option right now.'

'So he doesn't care where the mother of his child is?'

'That's not—' She broke off. 'He isn't an option. But

this isn't your problem, so don't worry. I'll figure something out.'

'I *will* worry. You have nowhere to go.'

'I'll be fine.'

'Jess—'

'Why are you pushing me?'

'Why won't you accept my help?'

'I *have* accepted your help. With all of this.' She waved her hand around them at the house. 'You've done enough.'

'Not if I leave you to figure things out by yourself,' he argued. 'Letting someone help you isn't going to rob you of anything, you know.'

'Not in my experience.'

He paused. 'What do you mean?'

'Nothing,' she said immediately, shaking her head. 'It doesn't mean anything.'

He studied her. Couldn't bring himself to look away from her. Not when her expression was so captivating. She'd been hurt before, he saw. And realised that hurt had made her lose something of herself.

Though he barely knew her, Dylan found his fists curling and his mind fantasising about being alone with whoever had hurt her. And since she was pregnant and didn't want to turn to the father of her child for help, Dylan was willing to bet he knew who he'd like to hurt.

He forced himself to relax. 'Okay, how about you get some of your clothes and come over to my place for breakfast? You can figure it out there,' he added over the protest he could sense would come from her.

But, instead of protesting, she said, 'That would be great, thanks,' surprising him. He watched as she got up— resisting the urge to help her when her movements looked the slightest bit sluggish—and waited in the passage leading to the front door while she packed.

He used the time to look at his sister's house. Just as

he'd told Jess the day before, he preferred the décor here to that of his own house. Though the architecture was much the same, the bright colours made Anja's house look more homely than his own. When he'd told Anja as much, she'd told him that if he'd been there, maybe he could have made sure his was homely, too.

It had been the first sign of the crack in their relationship, but of course, he'd ignored it. It had been easier to do than facing the fact that he should have been home…

Jess came out then, just in time to stop those thoughts from spiralling. He wordlessly took the small suitcase she had, and turned towards his place. He was almost surprised to see how sullen the sky had become, though he shouldn't have been. It was autumn, and the warmth of the past few days had been more of a fluke than the grey sky.

He opened the door of his house to an excited dog, who became even more excited when she saw Jess behind him. Though he could still see the fatigue in Jess's eyes, she dutifully gave Daisy the attention the dog wanted and then followed him into the kitchen.

It was strange having her in his house again. Which itself was strange, considering that he'd only been living in that house for eight days himself after being away from it for two years. And since the décor had changed while he'd been away, it was almost like living in a new place.

'You can have the guest room,' he told her, leading the way. 'My housekeeper comes in every second day, so the room should be okay to stay in. There's an en suite bathroom, too, so it has everything you need.'

'Thanks. I think I'll take a shower and change.'

'And I'll get breakfast ready.'

'Oh, you really don't have to—'

'I know,' he interrupted her. 'But I'm hungry, too, so it won't be that much of an effort.'

He left before she could argue with him, and started

making their breakfast. Cooking was one of the habits he'd picked up growing up that didn't annoy him. At first it had been for survival. After it had become clear his father wasn't going to come home, his mother had given up on most tasks, including feeding them.

So Dylan had used the money he'd found in his father's safe to buy food, but he'd quickly realised that the money wouldn't last if he didn't learn how to buy sustainable items. And that the items that *had* been sustainable required effort on his behalf. So he'd spent a lot of time watching cooking shows, had flipped through the faded cookbooks in his mother's bookshelf and had taught himself to cook. He'd soon realised that it calmed him, and had roped Anja in, hoping she'd feel the same way.

'You look better,' he said when he saw Jess walk into the kitchen. He plated the muffins his housekeeper had made.

'You mean better than the horror show I was this morning?'

'Not at all. I just meant—' He broke off when he saw her smile, and felt his stomach flip. He ignored it.

'Do you want something to drink?'

'Tea, please.' She settled onto the bar stool at the counter.

'I have more comfortable chairs in the living room.'

'I know. But I won't let this baby rob me of the opportunity to eat while I watch you cook.'

She gave him a cheeky grin, and he laughed. She *did* look better than before. Not only because now she wore a long-sleeved black dress that stretched down to her feet with a belt tied under her breasts accentuating her bump, but because she didn't look quite as tired, as restless, as she had when she'd first got there.

He wondered if that meant he could convince her to stay with him while the work on Anja's house was being done. The thought was as surprising as it was sudden, but when he thought about it he realised it wouldn't be such a bad idea.

Unless he thought about how things sparked between them. And how badly he wanted to kiss her lips, to taste her mouth and feel the fullness of her body against his again...

Which, of course, he wouldn't think about.

He told himself to wait until breakfast was over before he mentioned it, and slid the tea and muffins in front of her. 'Your wish is my command.'

'You're such a good man,' she breathed as she picked up a chocolate muffin.

He bit back a grin. 'Those are the first ones I go for, too.'

'They're delicious. Where did you get them?'

'My housekeeper made them for me.'

'They're *homemade*? You need to ask her for the recipe.'

'You cook?' he asked, and started cutting fruit. He didn't know what was in a pregnant woman's diet, but he figured he'd cover all his bases.

'That's *baking*, Dylan.'

'You bake?'

'No.'

His lips curved. 'So you cook, then?'

'Nope.'

'Then why did you correct me?'

'It seemed like a fun thing to do,' she said with a smile, and then sobered. 'I've been learning how to do both over the last few years. I'm not quite at the level of being able to say that I can cook or bake *well*, but I can feed myself. And these—' she lifted the muffin '—are definitely the kind of food I'd like to learn how to make.'

'What happened a few years ago? That made you want to learn how to cook and bake, I mean.' He set the fruit he'd been cutting up to the side, and began preparing the bacon and eggs.

'I…I moved out of my parents' house.'

He frowned. 'How old are you?'

'Old enough to have been out of my parents' house by then,' she said with a laugh, but it sounded forced. 'We used to have a cook, so there was never really a need for me to learn how to feed myself.'

'You had a cook?'

'Yes.' He glanced over to see the hesitation in her eyes. 'Extravagant, isn't it?'

'I wasn't thinking that.'

'I wouldn't blame you if you did.'

He turned to her and watched as she avoided his eyes. And suddenly he thought that perhaps he'd attributed the hurt he saw in her to someone who hadn't deserved it.

'So you had an…extravagant childhood?'

'I guess you could say that.'

'What would you say?'

'I…was always well provided for.' He could hear the care she'd taken with those words.

'Your parents are wealthy?'

'Yes.'

'So why—' He broke off, knowing that his question would veer into territory she might not be comfortable with. But she finished his sentence for him.

'Why am I working as a PA?' He nodded. 'Well, I wasn't…well cared for. Or cared for at all,' she added softly, and Dylan felt his heart throb. 'So, when I moved out, I stopped talking to them. Which meant I had to take care of myself, hence this job.'

Seconds passed as he digested this new information. 'When you didn't want my help this morning, were you… thinking about them?'

'Only about how they used to throw it in my face whenever I asked them for help.' She paused. 'I remember when I was younger, I started saving for a new laptop. I didn't want to use my dad's old one any more, so I got a job and put away every cent of it so I could buy myself a new one. But my dad's laptop broke before I had enough money to replace it, so I asked them to help me buy a new one.' She lifted a hand, brushed at something on her cheek that he couldn't see. 'I thought that having half of the money for it—that working for it—would make them proud, but—' she cleared her throat '—but it didn't. They helped me buy the laptop, and reminded me of it whenever I acted in a way they didn't approve of.'

He blew out a breath, his heart aching when he saw the fear on Jess's face. Fear he realised came from telling him something so intimate. 'I'm sorry, Jess.'

'Don't be,' she said, avoiding his eyes. 'It's not your fault.'

But still, silence stretched long and awkwardly between them.

Dylan wished he could find something to say to make her feel better. Clearly, she'd had a tough time growing up just like he'd had. So, in fact, he should have known *exactly* what to say to her.

But, instead of helping him to find words of comfort, that fact kept him silent. Because he *did* know how awful it was, and that meant that nothing he could say would make her feel any better. And though he'd only met Jess the day before, something told him she wasn't the kind of person who wanted fake consolation.

He appreciated that. Respected it.

And yet, when he looked at her again, he heard himself saying, 'I guess you and I have more in common than I thought.'

CHAPTER FIVE

'SEEMS LIKE IT,' Jess replied, and wondered why that suddenly mattered. Wondered why she wasn't alarmed by the fact that it did.

Perhaps it was because she couldn't deny how much… better she felt immediately after he said it. It made her feel like less of a fool for bringing up the subject of her parents when she knew she shouldn't have. When she knew that doing so would bring out that side of her that was bitter and resentful.

That *hurt*.

It left a terrible taste in her throat, and Jess drank desperately from her tea to try to take it away. Even though her mind told her the response was irrational. Even though she knew that that taste was imaginary.

Damn her parents for doing this to her, she thought. She squeezed her eyes shut, and then forced herself to open them again. When she did, she saw that Dylan was watching her. Heat rushed to her cheeks, and the air in her lungs grew terribly heavy.

'I'm sorry that they hurt you,' he said.

'It doesn't matter.'

'But they did.'

'And yours hurt you,' she replied primly. 'We survive.'

'Do we?' he asked with a half-smile. 'Do you think we're surviving?'

'You don't?'

'I…don't just want to survive if this is surviving,' he admitted quietly. 'If constantly worrying that I'm repeating the mistakes of my parents—that I'm disappointing the people I love—is surviving.'

'I…feel the same,' she said in surprise. 'About surviving.'

He didn't reply for a moment. 'When I was on the second floor of Anja's house earlier I noticed something strange.' He turned back to the stove and flipped an egg.

Confusion spread through her, but the change in topic and the fact that he wasn't looking at her any more had the breath in her lungs moving easily again. 'Yeah?' she replied, grateful that her voice wasn't nearly as shaky as she'd thought it would be.

She took a deep breath, and then busied herself with adding fruit and yoghurt to a bowl.

'Yeah. A chair,' he said, deadpan, and her hand froze. 'In front of a window.'

She forced herself to move. 'That *is* strange.'

'Overlooking my property.'

'Even stranger.' She set the bowl down in front of her and dug in.

She couldn't admit her guilt if she couldn't speak.

'I thought so,' he continued conversationally. 'Until I realised that that was the window you pointed out to me yesterday. Where you said you saw me fall from.'

'Was it?'

'*And* then I remembered you'd known I'd been here for a week.'

She pretended to think about it. 'I don't remember. Sorry, pregnancy brain.'

'Pity.'

Dylan set two plates—one with bacon, one with the

eggs—on the counter with the rest of the food, and then took a third and began dishing for himself. As he settled on the stool next to her, Jess tried to think of something to say to change the topic of conversation.

Except she couldn't think of anything. All she *could* think about was the fact that he knew. He *knew* she'd been watching him.

She rolled her eyes. Sighed. 'Okay, yes, fine. That's where I was watching you from.'

He lifted his eyebrows and didn't say anything.

Damn it! Why was that so *sexy*?

'I mean, I didn't know it was you. Doesn't that count for something?'

He cocked his head. 'You mean towards the imaginary scoreboard that gives you points for being a pervert?'

'I am *not*—' She cut off her own protest when she saw the amusement in his eyes. 'What would you have done if I was working outside in my bikini?'

'Would it make you feel better if I said I'd watch?'

'Yes.' She sniffed. 'Yes, it would.'

'Then I'd have watched.'

She couldn't resist her own amusement at the expression on his face now. 'With chips?'

'You watched me...with chips?'

'Yesterday it was chips.' She considered her next words. *What the hell?* 'The day before it was popcorn. And the day before that, chocolate.'

'Choc...' he said before realisation dawned. 'How many days have you been watching me?'

'Don't act coy now,' she replied. 'I told you you'd been home for at least a week, so that's how many days I've been watching you.'

There was a beat of silence before his face split into a smile and laughter spilled from his lips. It made him look younger, more carefree, and Jess realised how little of either of those his expression normally held. She thought about his earlier words—about what he'd said about surviving—and for the first time Jess felt sorry for her best friend's brother.

It had been easy to see Dylan as the unfeeling older brother who'd left his grieving mother and sister weeks after they'd buried their father. Easy because she'd only heard Anja's side of things. Because she'd only seen the aftermath of Dylan's departure.

But now, after the time—however short—she'd spent with Dylan, Jess finally considered the other side of the story. That clearly told her that her rash judgement was undeserved. She only had to look at Dylan's face when he wasn't laughing to realise it.

'I'm glad you find it so funny,' she managed, though her thoughts made it sound more serious than she'd intended.

'You don't?' he asked, immediately sobering.

'No, no, I do.' She forced a smile, but could tell he wasn't buying it. 'I'm sorry, I just… I just remembered I spoke with Anja this morning.'

It was the first thing she could think of to say. And when the words changed the air between them, taking away the ease of the minutes before, Jess instantly regretted it.

'What did she say?' he asked quietly.

'That we should do whatever we needed to sort things out.'

'About me, I meant.'

She'd known he had meant that, but had hoped he wouldn't ask. She cleared her throat. 'She has a few things to tie up in Sydney and then she'll be back.'

'When?'

'End of next week, she said.'

He nodded, and a long silence followed his words. She wished she hadn't said anything. Wished she hadn't let her stupid thoughts and emotions interrupt what had been an enjoyable breakfast. She couldn't figure out what to say to make him feel better. Or why she so desperately wanted to.

'You said she wanted to set up another yoga studio there?' She nodded, and more time passed before he said, 'I'll see her when she gets back then.'

'Will you?' Jess asked softly.

He gave her a small smile. 'You're asking because I've been a coward for the past week?'

'I wouldn't say coward—'

'Except I was. I didn't want to face her. Still don't, if I'm honest.' He stared off into the distance, and then his eyes moved to meet hers. 'But I'm going to. I *have* to. It's why I left the UK. Why I'm taking a break from working after doing nothing but work for the last two years.'

'You're a pretty decent guy, Dylan,' she said after a moment.

His lips curved. 'You didn't think that I was?'

'I didn't know you.'

'And you do now?'

'I...' He was right. She *didn't* know him. So how had her opinion changed now after only a few hours with him? 'Well, you helped me this morning. And made me breakfast. You really didn't have to.'

'And you no longer believe I only did it because I wanted you to tell Anja that I had?'

Her mouth opened, and then she shut it again. She'd forgotten about that. *Damn it.*

'Why do I feel like you might have changed your mind about me now?' he asked, and she looked up into his gaze.

'I haven't,' Jess said, though a voice in her head told her that it wasn't entirely true. 'I knew that, remember? And I respect that you want your relationship with your sister back.' Tired now, she slid off the chair as elegantly as she could. 'Do you mind if I rest in your guest room? It won't be for long, and then I'll start arranging where I'll stay while the whole thing next door is going on.'

'Of course you can.'

He stood with her—awkwardly, she thought, even though that word didn't really fit with a man who looked like Dylan.

'I'll see you in a bit,' she said, and then walked back to the room and felt her body sag with relief when she lay on the bed. It had been a tiring morning. Being pregnant had made it worse, but she suspected she would have felt that way even if she hadn't been pregnant.

But the fact that her thoughts and emotions were all over the place she *would* blame on her pregnancy. It was the only logical explanation for the disappointment that still lingered. It was the only way she could explain why Dylan made her feel the way he did. And why meeting him had made her think so much of her own family.

She hadn't been lying when she'd told him she respected that he wanted a relationship with Anja again. But she couldn't quite understand it. Not when she didn't have anything to compare it to. She felt absolutely no desire to repair her relationship with her parents. She didn't think they deserved her in their lives, and she sure as hell didn't think she deserved *them*. And if their actions—or lack thereof—since she'd moved out told her anything, it was that they didn't want to repair their relationship with her either.

Maybe that was why she'd felt so disappointed by what Dylan had told her. Because it had been a reminder of what Jess *didn't* have—a family who would fight for her.

She suddenly hoped Anja would give Dylan a chance. Her friend had gone deathly silent the day before when Jess had first called to tell her about Dylan's arrival. And then she'd politely thanked Jess and put down the phone.

When Jess had called that morning, her reaction had

been similar, though this time Anja had told her she would try to come home sooner and had asked Jess not to tell Dylan anything about the baby.

It was a fair request. In fact, Jess had fully intended not to say anything to Dylan about the baby. She would let Anja deal with that. After all, it was none of Jess's business.

Except that Jess *wanted* to tell Dylan. It felt wrong not to. Or, more accurately, Jess told herself quickly, she wanted *Anja* to tell Dylan. Sooner, rather than later. Because not all families wanted to fight to stay a family. That was special. But some things—some decisions—could break a family so completely that it couldn't be fixed, even if someone wanted to fight for it.

She didn't think Dylan leaving was that thing, that decision. Especially since she suspected that he'd left for reasons neither she nor Anja knew. Good reasons. But keeping this child a secret from him—keeping the circumstances around the child's conception a secret—might just be...

It exhausted her to think about it and she closed her eyes, pushing the thoughts and emotions away. She wouldn't let Dylan's demons keep her from sleeping.

She certainly wouldn't let her own demons do that either.

CHAPTER SIX

DYLAN LOOKED UP from the book that he was reading when Daisy lifted her head from where it rested on his leg and lumbered off the couch. His heart did something strange in his chest when he saw it was because Jess had walked into his living room, looking just as sleepy and mussed and sexy as she had when he'd opened his door to her that morning.

It didn't seem fair that she could do something strange to his heart when the way she looked was entirely by accident. When the waves of her hair just always seemed to be mussed, when the sleepiness was an unavoidable consequence of waking up.

As for the sexiness... Well, he didn't think she intended to make him think of her that way. Nor did he think she intended to make him picture how she'd look waking up in his bed. How imagining it made his body tighten with a need he didn't understand. With a need he *didn't want*.

'Sleep well?' he asked gruffly.

'Yeah, thanks. Sorry that it was so long.'

'It wasn't.'

'The insurance?'

'The plumbers have come and gone. The ceiling people called to say they'd only be able to make it out tomorrow. You left your phone on the kitchen counter,' he said at her confused look.

She nodded but didn't reply, and the only sound between them was Daisy's attempts to get Jess to rub her belly. He watched as Jess lowered to her haunches and then slowly sat down on the carpet over the wooden floor. With one hand on her own stomach, she gave Daisy what she wanted and the simple image again did strange things to Dylan's heart.

It made absolutely no sense.

How did a woman he barely knew have such a powerful effect on him? A woman who was clearly off-limits? Who was pregnant? Who was his sister's friend?

And yet Jess affected him. She *tempted* him. More than just physically, too. The picture in front of him made him *want*. And what it made him want was even more baffling because he'd never, ever thought about it before.

Family.

Seeing Jess pregnant made him think about having a family. About having his own wife, his own child on the way. It wasn't something he'd ever wanted. His family situation had taught him that some people weren't meant to have children. They weren't meant to be parents.

He wasn't his mother. He wouldn't knowingly bring a child into the world knowing the brokenness of the situation they'd be born into. And he *was* broken. Not as much as his father—his mother, maybe—but he certainly wasn't whole enough to become a father himself.

Which was why considering it made absolutely no sense.

He set his book aside, told himself it was being in the house, being with Jess that was driving him to insanity. 'I'm going for a walk,' he told her, and moved towards the front door.

'Can I come with you?' she asked from behind him and he turned, frowning.

'Why?'

'It's going to rain soon.' She pointedly looked out of the glass doors where the sky was dark, warning of what was about to come. 'I won't have a chance to do it in a while and I feel—' Her eyes went soft, almost apologetic.

'You feel what?'

'Suffocated.'

He lifted his brows. 'By me? Because then you probably shouldn't take a walk with me.'

'It's not you.'

It was the only answer she offered and he sighed. Nodded. She lifted her arms in response and, after a brief moment of hesitation, he strode forward and helped her up. He resented the heat that went through his body at her proximity and stepped away from her as soon as he knew she was steady.

And then he whistled to Daisy and the three of them made their way to one of the most important places of his childhood.

Once, there had been one large house on the property where he and Anja lived. They'd grown up there, and when they'd got older and their mother had moved to be closer to her family, Anja and Dylan had stayed.

'You're lucky,' Jess said from beside him as they walked the pathway to the large forest that stood just behind his property. 'I would have killed to have this in my backyard.'

'I *am* lucky,' he agreed. 'It's because of Anja.'

'What do you mean?'

'We lived here as kids, and she—'

'Wait, what?' He looked over to see confusion on her face. 'You lived here as kids? In…your house?'

'Our houses weren't always on adjacent properties. There used to be one large property, with one large house on it, where we grew up. But we tore the house down when my mother moved to Langebaan and built two separate houses instead.'

She nodded, but didn't respond as they made their way through the forest path he'd taken so many times as a child. The trees were tall and full, the kind that had always made him feel as if he was in a movie of some sort. Daisy immediately sprinted out of sight—as she always did—and she'd find him again as soon as he'd call to her on their way back.

'Why did you say you had this because of Anja?'

'Because she…she wanted me to have it.' His heart ached at the reminder of how generous she'd been. 'When we split the property, she was adamant that I have the pathway. That I have easy access to this place.' His feet faltered just as he passed the tree where his sister had once carved her initials. It was almost as if his feet knew he was talking about her. He forced them forward.

'It was special to you,' Jess said in that understanding way she had. 'To both of you.'

He cleared his throat. 'Yeah. We came here a lot as children. Well, until Anja stopped coming with me because I used to scare her so often.' His lips curled at the memory. 'She told me the place reminded her of a horror movie she'd watched, so how could I resist?'

Jess smiled. 'Naturally.'

'Anyway, after she stopped coming… I used to use this place to think. To…escape.'

'Escape?'

'From the responsibility of looking after my family.' His throat burned with emotion. 'Sounds terrible, doesn't it?'

'How old were you?'

'Fourteen.'

'Then no,' she said. 'It doesn't sound terrible for a fourteen-year-old not to want the responsibility of a family.' She paused. 'Your father left when you were fourteen?'

Of course she knew they'd been abandoned, he thought. She was his sister's best friend. A fact he conveniently seemed to forget.

'Yes.' He paused. 'What did she tell you about it?'

'Not much.' They stopped exactly where he'd stopped all those years ago—at the hilltop overlooking the busy hub of central Cape Town. Where he would dream about a life where his parents weren't such complete disasters. And he hadn't even known then what he knew now about his mother. 'Just that he had an…addiction and he left because of it.'

He nodded and let her words sit between them while he thought about what to say.

'It's beautiful,' Jess breathed after a moment, and he felt her pleasure soothe some of the hurt that always accompanied thoughts of his past. He could almost forget then that she'd been a part of the reason he'd wanted to come to this place initially. To get away from…*her* and everything she made him feel. But now he thought it was…nice that she was there with him.

What was *happening* to him?

'It is, isn't it?' he said instead of pondering the disturbing thoughts that had popped into his head. But they were only replaced by more disturbing thoughts—by what they'd been talking about earlier—and he heard himself speak before his mind had fully caught up with the words he was saying.

'I always thought it was strange that Anja wanted to live here.'

'You didn't?'

'No. The house…didn't exactly have the best memories for us. But the place did. *This* place did,' he added, gesturing around them. 'So we told ourselves that we'd

save that and tear down the rest. Build something new.'
He ran a hand through his hair. 'It was round about the
same time Anja met Chet, and she was convinced pretty
early on that they were going to be married. So, instead of
building another big house, we settled for two.' He paused.
'Didn't you ever wonder why they look so similar? We had
the same architect.'

'Actually, I hadn't noticed.'

He noted the tone of her voice. 'Anja didn't tell you
about any of this?'

She shook her head, the expression on her face reflecting the tone. 'She's pretty tight-lipped about some things.'

'Me, you mean,' he offered when it was clear she
wouldn't say it.

'No. Well, not only you,' she said when he gave her a
doubtful look. 'She's told me the major things. But the
details...she didn't really offer them, and I never wanted
to ask.'

'Why not?'

'I...' She faltered. Frowned. 'I guess I didn't want to
push her to talk about something she didn't want to talk
about.'

'Sometimes we need to be pushed to talk about the
things we don't want to talk about.'

'So I should force you to talk about why you left?' she
shot back, eyes troubled, and then she immediately shook
her head. 'No, I'm sorry. I shouldn't have said that.'

'No, you shouldn't have,' he replied. 'Not because
you're wrong—you're not—but you sounded...defensive.'

'No.'

'No?' he repeated. 'No, you didn't sound defensive? Or
no, you're not allowing me to call you out on sounding defensive?' She didn't answer him and he sighed. 'Jess—'

'You're right,' she said with a slight laugh. 'I'm being
defensive because I'm defending my decision not to push

my friend to tell me something just in case it ends up pushing her away. From me.'

Realising the enormity of what she'd just admitted—to him, to herself—Dylan said, 'She probably didn't tell you about the house because you didn't push. Because you knew not to push.'

'I...don't understand.'

'But you do. The fact that you don't ask her about it means you understand,' he told her. 'Anja wanted a clean start. We both did. So, new houses and no talk of the past.' He gestured for Jess to sit down and, after he'd helped her, he settled down himself, their legs dangling over the hill.

'It's easier that way,' she said. 'Except, for some reason, we keep talking about our pasts with one another.'

He didn't reply. Chose not to since all he wanted to say was that it made no sense. Nothing about what was happening between them made sense. All Dylan knew was that he felt as if he'd been caught in an alternate reality where it didn't *have* to make sense. Where all the reasons why sharing with Jess—why getting to know her—was a bad idea ceased to exist.

A voice inside his head screamed that he didn't want this. And yet he found it *easy* to ignore it.

And felt himself sink deeper.

'You told Anja about your parents, didn't you?'

'Yeah, she knows.'

'Good.'

'Good?' she repeated. 'Why's that good?'

'You shouldn't keep it to yourself.'

'I haven't been,' she said wryly. 'I've shared more with you than I ever have with Anja.'

'You...have?'

She gave a soft laugh that went right through him. 'She doesn't know about the laptop thing. Or that they used to hold things like that against me. She only knows that they

were…bad parents. That the money made them worse.'
She paused. 'Or maybe it's just easier for me to blame the
money instead of who they are.'

'There's more.'

'Isn't there always?' she asked with a small smile. 'But
you get the picture.' She lifted a shoulder.

He reached out and took her hand, and only really realised he had when she flipped hers over and threaded her
fingers through his. He didn't know how long they sat like
that, but he *did* know that it felt *good*. That for the first
time in a long time he didn't feel alone.

It had warmth spreading through his chest, even though
he could acknowledge that it shouldn't have. Even though
he could acknowledge that he should pull back, pull his
hand from hers, before things could become more complicated. Before the alternate reality became his real one.

Instead, he said, 'I'm surprised you're being so nice to
me, knowing what I've done.'

'And what's that?'

'Leaving.' He couldn't bring himself to look at her.
'Hurting Anja.'

'I'll admit, I didn't *want* to be nice to you.' Now he
did look at her, and she gave him a small smile. 'I started
working for Anja a couple of months after your father
died. More than a month after you left.' Jess's free hand
lifted, and she began to trace circles on her stomach. 'Of
course, I didn't know that then. Anja was always professional with me, though I could sense that something was…
off.' The circles grew larger. 'Then one day I found Anja
crying and she told me about your father's death, and…
how much she missed you.' Her hand stilled. Fell to her
lap. 'I think that was the day our professional relationship
changed into friendship. And I immediately took Anja's
side in it all.'

'You should have. I've been a terrible brother.' Shame,

guilt, anger washed through him. 'You *should* treat me like I'm a bad person.'

'But you're not.'

'I am to Anja.'

'No, Dylan. You just…hurt her. But you're a decent man, just like I told you this morning.' She squeezed his hand and then gently pulled hers out of his. He instantly felt a little emptier. 'And if I base my opinion of you on how you've treated me since we've met instead of what I thought I knew about you *before* we met, it's easy to be nice to you.'

'Even though I told you the way I've treated you might be because I want to get on Anja's good side?'

She laughed. 'Trust me, if you wanted to get on Anja's good side, being nice—or whatever it is you're being to me—would *not* be the way to go.'

'Why not?' Her expression changed, closed. 'Jess—'

'Do you plan on telling Anja why you left?' she said instead of answering his question. She didn't want to talk about it, he thought. Which he should respect. Even if it *was* strange that she'd drawn the line with that.

'Of course,' he replied, though he could hear the hesitation in his own tone. She nodded but didn't respond, and he watched as her hand went to her stomach again.

He frowned and, for the first time in a while, thought about her pregnancy. About the implications of her pregnancy. About how those implications meant he shouldn't have brought her to this place—to *his* place—which would, no doubt, always remind him of her whenever he came now. About how it meant that he shouldn't be talking to her like he hadn't to anyone else before, how he shouldn't allow himself to be comforted by her—to comfort *her*—when there was another man in her life.

Even if that man did appear to be absent for the moment.

'How has it been going?' he asked to keep himself from getting lost in the hope that thought brought. It was more urgent now, more pressing, and his mind had cleared enough for him to know he couldn't allow it to be.

'How has what been going?'

'Your pregnancy?'

'Oh, fine.' She waved a hand. 'I can't complain.'

'Can't? Or won't?'

She laughed softly. 'How is it that you can see through me so easily, Dylan?' The words felt like a punch in the stomach, but she didn't give him a chance to double over. 'I can't *and* won't complain. There are so many women out there who would love to be in my position.'

'Not entirely,' he murmured, and she gave him a confused look. 'I'm sorry, you probably don't want to be reminded of it.'

'I have no idea what you're talking about.'

She was going to make him say it, he thought, and sighed. 'You're pregnant and alone, Jess. You didn't even want to call to ask the father of your child for help this morning. I don't think that's a position many women want to be in.' He waited and then added, 'You don't have to pretend like it doesn't bother you.'

She blinked. And then she threw her head back and laughed. It sounded just as much in place in the forest as the birds he usually heard chirping in the trees. He wasn't sure what confused him more: that he'd thought that, or that she was laughing at her predicament.

'I didn't realise I'd made a joke,' he said stiffly.

'Oh, no, I'm sorry. I didn't mean to—' She broke off, bit her lip. And then she sighed, and the expression on her face changed to what he thought was resignation. 'I'm not pregnant and alone, Dylan. No man has abandoned me.'

'But—'

'I made you think that?' He nodded. 'Sorry. It's only because…it's complicated,' she said slowly. Seconds ticked by, turned into minutes, but neither of them spoke. Eventually Jess looked at him and something inside him flipped at the emotion in her eyes.

'Dylan…this baby…it isn't mine. I'm just…the surrogate.'

CHAPTER SEVEN

JESS HELD HER BREATH, hoping that she hadn't made a mistake. She knew she probably shouldn't have said anything to Dylan. But whatever it was that had her opening up to him—that had her telling him about her parents, that listened to his concerns about his past—had demanded that she tell him the truth. So had the part of her that had softened at his concern that she was going through her pregnancy alone.

It would be fine, she thought now, releasing her breath as she watched him. She wasn't betraying Anja by telling Dylan that she was a surrogate. As long as he didn't know that she was *Anja's* surrogate, it would be fine.

She hoped.

'You're...a surrogate?'

'That's what I said,' she replied lightly, hoping that it would defuse some of the tension between them.

'But...how? I mean, why?' Dylan shook his head and angled his body towards her.

'Well, I have a...friend who struggled to fall pregnant.' It was the best explanation she could offer.

'So you...offered to carry her child for her?'

She tilted her head, felt her heart sink. 'I did. Is that a problem?'

'No…no, it's not.' He lifted his eyes to hers. 'I'm not judging you, Jess.'

'Really? Because it really feels like you are.' And it was such a surprise that her throat felt clogged.

'It's just…a lot to take in.' Emotion crossed his face. 'I've never met…someone like you,' he said, looking away. 'I guess I'm struggling to understand why you'd do this to yourself.'

'Do what to myself?' Jess asked, cautioning herself to pull back when she wanted to snap the words at him. 'I get that you're trying to process this information, which is fine, I suppose, but you don't *have* to understand my choices.' She wanted to get up, storm off, but she knew she wouldn't be able to with her stomach in the way. She glanced down at the distance to the ground from where she was, and clenched her jaw. She couldn't risk it. 'Would you help me up? It looks like it's about to start raining and we should probably get back.'

He nodded and helped her up without a word. She felt even more annoyed when her skin prickled at his touch. When her body became so much more aware at his proximity.

But it gave her steam to storm off, and she walked ahead of him through the trees, leaving the buildings of Cape Town behind them.

It really was a beautiful place, she thought. And now that she knew how personal it was to him, she wondered why he'd let her tag along. Why had he told her things even Anja hadn't told her?

Why had *she* shared things with him? About her parents? She'd told him more about them than she'd ever told Anja. And why did she feel so disappointed by his reaction to finding out the baby she carried wasn't hers?

All of it worried her. And, just like she'd first thought when she'd met Dylan, it convinced her that she couldn't become involved with him. Or come between him and Anja. Anja was as close to family as she had, and she couldn't do anything to damage that. And she should probably stay away from Dylan if she kept that goal in mind.

Besides, she didn't *want* to become involved with Dylan...did she?

Just as she thought it there was a sudden clap of thunder, followed by the sound of rain. Not the steady, calming rainfall that often started rainy days, but a hard, angry downpour that had them both coming to a stop.

'I'm sorry,' Dylan said after a few moments. 'We should have left earlier.'

'Don't apologise,' she breathed, eyes on the rain. They were under the shield of the trees, which seemed to have formed some kind of canopy protecting them from the majority of the water. From where they stood, they could see the rain pouring down in front of them. 'It's all a part of the view.'

'I didn't quite anticipate this one,' he said with a soft laugh. 'Though it *is* something.' Neither of them spoke as the drops around them grew heavier.

'There's a part of me that wants to stay here until the storm is over.'

'Because you don't want to get wet?' Dylan asked, turning towards her.

'Because it's so beautiful. Angry, but beautiful.'

'Yeah, I know that feeling.'

Her eyes met his and she felt a shift in the air between them.

'What makes you think I'm angry?'

'Because of the way I responded to your...news back there.' His face tightened, but he didn't look away.

'It doesn't matter.'

'I think it does.'

His words stirred something in her chest, and she shook

her head. 'It shouldn't. Our lives, our decisions, don't affect one another.' Though those lives, those decisions *did* seem to be intersecting, she thought. 'The smartest thing we can do is to remember that.'

Silence followed her words, and she felt the change in him before she saw it on his face.

'Are you always…smart, Jess?' he asked slowly, taking a step forward. Breaching the gap between them.

In her mind she stepped back, maintaining the distance that would ensure she wouldn't do something that would prove the exact opposite of her words.

In reality, her feet stayed exactly where they were.

'I like to think so,' she replied, her voice husky.

She wondered why, and then got the answer when she suddenly found herself pressed against Dylan's body. She swallowed, and a voice in her head desperately warned her that she couldn't make this mistake.

It warned her to move, to run, and get a room in a hotel as far away as possible from the man who held her in place with only his eyes.

But then the voice was muted by another, louder one in her mind. One that shouted only one thing.

Stay.

'I don't think I'm being very smart now.'

'With me?' Dylan asked, his eyes heating, his arms going around her. 'Should I be offended?'

'Not unless you think I'm wrong?' When he didn't reply, she nodded. 'I didn't think so.'

She kept her eyes on his as she brought her mouth closer, closer still, until finally their lips touched.

Jess felt thunder boom inside her at the contact. Felt it break something, and then, like the rain, that something poured through her body into her blood, rushing through her as she sank into the pleasure of kissing Dylan.

Because the man could *kiss*. There was no hesitation

in the way his lips moved, no uncertainty in the way his tongue stole her breath. Her body trembled as her blood carried a headiness through her that she'd never felt before. As if its purpose had become more than to simply carry oxygen through her body. No, now it felt as if it carried thrills, sensations, *awareness* through her veins, and her hands tightened at Dylan's waist in response, as if they wanted to grip the feeling.

As if they wanted to capture it and never let go.

Dylan groaned as his hands moved over her body. Over the curves of her hips, her rounded belly, her breasts. They ached from his touch when his hands lingered, and then heated when he kneaded, softly, gently, adding more pressure each time so that the ache turned into longing, into desire, into *fire*.

He pressed her back until her feet hit a tree, the force of it sending a puddle of water right on their heads. But neither of them stopped. No, the coolness helped keep the fire at bay. Helped them start the kindling all over again.

Jess ran her hands over his back, over the muscles she'd admired ever since she'd first seen them in his backyard. Over the ridges she'd fantasised about. His shirt was plastered against his body from the water, and she moaned softly at how it saved her the trouble of going under his shirt to feel what she wanted.

Her fingers swept across the hardened planes, her hands moving from his back to his biceps, and then between them to his pecs.

It was so defined, so damn sexy that suddenly it felt as if she'd lost her breath, and she had to pull away so that she could breathe. His chest heaved as much as hers did as he rested his forehead against hers, and when their eyes met his lips curved into a smile that was the perfect illustration of what they'd just done.

Reckless. Spontaneous. Dangerous.

'It's raining,' she said huskily.

'Yeah, I know,' he replied with a soft chuckle. 'We both knew that before...*this* happened.'

'No, Dylan, I mean it's raining here, on us.' Just as she said it, drops splattered hard on both their faces. 'I don't think we can stay here any more.'

'No, we probably shouldn't.'

He took her hand and then whistled for Daisy. Seconds later, the dog came sprinting through the trees, wet and blissfully unaware of what her owner had just got up to. Together they ran for his house—although Jess couldn't quite call what she was doing running. But Dylan didn't seem to mind, and soon they were in the house, completely drenched.

'We should probably get out of these clothes,' she said, and felt her face burn as soon as she said it. 'I don't mean—'

'I know,' he said with a slight smile. Silence beat between them, and then he shook his head. 'But you're right. Besides, I should sort this little bugger out.'

He looked down at Daisy affectionately, and Jess felt something tumble in her chest. Not surprising, she thought, considering that everything inside her felt as if it had come apart.

'Dylan—'

'No, Jess,' he interrupted. 'We don't have to...talk about it.'

'I'd love to *not* talk about it,' she said with a bark of laughter. 'But how can we not? This—what just happened? It's not a good idea.'

'You think I don't know that?' Dylan answered, his expression serious.

'No, I'm sure you do,' she replied quietly, and felt fatigue seep back into her bones. 'So maybe you're right, and it's better that we don't talk about it.' Why did that make her so sad? 'I'm going to have a shower and then I'll call a hotel or something for the next few nights.'

'You can stay here.'

'No, I don't—'

'It won't happen again, Jess,' Dylan promised. 'And you being here is better. You'll be near if they need you next door. And you'll be able to call Anja if she needs to approve anything.'

They were good points, she knew, but still, agreeing felt like it would be the wrong decision. She didn't know how much of that was because her insides were still a mess from their kiss.

So she said, 'I'll think about it,' and walked to the room he'd shown her to that morning. She stripped off the wet clothing and showered quickly, and then dried the water from her hair before plaiting it and pinning the plaits around her head in a crown.

She pulled on thick woollen tights that she'd had the foresight to pack, and an oversized jersey that was just as thick, just as woollen. It made her look like an unshapen mess, but somehow that made her feel better. There was no way she would be tempted into seducing Dylan wearing that. No way he'd be tempted into seducing her either.

And because trying to find other accommodation seemed to require more energy than she had—along with going back out into the rain, getting the keys to her car, driving in the horrendous weather—her choice seemed to be made. She would stay there that night.

She should go out and tell him, she thought, but instead she climbed under the bedcovers, telling herself she would only rest for a moment. That she only needed comfort for a moment.

She'd made a mistake. Kissing Dylan had been a mistake. Because now that she knew what it felt like, she wanted more of it. And that wasn't an option.

She couldn't risk her friendship with Anja for more. It didn't matter that Dylan had been kind to her. That he'd listened to her. That it felt as if he understood her.

The attraction between them couldn't matter, nor the emotional connection. More than just being for Anja's sake, it was for *hers*, too. She didn't think that when Dylan found out whose baby she was carrying he'd understand why she'd kept it from him. Jess already knew that he'd be hurt because Anja hadn't told him about it, and she suspected *she* would be the target of the anger that hurt would turn into since he seemed so desperate to keep things civil with Anja.

It was easier to put some distance between them now, Jess told herself. Prevention was better than cure, and she needed to prevent the inevitable hurt that would come from entertaining anything other than a cordial relationship with Dylan.

Decided, she pulled the blankets closer around her and closed her eyes.

He was restless. Primed for a fight. Had been from the moment Jess had reminded him that their kiss was a bad idea.

The fact that she was right didn't have anything to do with it. No, he was upset because somehow she'd kept her mind when their kiss had made him lose his. When the kiss that *she'd* initiated had crossed the clear—albeit unspoken—boundaries between them, but *she'd* been the one to remind them of those boundaries after it had happened.

And yes, fine, maybe he'd wanted it to happen. Maybe he'd closed the distance between them in the forest because he'd wanted one of them to initiate a kiss. But he was only human. How was he supposed to resist the beauty, the vulnerability of her, wrapped up in that little bubble of anger?

When that bubble had screamed of the passion he'd got to experience only minutes after he'd thought about it?

It all made him feel so edgy that he knew nothing good would come from facing Jess in that state. So, after he took care of Daisy, he peeled off his wet clothes and replaced them with gym clothes, and made his way to his home gym to expel some of the energy.

If it hadn't been raining, he'd go back to his task of chopping wood. It was laborious work, something that kept his mind and body busy. Something that distracted him from the fact that he should have gone to speak with his sister.

Unfortunately, now he could only seem to keep his body busy. No matter how hard he pushed himself during his cardio, his strength training, his thoughts kept looping back over the last few hours. Over his words, hers. Over her reactions, his.

He finished his workout, showered and went back downstairs. All the while, he was trying to figure out what he should say to her. The only thing that he came up with was an apology, but what would he be apologising for? For kissing her back? For enjoying it? For facing the fact that they'd made their lives infinitely more complicated by acknowledging their attraction to one another?

None of it made sense, but he knew he couldn't avoid her for ever, so he told himself to man up and went to find her. He wandered around the house, but she wasn't in the living room or the kitchen, and for one sick moment he worried that she'd left without telling him that she was going. As a last resort, he checked the guestroom and relief flooded through him when he saw the shape of her under the covers.

His eyes swept over her. Her face was flushed from the heat of sleep, her hair in some kind of plait pinned at the top of her head. A woollen-covered arm rested on her belly on top of the covers, rounding off a picture Dylan knew he wouldn't be able to push out of his head with ease.

He shut the door just as quickly as he'd opened it, careful not to make a sound and wake her, and put as much distance between him and the room as he could. Daisy looked up at him from her station in the corner of the kitchen when he walked in and whined when he leaned over the counter, his heart beating so fast he couldn't catch his breath.

What *was* that? he asked himself eventually. What was that burst of emotion in his chest at seeing her? What was the fierce protectiveness that had surged inside him?

Whatever it was, it wasn't welcome. And yet it wasn't unfamiliar. It took him some minutes, but the image of Jess sleeping had him realising why he'd reacted so uncharacteristically to her surrogacy news.

He felt *protective* of her. And he was worried that this pregnancy would somehow hurt her. That he wouldn't be able to keep her from getting hurt.

In some part of his brain he knew that it wasn't his job to protect her. Knew that his need to do so could only mean trouble. But he couldn't figure out why he still wanted to, despite knowing better.

He sucked in a breath. It was going to be a long night.

CHAPTER EIGHT

Jess found Dylan in front of the fire in his living room.

Rain thrashed against the glass doors, lightning flashed every few moments. Daisy was curled up next to Dylan on the couch, whining ever so softly every time thunder sounded. Jess didn't blame her. It seemed that they were experiencing one of the famous Cape Town storms, and if Jess had been Daisy she'd be curled up next to Dylan, too.

Except she wasn't Daisy, and she'd given herself a stern warning against thoughts like that. Reinforcing her resolve, she walked towards them slowly. Daisy popped her head up when she saw Jess, but Dylan kept staring into the fire. As though there was something he could see there that no one else could. As though it held all the answers to life's mysteries.

'Hey,' she said softly after a few more seconds. Daisy immediately jumped off the couch and rubbed herself against Jess and, obliging the dog, Jess gave her the attention she wanted. But her eyes were still on Dylan. Stayed on him, too, when his gaze met hers and she saw the pain there.

There was a long, long pause before it cleared and then he said, 'Hey.'

'Are you okay?'

'Fine,' he replied. 'You fell asleep.'

'Yeah, I did. Sorry. It's been more of an exciting day than I'm used to. Knocked me out.'

'That's fine.' He paused. 'Did you figure out what you're going to do?'

'I was hoping that your offer was still on the table.'

'Of course,' he told her, though his tone made her uncertain.

'Thanks.' She waited for him to say something more and, when he didn't, she added, 'I can be out tomorrow.'

'Why?'

'You just don't seem like you want me here.'

'No, it's not that.' He leaned forward now and drained the glass she hadn't noticed on the table in front of him. 'It's just been…an exciting day,' he repeated her words.

'That's true.' She fell silent and, rather than contemplate his strange mood, decided to channel her energy into something useful. 'Would you like me to make us something to eat?'

His brows rose. 'I thought you said you couldn't cook?'

'I said I only started to learn a few years ago. That's a lot of meals, Dylan, so I think I can make us a…pot of curry,' she said, improvising.

'You're going to make us…curry?'

'Why not?' She'd made it a couple of times before. She was pretty sure she could do it again. 'It's the perfect meal for this kind of weather.'

'Oh, I'm not arguing about that. I'm just wondering whether— No, you know what? I would love some curry.' He patted Daisy, who'd curled up next to him again when it became clear she wasn't going to get any more attention from Jess, and stood. 'Come on, I'll show you where everything is.'

Jess would have found it hard to describe the next hour. But she *was* sure that no one would mistake it for any kind of cooking show. *Especially* not with Dylan watch-

ing her every move with amusement from where he sat
at the counter.

'You don't have to watch me, you know,' she said irri-
tably when she couldn't figure out how many cardamom
pods to use.

'You might need my help figuring out where everything
is,' came his reply. She rolled her eyes and counted out
five and then threw them into the pot, where her efforts
were looking more like a stew than a curry.

She hoped by the time the chicken started cooking
that it would be in better shape, but she was sadly disappointed. She sighed noisily, causing Daisy to look up in
concern from her corner, and Dylan to leave his post at
the counter to peer into the pot.

'This is your…curry?'

'It tastes better than it looks,' she said defensively,
spooning up some of the sauce and offering it to him.
His expression was neutral as he tasted it, and then his
eyes met hers and suddenly she wasn't thinking about the
sauce any more.

She'd seen scenes like this in movies before. Had wondered how feeding someone could ever really be erotic.
But clearly it could be, she realised, her eyes still caught
in his. Because now she wasn't thinking about Dylan tasting the sauce, but her lips.

Her skin.

Would his expression still be so neutral then? Or would
he offer her something to taste in return? Like *his* lips?
Like *his* skin? It would be so much better than the food
she'd made that evening, and she knew that the slight kick
in the sauce would have nothing on what would happen
between them…

She swallowed, and her hand faltered. She cleared her
throat. 'Well?'

A beat of silence passed before he answered. 'It's not bad.'

'Not…bad?'

'But it isn't curry either.'

She looked down at the pot, and then up at him again. 'Then what is it?'

'I'd say tomato stew.'

'But…but there's curry spice in it. It has a kick.'

'Well, the kick doesn't make it curry.' He narrowed his eyes. 'How many times have you made this?'

Heat immediately seared her cheeks. 'A couple.'

'Okay.' But she could see that he didn't believe her. 'Let's turn this into curry then, shall we?'

The next half an hour was distinctly different from her solo foray into curry-making. Mostly because of the way Dylan took her through the steps. It could have been a cooking show now, she thought. Or, more accurately, a one-on-one appointment with a cooking instructor.

Dylan was patient, and explained the steps to her before encouraging her to do it herself. She forced herself to ignore the thrill that went through her every time he touched her or drew closer to show her an ingredient or check how she was coming along.

But still, the time they spent fixing supper was lovely, and settled some of the tension that had still been lingering between them since that afternoon.

'I have to say this is pretty good.'

They were sitting in the dining room adjacent to the sunroom she'd admired the day before. This room was also enclosed by glass doors, the solid wooden table clear of decoration, with only a beautiful chandelier adorning the space. Simple and tasteful, she thought, and wondered if it was the room that had her thinking that, or whether her perception of the décor had been changed by the man sitting opposite her.

'Yeah, I think we're a pretty decent team,' Dylan replied with a smile. But almost as soon as he said it his smile fell away, and Jess heard herself speaking before the tension could return.

'You're an amazing cook. And unexpectedly patient.'

He laughed, and relief went through her. 'Yeah, well, I learnt patience when I taught Anja.'

She stared at him. 'Anja's a *terrible* cook.'

'Hence the need for patience,' he said with another laugh. 'It didn't take us long to realise cooking wasn't for her, and so she was relegated to sous chef for as long as we lived together.'

The silence that followed told her he was lost in the past. And, for the life of her, Jess couldn't figure out why she wanted to help him find his way back to the present. Or at least find a way to be in the past with him.

'It sounds like you two were quite a team.'

He looked up. Smiled. 'We were. I always told her we were a well-oiled machine.' His hands stilled and Jess kept herself from asking him if he was okay again. 'Did she tell you about that?' he asked suddenly, but continued before she had the chance to reply. 'No, she wouldn't have. You told me she didn't tell you the details.'

'Do you...' she started. Faltered. Cleared her throat. Tried again. 'Do *you* want to tell me?'

His eyes met hers. 'I probably shouldn't.'

'Of course,' she said immediately, insecurity dictating the thudding of her heart.

'But I'd like to,' he continued gruffly, and she nodded, too afraid she wouldn't have a voice if she tried to speak. She waited for him to find his words, eating in silence while he did. And when he started to speak she continued, knowing it would be difficult for him to share if she was watching him.

'Anja must have told you that my father was an...absent father, long before he actually left. He went to work every morning, came back home, showered, ate, and then left for the casino. Every day, like clockwork.'

Jess's eyes strayed to Dylan's face, her hands stilling, and she realised he was too engrossed in his story—in the emotion of it—to notice that she was watching him.

'But my mother was fine with that. She…she was able to handle that because she got to see him each day. Because some days he would return at night and sleep at home. She got to see him, and I think that was the most important for her.' He lifted his fork, ate, but Jess could see the actions were mechanical. 'And then he stopped coming home at all. I was fourteen, like I said. Anja was twelve. Both of us suspected he was gone when the routine stopped. When my mother checked out, we knew it was permanent.'

'That's…terrible, Dylan. I'm sorry.'

'I thought we already agreed we didn't have to apologise to each other for our crappy families?' he said with a wry smile. It quickly sobered. 'I remember thinking how strange it was. That even though my father barely spent time at home, not having him there at all changed… everything. We didn't used to have to worry about the house, about food, about my mother. And then—' he set his fork down, wiped his mouth with a napkin '—we had to worry about everything.' He threw the napkin aside. 'The house staff stopped coming. We had to take care of the things they used to do ourselves.' Jess saw him clench his jaw. 'And we had to take care of my mother.'

Her arms ached to comfort him, but Jess refused the urge. 'I don't understand. There was enough money. Why—?'

'Because my father had been handling all that money. He'd been running the house, paying the staff, making sure everything ran smoothly until the moment he stopped coming home. Then, everything stopped.' Dylan paused.

'Immediately after he left, I used to think the fact that he looked after us for those first fourteen years—that he hadn't used all his money on gambling—meant that he must have loved us. But then I'd remember that he *left* us, knowing that my mother didn't have access to his money, and all of the wishful thinking would disappear.' His words were so bitter, the ache in Jess's arms grew.

'Why did he leave?' Jess asked quietly, voicing the question she'd wanted to ask Anja for two years.

'I think gambling became more important to him.'

'I don't—'

'Or,' he interrupted, 'he lost control. It had been a tenuous control, anyway. Addicts...they can't indulge their addictions. If they don't get help...' He trailed off. Sighed. 'So really it wasn't about us.'

Seconds passed in silence, and again Jess resisted the urge—though it had become more pressing now—to comfort him. She told herself it was only because she understood what it was like to be abandoned. And she knew what it was like for that abandonment to be about the person who was doing the abandoning, and no one else.

Except you still think that your parents' attitude towards you has something to do with you.

Jess forced herself to speak. To distract herself from the annoying voice in her head. 'How could he keep gambling? Didn't the money ever run out?'

'The success of the family business prevented that from happening. My grandfather had made sure that my father would get a percentage of the profits every year, paid out monthly, until he died. He always had money.'

'And what about you? And Anja? And your mother?'

'My father didn't *quite* look out as well for us as his father had for him,' Dylan said with a thin smile. 'We were okay for a while after he left. My father kept cash in a safe for emergencies—that's what he told us, though now I realise it was probably for him, just in case he needed some quick cash to fund his habit—and we used that to keep us going for a while.' He picked up his fork again. 'Anja and I figured it out.'

'What happened when the money ran out?'

'I—' he cleared his throat '—I went to my father's work. I hoped I would find him there, ask him to come back.'

'But he wasn't.'

'No. Turned out his job there wasn't really that important. He was more of a…figurehead for the empire that held his name. My name,' he added. 'When I asked for him, they told me that he hadn't been there in months.'

'What did you do?'

'I asked to speak with someone who could help me.' He gave her a small smile. 'I was brazen for fourteen, but fear had forced it.' The smile faded. 'I was terrified I wouldn't be able to look after my family.'

'Oh, Dylan.' Jess reached over, laid her hand on his arm, before pulling back again.

'It worked out.' The smile was back, hiding some of the vulnerability she saw on his face. 'They sent me to the CEO. Ridge had worked closely with my grandfather, considered him a friend. He knew about my father's problems, but had no idea about what was happening with us. He made sure that we were taken care of until Anja and I got access to the trusts neither of us knew we had. My grandfather had set that up, too, though he died before we were old enough to know him.'

'How long until you got your trust?'

'Seven years.'

'So for seven years you were at this man's mercy?'

'It wasn't like that. Ridge was good to us. He taught me everything I know. Because of him, I could actually run the company my grandfather started when Ridge stepped down.'

'You've done a great job of it.'

'At what cost?'

'What do you mean?'

He shook his head, and Jess opened her mouth to press. But she stopped herself. Thought that maybe he felt as if he'd told her too much. So she didn't push. Instead, she thought about the man who had taught Dylan about his family's company.

When her stomach churned, and her memory stirred, she tried to push the thoughts away. But it was too late. Her mind kept replaying the thought. *A stranger taught Dylan about his company. Your own father wouldn't teach you about his.*

'It's been fine while you've been gone, you know,' she said suddenly. Desperately. 'They've both been fine. Anja and your mom.'

'I know. I've spoken to them. My mom—' His face tightened, his jaw clenched. 'I had her in London with me for Christmas last year.' When he lifted his eyes to hers, a pain she didn't understand shone in them. 'Anja wouldn't come.'

Why didn't she believe that that was the reason for the pain?

'She had her reasons,' Jess said instead of asking him about it. She thought about Anja's reasons for not spending Christmas with Dylan and their mother, and it took a surprising amount of strength for her not to tell him what those reasons were.

They'd done their second embryo transfer in December, and Anja had wanted to be around when they did the tests to find out whether Jess was pregnant.

It had been a stressful experience since the first transfer hadn't taken. Anja had told Jess she hadn't wanted to see her brother on top of it. Then, Jess had believed it was because Anja hadn't wanted to add to her own stress by seeing the brother who'd hurt her so badly. But now Jess wondered if it wasn't because Dylan knew Anja well enough to know that there was something on her mind, and Anja would have been forced to tell him about the baby before she was ready.

Perhaps, if things had been different, Anja *would* have joined her mom and brother for a happy Christmas, and the inevitable drama of Anja's return wouldn't be hanging around their necks like an invisible noose.

But things *weren't* different, and Jess only hoped that the fact that the second transfer had taken—that there was a baby on the way—would make Anja more open to her brother's return.

And why is that so important to you? an inner voice chided her.

'Do you have siblings, Jess?' Dylan asked, interrupting her thoughts.

'No, I don't.' She forced a smile. 'I'm an only child.'

'So you don't really know how long they can hold a grudge.'

'Maybe not,' she allowed. 'But I've had one against my parents for a really long time. Does that count?'

CHAPTER NINE

'Why?'

'I've already told you they're terrible people.' She laughed, but it sounded strangled. He watched her hand go to her stomach, fingers spread over the roundness of it as though she was protecting the child she carried from her words. His heart ached. 'There's really not much more to it.'

'You keep saying that, but we both know it's a lie.' He kept his gaze on her face. 'You said you haven't seen them since you moved out.' She nodded. 'What happened?'

'What do you mean?'

'What happened to make you move out?' he clarified. 'You knew they were terrible people long before you moved out, didn't you?' Her eyes dropped from his, but she nodded again. 'So what happened to make you leave?'

He was suddenly desperate to know. Perhaps because he'd done the same thing two years ago—walked away from his family. But he'd had his reasons. His father's death had caused memories he'd ignored for years to re-surface. Emotions he didn't want, didn't understand, had surged inside him.

And then he'd found out his mother had known his father had been an addict before she'd had children. She hadn't even tried to deny it when he'd confronted her. All of it had been too much for him to handle—or to keep from Anja—and so he'd left.

When guilt had nudged him, he'd tried again with his mother. He'd invited her to London, had thought they could work through it. But then, neither of them brought it up. Each day he'd told himself to, but he just…hadn't been able to. Much like he hadn't been able to walk over to Anja's house after he'd first arrived in Cape Town…

There were reasons he'd left, he thought again. So there must have been a reason Jess had left, too. He told himself he only wanted to know because he'd spilled his guts to her. But at the back of his mind he knew that wasn't true.

'What happened that made you leave, Jess?' he asked again, softly this time.

Her face went tight. 'There were…a lot of things. A lifetime of things.'

'Did they…hurt you?'

'It takes effort to hurt someone. I was nowhere near that important to them.'

His eyes took in her expression, her voice, the way her shoulders had suddenly hunched. He put his hand over hers. 'Why would they have you if they didn't think you were important?'

'Because my mother fell pregnant unexpectedly.' She paused. 'I was an…inconvenience. They didn't want me, but they didn't *not* want me either. At least not enough to do something about it.'

He stopped himself from apologising. Told himself to just listen.

'I wasn't a part of their plan. They told me that, over and over again, whenever I did something they didn't approve of. Even when I did,' she added softly. 'Remember I told you about my job as a lifeguard?' He nodded. 'I applied for it at sixteen so that I could buy my new laptop. And they *hated* it. It was at my father's country club, and they told me it made them look poor. And that looking poor wasn't a part of *their plan*. That dropping me off every day reminded them of how much it wasn't a part of *their plan*.' She stopped. 'What they actually meant was that *I* wasn't a part of their plan.'

Dylan wasn't sure what was worse. His situation, where his mother had willingly had them, knowing what they'd be born into, or Jess's, where she was made to feel unwanted for most of her life.

'You know what's funny?' she interrupted his thoughts. 'I think my father actually liked the idea of an heir.' She tilted her head. 'Until I actually appeared and I was nothing like either of them. I actually *cared* about people. Heaven only knows where that came from.'

'I guess you taught yourself more than just how to cook,' he offered quietly.

'Yeah, maybe.' She smiled, and scooped the last piece of her chicken into her mouth. 'That was wonderful, thanks.'

'Dessert?' he offered spontaneously, even though he'd stopped midway through his own dinner because of their conversation. Her gaze lowered to his plate and she gave him a pointed look before shaking her head.

'I've distracted you.'

'I think we distracted each other.' He smiled at her. Made a show of eating his food. She smiled back. And his heart flipped in his chest.

Stop, an inner voice warned, even as another part of him—a stronger part—told him that he'd opened up to her for a reason. Perhaps because there was…*more* there, between them. Perhaps because he *wanted* more.

He swallowed, and began to listen to that inner voice.

'There's not much more to tell you, you know,' she said, studying him. He wondered what she saw. 'When I left university I realised it wasn't my responsibility to point due north for them any more. They were adults. So was

I. And, like mature adults who didn't agree, we went our separate ways and now live separate lives.'

'They haven't tried to get in touch with you since?'

'No.' Sadness tinged her face before it was gone. 'But then, I haven't tried to contact them either. You should really finish your food,' she said, changing the subject 'It's delicious, prepared in the kitchen of one of the most revered chefs in Cape Town.'

She winked but stood, and started clearing her own dishes. Dylan might have thought it rude if it had been any other person at any other time. But he thought he understood why Jess she was doing it. She wanted to get away from him, from his questions. And, since he felt a bit raw himself, he understood.

So he finished his meal silently, and then cleared up his own dishes before joining her in the kitchen to help tidy their supper mess. The way he and Jess worked in tandem reminded him of how he and Anja had once worked. How it had been them against the world. Against their parents.

He thought about how he'd left Anja. Asked himself if that made him any better than his father. His stomach rolled with the fear of it, before it lurched with the knowledge that he *wasn't* like his father. His father hadn't needed them, but Dylan *needed* Anja. He'd discovered that when he'd been away. When he'd been plagued with how much he missed her. With how much he wanted them to be a family again, even just the two of them.

So he'd come back to try to make that happen…

But what if she didn't forgive him? What if he'd hurt her so much that, just like they'd done to their father, Anja turned her back to *him*?

The thought absolutely terrified him. Enough that he realised he couldn't afford to complicate the situation with his feelings for Jess, whatever they were. He couldn't afford to need Jess. To want her.

And so he wouldn't.

'Jess?'

'Yeah?' She was drying her hands and looked at him, and the homeliness of it sent a shot of something deep and unfamiliar through his body.

And strengthened his resolve.

'It won't happen again.'

'What won't?'

'You know, earlier...' It was strange, the heat rising up his neck. He'd faced much worse in his professional life—with his family—and yet here he was, embarrassed by a kiss.

'Oh. Oh,' she said again, her eyes wide. 'Okay.' She nodded. 'There's no hard feelings.' There was a beat of silence before she said, 'No, I didn't mean—'

'I know.' He cut her off with a slight laugh. 'Though it's a hell of a pun.'

'It was, wasn't it?' she said, chagrined. An unspoken attraction slithered over them as their eyes met again, and then she shook her head and stepped back, as if somehow it would kill it. 'Thank you for letting me stay here. I'll be out as soon as everything is fixed next door.'

'You can stay as long as you like.'

He didn't bother clarifying the implication, and she nodded and ducked her head.

But not before he saw a pretty red colour stain her cheeks.

She murmured goodnight, and left the room. Long after she had, Dylan stood in the kitchen, Daisy by his side, staring after Jess.

The next day passed in a blur of busyness.

The ceiling company had told them they would have to plaster certain sections and then repaint the entire ceiling. The good news was that they'd be able to do it all on the same day, so most of Jess's time was spent walking back and forth between Anja's and Dylan's houses, making sure the guys had everything they needed and checking on their progress.

She arranged for cleaners to come in the next day to make sure the house was one hundred per cent before she moved back in, and told herself it wasn't an excuse to spend more time with Dylan. She was *happy* about the busyness. It meant she didn't have to think about the attraction that had sunk its fangs into her the day before and wouldn't let go, no matter how much she wanted them to.

It also meant she didn't have to think about why she'd opened up to Dylan about her family. Sure, she hadn't told him everything, but she'd told him enough to make her uncomfortable. Or did she feel uncomfortable because he seemed to understand what she was telling him? That what he'd shared with her told her that he understood more than she even gave him credit for?

Unable to find answers for those questions, Jess stayed out of Dylan's way as much as she could. She answered queries about when Anja's next class would be, posted another reminder of Anja's absence on the yoga studio's social media. After a brief hesitation, she sent Anja an update on the house, and then thought it might be nice to send a picture of her baby bump as well.

It had only been two weeks since Anja had left, but Jess's belly had grown during that time and perhaps the reminder of her child would help Anja deal with her feelings about *other* members of her family.

She was trying to take the picture herself when Dylan walked in.

'I'm clearly interrupting something?'

'I'm just trying to—' She stopped the automatic answer before she told him the truth, and then gave him a smile. 'I want to take a picture of the bump for the mother and father.'

His eyebrows rose but he only said, 'Can I help you?'

'Yeah, please.'

She handed him the phone and a few seconds later she had it back with the pictures. She sent them to her laptop before shutting it. Things had suddenly become awkward and she didn't want to send the email with Dylan hovering around. It had guilt nudging her, and she realised how little she liked keeping this secret from him. But she couldn't tell him. She *wouldn't*. She had to think about Anja, and not whatever it was that had her thinking about Dylan.

'Why are you taking pictures of your stomach?' Dylan asked into the silence. 'Don't you see the parents? Your friends?'

Careful, she warned herself. 'Yes, but they're away at the moment, so I thought it might be nice to take a picture to send them.'

'How long have they been away?'

'Not too long. And they'll be back soon, too,' she added, anticipating his next question. 'They're good people, Dylan. This isn't the kind of situation that belongs in a documentary.'

She'd meant for it to be a joke, but he didn't laugh. After a while he said, 'I'm not judging your choice, Jess. Honestly, I'm not. I just can't help but wonder what happens to you after you give birth to this child.'

'I move on with my life,' she replied simply, though the question sent discomfort through her. 'It's a part of the agreement, when you do something like this.'

Though it wouldn't be for her, she thought. Not entirely. Because she'd still see the child every day when she went to work. She'd help Anja with the baby while Anja was on maternity leave, and then go back to her normal administrative duties.

That was her plan, at least. She'd taken Anja's PA job because it had seemed like the perfect opportunity to get away from her family, from their legacy. To create *her own* legacy. And while she enjoyed the organisational challenge of being a PA, it wasn't the only thing she was capable of.

She had a degree in finance. A choice that had been made when she'd still had hope her father would hire her after she'd graduated. She would be able to take over the family business one day, and finally be a part of the Steyn family. A real part. A *wanted* part. Except her father had no intention of including her, and that had been the straw that had broken the camel's back.

She told herself to snap out of thoughts of the past, but the present wasn't any better. Dylan's question had reminded her of a thought she'd shoved down a long time ago. That maybe it would be better if she didn't have to see the child she'd carried day after day. She didn't regret her decision, or think that she'd long for the child to be her own. She knew what she'd signed up for.

But she *was* worried about the things she couldn't anticipate. Like the emotion of childbirth. And the hormones that would overcome her once she saw the child who had grown inside her for nine months.

So perhaps making use of that finance degree would be a good move after she gave birth. She'd be able to give herself time to deal with the unanticipated without the emotional stress of seeing the baby every day.

But she wouldn't tell Dylan that. And she couldn't tell Anja that. But she *would* think about it.

'I appreciate your concern, Dylan. I really do.' And she meant it, she thought. 'But I know what I signed up for, and I know what it might mean for me.' She shrugged. 'I'll figure it out.'

He nodded, but his expression told her that he wanted to argue. She wouldn't let him.

'I'm going to take another look at what's happening next door.'

'No, I'll go. You were working before I got here.'

He was gone before she could protest.

CHAPTER TEN

DYLAN STAYED OUT of Jess's way for the rest of the day.

Her answers had irked him almost as much as the pull he felt towards her and was desperately trying to ignore. By the time it hit six o'clock, he was fed up with it, and decided they needed to get out of the house. Fortunately, the rain had subsided early that morning, so he made a few calls and went to find Jess.

'Hey,' he said when he found her in the sunroom. 'Not much sun to see any more.'

'You're about fifteen minutes too late. The sun's just set, and you have the perfect view of it from here.'

'I'll have to make time to see it then.'

'You never have?'

He smiled at the surprise in her voice. 'Not recently. But then, I haven't been home long. There'll be plenty of opportunities.'

'I suppose.' She paused. 'Have you come to find me because of my amazing culinary skills?'

'No,' he said, his lips slanting into a smile. 'I think we can both use a break from that tonight.'

'From my cooking? I'll try not to take offence to that.'

'From any cooking, actually,' he said, the smile turning into a grin. It was easier than he thought it would be, covering up the way his heart thudded in his chest. 'I thought we could go out.'

'Go out?' she repeated, straightening.

'Just for supper,' he added quickly. Less easy now, covering up the nerves. 'It wouldn't be a date or anything.'

'Of course not,' she said so stoically he swore she was teasing him. 'Because we're just—' She broke off with a frown. 'I was going to say friends, but I'm not sure that's what we are.'

'It's what we can be. What I'd like to be.'

But that was a lie, he thought, almost as soon as he'd said it. He didn't want to be *just* friends with her.

The realisation dislodged something in his chest he'd been ignoring since he'd met her. Since the night before, when he'd told himself he *had* to ignore it.

'Then we should seal our new friendship with a dinner out, I guess.' She smiled at him, but there was something behind the smile that told him she knew it wouldn't be that simple. 'I'm going to take a shower and then we can go. I'll see you in thirty minutes?'

'Great,' he said, and she nodded and left. A few minutes later he followed her lead, hoping that the pounding of the water against his body in the shower would give him back his ability to think logically.

Because he hadn't been. If he *had*, he wouldn't be taking her out to a restaurant. He wouldn't be entertaining their *friendship* knowing that there was something between them that could easily—*easily*—demand more.

And he couldn't have more. He'd told himself that just the day before. Had thought of all the reasons why he couldn't have more. He *knew* that he needed to focus on fixing things with Anja. On learning to forgive his mother.

Besides, there were too many complications with Jess. Too many reasons not to get attached, and risk being hurt. Too many reasons not to pursue any relationship—even a friendship—with her.

So why was he so excited to spend an evening with her?

He dressed quickly, and tried not to think about it. And then he went downstairs to wait for Jess.

His breath was swept away as soon as he saw her.

She wore a pretty blue dress that was printed with pink, yellow and green flowers over tights and boots. She'd twisted her hair up into that plaited crown again— so intricate-looking and yet so simple. He supposed the description could work for her, too. There was something so intoxicatingly intricate about her beauty, about her demeanour, and yet she wore it so casually, so easily that it seemed simple.

But he knew it wasn't. Nothing about her was.

'You look lovely.'

'Thanks,' she said with a shy smile, revealing yet another layer that wasn't simple. He'd never seen her shy before. Even when she'd been running her hands over his naked chest the first day they'd met. 'So do you, by the way.' She tilted her head. 'Maybe lovely isn't the right word.'

'Why not?'

'I don't know if your manly ego would accept it so easily,' she teased. 'So, I'm going to go with—you look very handsome tonight, Dylan.'

'Thank you,' he replied with a smile. He offered her his arm and she slid her own through it, the scent of her flowery perfume following them. He led her into the garage and opened the car door for her before sliding into his own seat and pulling out onto the driveway.

Then he took the road that would take them to the restaurant he'd only been to once before. Ironically, it had been on a date, and he remembered being so uninterested in the woman who'd accompanied him—he'd made mistakes in the past, too—that he'd spent a decent amount of time noting the details of the restaurant décor.

But he'd so been impressed that he'd thought that one

day he'd take someone he actually liked there to enjoy it with him.

'Where are we going?' Jess asked, interrupting his thoughts.

'It's a place not too far from here, actually.' He took a right, and drove the winding road up the hills that were so abundant in Cape Town.

'Are you going to tell me the name?' she asked, amusement clear in her voice.

'Buon Cibo. It's Italian for good food.'

'You're taking me to an Italian restaurant?'

'Yes.' His eyes slid over to her. 'Is that a problem?'

'No. In fact, I'm going to go out on a limb here and say that it establishes our friendship on a pretty great foundation.'

He chuckled. 'You like Italian food?'

'Love it. When I was younger...' She trailed off, and then cleared her throat and continued. 'When I was younger, my nanny was actually Italian. I'm not a hundred per cent sure where my parents found her, but I was glad they did.'

'Because of the food she made?' he asked, hoping to make her laugh. Felt warmth spread through him when she did.

'Yes. And because she was warm and kind. Things that hadn't really been a part of my parents' MO. Anyway,' she continued after a moment, 'she used to make delicious carbonara pasta. And a delicious lasagne. And— You know what? All of her pastas were delicious.'

He smirked. 'And this was before the baby?'

She stuck her tongue out at him. 'I guess we'll see if Buon Cibo delivers on their promise.'

She stopped speaking just as he pulled in front of the restaurant, and he enjoyed the way her eyes widened. The exterior of Buon Cibo was designed to look exactly like the little cafés in Italy, except it had two large trees on either side of the door that had been decorated with small lanterns. He helped Jess out of the car, and enjoyment turned to pleasure when she saw the interior. When her reaction told him she shared his opinion of the place.

Small round tables were spread throughout the room, suited for two or four people, making it clear the place was meant for intimate dinners. Chandeliers hung from the wooden ceilings, offering light throughout the dim room, accentuated by the flickering of candles on each table.

The wall opposite the entrance was glass, and revealed that the restaurant was directly next to the ocean. Water plunged against the rocks, against the glass, in a stormy and enthralling rhythm that spoke of a passion patrons could be tempted into repeating at the end of their date.

Not that this was a date, his inner voice told him. Nor was he interested in exploring passion with Jess when he knew they would never come back from it.

He was grateful for the distraction when the maître d' showed them to their table, though he didn't know how he felt about the fact that it was right next to the thrashing waves.

'This was not what I pictured when you said we'd be going out for dinner,' Jess said as they waited for the waiter.

'You don't like it?'

'No, I love it. I just wish I'd known how…intimate it was.' Her cheeks went a riveting shade of pink. 'I would have put on something a bit more appropriate.'

'How would you dress in an…*intimate* setting like this, Jess?' His voice had gone husky at her unintentional implication.

'I…no, I didn't mean it like that.'

'I know. But it's more interesting for me to think it,

anyway.' He grinned, hoping that teasing would cool the fire in his body.

'That's not how you're supposed to treat friends, Dylan.'

'I wouldn't know. My friends have never quite looked like you.'

'Stop,' she said softly. A warning, he thought, and instantly pulled back.

'We should ask about their specials, but I'd recommend the lasagne, if you're in the mood for pasta.'

'How could I not be?' she asked brightly. Gratefully, too, he knew, and mentally kicked himself for taking things too far.

'Why don't you tell me about what your life was like in the UK?' she asked once the waiter had taken their drinks order.

So he did.

He told her that the first thing he'd been struck by when he'd arrived was the cosmopolitan nature of London. It had reminded him a lot of Cape Town, and it had made him more homesick than he'd imagined he would be. He told her about the work he'd done. How he'd introduced himself to clients he hadn't yet had the opportunity to meet since taking over from Ridge.

And—though he didn't quite phrase it that way—about his obsession to bid for engineering jobs with clients who would enhance his company's reputation and portfolio. His success with those bids. How it had made him feel as if he was honouring his grandfather, the man who'd looked out for him and Anja even after his death.

How the success had made Dylan feel as if he was making up for his father's failures.

He told her how much he'd missed the warm South African weather. How he'd never quite managed to warm up even when they'd told him it was a summer's day. And, after the briefest moment of hesitation, Dylan told Jess about how much he'd missed home. And how often he'd wanted to come back.

'Why didn't you?'

'It didn't feel like the right time,' he answered. 'I... wasn't ready.'

'And you are now?'

'I don't know.' He gave her a wry smile. 'Maybe I just didn't care about the right or wrong time when I decided to come home.'

'You should tell them that. When you see them, I mean.'

'When I see Anja,' Dylan corrected automatically.

'No.' She frowned. 'When you see Anja *and* your mother.'

He opened his mouth to reply, but the waiter returned with their drinks just then and asked to take their order. Jess ordered bruschetta for her starter and went with the lasagne for her main. He ordered carpaccio and decided to have the carbonara for his main, telling her that she could have some of it if she wanted to taste.

She lifted her eyebrows. 'That's awfully kind of you, Dylan.'

'You sound surprised,' he said with a quirk of his lip.

'I'm not. Just...touched.'

He smiled at her now, and when she smiled back his heart flipped.

Get it together, Dylan.

'What were you doing before you started working for Anja?' he asked, desperate for a change of topic. One that wouldn't veer into the territory of his complicated emotions about his mother.

'Studying. I have a degree in finance.'

'Really?'

'Don't sound so surprised,' she replied, amused.

'I just...wouldn't have suspected that someone with that kind of degree would be working as a PA.'

'That's part of the reason I did it.' She fiddled with the salt shaker on the table. 'It was so different to the path I'd chosen to study, and I needed…different.'

'Why?'

The fiddling became faster. 'I studied finance because my father has an investment company. One of the largest in Cape Town.' Her fingers moved to the pepper. 'He inherited it from his father, and I thought he might want to share it with me some day.'

'But he didn't?'

'Nope.' She gave him a brave smile, but he could see the hurt. 'Apparently—' she blew out a shaky breath '—he'd been mentoring someone else at work.' Now she cleared her throat. 'To take over from him.'

'Someone who wasn't family?'

'Yes.'

'When did you find out?'

Her eyes met his. 'Just over two years ago.'

And, just like that, he got the answer to what had happened two years ago that had led her to move out. 'Did he make you believe that you'd be able to join the company some day?'

She laughed hoarsely. 'Not once.'

'Then why…' His words faded when he realised how terrible his question would sound. But she finished it for him.

'Why did I still want to? Why did I study a degree that would give me the necessary qualifications to be able to?' She dropped her hands to her lap. 'Because I wanted—' She broke off on a sigh. 'I don't know, Dylan.'

'What were you going to say?' he prodded gently. When she shook her head, he said, 'Jess, you don't have to pretend with me. Just tell me the truth.'

He held his breath during the pause after his words, and only released it when she answered him.

'I wanted to be a part of the family.' Anguish was clear in her voice, on her face. 'I thought that if I turned myself into someone that *could* be a part of the family—if I was a part of the business, if I stopped telling them where and why they were going wrong—they'd include me in their unit. It might not have been a conventional family,' she added, 'but my parents were a team. A—'

'A family that didn't include you,' he finished for her. 'Jess, I'm so—'

'Don't you dare apologise—' she interrupted him with a small smile '—I've moved on.' She paused, and Dylan thought she wasn't nearly as convincing as he suspected she wanted to be. 'And it wasn't that they wanted to exclude me entirely. My father *did* tell me I could marry the man he'd been grooming to take over.'

Dylan nearly choked on the wine he'd taken a sip of. 'He wanted you to *marry* the man? He actually said that?'

'Yeah, very seriously, too.' She rolled her eyes. 'He took my refusal just as seriously. It was clear then that what I'd wanted with my parents—what I'd hoped for—wasn't going to happen. So I moved out.'

'And you realised that what your parents did—how they acted—had nothing to do with you?' He had no idea why he'd said it, but when she looked up he knew she needed to hear it.

'It had *something* to do with me.'

'No,' he told her. 'If you believe that, then I need to believe that my father's addiction had something to do with me. That the fact that he didn't fight harder to overcome it—that he left us—had something to do with us. That my mother choosing to have us despite knowing my father had a—'

He broke off, realising what he'd said. Realising that he'd just told Jess something Anja didn't know.

Silence followed his words and, just before he could

start panicking, Dylan met Jess's eyes and something passed between them that had him feeling…calmer. As if they'd reached some unspoken agreement that told him Jess wouldn't tell Anja what he'd just told her.

It was a disconcerting feeling, and he cleared his throat. 'It's not you, Jess. It's not us.'

'Do you believe that?'

'Yes,' he replied honestly. 'Coming to terms with it, on the other hand…'

Her lips curved into a half-smile and she nodded. Again, something passed between them. But this time Dylan could identify it as a kind of understanding he'd never experienced before. Not even with Anja.

He felt it draw him in, though he told himself to fight it. Reminded himself that he wasn't interested in a relationship, in a future—that thinking of either was dangerous.

He struggled with it as the waiter arrived with their starters. They were about halfway through them when he tried to distract himself. 'Do you miss them?'

'My parents?' He nodded, and she lifted her shoulders. 'I had reasons for leaving them. I *have* reasons for not keeping in touch with them. Those reasons are more important than what missing them feels like,' she said quietly. 'But I guess I do miss them.' She paused, tilted her head. 'Or maybe I just miss the parents I wish they were.'

CHAPTER ELEVEN

JESS COULD SEE that Dylan was considering what she'd just said. It was obviously something that hadn't occurred to him before. He wore the exact same expression of surprise as when he'd told her that his mother had known about his father's gambling problem before he or Anja had been born.

Since Anja had never mentioned it—and Jess was sure it was something she *would* have mentioned—Jess knew that Anja didn't know. That it was part of the reason Dylan had left.

And somehow, without words, she'd promised Dylan *she* wouldn't tell Anja either.

She told herself it was because she didn't want to get in the middle of it. Of *them*. It was the only logical explanation. Any other explanation would be anything *but* logical.

It implied that Jess didn't want to tell Anja because *Dylan* didn't want her to. Which, in turn, implied that Jess felt a certain…loyalty to Dylan that trumped the loyalty she felt to Anja. Because if Dylan knew this and Anja didn't, it meant that he'd found out and hadn't told her. And, if that was true, Jess knew it would complicate Anja and Dylan's reunion even more.

So Jess would choose to believe that she'd agreed to keep the information to herself because she didn't want to get involved. And she would choose to believe that the guilt she felt was worth it to save Anja—and possibly the baby she carried—from the pain of a broken family.

'It's hard,' Dylan said suddenly, interrupting her thoughts. 'To face that the people who raised us weren't who we hoped they'd be.'

'Especially when they're gone and we have to face that they'll *never* be who we hoped they would be.'

He gave her a small smile, but they finished their starters in silence. Jess found herself looking at him every few minutes, and wondered if he realised how expressive his face was. Probably not, she thought, or he would have tried to hide the emotions that were clear there.

Compassion thrummed through her veins, followed closely by coldness when she realised that she shouldn't be bonding with Dylan. She shouldn't be learning the nuances of his face, of his voice. She shouldn't be understanding that he'd left because he'd been in pain.

Because leaving had caused *Anja* pain. Anja, her best friend. The only person in her life who actually seemed to deserve Jess's love. Who'd made Jess feel loved. Dylan was not her friend. No, he was the man who'd broken a piece of her best friend's heart. He was her best friend's *brother*.

So what if he seemed to understand her? If it seemed they had a lot in common? He was off-limits. And she couldn't—*wouldn't*—consider the dangerous emotions that were suddenly whirling around inside her.

Instead, she said the only thing that she could: Dylan needed to open up to someone else.

'You need to talk to someone about your father's death.'

'Excuse me?'

'You heard me. You need to talk through your feelings about your father's death, about him leaving. About—' she hesitated '—about your mother.' Left it at that.

'You mean...like a therapist?'

'That's not a bad idea, but it's not what I meant.' She let the words linger. 'I meant a…friend.'

Seconds passed before he said, 'I don't have that many friends.'

'You have Anja,' she told him. 'And your mother. No,' she said over his protest. 'I don't know the details of what happened with your mother, but if it can be salvaged, salvage it.'

'I…don't think that's going to happen.'

'Dylan—'

But the arrival of their main courses interrupted what she was going to say, and the turmoil on Dylan's face prompted her not to continue when the waiter left. Instead, Jess dug into her meal with a gusto she'd only experienced as a pregnant woman.

'Do you want some of mine?' Dylan asked, the turmoil now replaced with faint humour. It made him look softer, more handsome.

No, Jess!

'Yeah, thanks.' She took a forkful of spaghetti, but paused before she brought it over to her mouth. 'What's funny?'

'What do you mean?' he asked with an innocent expression that immediately had her narrowing her eyes.

'Are you *laughing* at my eating habits?'

'No.' But he laughed aloud now, and her eyes narrowed even further. 'I told you I was ordering this so you could taste it.'

'But then you looked at me like you thought I *needed* to taste it.'

'I did *not*.'

'You better not be lying to me.'

He chuckled. 'I'm not. Now, do you want to taste the pasta, or are you going to spend the rest of the night arguing with me?'

'I want to taste the pasta,' she grumbled, but winked at him.

The rest of the evening wasn't as tense as the first part, though the ghost of it hovered over them for the rest of the night. But, since neither of them brought it up, the conversation was light, happy, as though they hadn't spoken about their pasts that night.

It was late when they finished and as they walked out of the restaurant Jess paused to turn back. 'This was a really lovely evening at a really lovely place.'

'I'm glad you liked it,' he replied, standing next to her. 'Jess…'

Something about his voice had her turning towards him, and she sucked in her breath when she saw his expression.

'I know that this is probably the last thing that we should do after everything that's happened—after everything we've said—today,' he whispered, closing the distance between them and lifting a hand to her cheek. 'But I'm going to anyway.'

She opened her mouth to reply, but his lips were on hers before she could. It tasted sweet, a mixture of dessert and coffee. But beneath it Jess could also taste the man. That pure masculine taste that she'd only really experienced once before.

With him.

This time, though, the kiss wasn't as desperately heady as the one they'd shared in the forest. This kiss was soft and deliberate, a gentle sigh that had her heart racing. She felt the heat of his hand on her face as his other hand settled gently on her waist, a slow burn that went from the point of contact straight to her blood, warming her body as leisurely as a bath would.

With bubbles, too, she thought foolishly when he deepened the kiss—still tender, still cautious—and it felt as if there were bubbles in her stomach, on her skin. She gave a soft moan and pressed closer, her own hand sliding up from where it had rested on his chest to cup his cheek. His beard prickled, aroused, and it was strange that the feeling was more jarring through the contact of her hand than against her face.

She was breathing heavily when she pulled back, and she felt a flip in her stomach that had nothing to do with the way Dylan had made her feel. The hand on his face immediately lowered to the movement and, smiling, she looked up at him.

She wasn't sure what she'd expected. But it wasn't the following of his hand to where she'd put hers. It wasn't the reverent look on his face as he felt the slight pressure of the baby moving inside her.

It reminded her that he wouldn't be nearly as touched when he found out whose baby she was carrying. It told her that she was playing both sides. That she was betraying Anja with whatever was happening between her and Dylan. That she had betrayed Dylan by getting involved with him—even though it had been unintentional—when she was connected so deeply to his sister.

Tension crept into her body and settled in the muscles of her shoulders, her neck. She stepped back, away from him, and then walked to the car, waited for him to unlock it so she could get in. She didn't give him a chance to open the door for her this time—didn't give *herself* a chance to deal with the confusion on his face. She only shook her head when he said her name, and told herself to breathe when the tension inside her spread between them.

The ride back home was short, quiet, and Jess was almost relieved when they pulled into the driveway of Dylan's house.

Almost.

Except there was already a car in front of the house

when they got there, and Jess inhaled sharply when she recognised it. She let the breath out in a shudder just as Dylan said, 'Anja's home.'

CHAPTER TWELVE

THERE WAS A sick feeling in Dylan's stomach.

To be fair, he couldn't blame it entirely on returning from dinner with his sister's best friend to find said sister on his doorstep. No, the feeling had started the moment he'd felt the baby Jess was carrying moving against his hand. When he'd seen her face and worried that the wonder and amazement he saw there—that the wonder and amazement *he'd* felt—would turn into heartbreak when she gave that baby away.

The feeling had settled when Jess had walked away from him, breaking the warmth of their kiss and their connection that had grown during their dinner. And when he'd tried to do something about it and he'd got the cold shoulder, the silent treatment on the way home.

But now he was home, and his sister was back, and there would be no more time to think of it.

He pulled the car into the garage and then got out slowly. He heard Jess behind him as he walked to the front of his house where his sister was and, by the time he got there, Anja was standing outside, Chet next to her.

Dylan's eyes first went to their hands—to the tight hold he could see between them. And then he looked at his sister. Really looked. And really saw, for the first time in years. She'd got skinnier. And her face was tougher, its lines creased into a tight expression that told him she wasn't going to take it easy on him. But other than that she looked the same, and the emotion that clogged his throat had him wanting to walk right to her and pull her into his arms.

Instead, he shoved his hands into his pockets. 'It's good to see you, sis.'

'It's a…surprise to see you, Dylan.' Her voice was hoarse and she cleared her throat. 'How long have you been back?'

'Just over a week.'

'And you didn't tell us? Me or Mom?'

'I wanted it to be a surprise,' he said lamely, and belatedly thought that maybe it *was* lame. That maybe his plan to come home and reconcile with his sister was just plain *lame*.

'Well, it's certainly been that.'

Silence spread between them, and then Anja's eyes shifted to behind him and her stormy expression cleared. 'Jess!'

His sister stalked past him as if he wasn't even there and enveloped Jess in a hug. Jealousy beat an uncomfortable rhythm in his blood and all he could do was stand there as Chet walked past him, too, thumped him on the back in greeting and went over to hug Jess.

'Your stomach has grown so much!' Anja said and lowered to her haunches. Jess's eyes fluttered over to him, and something crossed her face that he couldn't quite read.

'Yeah. But it's only been two weeks, An.'

'Much too long for my liking,' Anja murmured to Jess's belly and Dylan's stomach dropped slowly, steadily, his mind still trying to comprehend what his eyes were telling him.

Anja straightened and turned to Dylan. 'Did Jess tell you?'

'Tell me what?'

'You asked me not to,' Jess interrupted, and her eyes went from Anja's to Dylan's. This time he could clearly see the apology on her face.

'So he doesn't know?' Anja asked, but the question wasn't directed at Jess. It was directed at him. Which made absolutely no sense. How was he supposed to know what he didn't know?

'I don't know what you're talking about.'

'Maybe we should take this conversation inside?' Jess interrupted.

'What conversation?' Dylan demanded, his heart thudding from the tension. 'Someone just tell me what you're talking about. Now,' he snapped, when Jess opened her mouth again.

'Relax,' Anja told him. 'This isn't Jess's fault. She's right. I asked her not to tell you.' She shifted closer to Chet and took his hand. 'Jess is carrying our baby, Dylan. Chet and I are going to be parents.'

And immediately Dylan knew why his stomach had dropped earlier. Why he suddenly recognised it as sick anticipation. It didn't matter that it made no sense—how could he have anticipated the news Anja had just told him? How could he have known that Jess was carrying his sister's child? *His* niece or nephew?

But all he knew for sure was that the feeling was there, and it made him feel foolish.

Just like trusting Jess did.

'Why?' he asked hoarsely. 'When?'

'We should go inside,' Jess said again. Dylan nodded, but he didn't look at her. Couldn't. Not even when she said, 'No, actually, you all should go inside. You need to talk about this and...' Her voice faded, though Dylan sensed everyone knew what she was referring to. Him. His return. Why he'd left. 'I don't need to be there.'

'You can be,' Anja said softly. 'You're as much a part of the family as any of us are.'

'No,' Dylan heard himself say. 'She's not. And she's right, this should be between all of us.'

'Dylan—'

'No, Anja, he's right,' Jess said. 'I'll be next door.'

'I thought you said the ceiling wouldn't be done until tomorrow?'

'They finished the painting today. I'll open all the windows and be upstairs. The smell shouldn't be as bad there.'

And then she was gone, leaving Dylan alone with his sister and brother-in-law.

It was silly to cry. Jess knew it, and yet she still felt the tears slip down her cheeks.

She could blame it on the hormones. And they probably deserved some of the blame. But most of it came from the look on Dylan's face after he'd discovered that she was carrying Anja and Chet's baby.

And the vicious reminder that she wasn't a part of their family.

Her breath shuddered out as she opened the windows of Anja's house, the fresh, brisk autumn air relieving the smell of paint in the house. It was better upstairs, as she'd thought it would be, and after she opened the windows her eyes fell on the chair that still sat in front of one of them.

Had it only been a week ago that she'd seen Dylan for the first time? It didn't seem right that she could feel his disappointment in her—his hurt *because* of her—so profoundly when she'd only known him for such a short span of time. And yet there she was, wiping tears from her eyes because of it, and trying to figure out what to do next.

She couldn't stay in Dylan's house any more. She suspected that she'd burnt that bridge, well and truly, though it hadn't been *entirely* her fault. Perhaps if Anja and Dylan's relationship hadn't been so damaged, things wouldn't seem so bad for him. Except that it *was* damaged, and Jess was carrying the reminder of the extent of it.

She knew now that every time Dylan looked at her he'd be reminded. Added to the fact that he'd been acting so strangely about her surrogacy even before he'd known who she was a surrogate for.

So she couldn't stay at Dylan's, and Anja's was out of the question with the smell of paint still lingering in the air. She could find a hotel—there was no way she'd find anything cheap at such short notice—but that would take from her savings. Savings she'd need after she'd given birth and needed to separate herself from Anja and Dylan.

It was clear that would be her only option now. Her friend would put up a fight, Jess knew, but Jess needed space. Away from the baby, and away from their uncle. Though she knew that wasn't the only reason.

She'd become comfortable with her life, just as she had been before she'd started working with Anja. Was it perfect? No, but she hadn't expected it to be. And perhaps that was why she'd lingered, avoiding what she'd needed to do, just as she had with her parents.

But she needed her independence. She saw that now so clearly that she wasn't sure why she hadn't before. She needed to stop relying on people she *thought* were family, and she needed to start relying on herself.

So she would drive to a hotel and spend the night there. And soon she'd move into her own flat. She'd save as much as she could while she still worked for Anja, but she'd start making plans. She *would* survive this. She'd survived worse.

Jess sighed and sank into the couch, her body aching from the strain of being pregnant and the tension of the day. The brisk breeze still drifted through the air and she pulled a throw over herself. She switched on the television, and waited for Anja to tell her their discussion was over.

She would pack up her things and go to a hotel, she thought, even as her eyelids started to close...

Dylan found Jess wrapped in a fleece throw in front of the television. It took him a moment to realise that she was sleeping, and seeing her like that wiped away all the righteous indignation he'd felt from the moment he'd offered to tell her she could come back to his house.

Instead, he settled on the opposite couch, his body and soul weary from the last couple of hours. He could do with a break from the tension between him and his sister. That was the only way he could describe what had transpired between them. He was exhausted, and the space he wanted so that he could figure out how he felt about everything was unavailable as Anja and Chet were sleeping over.

He had plenty of spare rooms—the house had been designed that way because he'd hoped one day to have a big family. To have his and his sister's kids playing around, having sleepovers. He wasn't sure that would happen any more. Which made sense considering that his sister hadn't even told him she was expecting a child.

Could he even call it that? he thought, rubbing a hand over his face. He immediately felt bad about it, and let out a shaky breath. It was all too much for him—Jess, the surrogacy, seeing his sister again.

Finding out his sister had had a miscarriage and how she'd struggled with it afterwards. Finding out Jess had offered to help them have a child when Anja had been so close to giving up. The unselfish reasons Jess had described to him when she'd told him about the surrogacy were so much more profound now. So was his fear for her when she had to give the child away, though heaven only knew why.

She was carrying his niece or nephew and *she hadn't told him*.

Did it matter that Anja had asked her not to? Maybe. But it still felt like a betrayal, that she'd broken his trust. Which was ridiculous, considering that he hadn't even known her long enough to trust her.

Logically, he knew that. But, just like he'd thought before, nothing about the situation with Jess felt logical. It hadn't been logic that had softened, warmed in his chest when she'd shown him her sympathy and told him he needed to talk about his problems. It hadn't been reason that had pushed him into kissing her. There was something more there that had nothing to do with logic, and it terrified him.

And maybe that was why he felt the way he did.

Or maybe it was all a distraction to keep him from thinking about how coldly his sister had greeted him. Or how stilted their interactions had been. They hadn't spoken about anything other than the baby since Anja had told him she was too tiredfor anything else.

He couldn't argue, considering she'd travelled eighteen hours to get home. But he knew it wasn't the travelling that had tired her. It was the first of many difficult conversations they were going to have.

It was going to be a process, he thought. One he couldn't speed up merely because he wanted to. He needed to give Anja time to process. Hell, he needed to give himself time to wade through all his thoughts, all his feelings. About his family, yes. But also about the woman who whimpered so softly in her sleep.

So he stayed in Anja's house for a while longer and, when he was ready, did what he'd offered to do. He closed all the windows and then lifted Jess into his arms and carried her to the house next door.

CHAPTER THIRTEEN

WHEN SHE WOKE UP, Jess wasn't entirely sure where she was.

It took her a while to figure out that she was in a bed. And that that bed was the one she'd slept in for the second time now...in Dylan's house.

So much for getting a hotel room, she thought. And then realised that being there meant someone had *brought* her there the night before.

She didn't want to spend too much time thinking about who.

Because though she knew Chet could easily have carried her the short distance to Dylan's house, he would have more likely woken her. Which left only one other option...

Pushing away fanciful thoughts of how sweet, how romantic it must have been, Jess got out of bed and had a shower. She hadn't brought another set of clothes with her, so she pulled on the tights from the night before—ignoring the way her heart sank at the memory of how different things had been when she'd worn them then—and her woollen oversized jersey with boots. It wasn't entirely new, but she hadn't worn this combination before.

Besides, who was she trying to impress? Certainly not the friends who'd seen her with her legs in the air while she'd been impregnated with their child. And *certainly* not the man who'd brushed her off so completely the day before.

With that in mind, she pulled her hair into a bun at the top of her head and began packing. Fifteen minutes later, she walked with her suitcase to the kitchen. She was surprised to find no one there, but she heard the deep rumble of male voices from the dining room. Leaving her suitcase in the kitchen passageway, she made her way there.

It was strange seeing Dylan and Chet there, talking as though there hadn't been a boulder of tension that had descended on them the day before. They stopped when she walked in. Chet smiled at her, but Dylan's face immediately soured before settling into a blank expression. She nearly rolled her eyes.

'I'm not sure how I ended up in bed here last night, but I'm willing to bet it was one of you.'

'Hey, you *are* carrying my child,' Chet replied with a wink, and she felt her mouth curve.

'Though, let's be honest, that wouldn't have kept you from waking me up and telling me to walk back to the house.' Her eyes went to Dylan and she felt the amusement waver. 'Thank you.'

'No need,' he replied smoothly.

She clenched her jaw. 'Well, I think there is, so I'm saying thanks. Also for letting me stay here while everything was happening next door.'

'You're welcome.' His eyebrow quirked. 'Better?'

'Much,' she replied, and then turned her attention to Chet. 'Where's Anja?'

'She went for a run. Said she'd see you when she gets back.'

'Well, she can see me next door. I'm going to head over, make sure everything's okay before the cleaners arrive in an hour.'

'You don't want breakfast first?' Chet asked.

'I'll make myself something at your place.'

'You sure about that?' Dylan interjected now.

'Why wouldn't I be?'

'Just because I've tasted your cooking and...' He let the words drift and annoyance stirred. Which was strange, since she was fairly certain that she would have been amused if it hadn't come from him.

'And yet I've survived for twenty-six years,' she said wryly. 'I'll see you next door, Chet. And...' she hesitated '...I guess I'll see you around, Dylan.'

She pretended that she hadn't seen the questioning look Chet sent her and picked up her bag, giving Daisy a head pat before she left.

It felt strangely as if she was turning over a new page. And perhaps she was, she thought, considering the plans she'd made the night before. Granted, it hadn't worked out for her to sleep at a hotel the previous night, but perhaps that was a blessing in disguise. Now she could keep that money in her savings.

When she got to Anja's place she made herself something to eat, ignoring the way her stomach wished she'd taken up Chet's offer to have breakfast next door. She could have had bacon and eggs instead, and tried to make up for the lack of it by making her single cup of tea for the day.

She was curled up on the couch when Anja walked in.

'Glad to see you're having a good balanced breakfast,' Anja said, flopping down on the couch opposite Jess. Her hair was still wet from her morning shower, the curls piled up on top of her head, much like Jess's.

'Eating for two and all that,' she said, tilting her bowl of oats for Anja to see. 'You can't have had breakfast yet?'

'I haven't, and I'm starving.'

'Why didn't you eat something before you came over?'

'Because it would entail spending more time with my brother?'

Jess's heart thudded at the mention of Dylan. 'Well, you *did* come back to do that…didn't you?'

'I guess. I don't know. I'm just so…*mad*.'

Jess bit back the *why?* on the tip of her tongue and nodded. 'You should tell him that.'

'I don't think it would go down particularly well,' Anja replied dryly.

'Actually, I think it might. He doesn't know why you're mad, Anja, besides the obvious reason. And it's about time you stop carrying it around with you, too.'

Anja narrowed her eyes. 'Since when do you push for family reconciliations?'

She choked out a laugh. 'Since you came back from Sydney as soon as you heard he was back?' A beat of silence passed. 'You can't tell me that you finished everything you wanted to?'

'We finished the last of the work on the studio. I'd hoped to do more…but I wanted to be here. The rest we can do via email or video chat.' Anja sighed. 'I guess you're right.'

'As usual,' Jess teased.

'Ha ha.'

Jess let Anja mull it over and finished her breakfast. She made some coffee for Anja and handed it over. Anja murmured her thanks, adding, 'How do you know? That Dylan doesn't know why I'm mad, I mean?'

She should have worn her hair down, she thought, when she felt the tell-tale heat of a blush start in her cheeks. 'We talked over the last few days.'

'About me?'

'About him, mostly.'

'And?'

Jess struggled to find an answer that didn't make her

feel as if she was betraying Dylan's trust. 'He's come back to make things right. I know,' she said when Anja opened her mouth. 'I know that things are messy and painful between you two. But he's come back, and so did you. For the sake of your child, his niece or nephew, and for *your* sake, you should at least try to talk to him about it.'

Anja rolled her eyes. Then threaded her fingers together. 'Low blow, Steyn.'

'I know,' she said sympathetically. 'But it wouldn't hurt if it wasn't true.'

They sat in silence after those words, and then Anja said, 'He *did* take time off work to be home. He hasn't since—'

'Since he left.'

'Since long before then, actually.' Anja gave her a strange look. 'Are you…is there something going on between you two?'

'What?' There was no stopping the blush now. 'No, of course not. Why would you say that?'

'Because my brother doesn't just share how he feels with people. Hell, I lived with him for almost two decades and I still don't know some of the things he felt then. That's part of the problem.'

'I was just there at the right time, I guess.'

'Maybe.' But Anja looked worried. 'You're not interested in him?'

'No,' she said immediately. *Not any more, anyway.* 'I was civil with him because of you. And this baby.' She didn't have to mention the kisses. 'I know it would be much too complicated, Anja.'

'It would be,' her friend agreed.

'Good thing there's nothing to worry about then, isn't it?' Jess replied, and ignored the sick feeling in her chest at the lie.

Because she *was* worried. She was *very* worried.

* * *

Dylan saw her as soon as he got there, and was about to turn back—coward that he was—when she turned and saw him.

'Oh,' she said softly. 'I'll leave.'

'No, you don't have to,' he replied immediately. Though he was still mad at her, Dylan hated that the easiness between them had been replaced by...by whatever was happening now. A mixture of tension and apology. Of words unspoken and words that had been said. 'I'll leave.'

'No, this is your place.'

She turned, and he could almost see her eyes taking in the magnificent view from the hilltop he'd taken her to a few days ago.

His place of comfort.

Where he'd opened up to Jess.

Where he'd kissed her.

He pushed away the memories when she turned back. 'You shouldn't have to leave just because I'm here.'

'I'm not,' he said in a short tone that proved exactly the opposite of what he'd said. 'I just wanted to be alone.'

'So I'll go.' She walked past him.

The words were out of his mouth before he could help it. 'Why were you here?'

The crackling of leaves and sticks under her feet went quiet. 'I wanted to think.'

'About?'

She gave a small laugh. 'Why don't you take a guess?'

He didn't reply. Couldn't, when what he would guess sounded incredibly self-centred. There was no way she was thinking about him. Even if *she* was part of the reason he'd needed time outside, to think alone.

After a moment he heard the crunching of leaves again, and he whirled around. 'Jess.'

She stopped, turned back to look at him. 'Yeah?'

'Anja and I…we had a conversation this morning.' It had been one of those conversations that had picked his emotions apart and left them out to dry. Naked. Raw. 'She told me you told her to give me a chance.'

She shook her head. 'I told her she needed to start thinking about her child.'

'The child you're carrying.' As if he could forget.

'Yes,' she told him. 'I see your opinion hasn't changed despite the fact that you now know I'm carrying your niece or nephew.'

'I have no opinion on this.'

'You and I both know that's not true.'

'Your agreement with my sister has nothing to do with me.'

He watched her face tighten.

'I'll remember that the next time I have to talk her into having a conversation with you.'

'So you *did* tell her that.'

'For her child's sake.'

'And yet she made it sound like it was for the sake of this family, too.'

'What do you want from me, Dylan?' she asked in an exasperated tone.

'The truth,' he growled.

'Fine. I told her to give you a chance. For the child's sake, for hers, and yes, for you, too.' The admission cost her, he thought, taking in the expression on her face. 'I care about… I care,' she finished, and lifted a hand to brush at her face.

'Why?' he asked, caught by her now. Anger had flushed her cheeks, making the golden brown of her skin almost luminous. 'Why do you care?'

'I'm asking myself that very question right now.'

'And what answer have you come up with?'

His back was turned to the view he'd returned to for

solace, the beauty in front of him now much more appealing. He shouldn't have noticed what a lovely picture she made. Standing in the woods, tall, dark trees around her, dull brown leaves at her feet. She looked like a woodland creature, though he couldn't blame it on the plaid shirt and jeans she wore.

He *did* blame it on the way she carried herself. The ease, the natural rhythm of her. Even when she was standing there, looking at him in annoyance, she looked as if she belonged there. As if her selflessness, her kindness, belonged in a natural setting.

'That I'm crazy.'

'You're not crazy.' If *she* was, then so was he.

But then, maybe that was the answer.

'No? Then how do you explain what's been happening over the last few days? Because you might not have known just how off-limits I was, Dylan, but *I* did. I knew the moment I found out the sexy guy living next door was my best friend's brother, the uncle of the child I carried. I *knew* that I shouldn't have got involved with you.'

She threaded her fingers together, as though she didn't know what to do with her hands. 'And yet, when you brought me here, when you told me all of those things about your family…I felt…I don't know, *attracted* to you.' She said the word with a disgust he struggled not to feel offended by. 'And, you know, because of all that—' she waved a hand at his body, and amusement coloured the insult '—and so I kissed you. And I went on a date with you. And none of that nonsense about us being friends,' she added, 'because we both know that wasn't a friendship date.'

He didn't know what to say. But he'd asked for it, he knew. He'd pushed her, and he couldn't be upset that she was giving him the information he needed. That he wanted.

The only problem was that nothing she was telling him turned off whatever it was that he felt whenever he saw her. It didn't matter how angry—or how raw—he was, his heart ached and his stomach flipped every single time he saw her.

'You know what the worst part is?' she asked. 'That I got in the middle of whatever's going on with you and Anja. I *ran* right in the middle of your family drama while running away from my own.'

'You've helped,' he said softly.

'Have I?' She lifted her brows. 'When you came here, your question was more accusation than gratitude.'

'I'm…sorry about that.' The apology was a surprise. As was the sincerity he felt as he said it. 'The conversation with Anja… It was tough, and I came out here to deal with…everything.' He shrugged, wishing the pain was as easy to shake as the words. 'I'm glad you asked her to talk with me.'

'She wanted to,' she replied after a moment. 'She just needed a shove in the right direction.'

He almost smiled. 'Thank you.'

'Sure.' Silence pulsed between them, and then she said, 'I'm going to leave before we get into another argument that tempts me into shoving more literally.'

He nodded. Told himself what he wanted to ask her wouldn't be worth the turmoil her answer would no doubt bring. And then he asked it anyway. 'Why didn't you tell me, Jess?'

'Anja asked me not to.'

'And it was just that simple for you?' Anger stirred, and then burrowed into him. 'It was just that simple to keep something I should have known from me?'

'Yes,' she replied quickly, and then exhaled sharply. 'That's what you want me to say, isn't it? That it was simple for me to keep this secret from you?'

'I just want the truth.'

'No, you don't, Dylan. You want another reason to be angry with me.'

Disbelief made him splutter his words out. 'You think I *want* to be angry with you?'

'Yes, I do,' she replied. 'Because it would be easier to be angry with *me* than with your mother. With your father. With…' she hesitated '…with yourself.'

'No,' he denied. 'I *trusted* you, Jess. You broke—' his voice went hoarse '—you broke my trust.'

'Because I was being loyal to the only person who's ever been loyal to me?' she demanded. 'Because I was keeping *Anja's* trust?' She shook her head. 'She's like family to me, Dylan. She *is* my family. And you know why that's so important to me.' She paused. 'Whatever you and I shared these past few days—' She broke off and he nearly protested, desperate to hear what she was going to say.

Instead, silence followed her words before she blew out a breath. 'It wasn't easy,' she told him. 'It wasn't simple. But Anja trusted me, too. And—' Jess lifted her shoulders '—being able to trust your family, knowing that they'll be there for you, that they'll do what's right for you, even when it's hard for them? That's what family's supposed to do.'

She stopped speaking then, her eyes studying his face, telling him that she had more to say. He wasn't wrong.

'That's why you're really upset, Dylan. Because your parents broke your trust. They left. Even though your mother was still there,' she continued, 'she wasn't *there*. Not in the way you needed her to be. And I'm sure…what you found out about her made that feel even worse.' Dylan felt the agreement inside him—felt the truth of it—but he didn't speak.

'You're angry at her because of it. And at your father, for all the horrible things he put you through. But you're also angry at yourself. For leaving,' she said when he looked at her, and he wondered how she knew things he hadn't even admitted to himself. 'So if you need to deal with that by being angry with me, go right ahead. But realising it and facing the anger you have is going to help you fix what's wrong with you and Anja.'

She left then, but he didn't follow. He needed time to think, especially since Jess had just added to the list of things he needed to think about, easily summarising feelings he'd struggled to figure out for the longest time in just a few minutes. By the time he made his way back to the house, Dylan knew just how right Jess had been.

And damn if that didn't complicate things.

CHAPTER FOURTEEN

DAYS LATER, ANJA told Jess that she, Chet and Dylan were taking a trip to the coastal town of Langebaan to see their mother. The news was unexpected, as was her insistence that Jess go with them.

'No,' Jess said, feeling ambushed. She was still staying in Anja's house, working, thankfully, which helped her keep her mind off Dylan and the inner voice telling her it was time to move on. She'd avoided Dylan as much as she could, which was possible since Anja mostly went over to his house after work. She stayed there for hours and when she came back looked exhausted and emotional. They were sorting it out, Chet had told Jess one night, since he was her only companion for the time Anja was away. And sorting it out was a process, Anja had told her the following day at work. It hadn't been easy since their issues extended far beyond what either of them had known, but they were working through it. And now the final step was to speak to their mother.

Jess's efforts to avoid Dylan were now in vain since he stood on the other side of Anja's lounge, leaning against the wall with his arms crossed. She suspected he was going for a nonchalant look, but he only succeeded in looking broody and sexy and Jess cursed the pregnancy hormones for making her notice.

'You don't need me there,' she said, looking from Anja to Chet. She studiously avoided Dylan. 'I'm just going to be in the way.'

'No, you won't be,' Anja told her. 'My mom wants to see you again. And, you know, the baby,' she said, which was a real punch in the gut for Jess. How could she say no?

Her eyes flickered to Dylan, and then back at Anja again.

Oh, yes, *that* was how.

'It won't be comfortable for me to sit in the back of your car,' Jess protested, clutching at straws now. 'Either of yours,' she added, looking at Chet.

Both of them had trendy little cars that were incredibly impractical for a pregnant woman—and for a family. Anja was planning to trade in her car before the baby was born, but there was no way she'd be able to do it before this impromptu little trip.

'We've already thought about that,' Anja said, her enthusiasm a stark contrast to the fatigue she'd shown over the last few days. Jess could feel her resistance weakening. 'Dylan will drive up in his car. He's agreed for you to drive with him.'

'Has he now?' she asked, and cocked an eyebrow at Dylan. He gave her a smile that made her want to punch it from his sexy mouth.

'Yeah, and he has more than enough space. Besides, Jess,' Anja continued, her voice softening. 'None of us want to leave you here alone.'

And, with that, her resistance broke all together. 'Fine, but don't think I don't know you were working me.'

'I was *not*,' Anja said in mock insult. 'If I was—and, I repeat, I was not—I would have mentioned how much we consider you to be a part of our family, and that any family trip would be incomplete without you.'

With a laugh, she ducked out of the way of the cushion Jess threw at her.

Though she'd been joking, Anja's words had stayed with Jess in the days before they took the ninety-minute drive to Langebaan, a tiny town on the West Coast of South Africa. It had made Jess realise how much she wanted Anja's words to be true. And that had made her wonder— or panic—about whether she'd offered to be Anja's surrogate because she so desperately wanted to be a part of that family.

Of any family.

At the time, it hadn't even occurred to Jess. She'd only offered because she'd wanted to help, and it had been a real, tangible way for her to do so. She loved Anja—more than the employer she was, or the friend she'd become. She loved Anja... Well, Jess imagined she loved Anja like she would a sister...

Except she'd never had a sister—or any sibling—so how could she possibly know?

Now she worried that she'd become Anja's surrogate because she'd wanted to protect that love. *Her* love. *Her* feelings. Because surely Anja couldn't turn her back on Jess when Jess had carried her child? She couldn't stop caring about Jess, or toss her away like Jess's parents had...

Unless she could.

Because Jess would have served her purpose then, wouldn't she? She would have done what she'd offered to do, and given Anja the child she'd always wanted. What would keep Anja from turning from Jess then? What would keep that bond she thought she shared with her friend from crumbling?

Jess had already learnt that she didn't have much purpose in her life. The degree she'd worked so hard towards was useless. No matter how hard she'd tried, her parents didn't want her. And if she didn't have a purpose—if she was useless—why would Anja want to keep her around?

Jess sucked in her breath. Told herself not to cry.

But the tears came anyway.

'I know this might not be exactly how you would have liked to travel,' Dylan said wryly. 'But we could at least try for some civility.'

He felt Jess shift beside him, but kept his eyes on the road. It was bad enough that he was stuck in such a confined space with her. He wouldn't look at her, too, and have that sexy and sweet look she had going for her distract him even more.

He'd been annoyed when his sister had told him about the plan. Partly because he'd had to put Daisy in a doggy hotel while they were away. Partly because he'd had to leave his house and he'd just grown comfortable living there again.

But mostly it was because he really didn't want to speak to his mother about the past. But as soon as Anja had found out that their mother had known about their father's gambling problem before they'd been born, she'd been determined to find out why their mother had decided to have them.

Though that determination had only come after the shock, the tears, the hurt, he thought. And knew that they were only in store for more of the same.

But they'd been making progress, and for the first time he'd been able to articulate why he'd left. Because he'd felt as if their mother had betrayed them. Broken their trust. Because she'd abandoned them by reacting the way that she had to their father's abandonment, even though she'd *known* what she'd signed up for.

Because he hadn't wanted to add the pain of knowing all that—pain he knew the extent of—to Anja's grief. Because he hadn't been able to deal with his own grief over a man who hadn't deserved it.

He hadn't mentioned his fear that maybe *he'd* abandoned Anja just like their parents had. Didn't want to in case Anja didn't feel that way, and he'd put it in her mind. No, he'd rather keep that to himself. And, even without disclosing it, Dylan felt…hopeful. Hopeful that maybe their family could move past the hurt, the abandonment, the betrayal.

And perhaps that was why he'd agreed to take the trip. For the sake of closure. And as for taking Jess along… what was he supposed to do? Say no? That would have for sure sounded his sister's alarms, and he knew that she already had her suspicions about his relationship with Jess. He suspected the only reason she hadn't asked him about it was because she'd had the conversation with Jess, and she'd chosen to trust her friend's word on it.

Good thing, too, or the progress he and Anja had made might have been wiped away.

'I'm sorry,' Jess replied, interrupting his thoughts. 'I didn't realise civility required words.'

'Well, we have over an hour left of this trip, so if you're happy with being quiet for the rest—'

'I am,' she said quickly, and he frowned.

They weren't on the best terms, he knew, but this withdrawn, sullen person wasn't the Jess he'd got to know. She wasn't even the one he'd fought with that night that felt like so long ago, or the one he'd had the terse but somehow productive conversation with in the woods.

'Are you okay?' he asked.

'I thought we were going to be quiet?'

'And if I thought that you wanted to be quiet because you were annoyed with me, I would have been. Except that isn't the case.'

'You're an expert in my emotions now?'

'No, but I'm a good businessman and that requires being able to read people.' He glanced over, and then looked back at the road. 'It helps that I *do* know you.'

'I think you're overestimating your knowledge,' she said, but he could sense her resistance was waning.

'Or underestimating it,' he replied quietly. 'What's wrong?'

He saw her shake her head and then bite her lip. He didn't push, didn't say anything else since he understood her hesitation. Understood that he was responsible for it. They'd been put in a hell of a situation, he knew, but his behaviour hadn't helped.

He'd overreacted. Or he'd just reacted, he thought, to his trust being broken while he was still trying to deal with his mother breaking his trust. While he was still trying to deal with all the other things Jess had pointed out to him.

So he needed to apologise for taking it all out on her. And perhaps now was the time that he did.

'Look, if it's about what happened with us—'

'It's not.'

'No?'

'No.'

There was a beat of silence while he processed that, but then he said, 'Well, I wanted to apologise anyway. I reacted too harshly about the baby. It wasn't entirely…your fault.'

'Entirely,' she repeated, and he felt her gaze on him.

He sighed. 'I felt betrayed, Jess. I told you that.'

'And I told you why I couldn't tell you.'

'Yeah, and I understand that. But—' his grip tightened on the steering wheel '—but I wish you'd told me. Warned me.'

She didn't reply immediately. 'I…I couldn't just tell you. Firstly, I barely knew you. And when I started to get to know you,' she said as he opened his mouth to protest, 'Anja had already asked me not to say anything to you about it. So I didn't.' She cleared her throat. 'But I am sorry for my part in…in hurting you.'

He nodded, but couldn't bring himself to say anything. He appreciated her apology. Her loyalty to his sister. But… Well, he'd wanted Jess's loyalty, too. To him.

And that was the real problem.

'If it makes you feel any better,' she said quietly, 'it wasn't simple for me. I *wanted* to tell you. It felt…wrong not to. But—' she lifted her hands '—I couldn't betray Anja's trust. So I settled on telling you the baby wasn't mine and hoped that it would help you, I don't know, understand.'

Dylan felt some of the pieces that had broken inside him come together again. 'I…appreciate that. Thank you.' He paused. 'And I'm sorry, too. For reacting the way that I did. I shouldn't have…been so blunt. I didn't mean what I said about you not being a part of the family.'

She nodded, and the words were the last they said for another few kilometres.

'It wasn't just about you, you know,' he heard himself say into the silence. 'It was difficult for me to hear it because—' He broke off. Told himself to get it over with. 'When I found out my mother knew my father was an addict before she had us, it felt like a betrayal.'

'When did you find out?' she asked softly.

'A few days before his funeral.' He took a deep breath. 'They'd put all my father's stuff in a box at work after it was clear he wasn't coming back. Gave it to me when I first started. I put it in a storeroom and never looked through it until I got the news that he'd died.' Dylan paused, took another breath. 'When I did, I found meticulous records of his expenses dating back long enough for me to see how he'd paid off the house. How he'd set money aside for the staff, for us. And how he'd used everything else to fund his habit.'

'That must have been hard.'

'What was worse was that it proved my father had his problem long before we were born. Before my parents had even married. And when I confronted my mom about it—' he lifted a shoulder '—it didn't go well.'

'Oh, Dylan,' she said on an exhale. In those two words Dylan heard everything that Jess wanted to say. That she understood his reaction now. That she was sorry it had happened. It soothed something deep inside him.

'Does Anja…?'

'Yes,' he replied when she trailed off. 'I told her about it a few days ago. Hence this little family trip.'

'Are you okay with that?'

He took a moment to think about her question. About how she'd known to ask it. 'I'm not thrilled. Things were… awkward when I saw my mother at Christmas, and we didn't even end up speaking about it.'

'Maybe things were awkward *because* you didn't speak about it.'

'Maybe,' he murmured.

'So this trip might be exactly what you need to move through it.'

He let the words settle in his mind. Felt the hope of it fight back against the burn of betrayal. Maybe things *would* get better after this trip. Maybe, after finally being honest with one another, they would become a family. A real one, without the weight of betrayal and hurt and resentment hanging over them.

But hearing Jess's opinion spoke to his biggest regret. And now all he could think about was how things could have been sorted out so much sooner if he'd just come home.

Or if he'd never left.

'Things seem to be better between you and Anja now,' she said into the silence.

'Better, but not the same.' He ran a hand over his beard. 'It's going to take some time.'

'Of course it will. But progress is progress.'

'Except—' He stopped himself before he could say what he'd been thinking.

'Except?'

'It's nothing.'

'Oh, so you're going to keep quiet *now*?' she asked dryly, and he felt his lips lift.

'Annoying, isn't it?'

She grunted, and his smile widened into a full grin. And perhaps it was that that had him saying, 'I can't believe she didn't tell me about the baby. About any of her fertility issues.'

'It was…hard for her to talk about.'

'But we're *family*. And we were close before…' He let the words linger. They were another reminder of the mistakes he'd made.

'She thought she was a failure,' Jess said. 'I don't think she wanted to tell you and have you believe that of her, too.'

'*What?* Why would she feel that way? Why would *I* believe that?'

'Because she wasn't thinking logically. She was only thinking about how she couldn't do the one thing that she was supposed to be able to do as a woman.' Jess shrugged. 'I was there, Dylan. She was so hard on herself.'

The words made pain splinter through him. 'I wish I was here. I wish I could have helped her through it.'

'I know.'

'I shouldn't have left, Jess.'

It ripped from him, the admission.

He was suddenly incredibly grateful that a business crisis had delayed Chet and Anja's departure and they weren't travelling behind him and Jess. Dylan had agreed to go ahead with Jess so that they wouldn't have to tell their mother they would be late. It meant that he could take a few minutes to regroup, to recover from whatever had made him tell Jess the thing he worried about most.

He took the next exit, which led to a pit stop that he only realised was familiar after they stopped next to the small café. They'd stopped there on family trips, he remembered, when they'd taken the short journey to visit his mother's family. He didn't dwell on why the familiarity of it was suddenly comforting, or why he held out his hand when he got out of the car, waiting for Jess to take it.

All he knew was that he felt better when she did. More so when they stopped in front of the little pond next to the café, birds frolicking in the water, making the most of the sunny autumn day.

They stood in silence for a long time while he figured out why he'd stopped. But Jess spoke first.

'Do you know why you left, Dylan?'

'Yes.'

'Why?'

So he told her all the reasons he'd figured out himself over the past weeks. And when he was done she squeezed his hand.

'It's normal to turn away from the things you can't deal with,' Jess said. 'We all do it.'

'Anja didn't. She stayed here and faced it. The memories of it. The grief of it.' He watched as a duck dipped itself under the water and shook it off.

'Anja had Chet, Dylan. She had me. She had a support system. One outside of the family that had caused her pain.' He looked down at her. 'It makes a difference.'

'Why are you being so understanding?'

'Why are you determined to torture yourself like this?'

'I'm not—' He broke off, and shook his head. 'It's not

torture. It's the truth. I *abandoned* her. Just like our parents did.'

'You didn't abandon her. You took some time to figure out how you were feeling about your parents. About your childhood that was cut short. Did you do it in the right way?' she asked. 'Maybe not. Maybe you should have told Anja about what you'd found out. Maybe you should have shared how you were struggling with your grief and the anger. But that doesn't mean you abandoned her.'

'But my mother—'

'Was a flawed woman. And your father was a flawed man. So are you. We're all flawed,' she said with a smile. 'We all make mistakes. But we move on from them. We learn from them. And you being back tells me you *have* learnt from it.'

She faced him when he didn't reply, and narrowed her eyes. 'You're not only scared about that though, are you?' And only when she asked did he realise that he wasn't. 'What is it, Dylan?'

'I—' He stopped himself, but only for a moment. It was too late to play coy, and he was so tired of keeping it all to himself. 'Why did his death affect me so much? Why am I so unhappy and angry about it when I only really knew him for fourteen years?' He ran a hand over his head. 'Even *saying* that is generous.'

Her hand fell from his, and then lifted to cup his cheek. 'Maybe it's because you're still stuck in the hope that he could have been different.'

CHAPTER FIFTEEN

'WHICH IS FINE,' Jess told Dylan, dropping her hand. 'There's nothing wrong with wishing you had something you didn't.' It felt as if she was talking to herself. 'But you have to let go of the unrealistic expectations if you want to move on. If you want to move forward.'

'You're right,' he said after a moment.

'Don't sound so surprised.'

His lips lifted, taking some of the torture out of his eyes. 'I'm not. It's just…we have a lot in common, don't we?'

'I wasn't talking about me, Dylan.'

'Maybe not, but, despite what you might think, I've learnt how to read you. Enough,' he said before she could protest, 'that I know you were thinking about yourself, too, just now.' He turned to face her and took a step closer. 'Enough to know that something's wrong with you. Has been since before we even took this trip.'

She wanted to tell him that something *was* wrong. She wanted to share her fears with him just as he'd shared his with her. But it wouldn't help. She knew because when he'd told her that he hadn't meant it when he'd said she wasn't a part of their family she hadn't believed him.

'We should probably get back on the road.'

He stared at her for a few seconds, and then gave her

a curt nod. She almost sighed, but was afraid the sound would break whatever control had convinced Dylan that he shouldn't press. They were on the road a few minutes later, and Jess settled on looking out at the rolling hills, interspersed with long stretches of green fields and cattle, that they passed.

It was a pleasant trip, driving along the West Coast. Soon they would take the road that led to the coastal town of Langebaan, home to one of the most popular casinos in the Western Cape. The realisation made her think about Dylan's father, and whether his parents had met here, in this town. Whether it had been the start of his father's addiction.

Jess hoped that what she'd been able to offer Dylan at the pond had given him comfort. That it would be enough to help him work through what he was going through. And that once he had he would be able to turn to Anja when Jess was no longer there.

Because the more she thought about it, the more she realised that she had to leave. If she didn't have a purpose, what use would she be? She only had to look at her parents to know that. She only had to remember that they'd abandoned her long before she'd abandoned them. They'd done it from the moment she was born, no matter how hard she'd tried to prove herself.

Her father had rejected her even though she'd tried to make herself useful in the company. Her mother… Well, her mother had never really paid any attention to her. They'd never let her forget that her presence in their life hadn't been something they'd wanted.

And it turned out that being unwanted, feeling rejected—abandoned—were all pretty close together on the 'make Jess feel crappy' spectrum.

She hated that feeling. And she was still dealing with the remnants of it from her parents. She didn't need it from her friends, too. So she'd do what she'd done with her parents after she'd realised they wouldn't change and welcome her into their team. She would pull away, put distance between them, so that when the day came and she left, they wouldn't be so surprised.

Because *she* would leave, she thought. She would leave them before they left her.

'You've been quiet today,' Anja said from behind her.

Jess forced herself to give her friend an easy smile— even more so when she saw that Dylan was behind Anja— and went back to looking at the waves of the ocean in the distance.

Mia Nel's cottage was small but it was situated in the perfect position. Just outside the small town of Langebaan, where it was close enough to get whatever she needed within an hour, and far enough that there weren't many tourists around.

The beach was basically her backyard and for that alone, Jess told herself, the trip was worth it.

'It's been a long day,' Jess said as Anja and Dylan settled into the comfortable outdoor chairs on the small outdoor patio.

'It has been, but that's never stopped you from talking before,' Anja teased.

'Maybe it's this baby I'm carrying,' Jess teased back. 'Crazy genes can do that to you.'

'Oh, don't you dare blame my baby for your sullenness!' Anja's eyes twinkled, and then she grew serious. 'Are you sure you're okay though?'

'I'm fine.'

She felt Dylan's gaze on her, but she ignored it and kept her own gaze on the sea in front of her. It was a fair question. Jess knew that she'd been quiet since they'd arrived. She'd been sociable, of course. Had calmly accepted the love Mia had overwhelmed her with the moment they'd met.

But she'd kept herself from becoming too invested in the emotion. Because she knew it wasn't for her. It was for the baby she carried, and she couldn't forget it or avoid it. Ever since Anja had returned, the idea that Jess's time was running out had only grown.

She shook off the weight that settled on her shoulders at the thought of it. It was for the best. *Reject them before they can reject you*, a voice whispered into her mind.

She closed her eyes for a moment before asking Anja, 'So, what are the final accommodation arrangements for the trip?'

It did its job at distracting Anja, and Jess felt the air loosen in her lungs in relief. Though she couldn't deny it was also because she and Dylan would be spending the night in Mia's spare rooms, while Anja and Chet stayed in a cottage they'd rented a few doors down.

She didn't want to be alone with Dylan now. Not with his piercing gaze. Not with the knowing looks.

She felt as if he was looking straight through her. No, it felt as if he was looking straight *into* her. Into the part of her that was cowering like the little girl she'd been when she'd first realised her parents didn't care for her like other parents cared for their children.

It was annoying, being dragged back into the past. Which was why, as soon as the conversation lulled between the three of them, Jess excused herself for the night. She still had to face her demons, but if she wasn't near Anja and Dylan she wouldn't be tempted to belong.

She hoped.

'She's acting weird, isn't she?' Anja asked Dylan as soon as Jess left for the night.

'Yep.'

'Did she say anything to you on the way over?'

Do words of wisdom about my own emotional problems count?

'No. I asked, but she pretty much gave me the same answer she gave you when you asked.'

'It's so *strange*,' Anja said with a shake of her head. 'Jess isn't like this.' There was a beat of silence before she said, 'Do you know if something happened?'

He debated with himself about whether he should tell Anja. The truth had been working out pretty well for them. His relationship with Anja was slowly improving because of it. And he knew once they had a conversation with their mother they would finally get some closure.

Honesty had brought him a lot of what he'd wanted since he got back. Honesty and Jess. He sighed.

'It could be the fact that we…that I…'

Probably should have figured out what you were going to say before you started talking, dummy.

'It could be because of me.'

'Because of you?' Anja repeated in that slow way she had that told him she was trying to hide her real feelings.

'Yes. While you were gone, Jess and I…' He ran a hand over his head, again unsure of how to describe what had happened between him and Jess over those days before Anja had returned. 'We got close.'

'Got close?'

'Are you going to keep repeating what I say?'

'Yeah, I am. If that's what it takes to keep me from knocking your head against the table.'

And there it was, he thought, and braced for the onslaught.

'Are you telling me, Dylan Theo Nel, that you are *seeing* my best friend? The woman carrying my child?'

'We're not seeing each other. Nothing that official.'

'Nothing…' He thought he saw the colour drain from

her face. 'Please don't tell me that "got close"—' she lifted her hands in air quotes '—is a metaphor for some kind of hanky-panky—' She broke off. 'I think I'm going to puke.'

'Oh, stop being so dramatic,' he said, though he'd expected the reaction. 'Nothing happened.' Not in the way she thought, at least. 'But we did have…something.'

'She told me I had nothing to worry about.'

'Because there was nothing to worry about when you asked her. We both knew something between us would be complicated, so neither of us wanted to pursue it.'

Again, not entirely the truth, but only because he was just realising what the truth was as he said it. *He* wanted to pursue it. He had wanted to pursue it from the moment he'd met her. From that first kiss. And still he wanted to. The realisation stumped him.

A long silence passed before Anja spoke again. 'When you say there was nothing to worry about when I asked, does that mean there is now?'

'Depends on whether you're worried about me and Jess being together.' As soon as he said it, he realised how much he wanted Anja to be okay with it. And suddenly the conversation took on a whole new importance. 'Are you?'

'Am I—? Hold on.' Anja lifted a hand. 'I'm trying to process everything you've just said in the last few minutes. It's going to take some time.'

Since he needed some time himself, he didn't say anything. Instead, he tested how he felt about this latest development.

Of course, he'd known there was something between him and Jess. What he *hadn't* known was how invested he was in that something.

It didn't make sense, he thought. At least not on paper. They'd only known each other for a few weeks. And only two days of that time had been spent on something resembling dating. The rest of the time they'd either been arguing or talking about things so difficult for them that dating had been the last thing on their minds.

But the facts couldn't explain why his heart thudded that much harder when she was around. Why he couldn't keep his eyes from straying to her. Why he wanted to see her reaction to jokes that were made, or stories that were told. Why he still thought about their kisses, and how much he wanted to repeat them.

It didn't explain why he felt so comfortable that he *could* talk to her about things. Or why he sensed that she was unhappy about something. No, the facts couldn't explain any of that. And it was finally occurring to him why that was.

He was falling for his sister's best friend. The woman carrying his niece or nephew. The woman he'd only just met.

And none of the reasons he'd told himself why that was a bad idea seemed to matter any more.

His lips curved.

'Okay, I'm done thinking,' Anja said, and Dylan hid his smile. He didn't want her to think that he was mocking her. 'I'm not going to say that I'm happy about this development. It's messy. And complicated. And, I don't know, it feels incestuous.'

Dylan frowned at what he once again thought was an exaggeration, but kept the opinion to himself.

'But clearly whatever's going on between you and Jess…means something. To both of you.'

'Not sure I'd go that far,' he muttered.

'No,' Anja said immediately. 'Me not totally freaking out about this does not mean I'm going to counsel you on Jess's feelings.' She frowned, and then sighed. 'Except to say that Jess was…hurt by her parents. It takes a long time for her to trust, and if you've done something stupid—which, knowing you, you probably have—it'll take longer

for her to get there. But now that you've mentioned it—'
she slid a hand through her hair '—I did notice *something*
between you. Coming from both sides.'

'Really?' he asked, and was only slightly disgusted by
the optimism he heard in his voice.

Anja's face broke into a smile. 'Yes, you dork. Now,
back to what I was saying. It's complicated, and it's messy,
but...but if it's what you two want, then I'll support it. Just
don't, you know, do it, until my baby is out of the way.'

'Firstly, what is wrong with you? And secondly...
thanks, An.'

'Don't thank me yet,' she said and stood. 'I'm going to
be pretty miserable about this for the foreseeable future.'

'Completely understandable.'

She narrowed her eyes, and then sighed. 'Don't complicate things if it's not worth it, okay?'

'Okay.'

'And don't...don't hurt my friend.'

'I won't.'

Anja left with those words, and Dylan sat back with
a smile, watching the waves crash into the boulders and
then pull away. It hadn't been the easiest conversation to
have but, once again, Dylan felt that his honesty had paid
off. Not only because he'd told his sister the truth about
things that had happened between him and Jess, but because it had clarified a lot for him.

First, it *was* worth it.

Second, he would do his best not to hurt Jess.

And third, he was going to convince Jess of both those
points, no matter how long it took.

CHAPTER SIXTEEN

'So,' Jess said the next afternoon, 'I just had a chat with Anja. And it was…surprising, to say the least.'

She and Dylan were at the restaurant where they'd all just had lunch. She'd spent the morning walking through town—if it could be called walking, considering the number of times she'd rested—while Dylan, Anja and Chet had spent the morning with Mia. She hadn't minded entertaining herself. Understood that the reason they were there was so that those conversations could happen.

But that afternoon they'd all had lunch together. Afterwards, Mia had an appointment with a friend, and Anja and Chet had decided to drive to the next town to buy some things for the baby. Which left her and Dylan alone.

Handy, considering she had a bone to pick with him.

'You told her that we kissed?'

'What? No, of course not.'

'Then why did she follow me to the bathroom to tell me that she's okay with us being together?'

'She did that?' His lips twitched, but he shook his head. 'I'm sorry, I didn't realise she would speak to you about it.'

'*It?* What is *it*?'

'I…might have told Anja that there was *something* between us. Not that we'd kissed or anything,' he said quickly. 'But that there was…something.'

She opened her mouth, and then shut it again. Figured it would be better to keep the first words that wanted to come out of her mouth to herself rather than hurl them at him. But the entire exchange had made her feel sick, and she drank from the bottle of water she'd ordered with her meal before she spoke.

'So, let me get this straight. You told my best friend— the mother of the child I'm carrying—that there was *something* between us.'

'Yes.'

'Why?'

'Because there *is* something between us.'

'No, there isn't.' He gave her a look, and she gritted her teeth. 'Maybe there *was*, but we both know that there can't be.'

'Why not?'

'Because…' She trailed off, realising now that her main reason had been Anja, and that no longer seemed to be a problem. 'Because I'm carrying your niece or nephew and you don't agree with that choice,' she finished triumphantly.

'*What?*' he said, his face twisted. 'That's not true.'

'Isn't it?' she asked mildly. 'Because I distinctly remember your objections to me being a surrogate for someone else.'

'That was before I knew it was Anja's baby.'

'So your concerns aren't valid any more because this baby is your sister's?'

He ran a hand over his head, and she recognised the action as something he did when he was thinking. 'No,' he said finally. 'They still are. But I guess at least I know I'll be there for you now. We all will be. So, you know, you won't have to go through whatever you go through alone.'

It took her a while to figure out how she felt about his words. About the fact that he assumed he would be there for her. That they all would be there for her. It was as if he knew exactly what her biggest fear was, and was speaking directly to it.

It melted her damn heart.

But it couldn't, she told herself. Because it wasn't real. She wasn't only deluding herself into believing that it was.

'So that made you comfortable enough to tell Anja about us?'

'Well,' he said, leaning forward, 'we both noticed you haven't been yourself the last few days. She asked me about it yesterday and I told her that…it might have been because of me.'

She stared at him, and then she laughed. 'You are *so* full of yourself.'

His eyebrows lifted. 'You're saying I'm wrong?'

'I'm pretty sure I told you that you were in the car on our way here.'

'So I don't have anything to do with the way you've been acting lately? Nothing?' he repeated, as though, somehow, repeating it would change her mind.

It didn't, but it *did* point out that while he wasn't entirely the reason for her pulling away, he was certainly a part of it.

'There's too much going on for me to simplify it like that,' she replied softly. 'And you telling Anja makes it… worse.'

'Why?'

'Because now she has another reason—' She stopped herself from saying the words. From saying that Anja knowing about whatever had happened between her and Dylan would just give her another reason to abandon Jess when it was all over.

She'd been surprised when Anja had spoken to her earlier, and her first thought—her first fear, she knew, remembering how her throat had closed—had been that.

And even though her friend had told her she was fine

with it, could Jess believe her? And if she could, how would that work? Would she date Dylan and be forced to see how little she meant to their family day after day?

'Jess,' Dylan said, his expression telling her that he'd been trying to get her attention for some time. 'What's going on with you?'

'Nothing.'

'It's *not* nothing,' he said, and slammed a hand on the table. She resisted a wince, and met his eyes evenly.

'You don't have to believe me. But I'm not going to tell you. No matter how hard you slam your hand against the table.'

'I'm sorry,' he said, but his jaw was still clenched. 'You're just so damn *stubborn*. It's frustrating.'

His brows were knitted together, the anger clear in the planes of his face. And all she could think about was how cute he was when he was angry. She sighed at the flutter in her stomach.

'Don't feel like you have to entertain me for the afternoon. I wouldn't want to frustrate you more than I already have.'

'Jessica.' It was said on a soft exhale of air, and again she watched Dylan rub a hand over his face. 'I don't know what I'm going to do with you.'

'You don't have to do anything with me.'

'Except that I want to.' His hand fell down to the table. 'Hell if I know why, but I want…you.'

Her heart thudded, and she gripped the napkin that had been beside her hand tightly in her fist. 'Is that why you told Anja? Because you *want* me?'

'I told Anja because I wanted to be honest with her. You encouraged me, remember?' She nodded, unable to speak. 'So I decided to go for it. To put everything on the line. And it's been working. Really well. We've finally made…progress. Real progress. In our relationship, *and* with Mom. So when she asked me, I thought I'd be—' he shrugged '—honest.'

She couldn't argue with his logic. Not when she could see how freeing it had been for him. 'I'm glad it's been working for you. I just wish you'd come to speak with me before you told her. Or, at the very least, warned me that you *had* told her.'

'I am sorry for that. But I meant what I said earlier. I didn't think she'd actually talk to you.' He shook his head. 'I should have known that she would, though. You're best friends.'

She didn't reply. Not when he made it sound so simple— so *special*—and she didn't know if it was.

'There's somewhere I want to take you.'

'What?'

'You said I didn't have to spend the afternoon with you, but as soon as I found out we'd be alone I knew I wanted to. So you don't have much of a choice.' He grinned at her, and called the waitress to get the bill.

'Are you kidnapping me?'

'Do I have to?' he said wryly, and she couldn't help the curve of her lips.

'It probably wouldn't look good for you, kidnapping a pregnant woman.'

'I could do it,' he said sombrely. 'For the greater good.'

She snorted. 'What greater good? Keeping your afternoon plans?'

'Exactly. Now, are you going to come with me, or do I have to resort to Plan B?'

'And you called *me* frustrating,' she replied, rolling her eyes, and got up with Dylan as soon as he paid the bill.

He chatted as they walked and, since that wasn't the kind of word she'd thought she'd ever associate with Dylan, it made her think that he was nervous. The thought was just as unwelcome as when she'd thought him angry and cute, but this time she didn't push it away.

Instead, she chose to indulge herself.

She was walking along the beach with a handsome man. A man who'd said he *wanted* her. The thrill she'd forced away before went through her spine now, and she relished it. It wouldn't be long before reality set in again. Before she was forced to face it and the fact that Dylan would tire of her eventually. He would figure out that *wanting* was temporary, and needing soon replaced it.

And no one had needed Jess in a long time.

So, for now, she would enjoy it.

Jess looked up when Dylan stopped walking, and for the first time noticed that they'd reached the pier.

'Are we going to be…watching the boats go by?' she asked when the seconds passed and he didn't say anything. It was the only thing she could think of, since there was no one around except a large boat at the edge of the pier and others in the distance.

'No,' he replied. Were those nerves she heard in his voice? 'We're going to watch for whales.'

'Really?' She perked up. 'That's awesome. Can you see them from here?'

'No,' he said again, and now she *definitely* heard the nerves. 'But we can see them from the boat.'

He nodded in the direction of the boat she'd noticed earlier, and she frowned. 'You mean we're going to…sit on that boat and watch the whales? I guess that would work, but—'

'No, Jess. We're going whale-watching in that boat. With it doing what it's supposed to do. You know, sail.' He lifted a hand, and then dropped it again. 'I hired the boat for the afternoon.'

CHAPTER SEVENTEEN

'YOU HIRED…?' JESS's voice faltered. And then she said, 'You hired a boat for this afternoon. For…a day trip? With a couple of people?'

Her reaction was making his spur-of-the-moment decision seem like a bad one. And he hadn't thought it was. At first. But from the moment they'd left the restaurant, he'd been thinking exactly that. She was *not* dissuading him of that notion.

'No, for the two of us. I wanted you to be comfortable, and I thought that it might give you a break from thinking about…whatever's going on with you.'

He held his breath as she considered his words.

'I have one question for you,' she said after what felt like for ever, turning to him. The wind fluttered through her hair, making the wavy strands of it stir. He felt the movement mirrored in his chest.

'What?'

'Are you going to take your shirt off?'

It took him a moment to realise she was teasing him, and the only reason he did was the saucy grin she gave him that had different parts of his body stirring.

'Only if you plan on watching me,' he said in a growl.

She pretended to think about it. 'Well, there *is* an art

to it.' Paused. 'And I *have* become somewhat of an expert on watching you without your shirt on—'

He cut her off with a kiss. Quick and hard. And pulled away before he could be tempted into savouring the taste of her lips—or the surprise on her face. Instead, he took her hand and led her to the boat.

He helped her on board, and then handed her a safety vest before putting on his own. When he was done, he nodded to the captain and they were off.

He'd been teasing her when he'd told her she should watch him. Which was ironic now, considering that he couldn't keep *his* eyes off *her*. She was captivating. She grabbed his arm whenever she saw something—or thought she saw something—her face alight with excitement. And clasped her hands together when that something turned out to be a whale.

They were lucky enough to spot a seal at one point, too, and the absolute glee in her expression made every reservation he'd had about taking her on a boat trip worthwhile.

'I can't believe I've never been on one of these before,' she said as the captain turned the boat around. She accepted the water he'd got from the bar, and drank from it thirstily before continuing. 'It feels like it should be a compulsory experience for everyone at least once in their lifetime.'

'I'm glad you enjoyed it,' he said with a smile, and sat back, enjoying his own drink.

'Oh, don't be so smug. There was very little chance I wouldn't have enjoyed it.'

'There was enough of a chance. What if you got seasick? A high possibility, considering you're pregnant.'

Her hand immediately went to her belly. 'I didn't really suffer from motion sickness before, and I'm happy to say carrying this little guy or girl hasn't changed that.'

'How has it been?' he heard himself ask.

'The pregnancy?' He couldn't pretend he hadn't asked. He nodded. 'Good, for the most part. I was exhausted the first trimester. Still am, though it hasn't been quite as debilitating since.'

'Do you enjoy being pregnant? You don't have to answer that if you don't want to,' he said quickly when she frowned.

'No, it's not that. I just haven't really thought about it.'

The hand on her belly started to move, and he watched as she drew little circles, over and over, around her stomach. It wasn't the first time he'd seen her do it, but it *was* the first time a small, unknown part of him had stirred.

'It hasn't been a bad experience so far,' she said. 'I know it can be, so I'm one of the lucky ones who doesn't puke at every opportunity. So, I guess physically I don't mind it.'

'You don't mind that your body won't ever be the same again?'

She gave him a look. 'Is that really the question you're going with?'

He felt heat creep onto his face. 'I didn't mean it like that.' And then he wondered what 'like that' meant, and the heat become fiercer. 'I just... I don't know. Forget it.'

She laughed and, mingled with the sound of the water crashing against the boat, it sounded magical. 'Oh, I know what you meant. It was just too good an opportunity to miss.' She tilted her head, and then looked out at the sea. 'It's not that I don't mind it. I just keep thinking that it'll be worth it.'

'Even though it isn't your child?'

She looked at him, and it almost made him regret asking. But she answered him.

'Yes, I think so.' There seemed to be a long time between her answer and the next words she said. 'Anja was... devastated after the miscarriage.' She lifted a hand. Let it drop. 'That doesn't even seem like the right word to use.

It's too…neat. Tidy. It doesn't describe how she sobbed every day for two weeks. Her entire body wrenched from it.' He saw her fingers curl, tighten. And couldn't blame her when he looked down and saw his fingers had done the same.

'Giving her the chance to have the child she wanted so badly without going through the fear of that again…' She lifted her shoulders. 'Yeah, I guess it is worth it. Even though it isn't my own.'

'You really love her, don't you?'

'I do.' Her eyes filled and she looked away from him. Even when he took her hand and squeezed.

The rest of the trip was quiet, and Dylan worried that Jess had pulled back into herself again. By the time they reached the pier again, he knew that he was right. But he didn't say anything about it as he helped her off the boat, and said his thanks to the captain.

'We should get back to your mom's place,' Jess said softly when they reached the edge of the pier.

'Sure,' he said easily. 'I know a shortcut. It cuts across the beach though.'

'I don't mind,' she replied after a second, and shifted, looking down at her shoes longingly.

He smiled. 'Need help?'

She gave him an embarrassed grin. 'Would you mind?'

'Sure.'

He bent down and helped her out of her shoes. While he was there, he took off his own and soon they were walking down the beach.

The sky was a soft orange-yellow colour, an indication of the time of day. It had been a nice day, he thought. One of the few they'd get before winter came in full force. Even now he could feel the chill of the cool autumn air, and looked at Jess, wondering if she was getting cold.

But her face was turned up to the sun, her eyes closed,

and his feet stopped. Hell, his entire world stopped. She looked like an angel. The light made her bronze skin glow, highlighted the brown of her hair. For the first time he saw the almost blonde strands in between the dark brown, and the discovery had him reaching out to her, taking her hand before he knew what he was doing.

She opened her eyes and turned to look at him, and the easy expression on her face turned guarded. 'What? What is it?'

'You're beautiful, Jess.'

Her face went red, and he kept her hand in his, not allowing her to turn from him. She wouldn't push him away this time.

'Don't do this, please.'

'Do what?' he asked her softly, tugging at her hand so that she came closer to him. 'Are you asking me not to tell you how beautiful you are? Because I'm not going to stop doing that, Jess. Not when you're the most beautiful woman I've ever seen.'

'Yes, that,' she said exasperatedly. 'You're making it harder.'

'What are you talking about?' But she only shook her head.

It angered him. And anger had him taking her hand and putting it around his waist. He reached his other hand around her waist, and now she had no choice but to look at him.

'You're driving me crazy, Jess. You have been from the moment we got into that car to come here. You give me cryptic answers to simple questions, and there's *pain* in your eyes, damn it.' He tightened his hold on her, afraid of what letting go might mean. 'Do you know what it does to me, to see you in pain?' He barely waited for the slight shake of her head. 'It *kills* me. I don't know how it happened, but I care about you and I can't seem to escape how much I want it to be the same for you.'

'You don't mean it, Dylan.' Vulnerability crept onto her face, and for the first time he saw more than pain. He saw *fear*.

'How can you tell me I don't mean what I feel?'

'Because you *can't*,' she whispered. 'How can you feel that way about me when my parents, who've known me my entire life, don't?'

He felt her arm drop from his waist, but she didn't move away from him. Because of it, he could see the sheen of tears in her eyes.

Because of it, he could brush them away from her cheeks when they fell.

'It's only a matter of time before you, and Anja, and Chet realise there's something about me that's...that's *unlovable*. You'll realise that I'm no longer useful once this baby is born and I'll have to pick up the pieces of my heart when I'm no longer in your lives.'

Her breath shuddered from her lungs, and she rested her head on his chest. It completely undid him. The simple action. The complicated emotions. He held on to her tightly. As though somehow he could squeeze those insecurities—those absolutely ludicrous insecurities—out of her.

But her words had cleared up a lot for him. She was afraid the people she loved most in the world would abandon her. And it made sense, too, since the people who were *supposed* to love her most in the world had.

And she was scared about her surrogacy. For once, he thought, she'd had a natural reaction to her unusual situation. And now he knew where *his* hesitation had come from, too. From a fear that she would be hurt. That giving the baby she carried to someone else would damage her in a way she wouldn't be able to recover from.

But *her* fear was much less selfish than that. She was

scared Anja wouldn't want her any more. And in that moment Dylan suddenly realised how much Jess loved his family. His thoughts went back to everything she'd said about carrying the baby, about doing it for Anja, and he realised that she already *was* a part of his family. She just hadn't realised it yet.

But, most importantly, her words had made him realise how wrong she was. Because she *was* lovable.

Because *he* loved her.

CHAPTER EIGHTEEN

IT WAS INCREDIBLE, the things Dylan could get her to reveal. She looked up into those eyes that saw everything, into the arresting features of his face, and knew she didn't have a chance against the onslaught of emotions.

If she added how full her heart felt because of the way his arms held her close to him, as though he would never let her go, she was helpless.

And hopelessly in love.

'I'm sorry, I shouldn't—'

'No,' he said, cutting her off. 'You should have. We might not know what we are yet, Jess, but you can tell me anything. And I'll be there to listen.'

A lump sat in her throat. 'You don't—'

'I do, and you're going to stop doubting it.' He pulled back from the embrace, both her hands in his now. 'I know you've been hurt. And abandoned. You shouldn't have been, Jess. You didn't deserve it.' His eyes were hot, serious, and she almost, almost believed him. 'You didn't deserve it, Jess. I'm saying it again because I need you to hear me. To believe me.'

Was her face that obvious to read? 'I do.'

'No, you don't. And that's fine for now. Because we believe what our experiences teach us, and your experiences haven't shown you that you can believe me.' He paused. 'Or they have, but you haven't seen it.'

'What do you mean?'

'How long have you been friends with Anja?'

'You know the answer to that,' she said softly. 'Two years.'

'Has she done anything in the last two years to make you believe that she wouldn't be there for you once the baby's here?'

She shook her head.

'Then why do you think that she won't be?'

She couldn't answer him when the lump in her throat doubled. It was accompanied by tears burning in her eyes. It took all of a few seconds for them to roll down her cheeks and, for the second time, Dylan brushed them away.

He had a tender look on his face, and she hated what it did to her heart. No, that wasn't true. She didn't hate it at all. But she *was* afraid of it. Because she'd never felt this way before, about anyone, and she didn't know if she could trust him...

'What's it going to take for you to believe me?'

'Kiss me,' she heard herself say. Surprised herself with the words. But then she wanted it more than she'd thought possible. 'I want you to kiss me and make me believe that—'

His lips were on hers before she got a chance to finish her sentence, and she sank into the kiss. Sank into the moment.

For her, the moment was goodbye. It was setting aside the hope he'd stirred in her, and placing the love she'd only just discovered she had for him in a box somewhere inside her, to visit, to cherish whenever she felt strong enough.

But goodbye had never felt so good in her life. It had never come with a strong man holding her in his arms, with his hands caressing her body. It had never caused her spine to tingle, and her breasts to ache. She pressed closer to him, wanting to give him all that she had inside. Wanting to tell him how much he meant to her. Wanting to make sure that one day, when she was no longer there, he'd remember this kiss on the beach.

That he'd remember the passion, the tenderness. That he'd remember how her hands felt on his body, sliding up, underneath his shirt, kneading, skimming. That he'd remember the moan he gave when she scraped her nails lightly over his back, and the one that came from her when he nipped at her lip in response.

They drew away from each other, breath shuddering from their lungs, and then Dylan lifted his hand and set it on her cheek, his gaze intense as it met hers.

'I'm not going anywhere, Jess. And I'm going to prove it to you.' His thumb grazed across her cheek. 'You can believe me.'

'Why?' she asked, her heart hurting. 'Why is it so important that I believe you?'

'Because I love you.'

He stopped her reply with another kiss, and this time she was swept away in it. She didn't think about what he'd just told her, only felt it, and allowed the sweetness of his kiss to convince her to believe it.

And it did.

The time when they kissed, when their tongues tangled with one another in a sweetly intense duel, Jess believed that Dylan loved her. That he wouldn't leave. She could see herself as a part of his world, as a part of his family. She would give birth to Anja's child, and she'd still be a part of their lives.

Her own life wouldn't change all that much. She'd get a new job and find her own place, but she'd still see the people who'd changed her life so much. And there would be a baby she'd share a special bond with, who would enrich her life further.

Fantasy, she thought, but gave herself a few more minutes of it before pulling back.

'Dylan,' she said hoarsely.

'Hmm?' He smiled when he looked at her, but it faded. 'What?'

'We can't—'

'No,' he said, taking a step back. She immediately felt colder, and only then noticed the sun had lowered and it was dusk. 'Don't say that we can't. Say that you don't. Because that would be the only reason why we can't.'

She opened her mouth, tried to say what she needed him to believe. But she couldn't. Because she'd been hurt in her life by rejection, by abandonment, she wouldn't hurt someone else in the same way. Especially when it wasn't true.

'You feel the same way.' The darkness that had been on his face lifted.

'I didn't say that.'

'Because you're scared.'

He saw right through her, she thought, and resented it so very much. 'How far is your mother's place from here?'

'Jess—'

'How far?' she asked tersely.

'A couple hundred metres.'

'So let's get to it.'

She walked in the direction she remembered he'd been leading them in, and sighed in relief when he fell into step beside her silently. She didn't want to talk any more. Not to him, not to Anja. All she wanted was to go home and—

She cut her own thoughts off when she realised she'd thought about Dylan's house when she'd pictured home. That she'd thought about *him*. It had her feet stopping. Had her grabbing his hand, pulling it and forcing him to stop with her.

'I love you, too, Dylan,' she said hoarsely. 'But it doesn't change anything. It can't,' she said when she saw him open his mouth. 'It can't change anything because I'm…I'm not strong enough to deal with whatever might happen if this doesn't work out.'

'It'll work out.'

'You don't know that,' she said, and shook her head. 'No, it's just better for us to…'

Her voice faded as she realised she didn't know what would be better. Or, she thought, what would be worse. For her to fall into this web of hope they'd spun around them, only to find out she'd been fooling herself—she'd been fooling her heart—in the process? Or to ignore it, and constantly be tempted by the hope—the *love*—that Dylan was telling her to believe in?

She had to figure it out, and she couldn't do it with Dylan by her side.

'I'm not going anywhere,' Dylan said softly, and for the briefest moment Jess thought that she'd spoken out loud.

'You say that now.'

'So, I won't say it any more,' he replied simply. 'I'll show you.'

He leaned forward, kissed her forehead, and then continued walking back to his mother's cottage. After a moment Jess followed, her head and her heart a mess.

Since Dylan had never told a woman outside of his family that he loved her, he wasn't quite sure what should happen afterwards. But having her avoid being alone with him… Well, it was safe to say that that hadn't even made his list of possible consequences.

Especially since she'd told him she loved him, too.

And yet, as soon as they reached the cottage that night, Jess excused herself for the evening. And then she made sure that there weren't any more opportunities for them to be alone for the rest of the trip.

It was fairly crafty—it clearly required a lot of manoeuvring—and, if Dylan was honest with himself, she impressed him with her efforts. She woke up before he did, disappeared for a walk on the beach and only returned when everyone had arrived for breakfast. If she woke up later than he did, she would only appear after his mother had already got up and would dive into the breakfast preparations, using it as an excuse not to speak with him.

She went to bed before he did. Stuck to his mother's side at every spare moment. When Anja arrived, she'd switch between the two. And Anja was the perfect deterrent, he thought, remembering how she only needed to send him a look when he tried to get Jess alone and he would abandon his efforts.

If he hadn't understood it—expected it, even, knowing what he did about Jess now—he would have been more offended. But he *did* understand. He understood that she was scared. Terrified, he corrected himself, thinking about her expression on the beach. And the only way she would get over that fear was if he showed her that she had nothing to be scared of.

Which he could focus on now, he thought, since his trip to Langebaan had been somewhat successful.

Their conversations with their mother had been... hard. Hard and painful and, at times, ugly. His mother had greeted him with the nerves, the hesitation he'd come to expect from her. That had always been her personality, though he couldn't deny that there had been a part of him hoping she'd come out of her shell after their father's death.

But it seemed his death hadn't changed that much for his mother. When Anja had asked her why she'd chosen to have them, knowing what their father was, she'd broken down. Had defended him at first and, when he and

Anja had refused to accept that, had admitted it had been selfish.

But the more they talked—and it had been strange going between tense, difficult discussions and meals with Jess where everyone pretended nothing was wrong—the more Dylan realised it had been more about *hope* than selfishness. He'd heard it loud and clear in the way his mother had described the joy of feeling them grow, move inside her. Of sharing that with their father.

She'd told them her pregnancies had been the only time he'd been the kind of man she'd always wanted him to be. And Dylan had finally realised that he and Anja had been his mother's hope that he would *stay* that man. That each day after they'd been born she'd hoped for that man to pitch up again. And each day, when that man hadn't—when it became clear he'd left for good—she'd mourned.

She'd broken down in front of them. Had told them how sorry she was for failing them by loving their father. By abandoning them. Hearing the words, the apology, had loosened something inside Dylan. Perhaps because for the first time he believed that she wanted to make up for it. And that maybe she would finally become the woman—the mother—Dylan had always hoped she would be.

It didn't magically allow him to forgive her. And it hadn't done much to change his opinion of his father. But it *had* made him think that things weren't as black and white as he'd thought. Perhaps if he'd still been alive, Dylan could have had the same conversation with his father. Maybe that would have given Dylan a glimpse into the psyche of the man he'd resented all his life. Maybe it would have helped Dylan to understand him.

Now, Dylan realised that his grief was part dealing with his father's abandonment, half wishing that he hadn't died so that Dylan could have tried to understand him sooner.

The guilt that came from that—the regret—had merged with his anger and that had made Dylan *grieve*.

He knew it would take him time to work through it all, but Dylan was choosing to move forward. Moving forward meant working on forgiving his parents for not being who he'd wished they had been. For abandoning them. It meant working on accepting who his mother was, and learning to move on from who his father had been. It meant appreciating the closeness he and Anja had started forging again, and making sure that she knew he would never jeopardise their relationship as he had in the past.

And, most of all, moving forward meant making sure Jess knew he was serious about showing her he loved her.

'This must be torture for you,' he said mildly into the silence in the car. Jess might have been able to avoid him in Langebaan, but on their way home it was just the two of them. He almost enjoyed the sound of her shifting in her seat.

'I don't know what you're talking about.'

'Of course you do,' he replied. 'You hate being alone with me.'

'That's not true.'

'Really? Because I clearly recall you honing the skill of avoiding it over the last few days.'

'I did—' She broke off when he gave her a look, and then sighed. 'I don't hate being alone with you. I just know that being alone with you is…tempting.'

He felt his lips curve. *'Tempting?'*

'Yes, tempting.' His head turned in time to see her roll her eyes. 'You know you are.'

'And I'm not even shirtless,' he said with a smirk, and chuckled when she slapped at his hand on the gear knob. He let the silence that fell on them sit, felt her get restless as it did. He didn't mean for it to make her uncomfortable enough to talk to him, but he couldn't deny he didn't appreciate it when she spoke.

'I don't get it. I don't get *you*.'

'What are you talking about?'

'Why are you…why is this…why don't you sound annoyed with me?'

'Oh, I'm annoyed with you,' he replied easily. 'I'm pretty annoyed, actually.'

'I know I shouldn't have avoided you, but it was easier than—'

'And that's why I'm annoyed,' he interrupted. 'Not because you avoided *me*, but because you're avoiding your feelings for me. That you see them as complicated.'

'And you don't?'

'No.'

'You really don't think our admission of love for one another is going to complicate our lives when we get back?'

His heart did a flip. 'No. Because it won't.'

Seconds passed, and Dylan felt himself grow anxious, the easiness of the silence before gone.

'You know I'm moving out of Anja's place soon, right?' she said finally, and he softly exhaled the air he didn't realise he'd been holding in his lungs.

'When?'

'Chet told me he'll be finishing work on my flat the end of next week.'

'Okay.'

Minutes passed this time. 'And I'm not going to work for Anja after the baby is born.'

'You're…' His hand tightened on the wheel. 'Does Anja know?'

'Not yet. I'll tell her, though.'

'When?'

'At the right time.'

'I don't think there's going to be a right time for that conversation,' he muttered.

But she replied seriously, 'Probably not. But I can't work for her any more. Especially not after I give birth.'

'Is that your plan, Jess?' he asked quietly. 'You're going to push away the people who love you?'

'I'm going to *protect* myself.'

'No, you're pushing us away.' Dylan told himself to stay calm. 'I know what it's like to be abandoned. And I know the fear that it'll happen again can make you want to abandon the people you care about before they can abandon you.' He only then realised how true his words were.

'I'm not abandoning anyone,' she said. 'I'm trying to make sure this whole process is…easier on all of us.'

He didn't reply immediately. Instead, he took his time thinking about what he wanted to tell her. 'Do you know what this trip made me realise?'

'What?'

'That that fear of abandonment will stay with you until you let the people who love you show you it won't happen.' He let out a shaky breath. 'After my father died, I didn't give my mother a chance to tell me why she'd done what she'd done. And, now that she has, it's helped me to understand and…it'll help me to forgive.'

'Are you telling me to…give my parents a chance?'

'That's entirely up to you. But no. What I meant was that you have to give people chances. You have to give *us* a chance.' He reached over, took her hand. 'We're your family, Jess. Give us a chance to show you that we won't let you down.'

CHAPTER NINETEEN

'BUT YOU'RE NOT my family,' Jess told him with a clenched jaw. 'That's the whole point of this. I'm *not* a part of your family,' she said again, her voice cracking. 'I'm not even a part of my *own* family.'

It still hurt. She *hated* that it still hurt. And that perhaps it always would.

'Then maybe it *would* help to give your parents a chance.'

Surprise had a laugh spilling from her lips. Not because his suggestion was funny, but because it was *ludicrous*. 'I *have* given my parents a chance. I've given them *countless* chances.' She paused. Let the hurt pass through her now. 'They haven't tried to find me in two years, Dylan. They've made what they think about my chances pretty clear.'

'You haven't tried to get in touch with them either,' he reminded her.

'Because I shouldn't have had to. *I'm* the child. I'm *their* child. If they don't care enough about me to find out where I am, why should I care about them?'

'And you're happy with that?'

'I have to be.'

'Jess—'

'Enough, Dylan,' she interrupted. 'Nothing you say is

going to convince me that I need to speak with my parents. I know where I stand with them. Even though they haven't heard from me in two years—even though they don't know where I am—they've never tried to find me.'

'You don't know that.'

'I do,' she said, exhausted now. 'And that's the point. I *know* they haven't looked for me. Their only child. I've made it easier for them by leaving. I've made it easier for *myself*. Now I don't have to constantly feel unloved and unwanted. Now I can just move on and—'

'And let *us* love and want you.'

'No.'

'Yes,' he disagreed. 'Look—' he sighed '—maybe I shouldn't have suggested you see your parents. But I just… I just wanted to help take away that pain in your voice.'

'I…appreciate it. But—'

'I'm not done yet,' he interjected. 'You might have had a painful experience with your own family, but you have a new one. A better one. *Our* family.' He reached over and set his hand on hers, where they rested in her lap. 'You're a part of our family, whether you like it or not, Jess. I've had conversations with Anja that have told me you were long before you agreed to carry her child. You are now. And you will be after you give birth, too.'

Tears burned in her eyes and of course there was no way she was able to hold them back. He looked over at her and a few seconds later he pulled the car to the side of the road and drew her into his arms.

She heard her sobs before her mind registered that she was crying. And, once it did, nothing could stop them from wrenching through her. He murmured comfortingly to her, pressed kisses into her hair, and she stayed in his arms as long as she could. Even when the sobs passed, she stayed. And wished she could stay for ever.

But she couldn't, and minutes later she withdrew from

his arms. She accepted the tissues he offered her—heaven only knew where'd he got them—and tried to compose herself.

'Sorry,' she said hoarsely.

'Don't apologise.'

'It's pregnancy.'

He smiled. 'Sure.'

'And…well, you know.'

His smile widened. 'I do.'

But, after a few more moments, Jess said, 'Thank you for this.' She waved a hand between them. 'And for all you've said. But—' she inhaled, and then blew out the air shakily '—I'm not ready to…be *in* this. Not until—'

'You're sure I mean what I've said?'

'No,' she said, and then sighed when he shot her a look. 'Okay, maybe. But we both have a lot to deal with when we get back. I have my new place, I need to find a new job, and there's—' she lifted her hands '—the baby. And you just got back after being away for two years. I'm sure you'll have a lot to do at work here, and with your family…'

She faded when she realised it all sounded like excuses. And when she saw the way he was studying her.

She wondered if he could see that her admission of love for him had broken something inside her. That it had healed something, too. That his admission of love had made her want, need, hope for things she hadn't dared give herself permission to want, need or hope for before. That all of it had fear and panic beating inside her in an uncomfortable rhythm and she needed time to deal with it.

'I can give you time, Jess,' Dylan said, and Jess wondered if she'd said aloud what she'd been thinking. Or maybe he could just see through her, like she suspected.

'I can give you all the time you need,' he continued, and something flickered in his eyes that made her heart throb. 'Just…don't push me away. Don't push any of us away. Let us figure it all out. Together.'

Feeling a little helpless, she nodded, and after another few moments Dylan pulled his car back onto the road. For the rest of the trip, Jess couldn't help but think about what had happened over the last few weeks. And each time she did, she wondered one thing:

What if I believe him?

'Do you think Anja will ever get over the fact that I got another job?'

They were at Dylan's house. A fire was crackling in front of them, rain slamming against the windows around them. Daisy was on the carpet in front of the fire, sulking because neither of them had left her enough space to lie on the couch with them.

It was officially winter, and the weather had given them little reprieve. But Jess didn't mind it so much since she'd spent a lot of it in front of a fireplace, doing exactly what she was doing now.

Dylan, Anja and Chet had helped her with her move. Most of her things had been in storage, and it had been fairly easy to move in. But since she was pregnant, headed into her third trimester then, she hadn't been able to do nearly as much as she'd wanted to. So they'd been her hands, and after a few days she was living in her own home.

Since she was still working for Anja, things had gone on the same for them. Most days she'd spent the evening at Dylan's place after he got home from work. He'd cook for her—or them, as Anja and Chet often joined them for dinner—and the evening would end with a cup of hot chocolate in front of the fire.

Then she'd go home, and do it all over again the next day.

It wasn't a routine Jess had thought possible after they'd

returned from Langebaan, but somehow she and Dylan had managed to develop a…relationship that had allowed for it.

Even if that relationship did have a lot more sexual and emotional tension than either of them would have liked.

'Speaking from experiencing how long she can hold a grudge, I think it'll probably take some time.' Dylan was stretched out on the couch next to hers, looking incredibly sexy. She wished she hadn't noticed, just as she had countless times in the last three months. And, just as it had countless times in the last three months, a voice in her head warned her that their current relationship wasn't enough for her.

'It's only been a week, Jess,' Dylan continued, interrupting her worrying thoughts. 'And it's definitely going to take more than a week. Though you should probably leverage the baby now as much as you can.'

'I don't understand why she's not upset with you,' Jess grumbled, forcing herself to play along. 'You're the one who convinced me to interview at your company. Hell, you're probably the reason I got the job.'

'That's not true,' he replied. 'I only recommended you to them. I wasn't involved in your hiring.'

'But what did you think was going to happen when you recommended me?' she asked. 'You're the CEO. If they didn't hire me—'

'I'd have fired them all?' he said in a tone that clearly told her he thought the idea was ridiculous.

She smiled. 'Exactly.'

But Jess knew it wasn't true. She'd been hired into a junior position—something that would have been appropriate for someone straight out of university. Which was fair, she thought, considering her experience meant that she *was* basically just out of university.

But none of the people she'd met had given her the indication that they'd been coerced to see her. And based on the professional, kind and fair way she'd been treated, she didn't think her interviewers believed hiring her would influence the way their CEO treated them.

So while she knew Dylan's recommendation held weight, she liked to think her organisational knowledge and the financial experience she'd gained assisting Anja with the new studio had been the push she'd needed to get the job. Though the fact that they'd agreed for her to start after she'd given birth was *definitely* Dylan.

'Well, it doesn't really matter now anyway since you've already accepted and signed the contract,' he told her. 'And as for Anja not being upset with me… I actually think she prefers you working in the company. It means she knows you'll be taken care of.'

'But she's still mad at me,' Jess complained, and tried to push herself up. When that failed, she tried to get comfortable with the pillow behind her. It was really a bit pathetic, but she couldn't do much since she'd ballooned in her final trimester. Now, even the simplest things were hard.

'Here, let me help.'

She wanted to protest, but she couldn't because, damn it, she needed his help. She tried to hold her breath against his manly scent, against the way it always made her body feel achy and needy. But just like her body had ballooned in the last three months, so had her feelings for him. And while she still wasn't ready to face what that meant, it had heightened her physical attraction to him to the point where she couldn't deny that she wanted more.

'Thanks,' she said when he was done, and leaned back against the pillows again. She'd hoped changing position would help with the strange feeling she had in her back, and for a brief moment she thought that it had. But as soon as she was comfortable again, it reappeared. Almost like a band stretching across the breadth of her back, tightening. It was a little painful.

'I should definitely leverage it,' she said with a huff. 'Being this pregnant is *not* fun.'

He smirked. 'I can't imagine it is. But at least you carry it well.' He sat back down, and she laughed when she saw that Daisy had claimed part of the couch after Dylan had got up.

'You have to say that,' she said once she'd sobered. 'You l—' She cut herself off with a frown. Was she really just going to say because he *loved* her? That went against all the rules she'd given herself about speaking about their feelings for one another. 'Because you love the little thing making me so uncomfortable,' she said instead.

'Well, he or she is family,' Dylan replied with a thin smile.

She knew that smile. It was the one he'd give her whenever he restrained himself from speaking about his feelings for her. He'd agreed to give her time, she thought, but he hadn't agreed to keep himself from talking about how he felt about her. She knew that the only reason he did was because he wanted her to feel comfortable.

And didn't that just make resisting him so much harder?

The band tightened around her back again, and she closed her eyes. Hissed out a breath.

'Hey, are you okay?'

When she opened her eyes again, Dylan was at her side, concern etched into every angle of his face. 'Yeah, I'm okay.'

She gestured for him to help her sit up straight and when he did she took a few moments to breathe.

'Jess, I think we should go to the hospital.'

'No,' she said immediately. 'It's just some…discomfort.'

'No, it's more than that.'

'Braxton-Hicks contractions then. I've been having them all day.'

'All day?' Dylan said with alarm. 'We've been together since this morning. Why didn't you say anything?'

'Because I'm *fine.*'

As she said it, Jess felt something shift and soon after warmth puddled between her legs. She sucked in her breath. 'Dylan.'

'Yeah?'

'Please tell me that you dropped some kind of liquid on me.'

'No, wh—?'

He broke off when he looked down and saw her stained pants. Jess would have felt embarrassed by it if her heart hadn't started pounding, nearly cutting off her breath.

'Jess, honey, I think your water just broke.'

'No,' she breathed. 'No, it's too early. I think you just spilled something on me.'

'I don't have anything in my hands.'

She hated how gentle his voice sounded. 'Then I peed myself,' she snapped. 'It's three weeks too early for my water to break.'

'So let's get you to the hospital and sort it all out. They can tell you whether you peed once you're there.'

'No.' Now she was pleading. And ignoring how strange it was that they were talking about *pee.* 'Dylan, please, it's not time.'

'You're worried.' It wasn't a question. He brushed the hair from her face and left his hand on her cheek. 'There's nothing to be worried about.'

'Not worried,' she rasped. 'Scared. Terrified. I don't know… I don't know if I can do this.'

'I know. I know you're scared. But you're strong. And you *can* do this. I haven't had more faith in anything than that.' He leaned forward and kissed her forehead.

And in that moment, as ill-timed as it was, Jess could

no longer deny that she wanted to be with him. She loved him. And he loved *her*.

'Stay with me,' she told him as the band tightened around her back again. 'Please.'

'I will.'

And he did.

Dylan didn't know he could be so tired. And *he* hadn't been the one to give birth!

He imagined that Jess was feeling a million times worse than he was, except that she was still awake, smiling faintly at Anja and Chet as they cooed at their newborn son.

A nephew, he thought, a grin curving his lips. There was a little boy in his family. Sure, right now he looked all rumpled and new, but one day he would be kicking ball with his uncle who lived right next door. He'd be going on hikes, doing outdoor sports. Dylan figured his imagination would have conjured up much of the same images had his sister had a daughter but, either way, thinking about it was pretty great.

And made all of the turmoil of the last few months worth it.

His eyes settled on Jess again, and he felt his heart swell. She was amazing. It wasn't the first time he'd thought it, and he knew it wouldn't be the last. But witnessing her today...

She'd been amazing.

As soon as they'd got to the hospital she'd turned into the quintessential woman, prepared to do exactly what nature intended of her. She'd screamed in pain—and internally he'd screamed, too, since she'd insisted on holding his hand throughout the process—but as soon as the contraction was over she would go quiet, and softly apologise for acting exactly as anyone else in her position would have.

Six hours later—*six*—Jessie Dylan White had been born. Named after his godparents, Dylan had been told, and he'd had to pretend to drink water when he'd heard to keep them from seeing how emotional he'd felt. Jessie was a good size, good weight and perfectly healthy. And he'd been welcomed into a family who loved him.

He was a lucky kid, Dylan thought. He had great parents, a grandmother who would do her best not to repeat the mistakes of the past, an uncle who was already willing to give him anything he wanted, and a godmother who was a warrior.

He'd seen Jess's face when Anja had told her the name of their son. Had seen the annoyance Anja had felt for Jess fade away after they'd embraced. He'd known that the annoyance was temporary, and only because Anja had yet to see how important it was for Jess to believe that she was loved not because she'd provided something but just because she was worth it.

He'd spent the last three months proving exactly that to Jess. He'd told her he'd give her time and he had, even when it had pained him to do so. But he'd run from pain before. He'd run from the people he loved. He wouldn't now. Because Jess needed to believe that he'd always be there for her.

So he had been. And it was worth all the anguish when he could see on Jess's face that she finally believed it.

Jess turned her head and met his eyes, and her lips curved into a soft smile. His heart galloped in his chest and he smiled back at her, wondering at how much she'd changed him. Before he'd met her, he never would have enjoyed feeling his heart pound for someone.

Now, he relished it.

The nurse came in then, ushering them out by telling them that Jess needed her rest. He stood when Anja set the sleeping Jessie back into his crib, smiled when she kissed his forehead and moved to follow them out of the room.

'Dylan,' Jess said before he could leave.

'Yeah?'

'You showed up for me.' Tears shone in her eyes. 'I...I believe you.'

'What do you believe?'

'That you love me,' she said with a smile. 'That you'll stay.'

His heart filled. 'I do. I will.'

'You made me believe you.'

'I know.'

'And you waited until I was ready to tell you I believed you.'

'I did.'

'I love you.'

It took him a moment before he could speak. 'I love you, too.'

'And this time I believe that it *will* change everything. Because I believe in you. And I'm going to—' she took a breath, blew it out '—I'm going to wade through the deep, dark waters of commitment for you.' She gave a small laugh. 'I'm really high on pain meds. Can you tell?'

He chuckled, and met the nurse's eye. 'May I?' he asked. With a wink, she gave him a nod and walked out.

And in two short steps Dylan was next to the woman he loved, pressing his lips to hers.

EPILOGUE

'IT'S BEEN TOO long since we've been here,' Jess said, stretching out on the reclined beach chair on what had once been Dylan's mother's back porch. 'Too long, I think.'

'Well, we've had a lot on our plates,' Dylan replied, scooping her into his arms and plopping her down on the day bed just next to where she'd been stretching out before.

She cuddled back against him when he joined her, before realising that she should have been offended by his ungentlemanly behaviour. But by then she was already enjoying where she was too much. In the sun at a beach cottage with the most handsome man she'd ever met.

Who *just happened* to be her husband.

'I guess, but it just seems like a waste. Like we missed opportunities to use this place as a holiday home.'

'We've had plenty of other, just as enjoyable, holidays,' he said, nuzzling her neck. Gooseflesh shot out on her body as it always did when he did that, and she smiled lazily.

'*Very* enjoyable.'

'I like your dirty mind, Mrs Nel.'

'It's something of a talent, I think.'

She smiled and settled back into Dylan's arms, thinking about how much had happened since they'd last been in

Langebaan. It had been three years. *Three years.* At first, there hadn't been a reason to return. Dylan's mother had moved to Cape Town once Jessie had been born, wanting to be closer to her family. Wanting to show them that she was different now. And, since Dylan owned the cottage, he'd had it renovated into a larger home since he'd believed their family would expand in the coming years.

He'd wanted it to be a holiday home for them. A place they could come to for some R&R. The renovations had taken a year to complete, and then they'd had their wedding and a brief working stint in Dubai and it had never been a good time to return.

Until now, she thought. She couldn't have planned it any better.

'Dylan?'

'Hmm?'

'I think we should go see my parents.'

Dylan shifted against her and when she looked at him she saw concern in his eyes. 'Why?'

'Well, it's been five years and... I don't know.' She sighed. 'I keep thinking back to what you told me after we left this place three years ago. But I wasn't ready to see them then. I didn't have anything, and I was afraid—' she turned onto her back, let her fingers flutter up to play with his hair '—I was afraid that going back would break me because I had nothing. But now...' She smiled at him, pushed up for a kiss. 'Now, I have everything. And it seems like the right time.'

Jess didn't want to carry around the weight of the negativity she felt towards her parents any more. They were always in her thoughts, the hurt she'd once feared always lurking in the recesses of her mind. She wasn't the same person she'd been when she'd left them—that hurt no longer had the same power over her—and that alone gave her the courage to speak with them. To finally get some closure, and accept whichever form it came in.

Good or bad.

And though she didn't think that they deserved the chance—especially after they hadn't responded to the wedding invitation she'd sent them—Jess now knew that *she* deserved it. She deserved to know whether they regretted their decisions. She deserved to leave them behind if they didn't.

She had a family now, and she wasn't so completely desperate for their love any more. She could move on if she had to. She *had* moved on. But she wanted the opportunity to tell them that she was happily married, successful in her career, and that...

'I'm also pregnant,' she said in a rush, 'and it feels like it's a good time to move on from the past and clear up all the what-ifs.'

She held her breath as she watched the stunned expression on his face.

'You're *pregnant*?'

'Yeah. And it's our baby,' she joked. It was a lame joke, she knew, but she was desperate to break the tension that had suddenly fallen between them.

'I've only known for a few days, and I know we haven't thought about it in some time, so I didn't want to tell you immediately, and we were coming here, and I thought that it would be the perfect time to tell you.' She paused, but he still didn't speak, so she continued, 'I guess I shouldn't have just blurted it out. I should have done something cute and filmed it and put it online.'

She barely paused to take a breath. 'And I shouldn't have sprung it on you after telling you I wanted to see my parents. But I was thinking about our child, and how we'd feel if some day they didn't speak to us. Of course, it's not the same, but—'

He cut her off with a kiss, deep and filled with so much passion and emotion that she felt raw. When he pulled back, he leaned his forehead against hers.

'You're pregnant.'

'Yeah,' she replied, her breath ragged.

'I…I'm going to be a father.'

'Yes.'

'We're pregnant,' he said again, and this time he laughed and gave her another kiss. And when he sobered he said, 'I have no idea how to be a father.'

'I have no idea how to be a mother. But we've figured out a lot together, my love. I think it's going to be okay.'

'Me, too,' he said with a smile.

'So…you're not mad?'

'Why would I be mad?'

'Because…we haven't spoken about it.'

'Recently,' he added. 'But we spoke about it after Jessie was born. And again, after we got married. Life's been so busy since then…' He shook his head. 'I don't know how to be a father, Jess. And heaven knows I had the worst example in the world. But I'll be there for this baby. Our baby.'

He set a hand on her abdomen, and the heat of it—the sweetness of it—seared through her body. His eyes met hers and what she saw there made her heart fill. 'Our baby, Jess. Yours and mine. We'll figure it out together. And if you need to talk to your parents to help you figure it out, we can.'

She smiled at him. 'I never thought this day would come for me. Where I'm a part of a family that's not broken, about to have my own child. You made that possible for me.'

'I could tell you the exact same thing.'

'Yeah, you could.'
He chuckled and pressed his lips against hers.
This time neither of them pulled away.

* * * * *

MARRIED FOR HIS
SECRET HEIR

JENNIFER FAYE

For Caitlin
From one book lover…
to another :-)

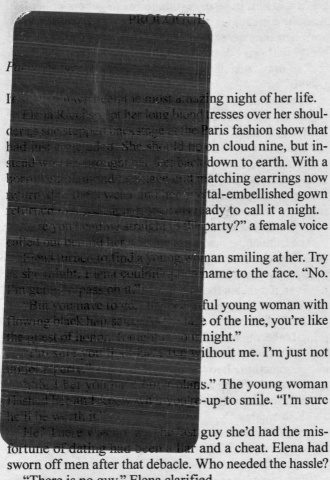

P...

It ... have been the most amazing night of her life.

Elena Ricci swept her long blond tresses over her shoulders as she stepped backstage of the Paris fashion show that had just come to end. She should be on cloud nine, but instead ... brought her feet back down to earth. With a borrowed diamond necklace and matching earrings now returned to the jeweler and her crystal-embellished gown replaced ... she was ready to call it a night.

"...se you heading straight to the party?" a female voice called out behind her.

Elena turned to find a young woman smiling at her. Try as she might, Elena couldn't put a name to the face. "No. I'm going to pass on it."

"But you have to go," the beautiful young woman with flowing black hair said. "... face of the line, you're like the guest of honor tonight ... night."

"I'm sure you'll ... be fine without me. I'm just not up to a party."

"Still, I bet your ... dans." The young woman flashed a knew-something-you're-up-to smile. "I'm sure he'll be worth it."

"He? There was no ... last guy she'd had the misfortune of dating had been a liar and a cheat. Elena had sworn off men after that debacle. Who needed the hassle?

"There is no guy," Elena clarified.

"Really? Then who's the man waiting for you at your station?"

Elena didn't bother answering. She just started walking. If it was Steven, she was having security escort him out.

She'd told him in no uncertain terms to get out of her life. And she'd meant it.

When she neared her station, the man had his back to her. "I told you I didn't want to see you again."

The man turned. "Is that the way you greet all your friends?"

Heat rushed to Elena's face. Before her stood the Earl of Halencia, Luca DiSalvo, her childhood friend. "I'm sorry. I, uh, thought you were someone else."

"I think I feel bad for the other guy."

"Don't. He doesn't deserve anyone's sympathy." She rushed forward and gave Luca a hug, finding comfort in his strong arms. And there was something else—a warm sensation that set her stomach aflutter. But she refused to examine the reason for her elated reaction.

The truth of the matter was, she'd grown used to shoving aside her emotions when it came to Luca. Their friendship meant the world to her, and she wouldn't do anything to risk it—even if it meant they would never be more than friends.

He pulled back and smiled. "That's better."

She looked deep into his tired eyes. There was something bothering him. This wasn't just a casual visit. Luca didn't do those. For him to come here unannounced, it meant something had happened—something big.

"What is it?" she asked. "Is it your father?"

Luca shook his head. "It's my mother."

"Your mother?"

Luca drew in a deep breath. "They caught her murderer. Actually, my sister did. Can you believe it? After all these years, it's finally over."

Elena wasn't sure how to react. On one hand, she was relieved they'd solved the crime, but she also knew how tough the years following the heinous crime had been on Luca and his estranged family. She couldn't imagine how he must be feeling at this point.

After the murder, Luca had withdrawn from everyone around him—including her. When he'd finished high school, he'd moved away. Soon after, she'd done the same and moved to Paris. Their friendship dwindled to an occasional phone call or an annual visit over coffee at a small café when Luca was in Paris on business.

Over the years, she'd told herself not to take the distance personally. It was Luca's way of dealing with the unimaginable grief. But she couldn't deny that losing the close connection with her best friend had hurt—a lot.

A million questions bubbled up within her. And yet she remained quiet as he gave her the highlights of how Annabelle had caught the murderer. The story was truly stunning.

"Annabelle just phoned me." His gaze didn't quite reach Elena's. "And I just needed to tell you." He paused as though considering his words. "I guess if I'd been thinking straight, I should have realized your mother would tell you."

Elena reached out and briefly squeezed his hand. "I'm glad you're the one who told me."

"You are?"

She nodded. "I'm so sorry this happened to you and your family. I hope the murderer's capture will help in some small way."

"Me, too."

There was something different about him. Instead of the usual cool aloofness that he wore like armor, he was uneasy, and there was a glimmer of vulnerability in his blue-gray eyes. Had he come here for yet another reason?

Refusing to let herself imagine that Luca was ready to become a part of her life again, she busied herself. She bent over and slipped on a pair of bright white tennis shoes with pink laces. Now that her makeup had been wiped away and the glittery, gauzy creations had been returned to the clothes rack, she felt like herself. Plain old Elena.

When she straightened, she found Luca staring at her. Her heart thump-thumped. She swallowed hard. "What is it?"

"Nothing. I was just looking at you."

Worried that she'd missed removing some of the sparkly blue eye makeup they used to make her up as a fairy for the new magical fashion line, Elena turned to the mirror. She didn't see anything but her own complexion. Her cheeks were a little rosy from the cleanser, but it was all her in the reflection. So why had Luca been looking at her so strangely? She shrugged it off.

"Can I persuade you to stay long enough to eat?" She hadn't eaten a bite all day. She'd been a nervous wreck about the show, and now that it was over, she was ravenous. "Or we could get one of your favorite pizzas from Pierre's and take it back to my flat."

"Your flat?" Luca shook his head. "Not going to happen. I hear you have some exciting news." He moved to the end of her makeup table and retrieved a champagne bottle. "We have to celebrate. It's nonnegotiable."

She wasn't sure either of them was up for celebrating. Before she could vocalize her protest, Luca popped the cork and Elena watched as pink bubbles rushed down the side of the bottle. Luca reached for a champagne flute and filled it up.

"For you." He held the glass out to her.

She accepted it. Luca was certainly acting out of character. Her gaze lowered to the glass as the pink bubbles rose and popped. If Luca and the designer of the line Elena now represented only knew of the mess she'd made of her private life, they wouldn't help her celebrate being chosen as the new face of the Lauren Renard line.

Elena felt like a fraud. They all thought she was so good—so deserving. But she was none of those things. Her judgment was way off where men were concerned. She'd been too trusting—too open—and in the end, she'd been lied to in the worst way. Now she didn't trust herself or men.

"Elena?"

She glanced up. Her gaze met Luca's. Tears suddenly rushed to her eyes. She blinked repeatedly, refusing to unleash the turbulent emotions that had been threatening all day.

"Hey, none of that." Luca raised his glass. "This is a moment for celebrating."

Elena forced a smile to her lips and lifted her glass.

Luca held his glass close to hers. "To the most amazing, wonderful tomboy I've ever known. And I might add that you clean up pretty good, too."

Her mouth gaped as their glasses clinked together. "That's not fair. I haven't been a tomboy since we were kids."

His eyes studied her. "I have one question for you."

"You can ask it, but I reserve the right not to answer." A nervous shiver rolled through her stomach. Had he heard about her romantic debacle? She groaned inwardly before taking another drink of champagne—a much bigger drink.

"When did you become so beautiful?" Luca's gaze caressed her, leaving her insides aflutter.

Heat rushed to her cheeks. "Be careful, Luca. If I didn't know better, I might think you were flirting with me."

"I am."

Her heart lodged in her throat. What had come over him? Luca was a constant flirt, but always with every other woman in the room. And now she didn't know how to react to him.

Luca grabbed the champagne and refilled their glasses. "Drink up. I'm taking you out on the town tonight. I'm going to show off the hottest lady in Paris."

He thought she was hot?

Maybe he was referring to the blush that had engulfed

her face. She resisted the urge to fan herself. Instead, she gulped another mouthful of bubbly.

Luca was far too sexy, and he was saying all the right things to sneak right past her meticulously laid defenses. If she wasn't careful, this evening was going to blow up in her face.

She swallowed hard. "But I'm tired—"

"Trust me. What I have in mind will wake you right up." He winked at her.

Her heart skipped a beat. She didn't know what to say. Instead she busied herself with another sip of champagne. As the alcohol hit her empty stomach, she realized that it wasn't her wisest idea and set aside the glass. "It's not that big of a deal."

"Of course it's a big deal. It's a huge deal." He smiled at her like he had something in mind. He'd been giving her that look since they were kids playing in the fields of wildflowers on the palace grounds in Mirraccino, and she knew it meant he had mischief on his mind. "We have to celebrate. And I have the perfect idea."

Why did it suddenly feel like Luca's reaction to her new role for the world-renowned Lauren Renard line was over the top? After all, Luca was an earl. He was royalty, for goodness' sake. His father was the Duke of Halencia. And Luca's mother had been the sister of the King of Mirraccino. Elena knew that her accomplishments didn't come close to stacking up to Luca's impressive lineage.

"Luca, it's really not that big of a deal." Heat rushed to her cheeks.

"Quit being so modest. You worked hard for this." He walked over to her and put his arm over her shoulders. "I'm proud of you. Just wait until my sister hears about this. In fact, she was just asking about you."

"She was?" When he nodded, Elena said, "Tell her I said hi."

"I will. Right after I tell her about you being world famous and the face of her favorite clothing line."

In truth, being the face of such a renowned line was truly a turning point in Elena's career. She wouldn't just have her face on the middle pages of a magazine. She would now dominate the covers. Her calendar would be filled with photo sessions. Finally, she was no longer just the daughter of the King of Mirraccino's secretary or the tomboy who followed Luca all around the palace grounds and played football with him until long after the sun set. She was now a successful international model—for however long it lasted.

"But after your news, I'd really understand if you didn't want to make a big deal of it."

"Indulge me," Luca said.

"What's that supposed to mean?"

"It means while you were taking your final stroll down the catwalk, I was on the phone."

"And? You were finding out the location of the next hot party?" She had no doubt there were parties with so many notable people in town this week for the line reveal, but that just wasn't her scene.

"There's only one party on my mind." He looked at her rather intently.

Her heart raced. "Luca, when did you become so mysterious?"

"Mysterious?" There was a glint of mischievousness reflected in his eyes. "I've been accused of a lot of things, but never that."

"Well, then out with it. What plans did you make?"

"Trust me. You'll find out soon enough."

She moved to retrieve her purse and turned back to say something when his lips landed on hers. That wasn't supposed to happen. Her heart jumped into her throat. So why wasn't Luca pulling away? Why wasn't she?

Maybe if she had held still just a moment longer, his

kiss would have landed on her cheek. Yeah, that was probably it. But now that they were in this awkward situation, neither moved. Could he hear the pounding of her heart?

Over the years, she'd wondered what it'd be like to feel Luca's mouth pressed to hers. But she'd never, ever thought that it would actually happen.

And then his lips moved over hers, tentatively and slowly, as though figuring out where they went from here. Her pulse raced, and any rational thoughts slipped out of reach. At last, her dream was coming true.

Her purse slipped from her hand as she reached out to him. Her fingers slid beneath his gray sports jacket to the black T-shirt beneath. As her palms slid over the defined contours of his chest, a moan swelled in the back of her throat.

Oh, yeah... This kiss—this moment—was so much better than she'd ever imagined. She definitely approved of this change in Luca.

His arms wrapped around her, pulling her close. Need, wonderment and eagerness consumed her. The rush of emotions was more intoxicating than the bubbly they'd just shared.

As their kiss intensified, his tongue slipped past her compliant lips. She leaned in closer, pressing the length of her body against his. If this was a dream, she didn't want to wake up.

A whistle followed by applause from the stage crew had her reluctantly pulling away. She wasn't sure what she expected to find when she gazed into Luca's face. Perhaps disappointment or regret, but instead he was smiling at her. It was one of those smiles that made his eyes twinkle.

"Are you ready to go?" Luca whispered into her ear, sending goose bumps racing down over her body.

"Um...yes."

"Good. I want to make this a very special evening for you."

It was already special. That kiss had been so unexpected and so much better than she'd ever imagined. This was a different side of Luca, and she liked it—she liked him—a lot.

After retrieving her purse from the floor, she slipped her hand into his and they rushed out the door. She refused to second-guess this decision. It was her one chance to be something so much more than Luca's friend.

At last, he'd seen her as a desirable woman.

CHAPTER ONE

Nine weeks later, Mirraccino Island, the Mediterranean

SHE'D HEARD IT said that you can never go home again. Maybe she should have heeded that warning.

Elena stared at herself in the full-length mirror in her bedroom at her parents' modest home on the royal estate of Mirraccino. This trip had not been her idea. It had come about rather suddenly when her mother broke her leg.

Her mother had called to say that she couldn't get around on her own, and since Elena's father was needed at the palace, her mother was home alone all day. As their only child, it was up to Elena to return home. And though the timing wasn't ideal with the start of the new campaign for the Renard line, Elena had worked feverishly to reschedule all of her appointments. She was more than willing to help her mother, who'd always been there for her.

But unbeknownst to Elena, her mother had exaggerated her condition. The fact that her mother had played on Elena's emotions was unusual, so she let it pass without comment. The truth was she didn't make it home often enough.

Don't think about it. Not this evening.

She hadn't even unpacked yet when her mother had handed over an invitation printed on heavy cream stationery sealed with a deep purple royal crest. A little confused, Elena had opened it, surprised to find that she'd been invited to Lady Annabelle's engagement festivities. The invitation had said the event was to be intimate and to dress casually.

Now, two days later, she'd tried on every single dress she'd brought with her from Paris at least twice. Some were too revealing. Others were too flashy. And some were too formal. What exactly did one wear to dinner at the palace?

She'd never been in this situation before. Although she was the daughter of the king's private secretary, she wasn't the type who received invitations to royal events. And this wasn't just any party. It was a weeklong series of events. And her mother had taken it upon herself to post an acceptance on Elena's behalf.

Knock. Knock.

"Come in."

Her mother smiled as she entered the room. Her long dark hair was pulled back and tucked up at the nape of her neck. Only powder accentuated her natural beauty. "I just wanted to see if you needed any help getting ready."

"I'm the one who should be asking if you need anything."

Her mother waved off the concern. "I'm fine."

"Isn't Father home yet? I thought he might stay with you while I'm out for the evening."

The smile slipped from her mother's face. "I don't see your father much lately."

Elena had noticed her father's increased absence. "What has him so busy?"

"The same thing as always—the king."

"Oh." Elena knew from growing up that her father kept his work to himself. And that was probably why he was the king's most trusted employee. "I'm sorry. I had hoped the king would be back to normal by now."

"I had hoped the same thing. Nothing has been right since they arrested that murderer. The news hit the king really hard."

"I'm sure it was quite a shock to learn there was a murderer wandering through the palace all those years."

Her mother shuddered. "I don't like to think of it. Your father saw that criminal every day. Just the thought—"

"Don't go there. It's all over." Elena hoped to reassure her. "Father is safe."

Her mother sent her a weak smile and nodded.

Elena turned back to the full-length mirror. She'd finally settled on a little black dress. It wasn't anything special. But the black suited her mood. She'd been sullen and reserved ever since her night with Luca. It had been just one more mistake on her part—a total error in judgment.

The only right decision she'd made was agreeing to be the face of one of the world's hottest designers. The work was now coming in droves. In fact, there were so many requests for appearances and photo shoots that she couldn't do them all. But once word got out about her condition, it would all end.

She was pregnant with Luca's baby.

Pregnant. The word still sounded so foreign to her.

She'd always kept track of her cycle—a little tick mark on her day planner. With the hectic schedule of a new campaign, she hadn't noticed right away that her timely cycle had suddenly drifted off course. But referencing her day planner to schedule future shoots, she'd stumbled across the missing tick mark. Her heart had clenched before panic ensued.

Four home pregnancy tests later, her worst fears had been confirmed. She was pregnant with Luca's baby. At this point, only Elena and her doctor knew the truth. And for the moment, that was how it'd remain.

"Is that what you're wearing to dinner?" her mother asked, studying Elena's black dress. A decided frown came over her face. "Don't you have something more cheerful?"

For some reason, her mother's disapproval decided Elena's attire for her. "I like this."

"You're awfully skinny." Her mother clucked her tongue disapprovingly. "While you're home, you need to eat more.

Thin is nice, dear. But when a man wants to wrap his hands around you and—"

"Mother, stop." She couldn't believe her prim and proper mother was talking about a man having his hands on her. It just sounded so wrong to hear her mother talk about sex. *Ew!*

"Really, Elena. I didn't think you were a prude, especially with those sexy outfits you model."

"I'm not a prude. It doesn't mean I want to talk about—about that—with you."

Her mother smiled. "I didn't think people your age were so shy talking about sex."

"Enough. You're really making me uncomfortable here."

"Okay. Okay. I'll stop."

"Thank you."

Ding. Dong.

Elena looked at her mother. "Are you expecting anyone?"

"Not that I recall."

"I'll get it." Elena made a move toward the door, immensely grateful for the interruption.

Her mother held up a hand. "You stay and finish getting ready. I'll entertain your date."

"I thought you didn't know who was at the door?"

"I, ah, just remembered." Her mother's gaze avoided hers.

"Really? That's interesting, because I don't recall making a date."

"I know, dear. That's why I arranged for one. After all, you don't want to show up at the palace all alone."

Stunned by her mother's matchmaking, Elena stood slack jawed as her mother used her crutches to maneuver out of Elena's bedroom. She even pulled the door shut behind her.

Elena didn't know what shocked her more—her mother's agility or the fact Elena had a date that evening and her mother hadn't even told her the man's name. At least with her mother doing the matchmaking, Elena knew the man would be honest and a gentleman.

The only problem was Elena didn't want a date. She was perfectly happy going to the palace alone. This wasn't the good old days when it was unseemly for a twenty-five-year-old woman to be seen in public without an escort.

She had to put a stop to her mother's meddling. After all, she'd returned to Mirraccino to take care of her mother, not the other way around.

Elena glanced back at the mirror. She turned, giving a side view. Would anyone be able to tell she was pregnant? She didn't think so. She wasn't far along. And so far she'd been able to avoid the dreaded morning sickness. A little nausea now and then and being a bit more emotional than normal were her only symptoms.

She turned away from the mirror and slipped on a pair of platform stiletto heels adorned with crystals. The added height to her five-foot-ten stature always gave her a boost of confidence. The peekaboo toes would give a glimpse of her pedicure. Thankfully, she'd had a nail appointment just before she left Paris. She'd hoped it would lift her spirits. It hadn't.

She pulled open the bedroom door and headed downstairs. "Mother, I—"

The words died in her throat. There, making chitchat with her mother, was Luca. Her heart lurched into her throat. How could this be? Luca never visited Mirraccino. And yet here he was, smiling and laughing with her mother.

He looked incredibly handsome with his dark hair cropped short on the sides and back while the top was a bit longer. He wore a charcoal suit that amplified his already broad shoulders—shoulders where not so long ago she'd rested her head. She squelched the thought as fast as it came to her.

Sans a tie, the top two buttons of his white dress shirt were unbuttoned, revealing a glimpse of his tanned chest and the gold chain that held his St. Christopher medal. He'd been wearing that necklace—a gift from his mother—almost as long as Elena had known him. She knew it meant a great deal to him.

He looked like he was ready to step onto a runway in Paris or Milan. He was certainly photogenic enough. He had it all—the looks, a title and money. He wanted for nothing. Even though he'd settled down with a job in the financial sector, she knew he traveled routinely. With his home base in Milan, he often traveled throughout Europe to the States and then to Australia before he started the expedition once again. And he certainly never lacked for companionship.

She should have known that Luca would be her mother's idea of an appropriate date. Her mother would like nothing better than to have her marry into the royal family. But Elena had made it clear that would never happen. She'd had enough of men. They only wanted one thing. Once they got it, it was game over and they were on to their next conquest.

Not so long ago, Luca had been the love 'em and leave 'em type. And the aftermath of their night together hadn't convinced her that this particular leopard had changed his spots. It was best that she trod carefully where he was concerned.

"Hello, Elena." Luca placed a practiced smile on his face, but there was a flicker of something dark in his eyes. In a blink it was gone, leaving her to wonder if she'd imagined it.

"Hi. I…I didn't know you were back on the island."

"I was told by my sister that if I didn't make an appearance for her engagement celebration, she would track me down and it wouldn't be pretty when she found me."

"I can imagine your sister following through on that threat."

"Me, too. So here I am."

"And since your appearance was last minute," her mother interjected, "Luca kindly agreed to be your escort. Isn't that right, Luca?"

His Adam's apple bobbed. "Yes, that's right. It looks like we're both without dates this evening."

"But that doesn't mean my mother should have imposed on you." Elena sent her mother a pointed look.

"I didn't." Her mother feigned innocence.

Elena's gaze narrowed on her mother, not believing her. "And I suppose Luca is now psychic and knew I'd be here this evening without a date?"

Elena could feel Luca's gaze on her, but she refused to face him. She was already embarrassed enough. How could her mother do this to her?

"I was just trying to help," her mother said. "Luca came round the other day to check on me. He'd heard about my accident, and he wanted to make sure I was okay."

It sounded innocent enough, but how that translated into a date was another story. "And that's when you hatched this scheme to impose on his kindness."

"Young lady—" her mother's voice took on a sharp edge of indignation "—I don't now, nor have I ever, hatched a scheme. I merely mentioned that you were flying in to town."

"And I suggested that we go to the dinner this evening— together." Luca was no longer smiling.

He was mad at her? She was only trying to undo her mother's meddling. She was certain her mother had more to do with this arrangement than she was letting on. Wait. Had he just said he was the one who'd wanted to go to the dinner with her?

Elena's gaze shifted to Luca. But it was like he had built a wall between them, and she wasn't able to read his thoughts. Drat! She felt as though she was standing on shifting sand and she just couldn't get her footing. The best thing to do was let him off the hook, gently.

"I appreciate your thoughtfulness, but you don't have to bother," she said, watching his eyes grow darker. "I don't mind going to the palace by myself."

"What about the palace?" Her father stepped through the doorway in his standard black suit, collared white shirt and black tie.

"Luca came to escort Elena to the dinner at the palace." Her mother beamed. "Isn't that wonderful?"

Her father's face was pale and drawn. Dark circles had formed under his eyes from being on call for the king at any hour of the day or night. Elena wished her father would set some boundaries in his life, but he insisted that his duty was to the king, and he could not be deterred.

Everyone stood quietly waiting for her father to speak. It wasn't like him to be so quiet. Usually he would tell her to have a good evening and be on his way.

"Are you all right?" Elena asked her father.

"I'm fine. Just a little tired." Her father moved to stand in front of Elena. He leaned forward and pressed a feathery kiss to her cheek. "But I'm feeling better now. How could I not with my wonderful family around me?"

Elena's mother nodded toward Luca. "Aren't you going to say anything to our guest?"

Her father grunted as though he'd forgotten. He turned to Luca. "Don't do anything to hurt my girl. Or else…"

Her father didn't finish the threat, but Luca's rigid stance and the firm line of his lips said that he'd gotten the message.

"I'll go clean up for dinner," her father said and moved toward the stairs.

"Shall we go?" Luca asked.

Elena had to try one last time to call off this awkward

date. "As I was saying before, I really don't mind arriving alone."

Luca sighed. "Ah, but see, I do mind. I hate showing up at these family events alone. There will be questions about who I'm dating, if it's serious and if I ever plan to settle down and get married. I'd rather avoid all that."

So she would be doing him a favor? By what? Being his decoy? A shield?

No. No. No.

She wasn't comfortable with any of those titles. Elena had enough of her own secrets. She didn't need to be drawn into anyone else's drama.

The past few months in Paris had consisted of making one bad decision after the other. It had gotten to the point where she had no faith in her own judgment. And now that she was pregnant, she had to make the right decisions. There was an innocent baby counting on her. She had mixed emotions about her unexpected condition. How could she tell Luca she was pregnant when she didn't even know how she felt about it?

That was why her mother's request for her to return home couldn't have come at a better time. She had hoped some downtime would clear her head. At the time, she'd had absolutely no idea that Annabelle was having a big celebration or that she would include Elena in the festivities.

Her gaze landed on Luca. He looked uncomfortable and anxious to be anywhere but here. Things had definitely changed between them. Where there had once been an easiness, there was now this crackling tension. If she needed any confirmation that they could never go back to how they used to be, this was it.

Tonight, she would be nervous enough being a guest at the palace. She really didn't need the added awkwardness she felt around Luca. If only he wasn't so insistent on being a gentleman and escorting her.

"I'm not quite ready to go." When he didn't say anything, she added, "I don't want to make you late."

"I don't mind waiting," he said. "It'll give me some more time to talk with your mother."

Her mother smiled. "And I just made a fresh batch of those amaretto cookies that you enjoy."

"They're my favorite," Luca said. "And I haven't had them in a very long time. You really are the best in the kitchen."

Her mother shook a finger at him. "You have grown up to be quite a flatterer. I'll just go get you a few."

"If you don't mind, I'll join you."

Her mother nodded and set off for the kitchen with Luca following closely behind. Elena stood alone in the entryway. What exactly had just happened?

CHAPTER TWO

Luca couldn't take his gaze off her.

Had Elena always been this beautiful?

Thankfully she'd turned her head to stare out the car's window at the passing fields of wildflowers while in the background the setting sun painted the sky with streaks of orange, pink and purple. But tonight Luca was in no mood to appreciate nature's beauty.

In the weeks since he'd last seen her in Paris, he'd convinced himself that everything about their evening together had been blown out of proportion by the champagne. He just couldn't accept that he was attracted to his childhood friend. He couldn't allow that to happen, because they could have no future.

He wasn't into commitments.

Not now. Not ever.

But there was something about Elena that pulled at him…even to this day.

And then he remembered how he'd woken up the morning after they'd made love and heard Elena sniffling. The sound had ripped him apart. No one had ever cried after spending the night with him. And the fact that it was Elena, of all people, made the situation so much worse.

He hadn't moved for an indeterminable number of minutes. Her muffled sobs had sliced through him. Clearly she'd thought their night together had been a mistake. Unable to think of anything to say to comfort her, he'd continued to breathe deeply as though he'd still been asleep. Each breath had been painful, as his entire body was tense. The memory was still so crystal clear.

He had done that. He had made Elena cry. And he felt awful.

If only he hadn't let things get out of hand. But he'd thought she'd been having a good time. Still, he should have resisted kissing her. He should have made their friendship the priority. If he'd been thinking clearly, he would have realized there would be no coming back from holding her all night long.

He swallowed hard as the limo glided through the estate to the palace. The ride only took a couple of minutes, but with Elena so close to him, time seemed to stand still. For the first time, he wasn't sure what to say or what to do.

Boy, he'd really messed things up between them. He resisted the urge to rake his fingers through his hair. He needed to look his best for the professional photos his sister would undoubtedly insist upon.

On second thought, this date is not a good idea.

Not good at all.

"Are you sure about this?" Elena asked.

"Yes." *Liar.*

She arched a brow. "You don't sound certain."

This was where he should reach out and squeeze her hand to reassure her, but instead he didn't move. He didn't trust himself to touch her. The images of their night together were still in the forefront of his mind.

He'd really mucked things up. The truth was he didn't want to be Elena's escort, but when her mother had mentioned Elena's return to the island, he'd been caught off guard. And when her mother had mentioned the party, Luca had spoken without thinking.

And now, well, all he wanted to do was sweep Elena into his arms and pick up right where they'd left off back in Paris. He wanted to feel her eager lips beneath his—ready and willing.

He halted his thoughts. This wasn't like him. When he ended a relationship, he moved on without looking back.

With Elena there had been no moving on. Since that night, no other woman had interested him.

When he closed his eyes, it was Elena's face he saw. It was the memory of her lips that tormented him. How was he ever supposed to get her out of his system?

So he didn't dare look at Elena right now. He refused to act on those desires. She'd made it abundantly clear that she regretted their night together—no matter how hot and steamy it had been.

He just needed to focus on something else—anything else. His mind drew a blank. Perhaps he should start a conversation. Yes, that was a good idea. But what should he talk about?

"I was surprised to hear you were back on the island." There—that sounded normal enough.

She shrugged. "I didn't have much choice, considering I thought my mother truly needed me."

"I take it she exaggerated her injuries?"

Elena nodded. "By the sound of her on the phone, she was on death's door."

Luca smiled. "I can imagine."

"What does that mean?" Elena suddenly sounded protective of her mother.

"I just meant that your mother would do anything to get you home."

"And how would you know? You're here even less than I am."

He shrugged, not certain he wanted to admit that he talked with her mother often enough. At first, Elena's mother had concocted any excuse possible to call him, but as time went by, he got used to hearing from her. He actually looked forward to it, because she would fill him in on all of Elena's accomplishments.

"I just remember how she used to be—always wanting you to stay close to home."

Elena shrugged. "She finally accepted that my future wasn't in Mirraccino."

"Speaking of which, how did you get time off from your new campaign to fly here?"

Elena glanced away. "I...ah, had a break in my schedule."

There was something more she wasn't telling him, but he didn't push. If she wanted him to know, she'd tell him when she was ready. The fact she was even speaking to him, he took as a positive sign. Maybe there was hope for their friendship after all.

The car pulled to a stop in front of the palace. Though he'd been staying here since he arrived a couple of days ago, he didn't want to attend this dinner any more than Elena. But he refused to disappoint his sister. He'd already hurt her enough by leaving home and allowing extended gaps between visits. He knew Annabelle wanted her family reunited, and now that their mother's killer had been caught, she thought it would fix everything.

It wouldn't.

Luca had witnessed too much. Experienced too much. And he couldn't be the son that his father needed—and perhaps deserved.

But now that Annabelle was getting married, hopefully she'd stop longing for the family she'd lost. When a family member was murdered, it seemed for the most part that families reacted in one of two ways. The horrific event either drew them together—the family against the world. Or it splintered them apart—each finding their solace in a different way. His family had been the latter.

Luca's car door swung open, interrupting his thoughts. It was for the best. He didn't want to dwell on how he'd disappointed his sister repeatedly over the years. Tonight was to be a celebration. And he would put on his biggest and brightest smile, which shouldn't be too hard since their father, the duke, was not to be in attendance. Tonight was an informal gathering of friends and some family. Annabelle wanted her groom to meet the people who had meant a lot to her while she was growing up.

An enormous wooden door with brass fixtures swung open. An older gentleman in a black-and-white tux stepped outside to greet them.

Elena put her hand on Luca's arm, pausing him from getting out of the car. She leaned over and whispered, "That's so strange."

"What is?" Luca glanced around, but he didn't notice anything amiss.

"That the butler is there to greet me—well, us. That's never happened in my whole life."

Luca smiled and shook his head. "I'm glad it makes you happy."

"It does."

Luca alighted from the car and turned back. He held out his hand to help Elena to her feet. "So what do you think?"

"I think that no matter where I go, this palace is the most beautiful building." Her gaze focused on the palace and not him. "What do you think? You've traveled even more than me. Have you ever seen anything so amazing?"

Luca turned to study the expansive building. He had honestly never really looked at the place. He was embarrassed to admit that he'd taken the centuries-old palace for granted. Over the years, it'd been expanded upon, which included the addition of the towering turrets. Though once used to keep an eye out for approaching enemy ships, they were now more a decoration and painted with stripes of yellow, pink, aqua and gold.

"It really is remarkable," Luca said, his gaze straying to Elena. "A beauty unlike any other that I've ever found."

Just then Elena glanced at him, and he turned away. Did she know he was no longer talking about the palace?

He hoped not. He didn't want to give her the wrong idea. They'd had their chance together—as brief as it might have been. There was no way of recapturing it. He refused to even consider it. Okay, maybe he had considered it, but he wouldn't act upon his desires.

Even if their lovemaking hadn't made her cry, they didn't belong together. He couldn't make her the promises she deserved. And he wouldn't have any woman waiting around for him when he had absolutely no intention of making a commitment.

Therefore, it was best that he shove aside those tempting images of her in his arms with that wanton desire reflected in her eyes. He swallowed hard. Could they ever be friends like before? He was feeling less assured about that with each passing moment.

The butler stood aside. "Welcome, Miss Ricci. It's good to have you back."

"Hello, Alfred. It's good to be back."

Luca held out his arm to Elena. She paused and looked at it as if she wasn't sure what to do. Boy, he really had messed things up between them.

"Go ahead," he encouraged. "I promise not to bite."

A small smile lifted the corners of her very desirable lips. She tentatively slipped her hand into the crook of his arm. When an unfamiliar sensation pulsed up his arm and settled in his chest, he stilled his body. He refused to give any indication that her touch affected him. Because it hadn't. Not really. It was just nerves. He was just worried about doing something to drive his best friend even further from him.

"Are you ready?"

Elena nodded.

Her face was void of emotion. He knew that look. It was her working face—the look she wore when she was strutting down the catwalk in some amazing outfit. He couldn't rightly describe any of the fashions she wore, because when he googled her, he was always caught up by the beauty of her face. It didn't matter what hair color or stylish cut she was sporting—ever since their night together, he'd been captivated by her.

He took sure strides up the steps to the open palace door. Inside, there was a host of palace staff to greet them and escort them to the dining room. It was odd, considering Luca had been running through this palace with his host of cousins since he was in diapers. That seemed so long ago now.

A flash went off, momentarily blinding Luca.

Elena came to a standstill. She released his arm. "The press is here?"

"Not that I know of."

Elena took a step back. "I should have expected this. Coming here was a mistake."

Luca glanced around. The photographer moved out of the dining room. "It's not the press. It's a private photographer. My sister is sentimental and wants to have pictures to remember these events."

Elena's worried gaze met his. "You're sure?"

He nodded. "Since when did you become so shy? I thought the camera was your friend."

"You thought wrong." And with that Elena brushed past him and headed into the dining room.

What had just happened? His radar was going off. Something was definitely amiss. And it frustrated the heck out of him that he'd wrecked their relationship to the point where she wouldn't even open up to him.

He rushed to catch up to her. "Tell me what's bothering you."

"Nothing."

"If it's nothing, why won't you even face me?"

She didn't stop. "It's nothing," she called over her shoulder. "Just drop it."

"Tell me what it is and I'll fix it if I can."

She stopped and turned to him. Wearing an indifferent expression like a mask, she said, "I don't know why you think I need help."

Luca reached out and grasped her arm before she could wander off. "I know things aren't right between us, but I also know you really well, and no matter what you say, I know there's something wrong—something big."

Elena yanked her arm from him. "You should concentrate on your sister. This is her big night."

As though his sister had heard her name mentioned, she rushed over to them. Annabelle's face was aglow with happiness. "Elena, I was so excited when I heard you were back on the island." She reached out and they quickly hugged. "Thank you so much for coming."

A strange sensation coiled through Luca as he watched the easy smile light up Elena's face. Elena certainly hadn't done that when she'd spotted him at her mother's house. In fact, her reaction had been quite the opposite.

He didn't know why he let it bother him. There were plenty of other women out there who would be happy to have his company. If only he had the slightest bit of interest in those other women.

He inwardly groaned with frustration. He turned away and went in search of something to drink. He wasn't really thirsty, but it was certainly better than watching Elena make nice with everyone—everyone but him.

He had to quit letting her get to him. He needed to withdraw. Wasn't that what he'd promised himself after his mother's murder? To keep people at a safe distance?

That was why he'd packed up and moved away from Halencia and Mirraccino. It hurt too much when people he cared about were torn from his life—whether by murder, grief or something else. He just couldn't go through that again.

And though he'd missed his sister and Elena while he'd been traveling, he'd been able to distract himself. He was always on the go. A new adventure. A new challenge. That was exactly what he should do now—set off on a new expedition. But he couldn't. Not yet.

Until the week was over, he had to make the best of this situation. And then he would be gone. He would return to Milan. He would make plans for some daring feat and forget all about these unwanted emotions.

CHAPTER THREE

AT LAST SHE was an invited guest.

Elena had never thought the day would come when she would be invited to the palace. It was the final confirmation that she'd gone from being a nobody to a somebody. She was no longer the shy child who was left out of all the elaborate royal birthday parties and the other celebrations Luca and his sister attended.

After waiting a lifetime for this moment, she was surprised to find it wasn't nearly as satisfying as she'd imagined. Truthfully, she wasn't enjoying herself. She was in no frame of mind to take part in such a celebration. Her life was a mess, and she had a feeling the worst was yet to come.

At dinner, Luca had been seated at the other end of the extremely long table. There was no chance of him probing her with his eyes—searching for answers to his unspoken questions. The problem with hanging out with her former best friend was that he could still read her like a book. And she just wasn't ready to open up to him.

During the dinner, she'd witnessed Annabelle's bubbly happiness. It was then that Elena made her decision. She would delay telling Luca about the baby until the end of the week. By then, the celebration would be over and the fallout from her announcement couldn't ruin this happy occasion.

The delay would be best for everyone. Until then, she'd have a chance to figure out her life plan and to find the right words to soften the blow for Luca. Not that she wanted anything from him—that she'd decided. But he was the father of her baby, and he deserved to know the truth.

She glanced around, finding Luca engaged in a conversation with Prince Demetrius. This was her chance to quietly slip away from the party. After all, who would notice?

Besides possibly Luca. But they'd been doing their best to avoid each other all evening. So perhaps he'd be relieved to realize that she'd gone.

Luckily, having spent her youth avoiding the guards and servants, she knew her way around the palace. She slipped into the hallway. A quick check both ways let her know that the coast was clear. Her gaze latched on the French doors at the end of the hallway. Although freedom was within reach, she forced herself to walk at a reasonable pace.

She inhaled a deep breath, hoping to calm her rising nerves. All she wanted now was to escape the curious looks and the inevitable questions regarding her showing up as Luca's date. When her hand grasped the brass handle, she glanced over her shoulder. So far, so good.

She let herself out onto the patio that was surrounded by the royal gardens. She looked left and then right. All alone. She breathed her first easy breath all evening. Whatever had made her think that coming here would be a good idea?

She moved to the far end of the patio and leaned her palms against the cold concrete balustrade supported by dozens of tiny pillars. The entire palace was a work of art. And just now the gardens were aglow beneath the full moon. It was breathtaking—

"There you are." Luca's voice came from behind her.

The breath caught in Elena's throat. She'd been so close to making a successful escape. Why had she stopped? Maybe because she knew this would be the last time she would be welcome at the palace. Once word got out about all her ill-advised activities, no one would want her around—most especially Luca.

Steeling herself, she leveled her shoulders, plastered a smile on her face and turned. "Luca, I didn't hear you approach."

"And I didn't hear you say anything about sneaking off into the night." His dark brows were drawn together.

"Who said I was sneaking away?"

"I did. And you were."

The smile was getting harder and harder to maintain. "Really, Luca? Sometimes you imagine too much."

"Don't try to brush me off. I know you, Elena. You put on a pretty good show this evening for the other guests, but I can see you aren't happy."

"Of course I'm happy. I'm honored that your sister still thinks so highly of our childhood friendship to invite me to such an event."

"Annabelle likes everyone." And then, as though he realized how that might sound, he added, "But you meant a lot to her, especially when our mother died."

Elena had tried her best to be there for both Luca and Annabelle, but he'd pushed her away. It was as if overnight Luca had built a wall around himself and no matter how hard she tried, there'd been no scaling that wall. Eventually she gave up.

"I don't belong here," Elena said.

"What? Of course you do."

She wasn't going to argue with him. Her gaze strayed to the sweeping steps that led to the garden. "I made an appearance, and now it's time that I go. Please tell your sister I had a good time."

Luca crossed his arms over his broad chest. "Tell her yourself."

The abruptness of his comment caught her off guard. "I…I will." A written message would be so much easier than a phone conversation where inevitable questions would arise. "I'll drop her a note tomorrow."

"This isn't about you fitting in. It's about us. Isn't it?"

She met his unwavering gaze. "Why would you think that?"

"Because I really screwed up in Paris. It was all a big mistake. I wasn't myself that night. And if you give me a chance to make it up to you, I swear it'll never happen again."

The more he tried to explain, the more his pointed words poked at her hope that they'd get past this awkward stage. But now she knew the unvarnished truth. And it was worse than she'd thought.

Having no response for him, she turned to continue walking.

"You can't just walk away," he called out.

Why did he have to keep pushing? He wasn't going to like anything she had to say. It was best to keep moving. She took another step.

"Elena, what is it going to take for you to forgive and forget?"

She turned, catching the frustration written so clearly on his face. "You don't understand. The past can't be that easily erased."

"What are you saying?" He stepped closer to her. "Elena, what is going on?"

Elena pressed her lips together. She'd said far more than she'd intended at this juncture. And now she'd aroused Luca's suspicion. There was one thing that Luca excelled at and that was ferreting out the truth. If she didn't get out of here soon, her secret would be out. And this royal scandal—the earl having a baby with a commoner, the daughter of the help— would be the talk of the palace and beyond.

She knew it would happen sooner or later, but she'd been hoping for later, after Annabelle's moment in the spotlight. After all Annabelle had been through tracking down her mother's murderer and then being held at gunpoint, her friend deserved this bit of happiness.

"I'm not leaving here until you talk to me," Luca said. "So out with it."

"I just meant we can't pretend that night didn't happen."

He didn't say anything for a moment, as though he were

considering the sincerity of her statement. "I understand. But I don't want to lose our friendship."

Before she could say a word, the sound of voices and approaching footsteps interrupted. Elena glanced past Luca and spotted Prince Alexandro alongside another of Luca's cousins. The prince glanced up and surprise flashed in his eyes.

"I'm sorry. We didn't know anyone was out here," Prince Alexandro said. "We'll go."

"No. Stay. You aren't interrupting anything," Elena hastily responded.

The prince's gaze moved between her and Luca. "You're sure?"

Luca hesitated and then nodded.

"Good," the prince said, approaching them. "Luca, we need you to settle a disagreement."

The men quickly got into a heated discussion about the upcoming European football season. Elena immediately tuned out the conversation. She wasn't a sports fan unless it was auto racing. There was just something about a hot guy and a fast car. Her mind immediately conjured up Luca in a sleek racecar. The image definitely worked for her. But just as quickly as the image came to her, she dismissed it.

With the men now deep in conversation, Luca had his back to her. She took advantage of the moment to follow through with her original plan to steal away into the night. Trying to act as casual as possible, she quietly strolled down the steps and entered the garden.

When she reached the other side of the garden, she slipped through the gate and entered the open field illuminated only by moonlight. At last, she was free.

With her hand splayed over her midsection, she said, "Don't worry, little one. We'll tell your father. The time just has to be right."

* * *

A late-night phone call was never a good thing.

In Luca's case, it always meant that his life was about to take a turn for the worse. He doubted tonight would be any different.

"Father?"

"Luca, you answered." Surprise rang out in his father's voice.

Was he that bad at accepting calls from his father? Perhaps. He had started to avoid his father's calls because the man kept hounding him to step up and take his place in the family business—a position Luca didn't feel comfortable assuming.

"Are you all right?" Luca asked, rubbing the sleep from his eyes.

"I'm coming to Mirraccino first thing in the morning. We need to talk."

"Is that code for you want to discuss how I'm wasting my life? If so, you're wasting your time—"

"I'm serious, Luca. It's imperative that we talk." There was a weariness to his father's voice that he'd never heard before. And it concerned Luca more than he'd expected.

"Can't you just tell me now?"

"No. We need to do this in person. And don't tell your sister. She'll find out soon enough, but for now she deserves to enjoy her engagement."

"Understood."

"Good. I'll see you first thing in the morning. Don't sleep in."

"I won't."

When they disconnected, sleep was the very last thing on Luca's mind. His father was far from melodramatic. In fact, after his mother's murder, his father had been the only calm person—perhaps too calm. At the time, Luca had resented the fact that his father hadn't fallen to pieces. In that moment, he'd been certain his father didn't love his mother. Not like he should have loved her.

That was the moment when Luca pulled back from everyone. Convinced that love was just an illusion, he'd refused to become a victim of romance and happily-ever-after. Because when the haze of lust lifted, someone would walk away and someone would get hurt.

And as much as Luca believed his father had not loved his mother, as the years slipped by, his doubts set in. His father never moved on with his life. He never remarried. Luca wasn't even sure his father dated. If he did, he used the utmost discretion. And the few times that Luca had returned to their home in Halencia, it remained the same. His mother's belongings were still where she had left them. It was so easy to pretend that she was just out for the day. It made Luca wonder if he'd misjudged his father. Had his father loved his mother in his own way?

Sleep was elusive for the rest of the night as Luca stared into the darkness. He knew as sure as the sun would rise that his life was about to change dramatically. It left him restless.

And then there was the matter of Elena.

She'd gotten away from him tonight. He didn't know what was bothering her, but he intended to find out. It wasn't like Elena to act so mysteriously.

Tomorrow there was a picnic. He wasn't sure what else Annabelle had planned for the day, but he was certain it wouldn't be boring. Nothing about the day would be mundane, because he had every intention of once again escorting Elena to the event. It would give them a chance to finish their prior discussion.

There was something going on with Elena, and he felt driven to find out what had this international fashion model cowering from the cameras. Perhaps it wasn't any of his business, but the worried look reflected in Elena's eyes haunted him.

He might not have been around much in the past few years, but he was here now. By helping her, he might be able to assuage some of his guilt over losing control in Paris. If he did, perhaps they could part on good terms.

CHAPTER FOUR

THE NEXT MORNING Luca paced back and forth in the palace library.

It was time he let his father in on his life choices. Luca couldn't help but wonder what his father would think of the fact that he'd gone back to school and received his degree in business management. He knew he was destined to run the family's citrus business one day. And he wanted to be prepared. In fact, for the past several years, he'd been working his way up in an investment firm in Milan.

Perhaps he should have told his father all of this sooner. He'd intended to, but it never worked out. Every time they got together, they argued. His mother used to say that they butted heads so much because they were so much alike. Luca had always taken it as an insult. He had never wanted to believe that he was as stubborn and infuriating as his father—

"Luca." His father's voice came from behind him.

Being so deep into his thoughts, Luca hadn't heard his father approach. He turned toward the doorway. "Hello, Father."

"At last we talk. You really ought to get a new phone so your messages don't get lost."

Luca had noticed the messages, but he kept putting them off for one reason or another. "I've been busy."

His father's dark, bushy brows drew together. "Humph… How can you be busy?"

Luca inwardly groaned. Did his father always have to think so little of him? And then he realized that it was partially his fault. His stubborn pride had kept him from revealing to his father that he'd followed the path his father had wanted him to take in the first place.

Luca cleared his throat. "What did you need to talk about?"

"Is that how you greet your father?"

"It's not like we're the mushy type. That's Annabelle's area."

His father broke out in a hearty laugh, surprising Luca. He had absolutely no idea what he'd said that was so amusing.

His father quickly recovered his composure. "Apparently you've spent as little time around your sister as you have me. Let me enlighten you so that you are not shocked this week. Your sister has grown up into a strong woman and a bit of a spitfire."

That would explain the adventure she'd gone on to track down their mother's murderer. "I'll definitely keep that in mind." Still not comfortable in his father's presence, he said, "Now, what did you want to talk about?"

His father's formidable presence melted away as his face seemed to age almost instantly and his broad shoulders drooped a bit. The duke closed the library door and headed for the tray of coffee and biscuits that had been left by the staff.

His father busied himself pouring a cup of coffee. "Would you like some?"

"I'm good." Then as an afterthought, Luca added, "Thanks."

He wasn't used to his father being thoughtful. This meeting must be serious. And right now, he was too wired. Adding caffeine to the mix would be a mistake.

After his father fixed his coffee with some sugar and a bit of cream, he turned. He took a long swallow before returning his cup to the saucer. "You need to move home."

Luca's body tensed. That was it? No explanation. Nothing but an order. Throwing around his authority was so typical of his father. But he must have forgotten that Luca was no longer a child to be bossed around.

"No." If his father would talk to him differently, he'd explain to him that he already had a job with responsibilities.

His father's eyes flared with anger. "You don't understand. You don't have a choice. It's time you stop partying and live up to your responsibilities."

"And if I don't?"

"You'll be cut off from your funds."

This was where he had his father. "If you hadn't noticed, I haven't touched that bank account in years."

His father's mouth gaped. A second passed before he regained his composure. "I...I didn't know. How are you getting by?"

Luca knew that he could continue to keep his father in the dark, but what good would that do? After all, he wanted to prove to his father—and himself—that he had changed. This was a good starting point. "I'm an account manager at an investment firm."

"You are?" His father leaned back against the table as though for support. The news appeared to have knocked him off balance.

Luca couldn't deny that he found a bit of satisfaction in being able to surprise his father. "Yes. I went back to school, earned my degree and I've been based in Milan ever since. But my work takes me around the globe."

"I see."

No *I'm proud of you.* Or *I'm happy for you.* His father seemed to absorb the news as though he'd just been told there was rain in the forecast.

"Well, I'd like to say that it's been great catching up, but we never were good at casual conversation. So if that's all, I should be going." Luca turned to the door.

"Wait. You can't go. Not yet." His father's voice took

on an ominous tone, causing Luca to turn back. "You need to know…"

When his father's voice faded away and his gaze centered on the coffee in his cup, Luca became suspicious that there really was a problem. His father never acted coy. Whatever it was had his father acting out of character.

"I need to know what?" Luca asked.

His father's hand shook just a bit as he turned to place the coffee cup on the table. When he turned his attention back to Luca, his eyes were dark and unreadable. "The family business is failing."

Failing? The grove of lemon trees had been in his family for five generations. It was a tradition. It was their history.

Luca had to be certain he understood his father. "And this is why you want me to move home?"

His father sighed. "I'm not getting any younger. It's time I pass the torch to you and step down. But before I do this, I need to know that you're up to the challenge. Are you ready to settle down and do the work necessary to save our business and our home?"

Sure, he'd been gone for a long time, but in all honesty, he never meant to be gone forever. His home in Halencia was where he planned to settle…eventually. He'd just never thought anything would happen to it. He always imagined it'd be there waiting for him when he was ready to accept his destiny.

But now his father was looking to him for help. What did his father think Luca could do that he hadn't already done himself? Luca didn't have any answers, but he did know this was his chance to prove to his family that he was someone they could count on.

After all, they had world-renowned lemons with a delicate taste and low acidity. Surely there had to be a market for them. They'd never had a problem in the past.

It would be so easy to turn his father down and go back

to his comfortable life in Milan. After all, he hadn't created the problem. It wasn't his responsibility to fix it.

But this was the first time his father had ever turned to him for help. How could Luca walk away from that? He was certain his mother would plead with him to let go of his pride and help his father.

It wouldn't be easy moving back to Halencia. His father might talk of retirement, but Luca knew his father wouldn't do it. The business was all his father had left. It was in his blood. So how would Luca work side by side with such a stubborn man?

Before he made up his mind, they needed to get a few things straight.

"Why do you want my help?" Luca asked, needing his father to admit that he needed him.

"I…I just told you."

"No, you told me the company is in trouble, but you didn't say why you turned to me."

His father hesitated. "Fine. I need your help. I can't do it alone. Is that what you want to hear?"

Luca nodded. "Yes, it is. And there's one more thing."

"I'm afraid to ask."

"Then just listen. If I succeed, you'll sign over the position of president to me."

His father's dark brows gathered and his mouth opened, no doubt to protest.

"You did say that you were planning to step down, didn't you?" Luca knew as sure as the sun was going to rise tomorrow that unless an agreement was in place, his father would never step down. Once the company was back in the black, his father would no longer have a reason to hand over the reins.

His father sighed as he shrugged his shoulders. "Okay. You'll be president if you succeed."

"And you'll put this all in writing?"

The duke's shoulders grew rigid as his bushy brows drew together. "My word isn't enough for you?"

"Let's just say, this way there will be no room for mis-understandings."

His father studied him for a moment. "The Luca who left here years ago never would have asked for such a contract."

"I was young then. And my mother had just died. It's not fair to throw that in my face—"

"Slow down. You didn't let me finish. I was going to add that I am impressed. You've grown up to be a man who isn't afraid to stand his ground, even against his father. I just hope you have that much resilience and guts when it comes to turning around the business."

"I will. Trust me."

Luca hoped he sounded more assured than he felt at that moment. His entire future and his family's legacy hinged on him pulling together a new business plan. And it was just starting to sink in that this endeavor might be much more important than proving himself to his father.

He had just signed on to save their home—the place where his ancestors had lived for generations. The place that was filled with memories of his mother. The thought tugged at his heart.

And at the moment, he didn't have a plan. He had to come up with one fast. And it had to be good—no, it had to be great.

At last her mother was resting.

Elena breathed a sigh of relief. Her mother was far too active. It was difficult to get her to stop and elevate her ankle like the doctor had told her to do. And her mother looked wiped out. She'd said her ankle throbbed at night and it kept her awake.

Today, Elena had promised to sit with her to watch an old black-and-white movie starring Cary Grant. Her mother seemed pleased with the suggestion, seeing as her father wasn't one for movies. He'd rather play checkers or cards to pass the time.

It was only a matter of minutes into the movie when her mother drifted off to sleep while sitting upright on the couch. Elena put a throw blanket over her and was on her way to the kitchen for another cup of coffee when there was a knock at the door. Not wanting her mother to wake up, she rushed to the door and opened it.

There, standing before her, was Luca in a blue button-up shirt with the sleeves rolled up, white shorts and boat shoes. He looked as if he'd just stepped off the deck of a luxury yacht. Dark sunglasses hid his eyes from her.

She ran a hand over her hair, realizing that she hadn't bothered to do much with her appearance that morning. "Luca, what are you doing here?"

"I thought we could walk together to the picnic."

"But last night—"

"You left before we finished our conversation. So are you ready to go?"

"I'm not going."

"You can't back out. It's a weeklong celebration and everyone on the invite list is expected. I was told this personally. Apparently my sister thinks I might skip out on her. So if I have to go, you do, too. And that includes the dinner and dance on Saturday."

"Your sister must be so excited." What did one even wear to such an affair? She wasn't certain, but she guessed frilly hats might be involved. She didn't own any.

"I'll give my sister credit for bringing together all our childhood friends. It was a good idea. And don't worry, the dance isn't a full-on ball. I imagine she's saving that for the wedding. Anyway, are you ready to go?"

He had to be joking. She glanced down at the ratty T-shirt she'd found in her old dresser as well as a pair of cutoff jean shorts. "Um, no. I'm looking after my mother. She had a rough night."

"I'm sorry to hear that. We could always stay here? I'm sure Annabelle would understand."

"But I wouldn't." Her mother's voice was immediately followed by the tapping of her crutches.

Elena turned to her mother. "But I'm here to take care of you."

"I can take care of myself. And if you go, perhaps I can take a nap without being interrupted."

"Sorry. I didn't mean to disturb you." Luca at least had the decency to look embarrassed.

Her mother waved away his worry. "I'm glad you stopped by. I remember a time not so long ago when you and my daughter were inseparable."

Was her mother trying to set them up again? Heat rushed to Elena's face. Of all the times for her mother to try to play matchmaker, this was the worst.

"That was a long time ago, Mother." Elena hoped to dismiss that subject.

"Not that long ago by my standards. You two got into all sorts of mischief. I was never sure which one of you was the instigator. I think you took turns, but regardless, you were always a mess by the time you got home. I can't begin to tell you how many outfits you ruined with mud. I was certain that one day you two would end up together—"

"Mother…" Elena lowered her voice, willing her mother to stop.

Elena didn't know if it was the embarrassment or something else, but suddenly her head felt a bit woozy and her stomach lurched. She pressed a hand to her forehead, hoping to settle her head. This wasn't good. Not good at all.

At least it wasn't the cramping she'd experienced just after she'd learned she was pregnant. That scare had sent her running to her ob-gyn. The doctor assured her that everything was normal, but she'd agreed to do a sonogram so Elena could see it with her own eyes.

The sight of her own itty-bitty baby with a heartbeat had brought tears to her eyes. She'd had them print out a photo that she carried in her purse everywhere she went. She was surprised she hadn't worn out the photo from holding it so much.

"Elena, are you feeling all right?" Her mother sent her a worried look.

Elena willed her body to cooperate. If only it would listen. "Sure. I'm fine."

Her mother studied her. "I don't know. You're a bit flushed and you haven't been eating much. Maybe you should stay home today and rest. I could call my friend and tell her that we'll play cards another time—"

"Nonsense. I'm fine. Nothing to worry about."

Her mother sent her a look that said she didn't believe her. With her mother, it was hard to say if the news that Elena was pregnant with the earl's baby would be welcome. It would either make her mother extremely happy or horrify her that it hadn't happened in the proper manner.

"There you go again," her mother said. "You look like you're about to pass out."

Why did her mother have to pick now, of all times, to make a fuss over her? Elena swallowed hard. "It's just a little warm in here."

"Warm?" Her mother's frown increased.

Elena chanced a glance at Luca, who was unusually quiet. He was staring right at her as though also trying to determine what was up with her. She just hoped that after their time apart his keenness at reading her thoughts would be skewed. After all, surely he wouldn't be able to figure out her condition just by looking at her.

Perhaps an outing was best. She was anxious to avoid

her mother's questions. "I really need to change my clothes. I don't want to be late."

Once upstairs and with the bedroom door closed, Elena took her first easy breath. It wouldn't be long now until her mother figured out that she was pregnant. And then what? Did she fess up that it was Luca's baby? Her mother would insist on a wedding. And that wasn't going to happen. Neither Elena nor Luca was interested in marriage. As it was, Luca had been doing enough backpedaling after their night together to make it clear that he didn't want more than friendship with her.

So where did that leave her? Saying she didn't know the father of the baby? No. That so wasn't her. And anyone who knew her would realize it was a lie.

That left her with refusing to divulge the father's name, saying he wanted nothing to do with her or the baby. But was that how Luca would truly feel? Would he turn his back on them both and walk away?

The Luca she'd known all these years would never do such a thing. No, he would stand by her out of obligation. But how would that work? She would make him miserable, and vice versa. Talk about a mess.

Elena switched into a dressy pair of shorts and a cotton top. She stopped in front of the mirror and decided to pull her hair up into a ponytail. She couldn't believe that in the midst of everything she was going on a picnic with Luca.

Five minutes later, she returned to find her mother and Luca deep in conversation about Annabelle's fiancé. They both stopped talking and turned to her.

"I'm ready," Elena said.

"Are you feeling better now?" Her mother sent her a concerned look.

"Yes. You're the one who needs to take it easy. I feel really bad about leaving you again."

"Nonsense. I'll be fine." Her mother smiled.

She and Luca said goodbye to her mother and headed outside. Once the door was shut, Elena said, "Sorry about that. You know how my mother can be."

"So there's nothing to her worries?"

Drat. Now wasn't the time to get into her pregnancy. It would wait until the end of the week, just like she'd planned. "No. I am not sick. I promise."

Luca arched a brow. "But something is wrong. I can feel it. Are you sure you're up for the picnic?"

She nodded. "It sounds like a lot of fun."

He paused as though evaluating her sincerity. "I still can't believe my sister is taking this long walk down memory lane with all these activities that we did when we were kids."

"I think it's sweet. She gets to share a bit of her past with her fiancé, and it's a way of saying goodbye to that part of her life before she sets out on a new journey."

Luca's smile broadened. "You got all that out of my sister's invitation?"

Elena nodded. "I think it's quite original and a lot of fun. Has she said what she's planning for the wedding?"

"She said the engagement is the fun part and her wedding will be formal. The best part, she said, will be the honeymoon."

"I like the way your sister thinks."

"And how about you?" Luca asked. "Have you met anyone special?"

"No." The answer came out too quickly and too vehemently. She inwardly groaned. "You know how it is with work and traveling. I hardly have a minute to myself."

Luca's inquisitive gaze was full of questions. "Is that the only reason?"

He was referring to their night together. She wasn't about to let him know that it had meant more to her than it should have. "Of course."

He nodded and looked away.

And then she knew exactly how to jerk him out of this train of thought. "The way you're questioning me, I'm starting to think you've been spending too much time with my mother."

"Ouch. That bad, huh?"

She smiled and nodded. "I'd rather talk about this picnic."

"Someone in your line of work probably doesn't eat much."

"Oh, come on. You know me. I love food."

He gave her an appraising look. "You sure don't look like it. You have all of the curves in just the right places."

A tentative smile pulled at her lips. "Well, thank you. I think. I'm just fortunate that I have a really fast metabolism, because there's hardly a thing I don't like."

He didn't say anything. They continued to walk along the dirt path to the bluff, and the silence dragged on. So much for their conversation.

She glanced over at Luca. She was surprised he hadn't chastised her for disappearing on him last night. Perhaps that was why he'd grown quiet.

"It's a beautiful day," she said, trying to break the tension.

He glanced up from where he'd been studying the ground. "Uh, yes, it is."

"Your sister seems to be having a good time this week."

"Uh-huh."

"I haven't been on a picnic since I was a kid."

"Uh-huh."

She doubted he'd heard a word she'd said. "I was thinking of cutting all my hair off."

"That's good."

She wondered what he'd say to this. "I'm thinking of dyeing it purple."

"Wait." Luca stopped walking and looked at her. "Did you say you're dyeing your hair purple?"

She smiled and nodded. "Wondered if you'd notice."

It was then that she realized she was smiling. That was something she hadn't done in what felt like forever. Her life had taken so many twists and turns in the past couple of months that she'd forgotten what it was like to unwind and enjoy the sunshine on her face and breathe in the sea air.

"I'd certainly notice something like that." Then concern filled Luca's eyes. "Please tell me you're joking."

She wasn't quite ready to quit teasing him. "I don't know. It'd certainly be different."

"Trust me, you don't have to go to those lengths to be unique."

She wasn't sure she liked that comment. "What exactly does that mean?"

He held up his hands as though to fend her off. "No offense meant. I was just referring to the way you left Mirraccino and made a name for yourself. Not many people achieve such notable accomplishments."

"You act like that's such a big deal. It's not like I'm an earl."

"I was born into that title. It had nothing to do with me. You, on the other hand, worked hard and earned a prestigious place as the face of the famous Lauren Renard line."

His words meant a lot to her—more than she'd expected. "Thank you."

Luca reached out, grabbing her hand. When she stopped walking and turned to him, he said, "Listen, I know I really messed things up in Paris, and I'm sorry. I don't want to lose our friendship."

With all her heart, she wanted to believe him—believe that their friendship was strong enough to overcome any obstacle. But that night had changed everything. And how would he feel toward her once he learned she was carrying his child?

She pulled her hand away. "Things are different now. We're not kids anymore."

"What's that supposed to mean? Are you saying you never want to see me again?"

"It means…" In that moment, she got choked up. She glanced away, not wanting Luca to see the unshed tears in her eyes. Darn pregnancy hormones. "I can't do this. Not here. Not now."

He placed a hand beneath her chin and lifted until their gazes met. In his eyes, she saw strength, but more than that, she saw tenderness and warmth. She latched on to that and found that between his touch and his gaze, her rising emotions had calmed.

Being this close to him had her remembering their brief Paris affair. Her gaze dipped to Luca's mouth—to his very tempting lips. What would he do if she leaned forward and pressed her mouth to his?

As if in answer, he turned away and started walking.

She stifled a sigh. If only things were different.

She rushed to catch up to him. The truth was in this particular moment, she didn't trust him. He'd said and done things with her in Paris that he now wanted to conveniently sweep under the rug. Was that how he'd feel about this supposed friendship once he found out they were to be linked for life?

She didn't know what to believe. She'd thought she'd known Steven, and she'd been horribly wrong about him. Now she didn't trust herself to make good decisions where men were concerned.

If he'd known she had been considering kissing him back there, he didn't let on. And that was fine by her. She'd had a moment of weakness. It wouldn't happen again.

CHAPTER FIVE

WHAT WAS GOING on with Elena?

Nothing had been the same since they made love. And he was left feeling—feeling…ugh! He didn't know how he felt, except confused and frustrated.

The rising sound of excited voices drew his attention. Today's guests consisted of the same group from dinner the prior evening minus the twin princes and their spouses. They all had prior engagements that they couldn't cancel. His sister took it all in stride. That was one thing Luca admired about his sister, her ability to handle the curves life threw her way with a minimum of fuss.

He wished he could be that way around Elena, but she got under his skin. She made him experience emotions he didn't want to feel and provoked him to act out of character. No one had ever had that sort of effect on him.

It was then that Luca noticed she was speaking with Alec, Luca's cousin. She smiled and toyed with her ponytail as it fell down over her shoulder. She was engaging and charming with his cousin. The thought of her being drawn into Alec's arms had Luca's jaw tightening. What was up with that?

The scene unfolding before him shouldn't bother him. After all, this was what he wanted, wasn't it? It wasn't like he wanted to romance Elena. The night they'd shared had been a mistake. Nothing more.

He turned away, refusing to keep watching. What Elena chose to do and whom she chose to do it with was absolutely none of his business.

He made his way over to his future brother-in-law, Grayson Landers. Luca was pleasantly surprised and relieved to find his little sister had chosen a really good guy. As they talked about Grayson's growing cybercafé business, Luca found himself periodically gazing in Elena's direction. She'd seemed to relax and unwind now that she'd moved away from him. The thought slugged him in the gut.

With lunch cleared, Annabelle let them know that it was time for games. A large white tent and a gentle breeze offset the warmth of the sun. But it was the heat he experienced when he was close to Elena that worried him. So when the guests set aside their hard lemonade and iced tea sangrias in order to play badminton, Luca made sure he played the opposite side of the net from Elena. And when it was time for bocce ball, he stood in the background sipping on a tall glass of ice water.

He had to keep all his wits about him, because something had happened back in that field—something intense had coursed between him and Elena. And it wasn't good. He knew what it was like to hold her in his arms, and now he wanted more. It wasn't logical. It wasn't realistic. But the desire was there every time they were within each other's orbits.

But even if she did want him, he could never be the sort of man she needed. He just couldn't commit himself to a lifetime of unhappiness. He'd watched it with his parents. They put on a good show for people, but they were very different behind closed doors. He forced away the memories of the secret arguments he had overheard as a child.

Annabelle had been too young to have noticed these things or else she didn't want to acknowledge that their parents' marriage had been far from perfect. And Luca had no intention of changing that for her. Their mother's murder had devastated both of them. Whatever comfort Annabelle found in her memories of their family, she deserved. They'd all endured far too much for one lifetime.

Once the badminton and bocce wound down, Annabelle

clinked a butter knife against her lemonade glass. Silence fell over the small group. "Okay. Everyone gather round."

Luca had an uneasy feeling as he took a seat at the large round table. His sister was up to something because she had a mischievous smile on her face. Every time she looked that way, he knew he was in trouble. It was just then that Elena drew a chair up next to his.

"Are you having a good time?" He didn't know why he'd asked. It wasn't like he really wanted to know if she was enjoying his cousin's company more than his.

She nodded. "Surprisingly, I am."

Annabelle again clinked her glass with her butter knife. She waited until she had everyone's attention. "I hope you all are having as much fun as I am. Thank you for joining in the celebration this week. And now it's time for a blast from the past."

The impish expression had yet to leave his sister's face, making Luca even more concerned at what she might be up to. Past experience told him he wasn't going to like it. He braced himself for what she said next.

She picked up an empty wine bottle and placed it on its side in the middle of the table. "Remember this?"

Remember what? Where was Annabelle going with this? He turned a questioning gaze to Elena. Her eyes widened, and then she turned a worried look his way. His gut knotted up tight.

"I can tell by the puzzled look on my brother's face that he doesn't have a clue." She looked directly at him. There was a gleam of devilment in her eyes. He was doomed. She continued, "It's called spin the bottle, Luca. Except that my version is a mix between spin the bottle and truth or dare."

His sister was always one to be creative with the rules. That was probably how she got herself in serious trouble with a killer. Thank goodness Grayson had been there.

The thought of his sister facing down their mother's killer shook Luca to the core.

And then guilt settled in. He should have been there to protect her—not that his sister ever needed anyone to play hero. She had a stubborn and independent streak, just like their mother. But that didn't lessen his guilt for not being there—for not uncovering the killer himself. Perhaps he had been gone far too long.

But now that he'd spoken with his father, things were changing. If all worked out, he would be around more for his family. But that didn't mean he had to stick around for this walk down memory lane.

He knew exactly how his sister would play the game—she would make people squirm. And he wasn't having any part of it. He started to get up to leave when Elena reached out, placing her hand on his arm.

She leaned over and whispered, "Please don't go."

His body tensed as he was torn between leaving before this day went horribly sideways and doing as Elena asked. It wasn't like he owed Elena anything. In all honesty, he wasn't even her official escort. He'd merely walked with her to the picnic. He knew he was just making up excuses in order to leave without a guilty conscience.

Then his gaze lifted and met Elena's. The worry was still there. No. It was panic. Why was she so upset about the game? Then again, who was he to question her when all he wanted was out of there?

He leaned toward her. It was then that a gentle breeze picked up and with it carried the not-too-sweet scent of jasmine perfume. He inhaled a little deeper. Every time he smelled that scent, he thought of Elena. She'd started wearing that perfume as a teenager. For some reason, he'd thought now that she was a famous model she'd have switched to a more trendy fragrance. Was it possible that everything about her hadn't changed?

And then, remembering he was supposed to say something, he whispered in her ear, "Come with me."

"I can't leave your sister's party."

"Sure you can. Come on."

"Luca, be serious. Everyone will notice."

He knew she was right, but that didn't mean he wanted to sit here and play a child's game. "I don't want to do this."

Elena squeezed his hand. "It'll be all right."

His fingers instinctively wrapped around hers. It was such a simple act, and yet his heart was racing. He loved the feel of her hand in his. His thumb stroked the back of her hand.

And then he remembered that they weren't alone. They had an audience that included his very astute sister. Thankfully the table and the white linen tablecloth hid their clasped hands from view. But not wanting to take any chances, he forced himself to release Elena's hand.

"Since I'm the bride, I'll go first." Annabelle smiled as she gazed directly at Luca.

He resisted the urge to shift in his seat. He would not be outmaneuvered by his little sister, and especially not over some childish game.

Annabelle spun the bottle. It circled round and round. Each time it neared him, the breath caught in his lungs. And then it started to slow down. His body tensed.

Thankfully the bottle didn't point at him. But it did point to Elena. He glanced her way, and she looked as pale as a ghost. Oh, no. This wasn't good. He wanted to tell her that she should have listened to him when he suggested they leave together, but he resisted.

Annabelle beamed. That was never a good sign. He wanted to speak up and tell his sister to back off, but before he could utter a word, his sister said, "Okay, Elena, you're first. Truth? Or dare?"

Elena looked horrified that she'd just been caught in his sister's crosshairs.

Luca leaned forward. "Annabelle, I don't think this is a good idea."

That was probably the wrong thing to say. His sister's eyes lit up. "Oh, come on, Luca. Loosen up." Everyone's gaze moved back to Elena. Once again his sister said, "Truth? Or dare?"

A moment passed as everyone waited for Elena to decide.

"Dare," she said so softly that Luca wasn't sure what she'd actually said.

"What was that?" Annabelle asked.

"Dare," Elena said louder.

Annabelle pressed her lips together as she made a show of making up her mind. She was having too much fun with this. Her gaze moved back and forth between him and Elena. What was she thinking? Surely she wouldn't—

"I dare you to kiss my brother."

Elena's mouth gaped, but nothing came out.

"Annabelle, enough is enough," Luca said.

"Tsk, tsk, brother." His sister shook her finger at him. "Since when did you become the serious one? I thought you enjoyed fun and games."

"But this is different—"

"Really? How so?"

He could feel all eyes on him now. What had he done? Was everyone going to guess that he had a thing for Elena?

Before he could find a way out of this mess, Elena leaned toward him. She grabbed the front of his shirt and pulled him toward her. What in the world?

The next thing he knew, Elena's lips were pressed to his. They were warm and so very sweet. His eyes drifted shut as a moan swelled in the back of his throat. Did she know how excruciating this was for him? Did she know how many sleepless nights he'd spent thinking of their lovemaking?

Remembering that they had an audience, he squelched the moan. It took all of his self-restraint to keep his hands to himself. He longed to crush Elena to him. He ached to feel her body next to him with their hearts beating in unison.

If they were alone, he'd kiss her slowly and gently at first. He'd let the hunger and desire build. And just when neither of them could take it anymore, he'd deepen the kiss. Just like before...

They'd been so good together.

It was like they'd been made for each other.

A moan started low and grew. Oh, yeah, her kisses were as sweet as berries and held the promise of so much more. If he were to pull her closer—

Elena pulled back.

And as quickly as the kiss began, it ended. His eyes opened to find her frowning at him. It would appear he'd lost his touch, and along with it he'd lost any semblance of a good mood.

CHAPTER SIX

"ELENA, WAIT!"

She didn't stop. She didn't slow down. In fact, Elena made a point of picking up her pace. The last thing she wanted to do now was deal with Luca.

She'd forced herself to remain at the party until it was over, but she'd made sure to keep her distance from Luca. She didn't trust herself around him. That kiss had reminded her of their night together. And that wasn't good. She had to keep her wits about her.

Steven and Luca weren't the first men in her life who had said sweet nothings to sway her to let her guard down. The others had been photographers, models and other men in the fashion industry. She'd done well navigating her way between the truth and the lies—until Steven.

She'd thought she'd known Steven. He'd seemed so sweet and charming when she'd met him in the Paris café. When she'd dropped her phone, he'd picked it up for her. A bit of casual chitchat led to him asking her to join him for a cup of coffee. From there they'd had dinner. To say it was a whirlwind relationship was putting it mildly. Maybe that was why she'd held back. Maybe there was something in the back of her mind that had said it was all too easy.

She wasn't used to things coming to her easily. Sure, she'd been raised on the royal estate of Mirraccino. But she was raised as an employee's child—someone who was forced to keep to the shadows. When there were grand functions, she had watched them from afar. She'd never had any illusions that she was anything but the help's daughter—a nobody.

When she'd moved to Paris, there was no modeling job waiting for her. She'd waitressed until she had enough money to have a portfolio made and then she started making the rounds of the modeling agencies. No part of her journey had been handed to her. But she'd never regretted any of it. She'd learned a lot and grown as a person.

So when Steven seemed more than willing to let their relationship escalate quickly, she'd put on the brakes. He'd been dropping hints about the future—their future. It had all been happening too easily—and too fast.

When their photo had been taken by an investigator his wife had hired, the whole truth about Steven came out. They had been caught kissing near the Arc de Triomphe, but luckily that was all they'd done. It was what she'd told Steven's wife when the irate woman had confronted her. No matter what Elena said, the woman refused to believe that it was a kiss and nothing more.

Elena had tried to explain how Steven had lied to her about himself and hidden the fact that he was already married. His family had conveniently been on vacation in Australia visiting his in-laws while he'd been sweet-talking Elena.

By the time Luca had arrived in Paris, Elena had been at her lowest. And Luca had been so vulnerable—so open. She'd let her guard down—perhaps too much. Obviously too much, or she wouldn't be pregnant.

She inwardly groaned. She shouldn't have chosen the dare. She could still feel Luca's lips on hers. She knew how easily his kisses could make her forget her common sense. The events of that night came crashing back to her. And the part that stuck out the most was how their night in Paris had all started with a single kiss.

And look where it'd landed them. But of course Luca didn't know yet. She was trying so hard to keep everything light and fun until the week was out, but at every turn Luca was making that increasingly difficult. Just like now. Couldn't he just let her go? Didn't he understand that she needed some alone time?

His fingers reached out, touching her shoulder. "Hey, slow down. What is this, a race?"

She came to an abrupt halt. She spun around and faced him. "What was that kiss back there?"

"A dare issued by my sister." He paused. Suddenly his eyes widened. "You surely don't think I put her up to it, do you?"

Elena crossed her arms. "I'm not sure what to think."

"Sure you do. We're still best friends. Just like always."

"Not like always. Things have changed."

"You keep saying that, but we don't have to let one night ruin a lifetime of friendship." His eyes pleaded with her.

"Why don't you understand that the bell can't be unrung?"

"I think you're making too much of things."

"Really? Then how would you explain that kiss?"

"What about it? It was a dare. A game. No big deal."

"This is me you're talking to," Elena said. "You can't lie to me. I was on the other end of that kiss, and you kissed me back."

He shook his head, not wanting to admit that there was something going on between them. "You're making too much of it."

"And you're working too hard to deny there was something to that kiss. Now why would that be?"

He ran a hand over the scruff lining his chiseled jaw. "It must just have been instinctive. After all, I'm not used to women literally throwing themselves at me."

Elena sighed. "Well, your sister saw that the kiss was more than a friendly peck. You know she's going to make something of it."

"Not if we don't let her."

Nervous laughter escaped her lips. "Have you met your

sister? No one tells her what to do, and that includes her big brother."

Luca's lips settled into a firm line. Apparently he didn't find it amusing. She didn't blame him. This whole thing was getting sticky. Maybe she should just fess up now about the baby.

But what did she say? Did she just blurt it out? No. It had to be handled delicately.

"Luca—"

"Elena—"

They both spoke at once. Both surprised, they stopped and stared at each other.

"Ladies go first." Luca looked at her expectantly.

Suddenly her nerve failed her. She needed more time. She had to think of the right words. "You go first. You look like you have something important to say."

He glanced at his phone. "I have to get to a meeting with Prince Demetrius."

"Oh." She noticed how he used the word *meeting*. "Do you two have business together?"

"I hope so." Then a guilty look came over his face. "Would it be all right if I left you here?"

"Seriously? You're worried about me walking home alone in broad daylight while on the royal estate—"

"Okay. Okay. I get the point. I just didn't want you to think that I was ditching you."

"I'll be fine. Go have your meeting. I hope it goes well."

He started to walk back to the palace, but then he turned back to her. "What was it you wanted to tell me?"

"It can wait."

"You're sure?"

"Positive." What they needed to discuss was going to take much longer than the couple of minutes that he had right now. And she was certain he wouldn't be able to think clearly after she told him. "We'll catch up later."

"You can count on it. Wish me luck."

"Good luck."

And with that he was gone. She was left to wonder what business he had with the crown prince. The last she knew Luca was into investments or some such thing, but what would that have to do with Mirraccino? And the last time they'd discussed his profession, he'd sworn her to secrecy until he told his father. So what exactly was he up to?

"I'm sorry—I can't help."

Luca stared at the crown prince, wishing he'd heard him incorrectly. This couldn't be right. He knew for a fact that Mirraccino was flourishing. So why was his cousin turning down his business plan?

"If it's the price," Luca said, "I'm sure we can negotiate it."

The truth of the matter was that he hadn't had near enough time to formulate any solid numbers. But the crown prince's schedule was kept quiet due to security concerns, and Luca didn't want to miss a chance to talk with him in person. His cousin was being groomed to take over the throne. And though Demetrius traveled often for diplomatic duties, he was also making business connections to keep Mirraccino flourishing.

Demetrius barely took his eyes off his young daughter. She was a toddler now, with a rosy smile just like her mother. She was into everything and getting faster on her toes each day. "It's not the price." When Princess Katrina landed on her diapered backside, Demetrius offered his hands for her to cling to while she got back on her feet. "This is just a really bad time. Perhaps we can revisit this in six months or a year?"

Luca had examined enough of the business's records to know there wouldn't be a lemon grove in six months, much less a year. It needed a large infusion of cash as of yesterday. But he refused to give up. If he hadn't let his ego rule his common sense, he would have returned to his home in Halencia long before now. He would have known the condition of his family's business.

"Perhaps I could speak with the king," Luca said.

"No." Demetrius frowned. Obviously he wasn't used to people not accepting the finality of his word. "My father is not seeing anyone."

Luca had noticed the king's absence since he'd arrived at the palace, but he'd thought his uncle was just feeling under the weather. "Is he okay?"

"I really don't want to discuss my father."

Princess Katrina toppled over on her backside once more, but this time she didn't laugh it off. She started slowly with a couple of unhappy grunts before it grew into a full-on cry. Demetrius immediately swung her little body up into his arms. "Is someone ready for a nap?" He shushed her before looking back at Luca. "I really am sorry. Now, I need to get this princess to her crib."

Luca watched the crown prince walk away. All the while Demetrius talked in soft, gentle tones that seemed to soothe his daughter. Luca wanted to be upset with him for immediately turning down his proposal without an explanation, but it was so hard to be angry with a man holding a baby in his arms.

Luca shook his head as he went to stand next to the elongated library window. He stared off into the clear blue sky. He couldn't imagine dividing his life between family and business. That was exactly what he'd been avoiding all this time—the complications.

He was so much better off alone.

CHAPTER SEVEN

THIS IS IT.

Today is the day.

Elena had awoken just as the sun rose the next morning. She hadn't slept well. Her thoughts wouldn't slow down enough for her to sleep more than an hour or two at a time. Finally she gave up.

By the time she stepped out of bed, she'd accepted that party or no party, she had to tell Luca about the baby. Keeping this secret was eating her up inside. They'd never kept secrets from each other until now. And this wasn't just any secret—it was gigantic and life changing.

She knew Luca had no intention of settling down with a family—ever. He said that families were too complicated and that love didn't last. She felt sorry for him. A lifetime was a long time to be alone.

She might have given romance a try and failed miserably, but at least she'd put herself out there. It bothered her that Luca wouldn't even try. What did that mean for their child? Would Luca insist on keeping their son or daughter at arm's length?

Elena hoped Luca would make an exception for his own flesh and blood. But he hadn't for his father or sister. Elena inwardly groaned. She'd been going in these endless circles all night. The only way to get some real answers was to speak to Luca.

After showering and dressing, she went downstairs to check on her mother. Elena found her in the kitchen about to prepare food for her invited guests. It appeared that Wednesday involved another card game.

Elena had her mother sit at the kitchen table while Elena set to work preparing a meat and cheese platter as well as a fruit and vegetable one. The whole time her mother filled her in on friends and family, who had married and who was expecting babies. Elena got the hint. Her mother was anxious to expand the family. She wondered what her mother would think if she knew the truth about Elena's condition.

"Are you sure I can't do anything else?" Elena asked as she placed the last platter in the fridge.

"No. You've done plenty by preparing lunch for everyone. Now, don't you have something to do this afternoon?"

"Mother, are you trying to get rid of me?" She eyed her mother, who suddenly looked flustered.

"Of course not. I'm not trying to get rid of you. It's just that there are four of us already. You would be a fifth person, and that wouldn't work well for cards."

"Okay." Something told her there was more to her mother shoving her out the door than setting her card game off balance. "Well, I should be going soon."

"Is Luca coming to pick you up?"

Elena rinsed off her hands in the kitchen sink. "Not that I know of." Of all the days she would welcome him picking her up, this would be the day he would skip out on her. "But I'm sure I'll run into him at the party. Unless, of course, you want me to stay home. I know you already have a foursome for cards, but I could take care of the food and clean up."

"That's sweet of you." Her mother reached out and patted Elena's arm. "But not necessary. You just go and have a good time."

Elena didn't know if she'd have a good time. Most likely it would not be a good day, but it was like her father taught her about peeling off a bandage—the faster you did it, the sooner the pain ended. Now it was time to yank off a very big bandage.

"I just need to get ready." Elena had changed outfits about a half dozen times. She couldn't tell if it was her imagination or not, but her clothes were starting to get snug—not that they'd been loose in the first place.

Elena glanced down at her stylish white cotton tank top, jean shorts and flip-flops with blue and white bows. The invitation had said casual dress. Maybe this was too casual.

Which meant once again rooting through her closet to put together just the right outfit—one that was casual but not too casual, dressy but not too dressy, and something that was comfortable, but again, not too comfortable.

"I'll be right back." Elena headed for the steps to the second story.

Twenty minutes later, she stared in the mirror at the coral sundress. It was actually one of the first designs she'd done. Designer Francois Lacroix had told her that she not only had to sketch her ideas but she also had to bring them to life. It wasn't frilly. It had a simple neckline with a beaded bodice that fit snugly. It was gathered just below the bodice and an embroidered hemline landed just above her knees.

She smoothed her hands over her midsection. She'd swear that she'd put on weight, but the scale in the bathroom said she hadn't gained an ounce. She turned to the side and puffed out her stomach, wondering what she'd look like months from now. They said your bustline expanded. She was looking forward to that part. Maybe then she'd be more than a padded B cup.

Everything about this pregnancy intrigued her, almost as much as all the unknowns and the forthcoming pain scared her. It might be easier if she had someone to go through it with her. Luca's handsome face came to mind, but she immediately dismissed it. He'd made it perfectly clear that he had no interest in extending his family line—title or no title. She'd never imagined that she'd end up a single mother, but sometimes you had to play the cards life dealt you—

"Elena! Elena, get down here." Her mother's voice was filled with urgency.

Oh, no! Elena rushed for the steps. Her mother must have reinjured herself. Elena had told her that she was doing too much, but her mother would not listen.

Elena almost missed the last step on the way down, but luckily she had her hand on the banister and was able to regain her balance. She rushed into the living room, where her mother was sitting in her favorite armchair.

"What's the matter?" Elena pressed a hand to her pounding chest.

Her mother's face was creased with frown lines. "This!" She turned the digital tablet Elena had gotten her for Christmas so Elena could see it. "Here. Take it. I can't look at it any longer. What are we going to do?"

Whatever her mother was going on about couldn't be nearly as bad as she was making it out to be. Her mother always did have a bit of an air for the dramatic. Elena took the tablet and gazed at the picture filling the screen.

It was an image of her...and Steven.

Elena's stomach plummeted down to her bare feet.

How could this be? They'd ended things the same day this picture was taken. She remembered wearing that exact outfit. This must be one of the photos the investigator had taken of them.

"Tell me it isn't true," her mother pleaded. "You'd never get involved with a married man. Right?" When Elena didn't say anything, her mother nervously chattered on. "I told your father that nothing good would come of you going so far from home. And now this. Well, what do you have to say for yourself?"

"Mother, I can't think when you keep going on like that. Just give me a second."

Her mother sighed but quieted down.

Elena scrolled down past the damning photo that was on a very popular tabloid website. The headlines read:

From Model to Home Wrecker!
Banking CEO Caught in Lover's Arms!
That Kiss Is Going to Cost Him Millions!

Elena's gaze stuck on the headlines as anger and humiliation churned within her. She forced herself to read the attached article. Word by painful word she choked down the lies and innuendo.

And the worst part was the press made it seem like that picture was new. It was more than two months old. She hadn't seen, much less talked to, Steven in that time. Nor did she intend to ever speak to him again. She'd been a victim here, but the press made it sound like she was a willing accomplice. She hadn't even known he was married. He'd conveniently forgotten to mention that part.

This was a disaster!

And it wasn't just her reputation that was on the line. It was going to affect her job, as her contract contained a morality clause. And when the paparazzi found out she was pregnant, they were going to jump to the wrong conclusion. It was like her life was a series of dominoes and now that the first one had fallen, the rest would follow. And it would end with Luca.

Luca!

She'd thought there would be time to speak with him. She'd thought she could break the news of her pregnancy to him gently. And now her best-laid plans were ruined. She had to get to him before he read these blatant lies.

"Well," her mother prompted, "what do you have to say for yourself?"

"I have to go." Elena turned to find her purse. She needed her phone. She had to call him. Had to warn him about the firestorm that was headed her way—and in turn their innocent baby's way.

"Go?" Her mother's voice rose to a screechy level. "Go where? We have to talk."

"I have something I need to do." Where was her purse? It had to be around here somewhere. She scanned the couch and the chairs in the living room. It wasn't there. *Think. Where did you leave it?*

Her thoughts were muddled and her pulse was racing. She was certain that all this stress wasn't good for the baby, but she wouldn't be able to calm down until she spoke with Luca.

She rushed to the kitchen. A quick scan of the house turned up her purse on the counter, where she'd placed it before preparing lunch for her mother and her friends.

"Elena, stop. You can't just rush out of here." Her mother balanced herself on her crutches in the doorway.

Elena paused at the front door to slip on her shoes. "I'm going. And you aren't going to stop me." Then, realizing that her mother was worried about her, she added, "Just concentrate on your card game. Don't worry about this. I have everything under control."

Her mother's face crumpled. Was she going to cry?

Elena hugged her mother. "I made a mistake. A huge mistake, and now it's coming back to bite me in a really big way. But it's not like the press is making out."

"Thank goodness. What can I do to help?"

"Forget you ever read that batch of lies." With her purse and phone in hand, she opened the front door. "I have something very important to do. Will you be all right?"

Her mother nodded. "Go ahead. I'm fine."

Elena rushed out the door and didn't slow down. She was a woman on a mission. She needed to speak to Luca before he read the headlines. Before he jumped to the wrong conclusion like the rest of the world.

Her fingers trembled as she reached for her phone. The display showed that she had three missed calls—all from

Lauren Renard. Elena's stomach knotted. The story was already making the rounds in short order. But Lauren would have to wait.

Right now, Elena's priority was Luca. She sought out his number on her phone. It rang once and went to voice mail. She disconnected and tried again. Once more, she was forwarded to his voice mail. She groaned inwardly.

"Luca, it's Elena. Call me when you get this message. It's important."

She disconnected the call. Where was he? And why did he have his calls forwarded to his voice mail today, of all days?

She could only hope he attended today's festivities. The invitation hadn't said what was planned for the day. It was going to be a surprise. Elena had to admit that initially she'd been quite intrigued with the mystery.

So far Annabelle had taken them on a fun trip down memory lane. Except for yesterday's spin the bottle game, Elena had enjoyed herself. Just the mere thought of that kiss yesterday sent heat rushing to her cheeks. She wondered if Annabelle was on to them.

Elena was still thinking all this over when she arrived at the far side of the palace. Before her stood a carnival, just like the ones they'd visited as kids. There was a Ferris wheel, game booths and food vendors. It was…it was amazing. Too bad she wouldn't get to enjoy any of it.

She walked around the small carnival, but she still hadn't spotted Luca. She couldn't imagine he'd miss it, not after he'd made the point that his attendance was mandatory.

"Elena, there you are." Annabelle and Grayson approached her. Annabelle wore a gleeful smile while holding cotton candy in her hand. "What do you think?"

It took Elena a moment to realize Annabelle was referring to the party and not to the nasty piece of gossip on the internet. "I think you've outdone yourself." Elena forced a smile on her face. "This entire week has been amazing."

"And it's not over yet." Annabelle reached for her fiancé's hand.

Elena did her best to act normal. "You're very lucky to have found someone so wonderful."

Annabelle blushed. "I know. Don't ask me how close I came to losing him."

"That wouldn't have happened." Grayson stared into Annabelle's eyes. "I know when I have a good thing. And you're the best."

"Aw…" Annabelle turned into his arms. She lifted on her tiptoes and pressed her lips to his.

Elena turned to walk away and leave the lovebirds alone—or as alone as they could be in the middle of a carnival. She really needed to find Luca.

"Elena, did you happen to see my brother?" Annabelle called out.

Elena turned back. "Actually, I was looking for him. I thought he would be here."

"I did, too, but he was distracted last night. He didn't even come down to dinner."

Oh, no. Had he heard something? Did he already know that she'd made a fool of herself in front of the whole world?

"So you haven't spoken to him since yesterday?"

Annabelle shook her head. "I wouldn't worry. It probably has something to do with my father arriving yesterday. Those two can get on each other's nerves."

"Well, if you see him, can you tell him that I'm looking for him?"

"I will. But before you go, I want to ask you something." Annabelle's expression grew serious.

"Um, sure. What do you need?"

"I, well, we wanted to know if you'd be in our wedding?"

"You want me to stand up for you?"

Annabelle smiled and nodded. "I know you're really busy now that you're a world-famous model, but the wedding is almost a year out. Please say that you'll do it. I know Luca would like it. A lot."

Elena wasn't so sure how to take Annabelle's last comment, so she just let it slide. "I'd be honored. Thank you for asking me."

Annabelle turned a triumphant look to Grayson. "I told you she'd do it. This wedding is starting to come together."

"I know it's going to be just as fabulous as your engagement," Elena said.

"Just not as fun," Grayson said.

"You'll just have to wait for the honeymoon." Annabelle sent him a devilish look.

Just then a man in a dark suit and sunglasses strode toward them. Elena guessed he was part of the palace security. She hoped nothing was wrong. But seeing as the man would want to speak with Annabelle, the king's niece, Elena was ready to make a quick exit.

"Looks like someone is searching for you." Elena pointed out the man.

"Oh." Annabelle frowned. "And here everything was going so well. I should have known it was too good to be true."

"Don't worry." Grayson rubbed his fiancée's shoulders. "Whatever it is, we'll get it straightened out and get back to the celebration."

Annabelle sent Grayson a worried look. "I hope so."

"I'll let you deal with it." Elena started to walk away.

"Ms. Ricci, could I speak to you?"

Elena paused at the sound of her name. An uneasy feeling inched down her spine. With great trepidation she turned to the man. "Yes?"

Out of the corner of her eye, she could see the surprised

look on Annabelle's face. Elena wondered if she was wearing a similar expression.

"Excuse me, ma'am. I was informed that you would be here."

"What can I do for you?"

"Ma'am, there are a bunch of reporters at the gate demanding to speak with you. What should we do?"

It felt as though the bottom had fallen out of her world. The article had just made the tabloid that morning and they were already seeking her out. She wondered what other information they had. She was certain that none of it would be good news.

"Did they say what they wanted?"

"No, ma'am."

Annabelle stepped up then. "Tell them to go away. Elena is my guest today, and she doesn't want to be hounded by the press."

"Yes, ma'am." The security guard pulled out his phone as he started to walk away.

"What do you think that's all about?" Annabelle asked.

"I...I have a confession." Elena's gaze dropped to the ground.

"That sounds awfully dire. Surely it can't be that bad."

Elena shrugged. "I guess it depends on how you look at it."

"I think I should go get another drink," Grayson said and slipped away.

"You don't have to tell me," Annabelle said.

"I do." Elena was so tired of keeping secrets. "There's a story in a tabloid and a photo linking me with a married man."

Annabelle's perfectly plucked brows rose, but she didn't say anything.

"It's not true. At least not like they are saying. I didn't

know he was married. He conveniently left that part out when we met. And it's been over for a while now."

Annabelle reached out and squeezed her arm. "It's okay. We've all made mistakes, but the paparazzi doesn't care about those mistakes unless you're an international public figure. I have a feeling this won't be your last time in the tabloids."

"I'd totally understand if you want me to go now. I don't want to ruin your party."

"Nonsense. You have to stay. We aren't going to let the paparazzi ruin our day."

"I don't think I'll ever get used to them."

"Me, either. We just have to stick together."

"Thanks for being so understanding." They shared a quick hug and then Elena said, "I think I'll go get a drink. It's a little warm out here today."

She moved away and spotted a lemonade stand. No doubt they'd used lemons from the DiSalvo lemon grove. They were the best. And she was thirsty. Hunting for Luca in the bright sunshine had her parched. And she didn't know where else to look for him...unless she was to search the palace. However, she doubted security was going to let that happen.

She stood in line for the lemonade. It seemed to be a popular stand. And she couldn't blame them. This was the best lemonade in the world. Not too sweet. Not too tart. It was just perfect. And any other day, she'd be excited to have some, but not today. Today she needed to find Luca before he stumbled across the lies and innuendos.

Once she had her refreshment in hand, she peered all around. He had to be here somewhere. But she couldn't spot him. She pulled out her phone and tried his cell. Again, it went to voice mail.

She'd just slipped the phone into her purse when she heard, "Elena, there you are."

She turned to find Luca approaching her. He was dressed casually in white shorts and a blue collared shirt with the sleeves rolled up. And she'd never seen him look more handsome. Of course, it helped that he was smiling right at her. He was like the sun, parting her clouds of gloom and doom.

He stepped up to her. "We need to talk."

"I know."

"You do?" Luca asked with a puzzled look on his face.

"Sorry. I thought you wanted to tell me about the press at the front gate."

He arched a dark brow. "No, but what are they doing here?"

She waved off his question, hoping he wouldn't make a big deal out of it. "It's nothing. We sent them away."

"We?"

"Your sister was here when one of the security guards stopped by. She instructed him to send the reporters away." And before he could question her further about the paparazzi, she asked, "So what did you want to talk to me about?"

Luca glanced around at the colorful tents. "It can wait until I win you a teddy bear at the ball toss."

So he really didn't know about the tabloid story. The breath that she didn't realize she'd been holding whooshed from her lungs. In actuality, she wasn't sure if this news made things better or worse for her. On second thought, it didn't do either. It just delayed the inevitable.

And then he paused and looked at her. She found herself staring into his blue-gray eyes. Some days they were bluer, but today they were a deeper gray. He had something on his mind. Just wait until he heard what she had to tell him. His eyes would turn dark and stormy.

"Elena, why are you frowning at me? I know I'm late to

the festivities, but you don't have to look that upset. What happened to bring the paparazzi here?"

She glanced around at all of the people they knew. This definitely wasn't the place to give him life-altering news. "I can't talk about it. Not here."

"Elena, there is obviously a problem. So out with it."

Just then her phone rang. She didn't even have to look at the caller ID to know it was Lauren again. She'd never called this many times in a row. With each phone call, Elena's hope of salvaging her job diminished.

"Do you need to get that?"

She shook her head. "It can wait. Can we go somewhere? Somewhere private?"

"Um, I haven't spoken to my sister yet, but she has enough distractions. I'm sure she won't miss me for a little longer."

They started walking toward the beach. All the while Elena searched for the right words. Was there such a thing? She hoped so.

"Elena? Hey, did you hear me?" Luca sent her a puzzled look.

"What did you say?"

"I said that you're really quiet today and you're starting to worry me."

He had no idea what was coming his way, and she felt bad for him. She didn't know whether to start with the tabloid story or the news of her pregnancy. Her stomach shivered with nerves.

Soon the worst will be over. It was the only positive thought she could dredge up, because her life was a scandalous mess.

CHAPTER EIGHT

WAS THERE ANY right way to say this?

Elena didn't think so. Maybe if they were a happy couple and madly in love. If that were the case, she'd do something cute—something memorable.

But in this case, she'd just have to settle for the blunt, honest truth.

They made their way down the long set of steps. She remained quiet, waiting until they were on the beach, where they wouldn't be disturbed. This conversation would be the most important one of her life. Once her feet touched the sand, she glanced up and down the beach, not spotting anyone.

"Okay. We're alone." Luca turned to face her. "What's bothering you?"

She gazed into his face. Her stomach started to churn again. And the words stuck in the back of her throat.

"Elena, you're really starting to worry me. Nothing can be this bad."

She nodded, trying to keep her emotions in check. "Yes, it can."

"Whatever it is, I'm here for you. You know that."

Her gaze rose to meet his. In his gaze, she found tenderness and warmth. She tried to impress that image upon her mind. She needed to remember this moment, because she doubted she'd see it again.

Where did she start? Did she blurt out about the pregnancy? Or did she start with the headlines? It was all such a mess.

She slipped off her shoes and started walking closer to the water. Letting the water wash over her feet always relaxed her in the past. She hoped it would do so again.

Luca walked beside her. He was quiet, as though giving her a moment to gather her thoughts. He was such a great guy. If he ever let down his guard, he'd make some woman a fantastic husband. It just wouldn't be her. They'd given it a shot in Paris, and it hadn't worked out. In fact, in the rays of the rising sun, it had gone from amazing to an utter disaster. The light of day had cast away all her silly romantic illusions and shed light on the stark reality—they did not belong together.

So what was she waiting for? It wasn't like they were a couple or even had a chance at a happily-ever-after. She might as well put it all out there and let the pieces fall as they may.

She stopped and turned to him. "This morning my mother found an article about me in the tabloids."

"And…"

She just couldn't look him in the eyes when she admitted the next part. She didn't want to see the disgust in his eyes. "And it had a picture of some loser kissing me. One of the headlines read, From Model to Home Wrecker!"

There was a slight pause as though he was digesting this news. "This is the guy you told me about in Paris?"

She nodded. "It's not true." She glanced up, willing him to believe her. "The whole thing is a twist of facts and lots of innuendo."

"I thought you ended things with him. That's what you said when I was in Paris."

"I did."

"Then how did they get a picture of you two kissing? And why is it showing up in the paper now?" Just as she predicted, his eyes were getting darker by the moment and clouds of doubt were forming.

Why did everyone in her life go for the worst-case scenario? Of course, the photo didn't help things. Before she could mount a reasonable defense, Luca pulled out his cell phone. And thanks to the beach being part of the royal grounds, the cell reception was excellent.

She wanted to beg him not to pull up the tabloid photo and article, but her pride resisted the urge. So what if he looked? It wouldn't change things. The tabloid was wrong. Surely he would see that. He knew her better. Knew that she would never knowingly cause problems in someone else's marriage.

She turned to stare out at the water. Usually she found it relaxing, but not today. Today all she could think about were all the mistakes she'd made in her life. And they seemed to be escalating this year. But that was going to stop. Here. And now. She had a baby to think about. She would do well by it.

She turned back to Luca. "There's more—"

"Did you read this?" His stormy gaze flickered to her and then back to the phone in his hand.

"It's nothing but lies."

"At the end, it says this jerk's wife filed for divorce. She's probably using this story as the basis for her multimillion-dollar settlement."

"And?"

He slipped his phone back in his pocket and stared at her. "Did you see this guy after you and I, well, after I visited you in Paris?"

"No. Of course not. Steven fooled me once with his flattery and lies. There's no way I would fall for his words again. I...I haven't seen anyone since you."

"And this story is the reason the press is at the palace gates?"

She lowered her head. "I had no idea they'd track me down here. I should leave Mirraccino."

"I can't think of any place better for you to be at this moment."

Her head lifted. "Really?"

"Yes. Here you have the best protection. No one will get near you. And eventually the paparazzi will get bored."

"I just don't understand why this is suddenly a story. I haven't seen Steven in almost three months."

His eyes momentarily widened, but then in a blink, his expression was unreadable. "Then I would say that picture suddenly appeared because the wife planted it, just in time for her to file for divorce."

"But the story made it sound like it just happened—as in yesterday."

"See, that's the thing. You were right here with me."

"Wait." She peered deep into his eyes. "You believe me?"

"Believe you? Of course I do. Why wouldn't I?"

She shrugged. "I don't know. I guess I'm just a bit on edge."

"Is this part of the reason you're in Mirraccino instead of in Paris, Milan or New York?"

She shook her head. "It has nothing to do with that story. In fact, there wasn't even a story until today."

"Then quit frowning. Everything will be all right. Give it one or two news cycles and the paparazzi will be on to another bit of sensationalized gossip." He reached out and pulled her into his arms.

She knew she should resist. She knew that things were complicated between them. But in that moment, she longed for the warmth and comfort she always felt in his arms. And so she let her body follow the pull of his arms.

Her chest pressed to his. Her arms wrapped around his trim waist. And her head landed on his broad shoulder. The stress ebbed away.

But then something happened that she hadn't been expecting. She breathed in his masculine scent, mingled with a spicy cologne. He smelled so good. She breathed in a little deeper. Oh, yes, she remembered being here—being held securely in his arms.

And it wasn't that long ago that they'd clung to each other like there was no tomorrow. Did he remember? Was that what he was thinking about right now?

Her whole body was alive with desire. It'd be so easy to turn her head just slightly and press her lips to the smooth skin of his neck. And then, realizing what she was about to do, she pulled away.

Luca gave her a puzzled look, and then he sighed. "Are you going to keep acting like this? Can't we just forget about what happened in Paris?"

She shook her head. "I can never forget."

"Sure you can, if you try. After all, we were friends a lot longer than we were lovers."

"Luca, quit trying to diminish it." That night had been very special to her even if it meant nothing to him.

He raked his fingers through his hair. "What can I do to make this better?"

"Nothing. Nothing at all."

"So that's it, we're always going to be awkward around each other? I can never put my arms around you to comfort you?"

"You don't understand. This isn't how I want things to be, but it's how they are."

"I don't understand. You're talking in circles."

He was right. She was being evasive on purpose. She was afraid to tell him that they would forever be linked.

"I'm pregnant." She hadn't intended to blurt it out, but at least it was finally out there.

"Pregnant?" Luca stumbled back a step as though the words had hit him with a one-two punch.

She nodded. The backs of her eyes stung with threatening tears. Darn hormones. She blinked repeatedly, refusing to play the emotional-woman card. She could get through the rest of this semirationally—she hoped.

His gaze searched hers. "You're sure?"

"Yes. I just saw the doctor last week for confirmation."

"Does he know? The guy in the photo?"

"Why would Steven know?"

"I would assume you'd tell the father, even if he's a total loser."

"I thought you believed me when I said it was only a kiss."

He shrugged. "People make mistakes. I thought maybe you were too embarrassed to admit it."

"First of all, he's not the father. Second, the baby's father is far from a loser. And lastly, I am telling him. Right now."

Luca's eyes momentarily widened. His lips pressed together into a firm line as the color drained from his face.

She'd never witnessed him speechless. He always had a quick comeback or a thoughtful comment. There was always something...until now.

The longer the silence dragged on, the more nervous she became. She had to do something, but what?

She knew this announcement was the last thing he'd expected to hear from her. "This was as much of a surprise for me as it is for you."

He shook his head as though he couldn't process it. He turned away and started walking—walking away from her. Just like he'd done in Paris. She'd let him go that time, but more than her broken heart was on the line this time.

She took off after him. "Luca, I know this is a shock. But we have to talk."

He stopped and faced her. The shocked look on his face told her just how caught off guard he was by this information. "Talk? Don't you think I deserve some time to absorb this information? After all, you've had how long?"

"A week or so. And I'm sorry I'm pushing this, but once the paparazzi finds out I'm pregnant, it's going to be a mess."

"Which won't be long, considering they're camping outside the palace gates." Luca turned and started walking again.

She walked with him. She hated having to push him, but the press was so close now. They were breathing down her neck—waiting for the next big headline. It was imperative that she and Luca do whatever they could to protect their child from scandal.

There was still so much to decide where the child was concerned. Would her child grow up here in Mirraccino? Doubtful. The only reason her parents lived on these amazing and sprawling grounds was because of her father's special affiliation with the king. If she wanted to move back to Mirraccino, she'd end up with an apartment in the city. Bellacitta was a thriving city that was a mix of old traditions and new technology. It certainly would be an interesting atmosphere to raise a child.

But she couldn't give up her future in Paris. If she remained there, her son or daughter would have the privilege of growing up in a city full of history, culture and endless ways to expand a young imagination. Luca could visit, or when she had time off, she could take their child to him. It would work out somehow.

But Luca wasn't helping her find any of those answers. She needed him to say something, or at least acknowledge what she'd told him.

She reached out, grabbing his arm. "Please, Luca, talk to me."

He stopped and faced her. "What do you want from me?"

"I don't know. I guess just to talk to me. Maybe to say that everything will be okay."

"Okay?" He ran his hand over the top of his hair, scattering the short, dark spikes. And then he expelled an audible sigh. "Just tell me one thing. Is it really my baby?"

Ouch! His question dug straight into her heart. Not so long ago, they'd accepted each other's words as fact without having to question. Obviously things had changed more than she'd ever imagined.

"I swear on my life that this baby is yours and mine. I didn't come to you expecting anything. I have enough of my own money to take care of the two of us. I just wanted you to know. It was the right thing to do."

"Then I would say, no, things aren't going to be all right. Those reporters at the palace gate, they are waiting for you and it has nothing to do with your work."

Elena's gaze lowered, and she shook her head. "They'll want some comment about the photo. But I didn't do anything they said. I went on a few dates with Steven. That's it. He told me he was divorced and lonely."

"How could you not know who he is?"

"He gave me a fictitious name, and quite frankly, I don't read the finance section of the paper. And he didn't give me any reason to doubt him." She worried her bottom lip as she internally berated herself. "I was such a fool."

"But smart enough not to sleep with him."

"Thank goodness."

There was one real reason why that wasn't an option for her. Steven didn't stack up to Luca. And though she tried not to, she couldn't help but compare everyone to Luca. Did that make her pathetic? She hoped not.

"And what will happen when they find out you're pregnant?" Luca looked worried. "The paparazzi is going to jump to conclusions, just like they did with that photo. They are going to tell the world that jerk is the father of my baby!"

There was so much emotion in that statement that Elena was caught off guard. Perhaps she'd been telling herself that he wouldn't care about the baby because he didn't care about her romantically—to soften his rejection. So where exactly did that leave them besides in a mess?

CHAPTER NINE

A BABY.

My baby.

Luca was having problems processing it all. A rush of emotions hit him like a tsunami. They swept away his breath and left him feeling unsteady.

I'm going to be a father.

Those were words he never thought he'd say. A tiny human was counting on him to get this right. Luca's gaze moved to Elena's still-flat midsection. It was so hard to believe there was a little human growing in there.

Luca raked a shaky hand through his hair. "Wow! This is a lot to take in."

"I know it is. Maybe I should go so you can think. Just know that I don't expect anything of you." She started to turn away.

"Wait. What?" Surely he hadn't heard her correctly.

"This mess with Steven, it's not your problem. I'll figure something out."

"Like what?"

She shrugged. "Maybe I'll just let the press have their say and ignore them. Eventually they'll catch on to a new story—a bigger story."

Luca shook his head. "No way. I refuse to let that scum be linked to our child."

"Like you can stop that from happening."

This was his moment to step up—to do the right thing. He'd never had anyone count on him so completely. The responsibility was enormous. He had no idea how to be a parent.

But he did know that no other man was going to take credit for fathering his child. No way! He refused to let that happen. He needed to head off the ensuing scandal. And there was only one way he could think of.

"We'll get married."

Elena shook her head in confusion. "I don't think I heard you correctly."

"Yes, you did. You and I, we're getting married."

"No."

"Yes. We have to. It's the only way."

Her eyes narrowed. "Did you just demand that I marry you?"

Had he? He supposed it might have sounded that way. Surely she had to see the logic of such a move. "This is what's best."

She shook her head. "No way. It's not what's best for me."

"Then think of our baby."

"I am thinking of the baby. And you forcing me into a loveless marriage isn't going to make any of us happy. Don't you remember Paris? That night—well, it didn't work out. Why in the world would you want to compound that mistake?"

"Because as you pointed out, this is about a lot more than you and me. There's the baby to consider. He or she will be the DiSalvo heir."

"Oh." The dejected look on her face told him that he'd said something wrong, but for the life of him he didn't know what it was.

"What does 'oh' mean?"

"Nothing. I'm just surprised."

"That I would want to marry you in order to protect our child?"

"I'm surprised that you would propose marriage at all. I thought you were a proclaimed bachelor."

"I was." He still wasn't comfortable with the idea of making a commitment. He hadn't had time to let it all settle in his mind. But time was running out before the press added two and two and got five. "Come on. Let's go."

"Go where?"

He sighed. Why wasn't she following this? "To get married. Once we do that, the problem is solved and the paparazzi will back off."

"Maybe it will fix one problem, but what about all the other problems it will create?" She shook her head. "I can't. I won't. I know you well enough to know that you don't want to get married, much less have children. I shouldn't have told you—"

"Yes, you should have. I don't know why you're fighting me on this. You have to see that I'm right."

"I don't see that. Just let me take care of this. You won't have to be bothered with me...or the baby. I'll go back to Paris and I'll refuse to name the father."

Was she even listening to what he was saying? She was going to compound this problem, whereas he planned to head it off from the start. "You'll just add fuel to the fire. The gossip will grow with every news cycle. By not naming me, it'll be like confirming that jerk is indeed the father."

She frowned. "Maybe you're right, but I can't do it. Binding us both to a...to a fake marriage, it just won't work."

He had to admit that she deserved better than to marry someone who couldn't love her the way she deserved to be loved. Perhaps he was broken inside. He hadn't chosen to shut down after his mother's death. It had just happened to him, like a raging case of the flu. No one wants it. No one expects it. And then pow! It hits you.

At least with the flu, you recover. Whatever happened to him the day his mother died, it hadn't gone away. His feelings just shut down—much like his father.

And so marriage had never been on his wish list. He knew it could become emotional warfare. All that emotional baggage wasn't something he wanted in his life.

But this was about so much more than what Elena deserved and what he wanted—there was now a baby involved. And this was no ordinary baby—it was the DiSalvo heir. His secret heir.

He cleared his throat. "Marriage is the only way I can think of to protect our child and give him or her a legitimate claim to their heritage."

Elena didn't move for a moment. And when she spoke, it was so soft that he had to strain to hear her. "Perhaps you're right." She paused as though gathering her thoughts. "On some level, your idea makes some sense—"

"Good. We have to do what is right for the child." He was finally getting through to her. He drew in a deep breath, hoping that everything was finally resolved. "Elena, I'm going to ask you one more time. Will you agree to marry me?"

"No." There wasn't even the slightest hesitation in her quick answer. She waved her hands, as though to chase away the idea. "I...I can't do this." A tear slipped down her cheek, and she swiped it away. "It's too much. Too fast. Too...wrong."

"Elena, don't do this. Don't do this to us—to our child."

This time it was Elena who took off down the beach, but she wasn't walking. She was running. Her long hair fluttered in the breeze.

Luca swore as he watched her run away from him. He'd never imagined if he proposed to someone she would run away in tears. Why did it seem as though he was always making Elena cry?

Part of him wanted to let her keep running until she wore herself out. And the other part of him wanted to go to her and comfort her. He was torn by the tumultuous emotions. And for a man used to keeping his emotions in check, this was a lot.

He realized that from this day forward, he would have

not one but two people to worry about—to protect. He knew just how unpredictable life could be, and he couldn't imagine living through another loss. His heart just couldn't take it.

And it didn't help that Elena was already a darling of the paparazzi. Her life was routinely on display for all the world to see—including potential stalkers.

However, his father would be thrilled to know the DiSalvo line would continue—someone to carry on the lemon grove. If there was still something to hand down. And that was Luca's fault. He shouldn't have let the distance between them become a yawning canyon with no footbridge to connect them.

But that problem was going to have to wait. First, he had to convince Elena to marry him. Knowing her as well as he did, she wouldn't make it easy on him.

And so he had to make it hard for her to turn him down.

He reached for his phone. This was going to take some work, but he would make her his bride in short order. And he would claim his baby—his baby. The words sounded surreal.

Life certainly did change on the spin of a coin.

Yesterday, he'd had a firm grip on his life. And today, he and Elena were having a baby.

And somehow, some way, they were getting married.

He'd make it happen. But it was going to take a little more forethought than he'd first envisioned. And he had no time to waste.

CHAPTER TEN

SHE WAS TRAPPED.

The paparazzi was camped out on the perimeter of the palace gates like leeches, just waiting to suck the life out of her.

Elena turned away from the roving cameras of the press. She'd been hoping that their fascination with her would end quickly, but that wasn't to be. It was open season on her life, and the reporter with the first exposé or telling photo would make a bundle.

And after speaking with Lauren Renard, Elena learned the painful truth—she'd been dropped from the fashion line. All her scheduled shoots had been canceled. Her contract was to be voided. And her name was on the lips of everyone in the know throughout Paris.

Without being spotted, Elena retreated to the royal gardens. Where she normally took solace in the serenity of the colorful blossoms and the gentle, perfumed air, today she didn't notice any of it. Her insides were tied up in knots. What was she going to do?

Luca's parting words kept repeating in her mind like a broken record.

Don't do this to us—to our child.

Normally, she'd blow off such a rushed, heat-of-the-moment proposal. No one would mean such a thing. After all, it wasn't like they were a couple. This pregnancy, it wasn't supposed to happen. *They* weren't meant to happen.

But a marriage proposal from Luca was different. He was not a man to throw around such words whether casually or in the heat of the moment. She knew him—or at least she thought she did. But everything had changed so dramatically between them since that night in Paris. Now, she questioned whether she'd ever known him at all.

Too restless to sit down, she started walking with no destination in mind. She moved past the garden gates and into the field of sunflowers. Blind to the world around her, she could only envision the *what if*s and *might have*s that this pregnancy had brought into her world.

She moved to the cliff overlooking the sand and sea. The breeze rushed past her, combing through her hair. Despite the beauty of this particular spot with the azure-blue sky, the sunshine dancing upon the water and the sailboat in the distance bobbing with each swell, all Elena could think about was that her life had come to a fork in the road.

The decisions she was about to make were so much more enormous than when she'd had to choose between attending college here on the island or pursuing a modeling career in Paris. To a young girl of eighteen who had led a sheltered life, venturing to a big city—even one as romantic as Paris—had still been a scary idea, especially when she knew absolutely no one there.

But now she had to make a decision not only for herself, but also for her child. The road to the left was one for just her and her baby. It would be them against the world. And if she took the road to the right, she envisioned herself holding her child's hand with Luca holding their child's other hand. Which was the right answer for all of them?

She started to walk again. Her head pulsed with chaotic thoughts of possible scenarios for her future. Her hand pressed to her midsection, feeling a protective instinct that she'd never felt before. She might disagree with Luca on numerous things, but there was one thing they agreed on. They had to do what was right for their child.

Their child.

The words stuck in her mind. As much as she wanted to make all the decisions about this baby, she couldn't.

They'd created this tiny life together, and it was only right that they share the decisions. It was her first solid resolution, and it felt right.

And then another thought came to her: she downright refuses to be dictated to by Luca or anyone else. In that moment, it didn't matter to her one iota that Luca was an earl or that his uncle was the king. They would make decisions together—she would not bend to his will.

Elena stopped walking. Suddenly she was feeling a bit better. Her jumbled thoughts were starting to gain some clarity. Even the pounding in her head was starting to subside.

When she glanced around, she realized that she'd been drawn back to one of her childhood haunts. And it was looking none too good. The little cabin had been abandoned eons ago, but as kids, she and Luca had worked to patch up the roof with branches and leaves. They made it into their secret clubhouse.

She stepped inside and glanced up, finding most of the roof was now gone. So much for their repairs. She smiled at the memory of them working so hard together. Back then, it was so much easier for them to communicate.

Why couldn't life be like it used to be?

The sound of an engine cut through her thoughts. It was getting closer. Who in the world would be riding around out here at the far reaches of the royal estate? And then she realized that it was probably the security guards making their rounds.

She stepped outside to let them know of her presence, not wanting to alarm them. But when her gaze adjusted to the bright sunshine, she found that it was not a guard seated behind the wheel of the navy blue Jeep with the royal crest emblazoned across the hood. It was Luca.

He jumped out. "So this is where you ended up?"

"I…uh, was just walking."

"That's some walk. It's been a few hours since you left me on the beach."

"I had a lot of thinking to do." She wasn't so sure she wanted to get into it all now. "How did you find me?"

"After I checked your parents' place and the gardens, this place came to mind. You always used to come here when you were upset." He stepped past her and entered the cabin. He looked around before returning to her side. "I wonder if our child will find this spot and make it their clubhouse."

"I...I don't know." She supposed that it was a possibility when she visited her parents.

Luca moved to stand in front of her. "Listen, I'm sorry about earlier. I didn't handle that very well."

"You're right. You didn't." And surprisingly, she wasn't furious with him any longer. "How about we write it off to shock? You didn't know what you were saying."

"But see, that wouldn't be the truth." He reached out for her hand, but she stepped back. "I did mean it when I said we should get married."

She shook her head. "Not like this. I don't want anyone to marry me because they have to."

"It's not that way." He shifted his weight. "I could walk away, but I'm not."

Elena let out a nervous laugh. "I can hear it now. At one of your sister's parties, someone will ask, 'And how did Luca propose to you?' And I'll say, 'He fell on his sword to save me and my child from the monstrous press.'" She shook her head, dispelling the awful scene. "Not exactly the romantic beginning to a marriage that a girl would hope for."

His eyes widened as though a thought had just come to him.

She didn't want to know his new idea. It was best that they end things here while they were still speaking to one another.

She lifted her chin and met his gaze. "I should be going."

"Wait." He reached for her hand. "I know I messed things up when I proposed to you earlier—"

"You didn't propose." Her gaze narrowed. "You practically ordered me to marry you."

His mouth opened, but nothing came out. And then at least he had the decency to look a tad embarrassed.

As much as she'd like to tell him that his idea of them getting married was preposterous, she couldn't. She hadn't thought of any other way to protect the baby and pass on the proper legacy their child deserved. If she were to marry Luca, their child would fit in—unlike her, who was forever on the outside looking in.

Luca craned his neck, looking at their surroundings. What was he looking for?

"Of all the places with flowers on this estate, why couldn't there be some here?" he said with a sigh.

"Flowers?" It took her a moment to realize that he wanted to collect them for her. Her heart picked up its pace at the realization that he was trying to do this proposal thing properly. "I don't need flowers. But I do need us to come to terms."

"Terms? What sort of terms?"

"I agree with you. Our child deserves to have their legacy. But this will be a marriage on paper only."

"Are you sure that's what you want?"

Was he hoping that she'd change her mind? She couldn't quite tell by his tone. Or was he making sure she didn't want more from him than he was willing to offer?

"I'm sure. We'll have separate beds and separate lives."

"Not so fast on the separate lives. If we want everyone, including the paparazzi, to believe the baby is mine, we're going to have to present a happy front."

He was right. Still, she hesitated. Could she really agree to this arrangement? It was so cold and calculated.

Luca took a steadying breath and then dropped to his knee. He took her hand in his. And then he gazed up into her eyes.

"Luca, what are you doing?"

"Proposing. If you'll let me."

"But you don't have to—"

"I want to."

"And what about your sister?"

He frowned. "What does any of this have to do with Annabelle?"

"It's her week. You know, *her* engagement celebration."

"And?"

"And we can't let anyone know that we've gotten engaged. It'll overshadow Annabelle's moment in the spotlight."

"First of all, I'm not proposing an engagement. I want you to elope with me. Today. Right now. As for my sister…" Luca rubbed the back of his neck. "We won't tell anyone about our marriage until after the reception on Saturday. Okay?"

Elena's heart was pounding so hard that it echoed in her ears. "But—"

"Shush. Let me do this before I forget what I'm going to say."

She pressed a hand to her mouth, but her gaze never left his. This was it. He was going to propose and then they were to be married. It would all be done so quickly, so neatly. No fanfare. No frilly dress. No romantic moments.

And yet, she could not deny that it was best for their child. She could no longer put her needs and wants first. She was about to be a mother.

"Elena, we've known each other since we were little kids playing in the palace gardens. You've been there with me through the best and worst times of my life. Somehow it seems fitting that we are pledging to join our lives officially. I promise to always be there for you and for our child. Will you marry me?"

Tears ran down her cheeks. Instead of tears of joy, they were tears of sadness. This wasn't how she'd imagined this moment working out. And her pregnancy hormones were working overtime, making her a sappy mess.

He removed the ring from his pinkie. "I know you're expecting a diamond, but I didn't have a chance to get you one. I hope you don't mind if I use this as a temporary substitute under the circumstances."

She gazed down at the gold ring with his family's crest engraved upon it. Luca held it poised at the end of her finger. She couldn't believe that this was all really happening. It was like she was moving through a dream.

And then she nodded her head. "Yes, I'll marry you—we'll marry you."

He placed one hand over her still-flat abdomen. With the other hand, he slid the ring on her finger. It was a little tight, but it would do.

This was the beginning of a whole new future for her, him and their baby.

CHAPTER ELEVEN

THE HEAVILY TINTED town car eased out of the palace gates.

It appeared the paparazzi was off chasing another story. Elena breathed a sigh of relief.

But that was just the first hurdle. They still had to conduct a secret wedding. Just the thought of exchanging *I do*s with Luca made her stomach quiver. When she was a teenager, she'd imagined that one day they might marry. But that was when she was still young and foolish. After all, he was an earl, one day to become a duke, and at the time she'd been a nobody. Why would he have ever considered marrying her?

It wasn't until much later in life that she realized all of Luca's grumbling and resentment about the institution of marriage wasn't just a smoke screen to keep her at bay. He really meant it. She'd felt sorry for him. She couldn't imagine living such a lonely life and never allowing anyone to get close.

And now she was dooming herself to a loveless marriage. She banished the thought as soon as it came to her. There was no backing out now. Luca had made a flurry of phone calls. The arrangements were in motion.

Elena pressed a hand to her abdomen, thinking about their unborn child. At least their son or daughter would now be legitimate. They wouldn't be excluded and press their nose to the glass to see all the dressed-up people at the formal dinners and balls. That thought was what kept her quiet as the black town car ushered them through the streets of Bellacitta.

They'd already stopped at the jewelry store, the courthouse and the dress shop, and now they were headed to a little chapel just outside the city—a place where they would have the privacy to say their vows without the paparazzi lurking about.

She nervously played with Luca's ring that was still on her ring finger. She remembered when he'd received the ring from his father. He'd been thirteen. His father had told him that he was growing into a man and this was his future—his destiny.

She had been awed not only by the beautiful ring with the intricate crest, but also the fact that Luca had a destiny to fulfill. She didn't have any such thing. Her family was ordinary, and she'd always longed to be extraordinary. And she'd almost done it. She had been on her way to having one of the most famous faces in the world.

But now she was pregnant. Her future as a model was over. Sure, she could lose the weight. Maybe she could avoid stretch marks. But even if she could regain the same figure—and that was a big *if*—she would have lost her traction in the business. Her slot would be filled by younger, more glamorous girls. She would forever be playing catch-up, and in the process, her child would only get bits and pieces of her time.

"What has you so quiet?" Luca asked as he leaned back against the black leather upholstery.

"Just thinking how far we've come since you received this ring from your father."

"It seems like a lifetime ago."

"Will your father be happy about the baby?" She hoped so. She wanted her child to be surrounded by love.

"My father will be over the moon that I'm finally doing what he's always wanted—settling down with a family and taking over the business."

"Wait." She sat up straight and turned to him. "You're taking over the business? Since when? What about your job in Milan?"

"Things have changed since I've been here. Certain matters have come to light, but we don't need to get into all that now. We have a wedding to go to."

"You're sure you want to go through with this marriage?" Elena asked for about the fifth time that afternoon.

"Quit asking. The answer is always going to be the same. Yes, I want to marry you."

If only he meant that for all the right reasons. She had no illusions about this marriage lasting, and so she would have to guard her heart. Letting herself think this marriage was anything but a show would be a disaster for her and her child. She had to stay strong for her unborn baby.

He'd never imagined that he'd be doing this.

Luca stood at the front of the chapel in his new suit. While Elena had picked out a white dress for the ceremony, he'd decided that a new suit was in order. Luckily, they had one in his size.

He resisted the urge to tug at his collar as the pianist played the wedding march. This was it. He was doing the one thing he'd vowed never to do—getting married.

But if he had to marry anyone, he was thankful it was Elena. They were compatible. Or at least they used to be. They'd shared more than twenty years of friendship. Surely they could draw on that and find common ground.

And then she appeared at the end of the aisle. It didn't matter that there were no guests. They had asked the photographer and his assistant to bear witness, and that was all they needed. The only important people were standing right here in this historic chapel.

As she made her way up the aisle, the photographer took numerous pictures. Elena seemed surprised that there was a photographer present, but with the help of Luca's assistant, he'd tended to as many wedding details that he could think of. And he figured that with the lack of any family present, Elena could share these photos with family and friends.

But he wouldn't need any photos.

There was no way he would forget his beautiful bride. Her dress was white and tea length, falling just below her knees. The straps were off the shoulder and the bodice fit her snugly. It was as if the dress had been made for her. She took his breath away. Too bad this wasn't a real marriage—wait, had he really thought that?

Before he could delve further into his thoughts, Elena stepped up to his side. With one hand clasping a colorful bouquet of pink and white peonies, she slipped her free hand into his.

The older minister peered at them over his reading glasses. "Have you both come here of your own free will?"

Luca felt the initial tightening of Elena's hand. He willed her to stay calm. He knew she didn't want to marry him but that she would do it for the love of their child.

"I have," Elena said softly.

"I have, too."

And so the minister went through the ceremony. Luca didn't know what he expected to feel, but as the minister said, "Until death do us part," Luca felt the walls go up around him. He knew he shouldn't shut down, but he couldn't help it. The devastation of his mother's murder still had lingering effects.

He'd witnessed how his father had utterly withdrawn from their family after his mother died. His father had always been working and never had time for his children—children who were hurting, too, and left to find their way through the darkness alone.

Luca couldn't imagine giving his heart to Elena—if she even wanted it—and then losing her. It was better to keep a wall between them. It was safer. For both of them.

But above all, this marriage would allow Luca to claim his heir—the future of the DiSalvo name. Luca's father would have no choice but to recognize that Luca was now all grown up and responsible—responsible enough to take over the family business and turn it around. Where he'd once felt a family obligation to fix things when his father asked for help, Luca now felt driven to keep the business and the title viable. It was a new experience for him.

"I now pronounce you husband and wife. You may kiss the bride."

Elena looked at him with a wide-eyed stare. It wasn't exactly the passionate look that he'd expected to find on his bride's face. Still, it was up to them to convince people that the marriage was real—no matter how temporary.

His gaze dipped to her pink, glossy lips. Her mouth had tormented him each night in his dreams. Her sweet kisses had left him longing for more. And now he had the perfect excuse to kiss her once more.

But he hesitated. Common sense told him to make it a quick peck. He could feel the minister's expectant gaze on him.

Luca pulled Elena close. And for a moment, he stared into her eyes. They were the most beautiful shade of forget-me-nots. The name was most fitting, as her eyes were quite memorable. In fact, they were totally unforgettable. Every time he stared into her eyes, it was like she spun a spell over him. Just like now...

His head lowered and he claimed her lips. And then, forgetting about this being a quick peck, he drew her even closer. In that moment, nothing mattered but them. Forgetting that they were still in the church, he deepened the kiss. Elena opened her mouth, welcoming him inside. Her kiss was extraordinary, and he didn't think he would ever take it, or her, for granted.

He didn't want to let her go. Because once he released her, he knew that the wall dividing them would immediately come back up. And though it might be safe behind that wall, it was also cold and lonely. But with Elena in his arms, there was a warmth growing and spreading within his chest.

Just then Elena pressed her palms to his chest and pulled back from him. Reality came crashing back in, popping the bubble of happiness that had momentarily encapsulated them. Luca glanced away, not wanting her to realize how that kiss had moved him.

Luca realized that going forward he had to be careful around her. Happiness didn't last. He'd learned that lesson the hard way. First, with his mother dying. And finally with his father hiding within his work and ignoring his children.

Luca had done the only thing he knew how to do at the time—let loose and lived life to its fullest—even risking life and limb routinely. But now he knew how to curb those urges. He knew how to tuck his feelings into that little box in his chest.

He could do this—he could be the public husband Elena needed. And he could be the father to his child that his father had never been to him.

CHAPTER TWELVE

SO NOW WHAT?

Elena sat next to Luca as their chauffeured car made its way across the city. She stared at her bridal bouquet. She was now Mrs. DiSalvo.

With the shock of what they'd just done starting to wear off, reality was hitting her hard. A whole gamut of emotions warred within her, leaving her stomach in a knot.

Elena DiSalvo. Mrs. DiSalvo. Mrs. Luca DiSalvo.

And what was up with that kiss at the altar? If that had all been for show, it was quite convincing—too convincing. There was more to that kiss than Luca doing his husbandly duty. If he was hoping to change her mind about sharing a bed, it wasn't going to happen. No matter how many heart-fluttering kisses he plied on her.

She glanced over at Luca, but he appeared preoccupied with his phone. She wondered if this was what their future would be like if they were to stay together—awkward and quiet. The funny thing was, before they'd slept together, their relationship had flowed easily. Before that night, they'd been able to laugh and joke around. But now, post-sex, things were so different.

She gazed out the window at the passing cityscape. This definitely wasn't the way back to the palace. "Luca, where are we going?"

"You'll find out soon enough."

"But your sister will be wondering where we went."

"I'm certain my sister is well distracted by her new fiancé."

Elena couldn't argue with that statement. Annabelle had never looked happier than she had this week. She was practically glowing.

That was the way a woman should look when she was getting married. It wasn't how Elena had looked today. And she knew it was selfish, because they'd done what they needed to for their baby. But she couldn't help but feel as though she'd missed out on something very profound and moving.

Sadness crept over Elena. This wasn't how she'd envisioned her wedding day. When she was younger, she'd dreamed about her wedding being the happiest day of her life. Of rose petals lining her path, with her family looking on and her eager groom awaiting her at the end of the aisle.

She stared blindly out the window. Tears pricked the backs of her eyes, but she blinked repeatedly, willing them away. After all, those had been dreams of a gullible young girl. She was now a mature woman who knew that life rarely lived up to anyone's dreams.

This marriage was a means to an end. A business arrangement of sorts. Try as she might, none of those explanations soothed the throb in her chest.

The car slowed down and turned into an underground garage. Elena was jarred from her thoughts, but it was too late to look around to figure out where they were. She was certainly confused.

"Luca, what have you done?"

His brows scrunched together. "Why do you make it sound like I've done something wrong?"

"I don't know. Have you?"

"Certainly not. I just thought the occasion deserved something extra."

"Extra?" She had no idea what he meant by that comment.

And Luca wasn't offering any other clues.

When the car pulled to a stop, the driver opened the door for her. She stepped out into the garage next to a bank of elevators. Luca rounded the car and took her hand. He led her to the farthest elevator and pressed a button. Instantly the doors swept open. Inside he swiped a card and pressed another button labeled PH1.

"Luca, what are you up to?"

"It's a surprise."

"Don't you think we've had enough of those for one day?" The excitement of the day really had taken a lot out of her. Especially as she found herself getting tired easier than normal since she'd become pregnant.

"I promise, soon you can rest."

She sent him an I-don't-believe-you look. "Just tell me what you're up to."

He didn't say a word as he stared straight ahead.

The anticipation was getting to her. She had to admit that normally she loved surprises and Luca knew it. But today was far from normal. What in the world did he have planned?

The doors swished open to reveal an expansive suite decorated mostly in white with strategically placed wine-colored accents. One wall consisted of floor-to-ceiling windows that looked out over the beautiful city. The soft golden rays from the setting sun gave the place a warm, inviting glow.

She turned to Luca. "I don't understand."

And then, without warning, Luca lifted her into his arms.

"What are you doing? Put me down."

"Smile for the camera." Luca smiled and nodded toward the photographer and his assistant, who had been at the church.

She forced a smile while the photographer snapped one photo after the next.

"Could I have one of you two kissing before you put her down?" the photographer asked. He obviously wasn't in on the fact that their marriage was for show only.

"Of course," Luca said a little too eagerly. And then he looked at her as though begging her to just go with it.

Luca's hands gripped her tighter as he rolled her body closer to his. As his face drew closer, her pulse raced. This wasn't a good idea. And yet neither moved to stop it.

Their gazes met and held. In the background, the camera flashed. But for Elena, all she could see was the desire reflected in Luca's eyes. Was she looking at him the same way?

He didn't have to beg. The truth was that she enjoyed his kisses, a lot. A whole lot.

Just then he pressed his lips to hers. Was it wrong that she was grateful for this excuse to kiss him? And what would happen when their excuses for being intimate faded away?

She'd be left with these delicious memories. And so she took advantage of the moment. She wrapped her arms around his neck and deepened the kiss. He tasted minty and delicious. And his kiss was filled with passion and promises of more.

Elena couldn't write off the rush of desire as a little too much champagne, because she hadn't had any. Nor would she have any in her condition. So did that mean all these rising emotions were real?

Luca pulled back and gently lowered her feet to the ground. His gaze met hers. They stared at each other for a moment as though they were each trying to figure out what had just happened. But with the photographer walking them through various poses—from sipping nonalcoholic apple cider to cutting the cake—they didn't get a chance to discuss what had happened during that kiss. Maybe it was for the best. Emotions were running high today, and it was hard to tell what was real and what was an exaggeration.

And then there was their first dance as husband and wife. Luca knew she enjoyed jazz, and so he put on "It

Had to Be You" by Tony Bennett and Carrie Underwood. The volume was just right to wrap around them, cocooning them from the outside world and transporting them to a place where normal rules didn't apply.

She paused for a second, wondering if Luca had picked out this specific song on purpose. It wouldn't be unrealistic. She hadn't missed his detailed level of planning for this rushed wedding. If she wasn't careful, she'd start to get caught up in this fantasy and believe that this wedding was real in every aspect.

The rays of the setting sun on the distant horizon painted the penthouse a warm gold. The piano music played and Tony Bennett's soft voice filled the air about them. This whole scenario was amazingly romantic.

As Luca's arms wrapped around her, her thoughts went back in time. When they were kids and weren't permitted to attend the palace balls, she would put on her finest dress and Luca would be in his school uniform. They would dance in the grand foyer. They'd both ended up laughing as they pretended to be all grown up and used proper mannerisms.

But tonight there was no pretending. They were adults, and being proper didn't appear to be on the agenda this evening. Luca held her close—quite close. And it was taking all of her will not to rest her cheek against his shoulder.

When her body accidentally brushed against Luca, need flared within her. She wanted her husband with every fiber of her body. Her insides heated up as desire pooled in her core.

The breath caught in her throat. *This can't be happening.* She couldn't give in to her longings.

Luca leaned close and whispered, "Relax."

The way his breath tickled her ear sent goose bumps racing down her arms. All the while, she had to think about something else—anything but the way her body was responding to Luca's. She focused on the lyrics of the song playing in the background. It was a duet, and they were singing about finding that special someone and how fate played a role.

But Elena hadn't found that special someone. She wasn't even looking. She didn't want to be lied to again.

Not that Luca would lie. He'd tell her straight up that he didn't love her. He had a double-reinforced wall about his heart and there was no breaking through it. He made sure of it.

The thought made her sad.

This wedding—this whole day—was too realistic. And yet, it was all a show. She couldn't let herself get caught up in it. Even the song was surely just a coincidence.

The backs of her eyes burned with unshed tears. These darn hormones had her reacting to things that she would otherwise be able to shrug off.

Luca continued to twirl her around the floor. She attempted to put a respectable distance between them. Because if she wasn't careful, she was going to get swept up in this piece of fiction. In the end, she would have nothing but a broken heart. And that would forever ruin her relationship with Luca. How could they raise a child together if nothing existed between them but hostility?

Just then the music switched to a love song by Frank Sinatra. The beautiful lyrics made her think of everything they were both deprived of by this empty marriage. They were doomed to live a lie.

Oh, no! This is just too much.

Elena pulled herself out of Luca's arms. Her gaze sought out the hallway and then she ran. She didn't know where she was running to, but she just couldn't pretend to be the loving bride any longer. The photo session was over. The whole thing was over. This was a mistake. A big mistake.

She just needed a few minutes to gather herself. And for

those stupid love songs to stop playing. She didn't want to think about how things were supposed to be. She was having enough problems dealing with how things were.

Elena ran to the first bedroom she came across and threw the door shut with a resounding thud. She willed Luca not to follow. She didn't know what to say to make this situation all right for both of them.

CHAPTER THIRTEEN

ONE MOMENT SHE was in his arms...

The next she was gone.

Luca stood there, watching as his wife ran away from him.

What had happened? He thought he was doing a good thing. He knew that Elena never imagined this for her wedding, but he'd wanted to give her some nice memories. He'd tried to remember all her favorite things, from the chocolate cake with raspberry ganache to the jazz music.

It hadn't been easy to arrange this evening on the spur of the moment, but thankfully he had a well-connected assistant. He had every intention of bribing her to follow him to Halencia. He could well imagine his perfect assistant handling the business while he was spending time with his family.

That was, if he still had a family. Why had Elena run off?

Maybe he'd tried too hard.

The thought was driven home by the lyrics of love reverberating off the walls and enveloping him. That had definitely been a miscalculation. What did they say? That hindsight was crystal clear? In that moment, he knew exactly what that meant.

Luca strode over to the stereo system and switched off the music. And then he turned to the photographer and his assistant. After thanking them for making room for them in their schedule, Luca showed them to the door. He didn't give them any explanations—mainly because he didn't have any.

He wished he knew exactly what had upset his bride.

Was it the music? Was she that miserable being married to him? Or was it the pregnancy hormones?

Was it wrong that he hoped for the last option?

Luca rubbed the back of his neck and stared down the hallway. It seemed like a lifetime since he'd been able to talk to Elena casually. Before Paris, he'd known how to make her smile. He'd known which words to say to encourage her when one of her projects seemed insurmountable. He'd known how to make her laugh out loud until happy tears pooled in her eyes.

And yet, he realized it really wasn't that long ago that he'd had his best friend. If only he hadn't broken the cardinal rule of best friends—don't sleep together. Since that unforgettable night, he'd lost his ability to speak to Elena without upsetting her. And this evening was no exception.

With much trepidation, he stopped in front of the closed bedroom door. He still didn't have a clue what to say to her. *I'm sorry*? But he wasn't sure what he was sorry for.

He rapped his knuckles on the door. "Elena?"

No answer.

"Elena, please talk to me."

Again, there was no answer. Worry settled in.

He knocked again. "Elena, I'm coming in."

He tried the doorknob, but it was locked. Surely she didn't feel that she had to lock the door around him. What in the world was happening to them?

"Elena, you're worrying me. Please tell me you're all right."

"I'm fine."

He breathed a sigh of relief. "Will you let me in so we can talk?"

"No. I don't want to talk."

Now what? He wasn't just going to walk away. There had to be a way to fix things. He lowered himself to the floor. He leaned his back against the doorjamb.

"I'm not going anywhere," he said as a matter of fact. "I'm going to stay right here until we work this out."

No response.

He would keep talking and hopefully he would get through to her. It'd worked in the past. But that had been when they were kids, when Elena hadn't understood why he got to do things at the royal palace that she was not permitted to do. At the time, he hadn't understood, either. When you're a kid, social status doesn't mean anything, especially when the person in question is your best friend. But now that their circumstances had shifted dramatically, he didn't know how to deal with the changing landscape.

If he was this confused, he couldn't imagine that Elena was doing any better, considering she was pregnant. The thought of the baby—his baby, *their* baby—was still mind-blowing. And maybe the wedding celebration on top of it all had been a bad choice.

He leaned his head against the door. "I only meant to make you happy today. I heard you on the beach when you said you wanted to be able to tell people about your engagement. I thought that would extend to your wedding. I wanted to make it a special memory for you. I knew I couldn't give you the magical day you've always dreamed of, but I tried to make it not so depressing."

This was so much harder than he'd ever imagined. "I know ours isn't a marriage made of love, but it's one based on a lifetime of friendship. Maybe it will be stronger than others. Because whether you believe it or not, I'm still your friend. I know that you hate peas. That you're afraid of horror movies. And that your favorite color is purple. And I really, really miss my friend. Is there any chance I can have her back?"

The silence dragged on, and he didn't know what else to say.

Then the lock clicked, and the door snicked open. And

there stood Elena. He got to his feet. The sadness in her eyes ripped at his heart. Was he responsible for all this?

He didn't think about it; he just reacted. He reached out and pulled her into his arms. And to his surprise, she wrapped her arms around him. Her head rested on his shoulder.

This right here—it was right. He felt calm and centered when she was in his arms. Or maybe it was because she wasn't upset with him any longer. It didn't matter. He just had to keep the peace. It was good for them and it was good for the baby.

When they pulled apart, he noticed the tear marks that had smudged her makeup. He didn't say a word about it and pretended he didn't notice. He took her by the hand, which he immediately noticed was cold.

He guided her over to the bed, where they sat side by side. She picked up something. It looked like a slip of paper. The way she held it made it seem important.

"What do you have there?" he asked.

Her gaze moved to him and then back to the paper. "It's a picture of our baby."

That was the last thing he'd expected her to say. The thought of seeing their baby for the first time filled him with anxiety. It would make this so real— so binding.

Suddenly he felt trapped, and the walls were closing in on him. He got to his feet and started to pace. This wasn't how an expectant father was supposed to feel. What was wrong with him? He'd failed his family, and now he was about to fail his child.

"Don't you even want to see it?" Elena's voice interrupted his thoughts.

He stopped next to her.

She handed over the black-and-white photo. He stared at it. This was his baby?

He squinted, trying to make out more than a blob. Try as he might, he didn't see anything that resembled a baby.

"What's the matter?" Elena asked.

"Ah…what?" He wasn't sure what to say that wouldn't get him in more trouble.

"You were frowning when you looked at the sonogram. If you don't want anything to do with the baby, just say so."

Luca shook his head. He decided to leave his uncertainties about his parental abilities unspoken. "It's just that I can't make out the baby. It's just such a…"

"Go ahead. You can say it. It's a blob. I call it my little peanut. That's the gestational sac. It was too early to make out the baby."

"Oh." He sat down on the edge of the bed and gave her the photo. "I thought I was missing something."

"Just relax. We both have a lot to learn."

It was nice to know that he wasn't in this all alone. "I'm really sorry I made such a mess of things today with the wedding and the reception."

She looked at him. "You didn't. It…it was really nice. It just wasn't real."

"But it was real. We are married."

"But not for the right reason." When he went to protest, she pressed a finger to his lips. "Do you love me? Not like a friend, but like a lover with that I-can't-live-without-you passion?"

He wanted to tell her that he did, but he couldn't lie. He never allowed himself to love anyone. Maybe it was his parents' numerous fights behind closed doors—fights they didn't think anyone ever heard. But he had, and he distinctly remembered his mother saying that she wished she'd never married his father.

He'd only been ten, but that night he was certain the world he knew would never be the same. Because his mother did pack her things. She took him and his very young sister and they went to his uncle's. He'd never thought his parents would work it out. But somehow, some way, they did return to his father in Halencia. He never did learn if his mother had married his father out of love or duty.

Or maybe he'd dismissed the idea of love when his mother had been murdered. When he learned that life ended in a split second that you could never be prepared for. He watched his father—the strongest man he'd ever known—disappear within himself and become a shell of the man he'd once been.

If that was love, Luca was certain that he didn't want any part of it.

"No. I'm not in love with you." His voice was soft, as though that would ease the blow.

"Good." Elena blinked repeatedly and swallowed hard.

"Good? I didn't think you'd say that."

"Why not? I've already had one man lie to me. At least you're honest."

He was quiet for a moment as he digested her words. "So you're okay—I mean, you don't have any expectations about us?"

"I expect that we'll do whatever it takes to protect our child."

"Agreed. But earlier—"

"Was pregnancy hormones and exhaustion."

"You're sure?" When she nodded, he said, "Then we should get you home." He got to his feet. "Stay here. I'll be right back."

He strode out of the room. He grabbed his clothes from earlier and changed into them. This evening hadn't ended the way he'd planned—with a fancy dinner including all of Elena's favorite dishes. But he'd never been around a pregnant woman before. In the future, he'd see to it that she didn't overdo it.

Now dressed in shorts and a collared shirt, he returned

to Elena's bedroom. The evening had come to an end. He should feel relieved, but he didn't.

She looked at him, and her eyes momentarily widened. "What happened to your clothes?"

"What?" He glanced down at his outfit. "They look fine to me. And here are yours. Hurry and change. I'll have the car brought round."

Before she could protest, he closed the door and walked away. He strode back to the living room, where he blew out all the candles that adorned the room. This whole evening had gone astray. And now Luca had to face spending his wedding night without his bride.

And try as he might, he couldn't stop thinking of that kiss at the chapel and then the one here at the penthouse. He hadn't married Elena out of love, so what was up with the feelings that had bubbled up inside him when the minister pronounced them husband and wife?

CHAPTER FOURTEEN

WHY HAD HE suddenly gotten so quiet?

Elena sat in the back of the town car as it eased down the private lane to her parents' house. Luca sat beside her, staring out the window. Ever since he'd seen the sonogram, he hadn't said anything about the baby. Was it possible he was having second thoughts about being part of the baby's life?

She wanted to ask him then and there, but she couldn't. She didn't want the driver to overhear.

And then the car pulled to a stop in front of her parents' house. They got out and strolled up the walk. Before they made it to the stoop, Elena stopped and turned to Luca. "Don't forget your promise to keep the marriage and the baby a secret."

"I won't." In the moonlight, Luca looked so handsome. He'd worked so hard to make today memorable, but she'd gone and ruined it. The guilt weighed on her. She would make it up to him. She wasn't sure how just yet, but something would come to her.

Luca cleared his throat. "And now you and that little one need to get some rest."

This was the opening she needed. She swallowed hard as her stomach quivered with nerves. "Do you want the baby?"

His eyes widened in surprise. "I married you, didn't I?"

"Answering my question with a question isn't an answer."

"It's all you're going to get tonight. It's getting late and we're both tired."

"That's it?" Her voice started to rise. "You're dismissing me and my concerns."

Luca shushed her. "We don't want to make a scene. We'll talk later."

"Sometimes you can be the most frustrating man."

He smiled at her like she'd just paid him a compliment. Then Luca swiped aside a strand of her hair and tucked it behind her ear. He leaned toward her. Her heart lodged in her throat as she realized he was going to kiss her. She should turn away and rebuff his attempt to smooth things over. But she couldn't move.

Then his lips pressed to her forehead. Her forehead? Really?

His voice was deep when he said, "I'll see you tomorrow for Annabelle's party."

She didn't respond.

And then her husband retreated to the waiting car.

Elena stood there watching as the car pulled away and the taillights eventually faded into the night. Had today really happened? And then she glanced down. The light along her parents' cobblestone walk reflected off her brand-new diamond ring.

Wondering if Luca had forgotten about his ring, too, she pulled out her phone. She dashed off a quick text. Seconds later, he texted her back.

Thanks for the reminder.

"Elena, is that you?" Her mother's voice came from the doorway.

"Yes, it's me."

"Well, what are you doing lurking around in the dark? Come inside."

Elena slipped the rings from her finger and slid them in her purse. It felt wrong to be hiding them, but how could she explain this to her mother when she couldn't even explain all the conflicting emotions she was experiencing?

Not that her mother gave her much time to think about

the wedding as her mother launched into a series of questions. "Did you talk to the reporters today?"

"How did you know about them?"

"Everyone on the palace grounds knows. What they don't know is what they wanted with you. Lucky for you, the people who live around here aren't up on reading the tabloids. But my friends read them, and I've been fielding calls all day. I don't know what to tell them."

"Tell them the stories are all lies."

"Even the one about you being pregnant—"

"What?"

"Yes, they have photos of you visiting the doctor's office, and some unnamed source let it slip that you're carrying that man's baby."

She wanted to tell her mother the whole truth, but she'd promised Luca to keep this secret for a few more days. And her mother was known for her lack of discretion, which was why her father never talked about his work at home.

"That...that is another fabrication."

Her mother eyed her. "Are you sure?"

"I'm sure that I'm not carrying Steven's baby. It's not even a possibility. Now, I'm tired and I have a busy day tomorrow, so I think I'll turn in—"

"Are you going to Annabelle's party?"

Elena nodded.

"With Luca again?"

"We don't have any plans, but I'm sure we'll run into each other, since I'm a guest and he's the brother of the hostess."

"Have a good time."

"I will. Good night." She made her way to the steps, anxious to get to her room and be alone with her thoughts.

But sleep didn't come easily. She kept replaying the events of the day. She wondered if they had made the right choice to marry. She'd always believed that people should marry for love, and now she'd done the exact opposite.

Because there was definitely no love in the relationship—not the kind that should exist between husband and wife. And she wasn't about to put her scarred heart on the line, especially for a man who'd repeatedly rejected love from those around him. She wondered if he even knew how to love someone.

She knew his mother's death had left a scar on him. It had set him adrift and made him willing to take needless chances with his safety. In fact, she'd worried more than once that his daring stunts of cliff diving and bungee jumping would cost him his life, but he'd made it through that rebellious period with only a couple of broken bones and a bruised ego.

He'd worked so hard to distance himself from his family. She knew what he'd been doing—protecting himself. Because the family that he knew had crumbled.

Was that what he was doing now? Was he holding her at a distance because he was afraid that if he let her in and it didn't work out his life would crumble again? Or did he feel absolutely nothing but friendship for her?

He could do this.

He could pretend he hadn't just married the most beautiful woman in the world.

Thank goodness Elena had thought to text him the night before about his ring, because it had completely slipped his mind. He'd almost blown it, and just after he'd promised Elena that he would keep their marriage under wraps until Sunday, when Annabelle's engagement festivities were officially concluded.

But he had to admit to himself that spending his wedding night alone was a complete and utter downer. He'd never considered marrying, but that didn't mean he didn't understand that the wedding night was supposed to be quite memorable. Instead, he hadn't even gotten a good-night kiss. Was this the sort of future he'd doomed them to?

He recalled their conversation before they said their vows. Elena had made him agree that they wouldn't share a bed. At the time, he'd been so concerned about claiming his son or daughter that he'd have agreed to almost anything. It wasn't until now that he'd realized what this concession truly meant.

He never contemplated what it would be like having a platonic marriage with a woman as beautiful as Elena, both on the inside and out. After all, he was a man. He couldn't just not notice that she was stunning. He wasn't the only one who noticed her rare beauty. She couldn't even walk down the street without men whistling.

But what none of them knew was that she was now his legally and otherwise—although the *otherwise* had a bit of a hitch. His thoughts rolled back to the kiss they'd shared yesterday after the wedding. It had caught him off guard. He'd thought he could do this whole fake marriage thing, but now he was having serious doubts.

"Luca, what are you doing all the way over here?"

He blinked and realized that he'd been totally lost in his thoughts. And then somehow the object of his daydream appeared before him. Elena stood there giving him a strange look.

"What did you say?" he asked.

She waved away his words. "It doesn't matter. You look like you have something on your mind. What is it? Or do I already know?"

"You know?" And then he realized that his voice came out a bit off-key.

She sent him a strange look. "Yes, I know. My mother told me about the latest story in the tabloid. I'll give them this much—they sure don't waste any time in going after a person."

"I take it there was another story about you?"

She nodded. "I thought you knew."

"Um, no. Do you think they went digging up more information on you when you didn't appear at the gate yesterday to answer their questions?"

"Something like that. Apparently they have a photo of me visiting my doctor's office."

"So what does that mean? You can't be the only woman who visits her doctor."

"Apparently they've got an unnamed source in the office, and they told them I was pregnant."

"And your mother knows."

Elena nodded. "But I hedged around her questions. So she doesn't know what's real and what's lies. I hate this."

He took her hand in his and gave it a squeeze. "I know you do. But it's almost over. If you want, we can just tell everyone today."

"The idea is so tempting, but Annabelle is so happy. I don't want to ruin this once-in-a-lifetime experience. Your sister really went all out for this celebration, and I noticed that you two are getting closer."

He nodded. "She's a little less angry with me for being gone all these years."

"So then there's good coming out of this week?"

"I suppose you could say that."

"Then I will put off my mother for a bit longer. If only I could disconnect her internet for the rest of the week, it would certainly help."

"Would you like me to borrow a pair of wire cutters from the palace staff?"

"You have absolutely no idea just how tempting that idea is."

They both laughed. And he couldn't help but stare at her. Her face lit up with happiness. Her eyes twinkled. And once again he felt an odd sensation in his chest—a warmth.

CHAPTER FIFTEEN

EUROPEAN FOOTBALL.

Elena stood on the sidelines and smiled. Thankfully Annabelle had given them a heads-up about today's activities so she could dress appropriately in shorts and a yellow cotton top. It'd been more years than she wanted to count since she'd hit the field, but she did have to admit that she'd played pretty well in her day.

"Okay, everybody, gather round." Annabelle waved everyone over. "What should we do? Pick two captains and let them choose teams? Or should we play guys on girls?"

The second option definitely got more votes from the women. But the men were shockingly quiet.

"Well, it seems it's a draw." She turned back to Grayson, and they whispered back and forth for a minute. Then he handed her something. "Okay. Since it's a tie, we're going to toss for it. Heads we do coed. Tails we do boys versus girls."

Annabelle flipped the coin high in the air. It turned end over end, reflecting the sunlight in the process. She caught it and looked up with a smile. "Looks like it's coed. Now for captains. Let's see."

"You and Grayson should be captains, since it's your party," one guest interjected.

Elena liked the idea. "Yeah, go for it."

As more and more people cheered on the idea, Annabelle waved her hands, trying to silence everyone. "I hate to disappoint everyone, but I'm not playing. As most of you know, I'm not coordinated in the least. So I'm going to be the cheer squad." She rushed over to a chair a few feet behind her and grabbed two little white pom-poms. She shook them and smiled broadly. "I came prepared. In my place, I elect Elena."

Elena couldn't help but smile. She liked that after all these years, Luca's sister still thought so highly of her. And since they were now family, it would certainly help matters.

But Elena thought of her condition—she didn't think playing football with the guys was such a good idea. One misplaced ball could hit her abdomen. But how in the world did she gracefully back out without upsetting Annabelle?

Annabelle gestured for Elena to step up beside her. Maybe it'd be possible to coach from the sidelines. That sounded like a good plan. If anyone said anything, she'd blame her lack of activity on her job and not wanting to return with a black eye or broken nose.

Elena took her place next to Annabelle. It was then that she noticed Luca. He was staring directly at her with a distinct frown. What had she done now?

She glanced away, hoping no one would notice his odd behavior. If he didn't lighten up, people were going to start suspecting that something was up between them.

Annabelle took both Elena's and Grayson's hands and raised them above her head. "Okay, these are your captains. And just like when we were kids, they are going to take turns picking players. Good luck—"

"Wait a second," Luca said. "I don't think that's a good idea."

Annabelle's smile faded. "What? The game?"

"No," Luca said, approaching them. "I don't think Elena should play football."

Annabelle's forehead creased. "Is there something we don't know?"

Elena knew what he was up to, and she didn't like it. Her hands balled up at her sides. They might be married now, but she could take care of herself and their baby. Perhaps it was time they laid out some understandings about this nontraditional arrangement.

Not about to let Luca make a scene, Elena spoke up.

"What's the matter, Luca? Are you afraid that I'll beat you like when we were kids?"

"No, I was thinking that you might not want the ball hitting you. You know, to the stomach or, worse, the face. A broken nose probably won't help your career."

They might be thinking along the same lines, but that didn't mean she was going to let him tell her what to do. "And that's why I was planning to coach from the sidelines."

"Or you can keep me company." Annabelle gave her a hopeful look. "I'll share my pom-poms with you."

Before Elena could respond, Grayson spoke up. "Actually, this will work out. As it was, we were going to have an extra person. Now the teams will be equal."

"What do you say?" Annabelle asked.

"Looks like I'll be joining the cheering section." Elena refused to look at Luca.

Annabelle glanced around. "And now I need a replacement captain. Luca, since you caused the ruckus, you can be the captain. Get over here and start picking players. We have a game to play."

Elena joined Annabelle off to the side of the field that had been painted up with white lines just like a regulation field. Even nets stood at either end. And the part Elena liked best was the hot dog and refreshment cart. She was getting a little hungry...and since she was eating for two now, she had the perfect excuse to ditch her diet for the day.

"So what's up with you and my brother?" Annabelle took a seat in one of the fold-out chairs.

Elena sat next to her. She willed herself to act normal. "Not much."

"Sure seems like something to me. The looks you two were sending each other were rather stormy. I hope you two aren't fighting. You barely see each other anymore."

"Oh, we're not fighting. I promise." At least not yet—not until she was alone with Luca.

"You're sure? Because I could say something to him. Now that my brother has reemerged into our lives, he seems to think he knows what's best for everyone. Don't let him push you around."

"Trust me, I've known him long enough to know all his tricks."

"Good." Annabelle smiled. "Us girls, we have to stick together."

"Yes, we do."

Was it wrong that Elena was starting to feel like she would have an ally in Annabelle? Her friend didn't even know the truth yet. Would Annabelle be upset when she learned that her brother had eloped? Would everyone think that he had married beneath himself?

Elena lifted her chin a little higher. She was, after all, famous. That had to count for something. She would make sure people respected her, starting with her husband.

"What was that back there?"

The hiss in Elena's voice drew Luca up short.

He stopped on the beach and glanced around to make sure they were alone. They'd meandered toward the beach while everyone else headed back to the palace to get cleaned up before dinner. But right now, food was the last thing on Luca's mind.

He turned back to her. "What are you talking about?"

"That scene you made before the football game. You shouldn't have done it."

"Well, excuse me for worrying about my—" he caught himself before he said *wife* "—my child. I was just doing what I thought was best."

"That's not for you to do. I can take care of myself. I was about to back out of playing the game before you interrupted."

"I didn't know." He suddenly felt as though he'd done

something wrong when all he'd meant to do was make sure that everyone was safe. Being a husband and father was trickier than he'd imagined.

"I think the problem is that we rushed into this marriage and we didn't take time to figure out how it was going to work."

He had a distinct feeling he wasn't going to like what she said next. "And how do you think it should work?"

"Well, my life is in Paris. I plan to return there."

He didn't like the thought of her being so far away. "When do you plan to leave?"

"My flight is scheduled for next week."

He nodded, but he didn't speak right away. Time was running out for them. He took a moment before he spoke. He'd already learned the value of carefully considering his words where Elena was concerned. "You do realize the paparazzi is going to follow you around and dig up whatever dirt they can find?"

She shrugged it off, but he caught a glimpse of the worry in her eyes. She didn't like living her life in the spotlight. So why was she in such a rush to get back to that world? Was it truly her career? Or was she anxious to get away from him?

"How will you work? Soon you'll be showing."

She said something, but it was so soft that he couldn't quite catch it. "What did you say?"

"I was fired."

"I'm sorry. I didn't know." And then another thought came to him. "So this means you don't have to leave?"

"I've been hoping to work in another area of the fashion industry. Something behind the scenes. So my pregnancy won't be an issue."

His hopes were dashed. "And this work, it's that important to you?"

She nodded, but her gaze didn't quite meet his. "I'm

being mentored by Francois Lacroix, one of the greatest fashion designers in the world."

When she mentioned the name, Luca was surprised. Even he had heard of the man. As she talked about this new endeavor, she became animated. Her face lit up and it was obvious that she'd found something that brought her tremendous joy.

Luca could see why this was important to her. "He must see a lot of promise in you. I'd like to see your designs."

Elena's blue eyes widened. "You would?"

"Sure. I think it's great that you are doing something you're passionate about."

"I don't know why I was worried that you'd try to talk me out of it. You always supported me, even when everyone else washed their hands. Like when I wanted to test out of school early so I could move to Paris."

"How could I tell you to stay put when I didn't?"

"But it was more than that. You always told me that I could do whatever I put my mind to. Unlike my mother, who thought I should stay close to home and find a suitable husband. She never did understand my need to venture into the world and find my place."

"So you're really happy in Paris?" He braced himself for her answer.

"I am happy. I don't know if it's Paris or the fact that I'm chasing my dreams. Can you imagine, instead of me modeling someone else's clothes, one day it might be my name up there and someone else might be wearing my fashions?" A broad smile lit up her face.

He didn't want to stand between Elena and that happiness. But they did have a marriage and a baby to consider. That had to be their priority. Surely she'd agree.

"And what of the baby and our marriage?" he asked.

"I gave it some thought last night, and I think I have a compromise of sorts."

"I'm listening." He doubted he'd like this suggestion, because it probably had to do with Paris.

"I think you and I should stay married for the next year. By then the baby will be born, and we can decide whether to continue the marriage, or if either of us wants out, we can end it."

Well, that sounded good so far. "I think that's agreeable."

"As for the living arrangement, I'll be spending the bulk of my time in Paris, and I'm sure you'll be spending most of your time in Halencia."

"No."

"What do you mean, no? You won't be staying in Halencia?"

"No, we aren't going to live apart."

She frowned. "Of course we are. We can visit each other on holidays. This doesn't have to change things between us unless we let it."

His jaw tensed. It had already changed everything. As soon as he said, "I do," his whole world seemed to shift, and he had yet to regain his footing. "And the baby? Am I never supposed to see it, either?"

"You're impossible to talk to when you're angry." She turned and started to walk away.

He reached out, catching her wrist. "Elena, don't walk away. We need to get this all out there. What about the baby?"

She sighed and turned. "He or she will live with me in Paris. You can visit as much as you like."

"And that's it?" he ground out between clenched teeth. "I'm just going to be the absentee father?"

She moved the sand around with her foot. "I thought about it, and I just don't see any other alternative—at least not until the child is older."

"And by then I'll be a stranger to them." His voice was filled with anger. He hadn't even realized until this moment just how passionate he was about playing an important role in his child's life. "Is that what you want?"

"I...I don't know. What else can we do?"

At this point, he was the one to turn and walk away. He had to put distance between them, because he didn't trust himself to pick the right words in the heat of the moment.

Didn't Elena understand what she was asking of him?

Sure, maybe he'd never expected to be a father, but that choice had been taken out of his hands. And now, well, he was starting to imagine a little boy, inquisitive and daring, or a little girl with her mother's forget-me-not blue eyes and blond locks. He was starting to put images to the concept of Elena being pregnant. With each passing day, it was becoming more of a reality to him.

And he wanted to do more for his child than give them his name. But now Elena was blocking him from doing that. She'd essentially written him out of her life as well as the baby's. Now what was he going to do about it?

He'd really mucked things up.

Later that evening, Luca sat at the enormous wooden desk in the palace library. The remainder of the lemon grove's financial reports had shown up while he was out. Now it was his job to formulate a plan to salvage his legacy. He needed to turn things around. He just couldn't fail his family again.

But instead of figures and projections, all he could think about right now was Elena. After telling himself that he'd keep his cool and watch what he said, he'd blown it. He just couldn't stand the thought of not playing a vital role in his child's life. That fact should shock him after telling himself for years that he wouldn't have a family, but instead the decision to be an active part of his child's life came easily to him—as natural as breathing.

And for Elena to try to cut him out of that experience

was unthinkable. He'd thought he knew her, but perhaps he was mistaken. Could that be right? Was Elena really a stranger to him?

"How does it look?" his father asked as he strode into the room.

Torn from his thoughts, Luca glanced up. "Are you sure this is everything?"

"Of course. Why? What are you missing?"

"Profits. And your debt ratio is astronomical."

His father's face was pale and drawn. As he looked at his father, Luca could see the toll the years had taken on the duke. He didn't look good. Luca truly had been gone too long. It had been easier to be secluded from his family than to have to deal with all the problems and responsibilities family entailed—like the problems facing him now.

But those days were over. If he were honest with himself, that decision had been made when his sister invited him back to Mirraccino for this celebration. He hadn't fully realized it then, but where he normally avoided family gatherings, he was drawn to this one. Of course, that might have had something to do with the fact that his sister had also told him that Elena had been invited.

Luca just never imagined that he would arrive to find out that his father was in such deep financial trouble. It would be a miracle if they'd be able to keep their home.

His father pulled a wooden chair next to the desk and settled on it. "I tried. It just got away from me. I thought I could turn things around."

Luca focused on the summary spreadsheet that he'd created on his laptop. "I've done an overview of your debt, expenses and revenue. Without a major influx of cash, I don't see being able to turn things around." When he glanced over at his father, he caught him blinking repeatedly. This display of emotion from his stalwart father shook Luca to the core. "I'm sorry."

His father sniffed back the rush of emotions. "You have nothing to be sorry for. I am to blame."

"I should have come back sooner instead of letting you deal with it all on your own."

"What can we do?"

Luca leaned back in his chair and rubbed his jaw. "I'll be honest—it isn't good. If you were one of my clients, I'd tell you to sell everything, make settlements with your creditors and start over."

"But our home—I couldn't bear to lose it. It's full of memories…"

Of Luca's mother? Was it possible that his parents cared more for each other than he would ever know? Perhaps relationships were more complicated than he'd imagined. He was certainly learning that with Elena.

"Can I ask you something?" Luca uttered the words before he evaluated the ramifications of what he was about to ask.

"Sure. You know that you can talk to me about anything."

Luca had never felt that way about his father, but perhaps the years and loneliness had mellowed the man. "It's about Mother."

"What about her?"

"Did you ever love her?"

His father leaned back as though the question struck him physically. "Why would you ask such a thing?"

This was where it got difficult. Luca swallowed hard. "I heard you two. When I was little, you would fight, a lot. Annabelle was too young to remember, but I do. I remember Mother saying that she wished you two hadn't married."

His father's shoulders drooped. "I'm sorry you overheard us. We thought that we were being discreet." His father took a moment as though to sort through his memories. "Your mother and I were practically strangers when we married.

It was arranged to strengthen alliances between Halencia and Mirraccino and it took us a long time to find common ground. With each passing year, our respect for each other grew, as did our friendship. It was hard won, which I like to think made our relationship stronger."

"Why did I never know any of this?"

His father shrugged. "I guess you never asked and I never thought of it."

"But you two ended up loving each other?"

"How could I not love your mother? She was the most amazing woman I'd ever met. She was gracious and kind, not to mention a beauty. But she had a strong spirit and was quite determined to do things her way. There were numerous areas where we had different views, including her allegiance to her brother, the king. That's what most of our heated exchanges were about. But what you heard were words spoken in the heat of the moment. What you didn't hear were the apologies."

Luca couldn't quite digest all this information. He wasn't sure what to make of it. His parents' story certainly wasn't like the fairy tales. Theirs was complicated and messy.

And Luca didn't do messy.

"Thank you for telling me," Luca said.

"I hope it helps you."

Luca wondered if his father knew more than he was saying, but Luca wasn't going there. They had another matter to discuss.

"I've gone over these numbers for the past few hours, and at this point, I know that if something isn't done right away, you'll lose everything." He took a deep breath. "I have some money set aside, which, along with my trust fund, we can use to pay off some of the more pressing debts, but it still won't be enough to make the company solvent. However, it should give us some breathing room."

"You…you would do that?"

"Why do you sound surprised? This is my legacy and that of my children. I want to hold on to it as much as you."

"Children?" There was a hint of glee in his father's voice. "Does this mean you've decided to settle down with a family?"

Avoiding the question, Luca said, "It means I have a vested interest in making this work. And it means I need to step up my efforts to bring in a new revenue source, and I think I know of a way."

The answer was the king. He had connections far beyond the normal businessman. In fact, the Mirraccino palace in many instances acted as an agent for its citizens. Now, granted, the lemon grove was not part of Mirraccino, but they were family. Luca could only hope that the king did better by his extended family than Luca had done by his immediate family. Guilt weighed heavy on his shoulders for pushing away his family and ignoring his obligations after his mother's death.

Everything was now in jeopardy—his tenuous relationship with his father and his sister as well as the lemon grove. He had to hope that if he fixed the business then his relationships would continue to fall into place. But how could he get to the king when he was sequestered behind guarded doors?

Elena's image came to mind. Her father was the only person the king had been seeing since the truth of Luca's mother's murder had been revealed. The news had hit the king especially hard, since Luca's mother had been trying to protect him from one of his own trusted employees.

Luca dismissed the idea of involving Elena. It didn't feel right. Besides, with the way they'd left things, she wouldn't be in any frame of mind to help him. There had to be another way.

CHAPTER SIXTEEN

THERE WAS NO avoiding this evening's festivities.

As it was, Elena had pleaded a headache the day before and stayed home, missing out on the croquet and bocce ball tournaments. She had been looking forward to them, too, because they were activities she could do and not worry about the baby. She had to admit that she did have a bit of a competitive streak.

But she knew that Luca was upset with her. In fact, their last conversation had been the angriest she'd ever seen him. He was usually so laid-back and let things roll off his shoulders. But this thing with the baby—it really got to him.

Was it possible the self-proclaimed bachelor was more excited to be a father than he was willing to admit? If so, it would be the first sign that Luca was letting his guard down. Was it possible? Or was she only seeing what she wanted to see?

Elena rushed around her bedroom in her parents' home. Tonight was a dinner and dance that would wrap up the weeklong celebration. This morning Annabelle had phoned to check on her and make sure that Elena would be in attendance for the evening's festivities.

Knock. Knock.

"Dear, are you almost ready?" Her mother's voice echoed through the closed door.

"Almost."

"I just don't want you to be late. And the car is here—"

"What car?" Elena rushed to the window.

Was Luca out there waiting for her? Her stomach quivered with nerves. They'd left things in such an awkward spot that she wasn't sure what to say to him. She had no answers, just more questions.

"I assume Annabelle sent it for you."

Not Luca. Okay. "I'll be down in a jiff."

"Do you need any help?"

"No. Thanks. I've got it." She rushed back to the full-length mirror.

Tonight she was wearing another one of her own creations. It was a light blue material. The shade was similar to her eyes, or so she'd been told. It had a strapless beaded bustier and attached to it was a long chiffon skirt in the same shade. It wasn't one of her more daring designs, but this was, after all, an appearance at the palace. Traditional trumped experimental in this particular scenario.

She wondered if Luca would like it. He had no idea that she was going to wear an Elena Ricci original. But on second thought, her clothes would probably be the last thing on his mind tonight. She'd hoped that he would have calmed down enough to call her by now, but there was still no word from him.

She slipped on white sandals that strapped over her pink-painted toes and wrapped around her ankles. She pulled up the zipper in the back of each shoe. When she grabbed her clutch purse from the bed, it was time to put on a show.

With each step, her nerves became more taut. She had no idea what to say to Luca, and there was no avoiding him this evening. She truly wanted to make things better between them. Their marriage had barely made it twenty-four hours before they'd had their first major fight. If she believed in omens, this would be a worrisome one.

The clap of hands had her gazing at the bottom of the steps. There stood not only her mother but also her father.

"Father, what are you doing here? Shouldn't you be with the king?"

"Your mother told me you were getting all dressed up tonight and I couldn't miss it."

She rushed over and gave him a kiss on the cheek and a

hug. She loved her father. He might not have been around as much as she'd wanted, but when he was there, he was alert and attentive.

And then she turned to her mother, who now had tears in her eyes. They hugged. Her mother might be difficult, but her heart was always in the right place.

As Elena made her way out the door, she realized her child deserved a loving home just like that, not a home filled with heated words or, worse, stony silence because the parents were frustrated with having to give up their dreams. If she couldn't find a way to build a genuine marriage with Luca, she knew she'd have to end things. Otherwise, it wouldn't be fair to any of them.

This acknowledgment hit her in the chest, knocking the air from her lungs. What would happen to Luca if she walked away? In the end, would he be relieved?

She halted the disturbing thoughts. She was jumping too far ahead. First, they had to get through this evening, and considering where they'd left things, it would be a challenge.

The car ride to the palace was short, and in no time she was being ushered inside. The grand dining room was set for the party. The table was the longest Elena had ever seen in her life—it would easily accommodate fifty.

Elena had only been in this room once. She had been quite small, and she and Luca had been sneaking around the palace. The room had been opened up for cleaning, and she had been floored by its vastness. She knew instantly that she didn't belong there, but it didn't stop her from having a quick look around. She had been a curious kid, anxious to find out what she'd been missing out on.

Now as an adult, she was still awed by the room and its elegance. The room was decorated in red brocade wallpaper. On each wall were portraits of family ancestors. Crystal chandeliers lined the long table.

And once again, she didn't feel as though she belonged in this room with royalty, statesmen and dignitaries. Even if she had known them when they would play in the flower gardens and swim in the sea, she wasn't one of them. Even with her secret marriage to Luca, she didn't feel like a member of this prestigious group.

It looked like everyone had arrived. They were all standing off to the side of the table in small groups, enjoying wine and appetizers served by the staff. They were done reliving some of the highlights of their childhood. Tonight they were all elegantly dressed adults, here to honor Annabelle and her soon-to-be husband.

Elena was so relieved that she and Luca had kept the scandal, the elopement and the baby all under wraps. After tonight, they wouldn't have to keep choking down the truth. They could be themselves, and maybe once the pressure was off they could figure out what the future held for them.

She scanned the room, but Luca was nowhere to be found. How could that be? This was his sister's party. He wouldn't miss it, not now that he was trying to make up for the past.

"There you are." Annabelle rushed over. Her off-white gown was figure fitting and accentuated all her attributes. She looked stunning.

"Sorry. I didn't think I was late."

"You aren't. Everyone just wants to get an early start on the evening." Annabelle gave her a worried look. "Are you feeling better?"

"Yes." Elena felt the heat swirl in her chest and rush to her cheeks. "I'm really sorry about yesterday. I just wasn't up for a day in the sun."

"I understand. With headaches, the bright light is the worst." Annabelle took her by the arm and led her over toward a cluster of people. "Let's get you a drink."

"Actually, I was going to ask you if Luca is coming this evening."

Annabelle glanced around. "He should be here. I know that he had an important meeting earlier, but he promised that he would be here. I'll go find him."

"No, let me."

Annabelle nodded. "But don't you go and get lost, too."

"I won't. I promise."

Perhaps it was best she met up with Luca away from prying eyes. She had no idea how it would go, because she'd never been in such a serious situation with Luca before.

She hoped they could find a way to smile and get through the evening. Just tonight and they would have made Annabelle's celebration perfect.

She started for the door when Luca stepped inside. Elena stopped in her tracks. She observed the frown on his face and the way his eyes were full of turmoil.

Oh, no! This was not good. Not good at all.

The situation was dire.

More so than Luca first thought.

How in the world was he supposed to convince Elena to stay with him in Halencia now? There was no way he could provide her with the life she would expect and deserve, not unless there was a miracle. The only thing he did know was that the news could wait until tomorrow.

Luca tugged at the collar of his white dress shirt. This was the last place he wanted to be. He did not like tuxes. They were stuffy and uncomfortable. They had to have been created by a woman, because he couldn't imagine a man designing something so miserably uncomfortable.

He hadn't even worn a tux to his own wedding. So when his sister insisted that he wear one this evening, he'd almost blurted out about the wedding. But he caught himself in time. So the only reason he was wearing this monkey suit was to appease his sister and possibly Elena.

He'd really messed things up on the beach the other day.

He'd lost his cool, and she'd been avoiding him since then. He'd thought of calling her, but what they needed to say to each other was better said in person.

And then his gaze latched on to Elena. She was standing there in a beautiful dress, but it was the expression on her face that made the breath catch in the back of his throat. She was staring at him with a lost look on her face. She was looking at him like he was a stranger. The knowledge dug at him.

They approached each other, their gazes never wavering.

At the same time, they said, "We need to talk."

"There you are, brother. I was worried you got caught up in something and forgot the time." Annabelle rushed up to them.

"I could never forget you," he said and forced a smile.

"Good. It's time to sit down." Annabelle pointed to the table.

"So much for talking," Luca whispered in Elena's ear.

He knew his sister had done a formal seating chart, which meant he wouldn't be seated next to Elena. She would probably be at one end while he was seated at the other with a chatty woman next to him. Tonight he wasn't in the mood to make light conversation.

When Luca started searching out his seat, his sister said, "You're up here, next to me." And then before he could ask, Annabelle said, "And Elena is right next to you."

That was very unorthodox, and his sister always maintained formality at these occasions. She was up to something, but he was so off lately that he couldn't put his finger on exactly what his sister had planned.

Annabelle clinked her glass. "Everyone, please have a seat."

It took a few minutes until everyone was seated. It was then that Luca noticed there were three empty seats—all directly across from him. What was she doing?

Annabelle remained standing. "I have a few more guests."

Through a side door Elena's mother entered, followed by both of their fathers. Oh, no. They were so busted. He didn't dare look at Elena. He could already feel her gaze boring into the back of his head.

Annabelle started speaking with a very serious expression. "Ladies and gentlemen, thank you all for coming." As she kept talking, she gave him and Elena some strange looks. "I'm thankful that my big brother is home with his family. And if the news I've uncovered is any indication, I think he'll be spending more time here."

A murmur rippled around the table.

His father sent him a questioning look, but Luca pretended not to notice. This was not good. Not good at all. The parents hadn't even been clued in and here was his sister about to blow the whistle in front of the whole family and their closest friends.

It was like watching a crash in slow motion and being too stunned to act. His sister was standing there smiling and getting ready to reveal their secret marriage. How was everyone going to react?

CHAPTER SEVENTEEN

THIS WAS GOING to be a disaster.

Elena lowered her gaze as Annabelle continued to address the guests. Why was she doing this? Had Luca told her? Elena couldn't believe he would tell his sister without mentioning it to her, but obviously someone had told her about the marriage.

And then Elena wondered just how much Annabelle knew. Did she know about the baby? *Please don't let her blurt that out.* Elena really wanted to tell her parents when the time was right. They deserved to know first.

"It has come to my attention that my big brother has been keeping a rather large secret from us," Annabelle said.

All eyes trained on Luca, followed by the murmur of voices. Everyone was trying to guess the news. But they were never going to guess that they'd eloped.

Heat engulfed Elena's chest, neck and face. If Annabelle was trying to punish them for keeping this secret, she was doing a good job. If only Elena could fade into the woodwork, she would—in a heartbeat.

Luca glanced at her. Her gaze searched his to find out if he'd known his sister was going to do this. As though he could read her thoughts, his brows rose and he gave a slight shrug.

Great! Annabelle was running loose. And who knew what she was going to say. Elena reached out for Luca's hand. They were in this together. He squeezed her hand, but the reassuring gesture did nothing to settle her queasy stomach.

Annabelle continued, "And now for the news that has come to light." She paused as though for dramatic effect. "My brother and the lovely Elena have eloped."

Gasps ensued around the table.

Elena chanced a glance at her mother, who was all smiles. Thank goodness! At least one person was happy for them. Elena wasn't sure whether Annabelle was happy or angry. Not that she would blame Annabelle for being upset. This was supposed to be her time in the limelight.

Annabelle said, "Tonight's celebration has turned into a wedding supper and reception in the ballroom." She turned to them. "Come on now, stand up, you two. You surely didn't think you were going to get away with this, did you?"

Neither of them answered. They just held on to each other's hands.

"Ladies and gentlemen, please allow me to introduce my brother, the Earl of Halencia, and his wife, Elena."

Everyone clapped and smiled, including all the parents and most of all Annabelle, who rushed over to hug Luca.

And then she moved to stand in front of Elena. "I can't believe you kept this a secret."

What was she supposed to say to that? "I'm sorry."

"Don't be. If you're happy with my stubborn brother, then more power to you." Annabelle smiled broadly and held out her arms. "Welcome to the family, sis."

"Thank you."

Elena hugged her back. But she couldn't help wondering if this was all for real or if Annabelle was trying to make the best of an awkward situation. Maybe in the rush to the altar, they should have given more thought to their families. Suddenly Elena felt very guilty for leaving them all out of it.

There were hugs all around with the parents and words of congratulations exchanged. Everyone seemed to be taking the news well.

Before the rest of the guests could congratulate them, the staff arrived with trays of food. Everyone took their seats to make things easier for the waitstaff.

Luca leaned over to Elena. "Did you know about this?"

"I had no idea. So how did your sister find out?"

"I don't know, but I intend to find out." He leaned over to his sister. "So how exactly did you find out the news?"

Elena, curious to know the answer herself, leaned closer.

"You mean besides you two acting rather oddly?" When Luca frowned, his sister continued, "Well, there was a delivery for you from the courthouse. I happened to be in the foyer at the time. So I signed for it."

"You read my mail?" Luca asked.

"No. But I do have eyes, and I read the return address. It wasn't hard to put two and two together. With a little research, I had confirmation. It would have been nice if you'd told me."

"We were trying not to ruin your big week."

"You didn't ruin it. I couldn't be happier to know that you are settling down, and with the one person in the world I've always thought was made for you." Annabelle reached out and squeezed his arm.

"Thanks, sis."

Elena blinked repeatedly, hoping to keep her makeup from smearing. She had no idea that his sister's opinion of their marriage would hit her so emotionally. These pregnancy hormones were going to turn her into a crier if she wasn't careful.

When Annabelle's gaze met hers, Elena mouthed a big thank-you.

All the while Luca continued to hold her hand. And it was like a weight had been lifted from her shoulders. Now if only everyone was excited about the baby, but that would wait for another time.

His sister hadn't been kidding.

Luca was impressed. Somehow in such a short amount of time, she'd thrown together a beautiful reception. There was a receiving line, where he and Elena were given best wishes by everyone. Hugs abounded, including another from his father. Two hugs in one night was a record for sure. Maybe the years *had* mellowed his father.

Small tables with white tablecloths surrounded the dance floor. Each table had candles as well as pink, purple and white flower centerpieces. Purple, blue and pink spotlights added a fun vibe to the room. Luca wasn't much for decorations and weddings, but he was touched that his sister had gone to so much trouble for them.

There was only one thing missing from this impressive event—his uncle, the king. It saddened Luca to know that the king was so distraught over events that were not his fault. Still, it was the king's lord-in-waiting who had not only been a spy, but had also murdered the king's sister—Luca's mother.

The king had taken the responsibility for the horrific event personally. His dubious health had declined even further, and he remained sequestered, only dealing with his secretary—Elena's father. It was a sad state of affairs, but Luca refused to let it ruin this moment.

In the background, a live band played. His sister insisted that he and Elena have the first dance. With so many people watching them, it wasn't nearly as intimate as the dance on their wedding night.

He glanced down at Elena, who was suspiciously quiet as they moved around the dance floor. A frown pulled at her lips, but when she noticed that he was looking at her, it disappeared.

"Is everything all right?" he asked. "I mean, you are feeling all right, aren't you?"

"Yes. Why do you ask?"

"Just checking. I'm not used to being around a pregnant woman. So if there's anything you need or want, let me know."

"I will."

They continued dancing. He glanced around at the people and the decorations. "Can you believe my sister went to all this trouble?"

"It's beautiful. But I feel bad that we ruined the last night of her festivities."

"You have to admit that we did try our best to keep a lid on the news. And we almost pulled it off. Don't worry. She's really happy for us."

"I'm glad."

"Then why aren't you smiling?"

A smile blossomed on Elena's very kissable lips, but it didn't quite reach her eyes. Something was bothering her, but this wasn't the time to delve into it.

When the dance concluded, they were about to leave the dance floor when his sister started to chant, "Kiss. Kiss. Kiss."

It didn't take long until everyone joined in, cheering them on.

His gaze moved to Elena's. "Shall we?"

Elena's cheeks took on a rosy hue. Her gaze met and held his. She looked so beautiful, and she was his wife—a concept he was still getting used to. And then she nodded.

He pulled her close and claimed her lips. They were sweet like the berries they'd enjoyed at dinner. And though her kiss was reserved at first, it didn't take long until her arms slipped up around his neck and her lips met his move for move.

Oh, yeah, there are definitely some amazing perks to this fake marriage.

The whistles and applause brought him back to earth. With great reluctance, he released her. Elena's gaze met his once more, and he could see that the kiss had gotten to her as much as it had him. But where did that leave them?

Her life was in Paris. She'd made that abundantly clear.

And he had nothing to offer her—he was about to lose his legacy to creditors. The future looked dismal at best.

At that point, they moved off the dance area to make room for the other couples to take a spin around the floor. Elena's mother came over to speak with her daughter at the same time as his cousins, the twin princes, came over to congratulate him.

Soon the conversation turned to sports. Their group expanded with more men, all giving their thoughts about the upcoming European football season. As usual with this group, opinions were plenty and the conversation was heated. Some things hadn't changed, no matter how much time Luca had been away.

He had no idea how much time passed before he broke away to find his beautiful bride. He'd looked everywhere for Elena. He even asked his sister to check in the ladies' room, but there was no sign of her. Was it possible she'd left her own reception?

He was just about to give up when he noticed that the door to the balcony was slightly ajar. He moved to close it when he noticed a figure in the moonlight standing at the far end that overlooked the gardens.

He stepped outside to get a better look and then realized it was indeed his bride. She hadn't left him after all. A smile pulled at his lips.

He started across the balcony. When he got closer, he noticed that she was frowning again. It was the same look he'd caught on her face earlier when she didn't think anyone was looking. Something serious was on her mind, and he needed to know what it was so he could fix it. It just wasn't right that the bride wasn't having a good time at her own reception.

Even for tonight, he'd set aside his massive problems with the lemon grove and dealing with his father. There was no point in letting them ruin this evening, since there was nothing he could do tonight to change their situation. He just had to hope that tomorrow would bring him the answers he needed.

He made his way across the balcony to Elena's side. "What are you thinking?"

"Nothing."

He didn't believe her for one moment. "It is definitely something."

She turned to him. "Do you really want to know?"

He nodded, because he didn't have a clue why she was upset. Everything had gone so well tonight. Everyone was happy for them. They should be celebrating that their plan was working out.

"You. Me. Us. This phony marriage."

"What about it?" When she didn't immediately respond, he said, "If you don't talk to me, there's no way I can help."

She licked her lips. "I…I've been an outcast my whole life—"

"What are you talking about?"

"I'm talking about growing up here, on the royal grounds. I was never a real part of you and all your cousins. Sure, I got to live here and it was amazing, but I always felt like I was on the outside looking in."

"That's not how any of us saw it. You were always one of us."

"No, I wasn't. I was the daughter of the help."

"You were more than that and you know it." He reached out to her, but she backed away. "We included you in everything."

Elena shook her head. She clearly remembered all the formal events, dinners and parties she had been forbidden to attend. "Not everything."

"Those other occasions weren't important—"

"Maybe not to you, but they were to me. While you and

your sister and cousins were all getting dressed up for a fancy party, I was left alone. I was the only one not invited."

"I'm sorry. You know I would have included you if I could have." Luca frowned. "But I don't understand. That was all a very long time ago. What does any of this have to do with our marriage?"

"I'm getting to that. After feeling like an outsider my entire childhood, I will not be left on the outside of our marriage."

"What's that supposed to mean?"

"That if you can't open up and tell me how you feel about the baby, I can't do this."

What did she mean, she couldn't do this? He was too afraid to ask. He didn't even understand what had brought this on, but he refused to let his marriage fall apart at their reception. That just seemed epically wrong.

"Elena, I do open up to you, as much as I open up to anyone."

"But that's the thing—you don't. You play everything close to the vest. I don't even know if you're going to let down your guard and love our baby."

"Luca, is that you?" Annabelle called out. She came closer. "Oh, Elena, this is where you've been. Somebody we both know—" she nodded toward Luca "—got worried when he couldn't find you."

"Sorry," Elena said. "I just needed a little fresh air."

"No problem. But as soon as you two are ready, it's time to cut the cake."

"We'll be right there," Luca said. He waited until his sister walked away and then he said, "Elena, I know you want a lot from me, and I'm trying my best. Just give me a little time."

"What makes you think that time will help?"

"This does." He leaned forward and pressed his lips to hers.

When they kissed, everything seemed right in the world. There was no need for words. Problems got lost in the haze. There was just him and her, lost in the moment.
Lip to lip. Heart to heart.
If only life could be so simple.

CHAPTER EIGHTEEN

WHAT ARE WE supposed to do now?

Elena looked at Luca, who was wearing a bewildered expression that must have matched hers. They stood just outside one of the elaborate guesthouses on the estate. They were secluded.

Just the two of them.

And now they would have to talk.

They stood there for a moment in the dark with the stars twinkling overhead. In any other scenario, this would be so romantic. But what their families didn't know was that Luca was not in love with her.

"Shall we go inside?" he asked.

She nodded. "It's late and I'm tired."

In the next moment, she was swept off her feet.

"Luca, you don't have to do this. There aren't any photographers around this time." And then she had second thoughts about her assumption. "Are there?"

"Why are you asking me? I didn't plan this."

And then Elena realized that Annabelle had planned this special evening. And that could only mean one thing—Annabelle approved of the marriage. At last Elena felt as though she'd been accepted. She was one of them—for however long it lasted.

Luca arched a brow. "And what has you smiling?"

Elena realized that she was indeed smiling. She shrugged and then went with the moment. She wrapped her arms around his neck as he carried her into their temporary home. They had been explicitly told that they were to stay put until Monday—or longer if they liked.

"What's up with you?" she asked.

"Me? Why does something have to be up?"

"Because you've been acting surprisingly happy tonight."

"And the problem with that is?"

"The last time I saw you, we'd argued and you'd walked away mad."

"Maybe I had time to cool off and regret walking away."

What was he saying? She wasn't quite sure. But as he carried her into the cozy cottage, she noticed the soft, jazzy tunes filling the air. Her gaze scanned the dimly lit room. Candles were scattered about, from the mantel of the fireplace to the coffee table. The French doors stood wide open with the gentle breeze off the sea rushing into the room.

Elena wasn't sure she wanted to ruin this moment with any serious conversation. Perhaps the reality of their situation could wait until tomorrow. After all the effort that had gone into this setup, it'd be a shame not to enjoy it.

She leaned close to his neck, brushing her lips gently across his skin. Mmm…he smelled like soap combined with his own manly scent. She breathed in deeper.

"What are you doing?" he asked.

"Smelling you."

"What?"

She couldn't help but smile at his startled tone. "You smell good." She leaned in close again. "Really good."

He lowered her feet to the ground. "It's probably best if you don't do that again."

But her arms were still looped around his neck, and she didn't feel like letting go. Maybe it was all the romantic songs that had filled the ballroom. Or maybe it was dancing with him most of the evening and staring into his eyes. Whatever it was, she was going with it.

"Loosen up. This is our wedding night do-over."

"We can't have a do-over." He loosened her arms from his neck and walked over to the open French doors.

"Sure we can—"

"A do-over implies that we had a first wedding night. And I distinctly recall spending that night alone. Remember?" He turned away from her and stared out at the star-studded sky. "It was one of your stipulations to our marriage."

"And a woman reserves the right to change her mind."

She walked up behind him. With his back to her, she leaned her cheek against his shoulder while slipping her arms around him. Her hand rested over his chest, where she felt the beat of his heart. It was strong and fast.

He cleared his throat, but when he spoke his voice was a bit raspy. "You were very serious that day."

"I'm sorry about that. It was a very emotional day and it crashed in on me."

"I think it's best we stick with the original agreement."

What was that supposed to mean? Her mind jumped to all the wrong conclusions. But then she stopped herself. In the past, jumping to conclusions had done nothing but get her in trouble.

With great trepidation, she asked, "Why is it for the best?"

"You know why."

She pulled back. "No, I don't. But I'd like you to explain it to me."

He shook his head. "Let's not get into this now. It was a nice evening. Let's leave it at that. I'll sleep on the couch. You can have the bed."

"No."

He turned to her. "No, what?"

"No, I'm not going to leave it at that. I want to know what you meant."

"Why do you always have to be so stubborn?"

"I guess I was born that way." She pressed her hands to her hips. "Now quit trying to change the subject."

He raked his fingers through his hair and sighed in defeat. "Because the one night we spent together, I awoke in the morning to find you crying. You regretted our night together. And I don't want a repeat of that experience."

He'd heard her? He'd never said a word about it. If he had, would it have changed things between them? She wasn't sure, but she wanted to clear the air now.

"I wasn't crying because I regretted that you and I had gotten closer. It was quite the opposite. I enjoyed it and that scared me."

"Scared you?"

"Yes. I knew you didn't want a serious relationship. And without us being able to move forward, I knew I would lose you—lose our friendship. I thought I'd once again made a huge mistake. What you saw was me being afraid of losing you."

His eyes searched hers. "Really? That's what you were upset about?"

She nodded. "After all, we've been through thick and thin. I couldn't imagine never speaking to you again."

"You never have to worry about that. I don't know how this whole thing with us is going to work out, but I will always be here for you. That I promise."

"I will be here for you, too. Always and forever."

His head lowered, and he claimed her lips. It seemed so natural, so right. Maybe that was because they were, in fact, newlyweds. Or more likely it was because they'd been made for each other, but one of them had just been too stubborn to see it until now.

But suddenly Luca pulled back. "We shouldn't be doing this."

"We just talked about this. Everything is okay now." She lifted up on her tiptoes to continue the kiss, but Luca leaned back.

"There are still things we need to talk about."

"It can wait. I promise, it'll be all right." She ran her hands up over the front of his shirt to his shoulders, where she slipped off his tux coat. It fell to the floor in a heap. "Tonight isn't for talking."

"It isn't?" His voice was deeper than normal.

"No." She pulled on his bow tie, loosening it. And then she undid the top button of his shirt. "I can think of other, more pressing matters."

"I think I'm getting the idea, but could you be a little clearer about what's on your mind?"

Her fingers undid another button. And then she lifted up on her tiptoes and pressed a trail of kisses along his neck. "Are you getting the idea?"

"Uh-huh." He moved just then and claimed her lips with his own.

This time his kiss wasn't tentative, but rather full of raw desire. As their kiss deepened, hope welled up inside Elena that this was the turning point in their relationship. That, at last, Luca was letting down the walls around his heart and allowing her in. There were still a lot of details to be sorted out, but as long as she knew Luca wanted this marriage for the right reasons, she would meet him halfway.

In the background, the Frank Sinatra love song that had played on their wedding day started up. She would never hear that song again without thinking of this moment. She leaned into Luca like she'd been wanting to do all week. She gave in to the passion that welled up within her, slipping her hands up over his shoulders and wrapping them around the back of his neck. Her fingers combed through his hair.

A kiss had never tasted so good. He tasted of sweet wine and chocolate. His touch was gentle yet needy. Joy filled her knowing that at last they were on the right page.

He pulled back ever so slightly and rested his forehead against hers. "Mrs. DiSalvo, shall we have our wedding night?"

Her heart fluttered. "Oh, yes."

And she sealed it with a kiss. Words were overrated in

this moment. They could communicate lip to lip, hand to hand and body to body.

In the next moment, he swept her up in his arms. With the warm sea breeze caressing them, he carried her over to the four-poster bed draped with a sheer white canopy.

He lowered her onto the fluffy white comforter and stared into her eyes. "It's as if I'm seeing you for the first time."

She smiled up at him. "I hope you like what you see."

"Oh, definitely." But then a worrisome look came over his face.

"What is it?"

"I just don't want to do anything to hurt you."

"You won't." She was trusting him with her heart. "Not unless you don't come closer and kiss me some more."

"That I can do."

He leaned down and pressed his lips to hers.

CHAPTER NINETEEN

THAT HAD BEEN a mistake.

A big one.

Luca slipped out of bed, dressed and went out to stand on the deck overlooking the sea. He shouldn't have let things go so far last night. Sure, he'd wanted Elena more than he'd ever wanted any woman he'd ever known. And yes, they were married, so it was expected.

But what he hadn't done was be totally up front with Elena.

Ever since they'd said their wedding vows, he'd been seeing her in a different light. He'd always thought she was pretty, but now when he looked at her, she took his breath away. And with the pregnancy, she wasn't as thin as she was for the catwalks. He liked those emerging curves a lot—a whole lot.

But he had to tell her that his situation had changed—and not for the better. He was not the man she thought she'd married—

"Hey, what are you doing up so early?" Elena's sleepy voice came from behind him.

He turned around to find her wearing his white dress shirt from last night. The shirt stopped halfway down her thighs. Her long blond hair was tousled. And she'd never looked sweeter.

She reached him and wrapped her arms around his neck before lifting up and pressing a kiss to his lips. Memories of their steamy night together sprang to mind. His body was immediately ready for a repeat.

No. He steeled himself. He was not about to cave again. He had to settle things between them.

Elena pulled away. "Can I get you some coffee?"

"I didn't think you were allowed that now that you're pregnant."

"I'm not. But that doesn't mean I can't get you some. I'll just have some juice or whatever I find in the fridge."

"Oh. Okay. That sounds good." Maybe some caffeine would help straighten his thoughts.

"You know, I've been doing some thinking about our situation," Elena called out from the kitchen. "I'll tell you in a few minutes."

There was a knock at the door.

"I wonder who that can be," Elena said. "I'll get it."

Luca leaned his arms on the railing surrounding the balcony. He stared off in the distance. He couldn't believe that he finally knew what he wanted, but it was just out of his reach.

It was like having an angel on one shoulder and the devil on the other. One prompted him to use his relationship with Elena to gain an audience with the king. It was the only viable way he could get a quick resolution to the lemon grove's troubles.

But the other prompted him to put Elena first. It was a tremendous favor to ask her to get an audience with the king while he was sequestered. The only way to do it would be for her to sneak him in. And that would leave her in a very awkward position with her father.

"These arrived for you." She handed over a newspaper and a big manila envelope.

"Thank you." He glanced at the return address on the envelope. He knew the significance of both items and set them aside.

"Aren't you even going to look at the package? It might be important."

"The envelope contains our wedding photos. I thought you might want them, so I had the photographer rush over the proofs."

"Oh. Okay. And is there any significance to the newspaper?"

He nodded. "We're in it."

"What?" She rushed over, grabbed it and found their photo on the front page. "But how did they get this? The picture is from our wedding at the church."

"I leaked it to the press."

"But why?"

"Because I was tired of their lies. I wanted them to have the truth. Now the world knows we're married."

Her gaze searched his. "You don't care if everyone knows that you married a…" Using air quotes, she said, "'Home wrecker'?"

"You are anything but. In fact, I should make that Steven guy come clean to the world—"

"No! Don't." When he sent her a puzzled look, she added, "It'll just dredge up that mess all over again."

He sighed. "I guess you do have a point. I just hate the thought of him getting away with lying to you."

"He's not. Not exactly. His soon-to-be ex-wife is making sure he's miserable."

"Nothing like a scorned woman."

Elena smiled. "Exactly. I'm sure she can make him squirm in ways you can't even imagine."

"Hmm… I'll have to make sure I don't get on your bad side."

"True." She smiled broadly. "But you don't have anything to worry about after last night. Right now, I feel like anything is possible—"

"Elena, don't go getting too excited."

"Don't worry. I know that we still have steep hurdles to cross. But if you give a little and I give a little, maybe we can meet somewhere in the middle. And our child will win by having both parents in their life."

Guilt assailed Luca. He'd been so caught up in the surprise reception last night and then being alone with Elena that he hadn't been thinking clearly. She'd been so different—so bold. And he was weak when it came to her kisses.

He took a big gulp of coffee. He swallowed, and his stomach churned. Maybe coffee on top of guilt was not a good combination for this morning. He set aside the coffee.

"Elena, come here." He guided her over to the wicker chairs. "There's something I need to tell you."

She looked at him. "I know."

"You do?"

"Yes. Your sister told me last night that you are going to be working with your father in Halencia. So you'll want to spend most of your time there. And that's why I've been thinking—"

"Wait." He waved his hands to gain her attention. "Is that all my sister told you?"

Elena's forehead creased. "What else should she have told me?"

"Nothing. Because she doesn't know this yet."

"Know what? You're worrying me."

He blew out a long breath and leaned forward, placing his elbows on his knees. "There's a problem with the estate. Huge problems."

"What kind of problem?"

"Financial. My father—he ran the estate into debt."

"Oh, no." She reached out and placed her hand on his shoulder. "I'm so sorry to hear this."

Luca's worried gaze met hers. "It isn't like my father to fall behind on his credit payments. He's used the estate, our home, to secure loans—loans that he doesn't have a prayer of paying off."

When Luca chanced a glance at her face, it was pale. She was getting the drift of the severity of the situation.

He didn't want to, but he had to go on. "I've had to use

my savings to stave off the creditors. And now I have nothing to offer you."

"Of course you do. I didn't marry you for your title or your money—"

"But you have a right to expect those things. And I can't give them to you. Well, I still have the title, but at this point it isn't worth much."

"It's okay," she said confidently. "I've got enough money to support both of us and the baby."

"No!" He jumped to his feet and moved to stand by the wall. "I'm not having you do that."

"You mean you're too proud to take money from a woman?"

"No, what I mean is that for a long time I shirked my responsibilities, and I won't do that again. I have to make this right and not take the easy way out. If I did that, if I counted on you to pull me out of this mess, how would our child ever respect me?"

He couldn't just stand there. He knew that Elena must now think less of him for letting things get to this point. If he was a proper son, he would have been there for his father before the business hit this critical juncture.

Luca took off down the steps of the decking bordering the cottage. He didn't have a particular destination in mind. He just needed space to figure out his next step.

"Luca, wait!"

He couldn't face her, not after he'd let her down. He kept going—kept moving down the beach.

"Luca, stop!" Elena cried. "There has to be a way to fix this. We just have to think about it."

Luca begrudgingly stopped and turned to the deck. "I did. And... Oh, never mind."

"No, you were going to say something. I want to know what it is." When she reached him, she placed a finger beneath his chin and lifted until they were eye to eye. "Speak to me."

"The only way to save the estate and the business is to find an immediate influx of cash." Maybe he'd been wrong. Maybe it was his pride and not some do-gooder notion that had him refusing to ask for her help. "I suggested that my father take on a partner with deep pockets, but he outright rejected the idea. He said that this was our legacy and only a DiSalvo would ever own the lemon grove."

"Even if it means losing his business and his home?"

Luca sighed. "Yes. He's a very stubborn man."

"Maybe he sees this as his chance to reconnect with his son."

The same thing had crossed Luca's mind. "I shouldn't have let things get to this point."

When Elena didn't interrupt, he was inclined to expand on his statement. The truth of the matter was that he hadn't opened up to anyone about this part of his life. By not talking about it, sometimes it was easier to pretend that his mother hadn't been stolen away and his family hadn't fractured under the weight of grief.

"It wasn't always this way," he said aloud as a way of convincing himself. "After my mother's death, I needed my father's assurance that everything would be all right—that we would be all right."

Luca drew an unsteady breath as his thoughts rolled back in time. He didn't want to go there and experience the too-familiar pain. Still, he needed Elena to understand how important his endeavor to save the lemon grove was to him. It was his plan to undo some of the damage that had been done to his family.

"My father withdrew from my sister and me. He was cold. He didn't cry. He didn't speak of my mother. I was convinced he didn't love her."

Elena sat down on the beach and patted a spot next to

her. When he joined her, she said, "Maybe he was in shock. I don't know. But anytime I saw your parents together, there was obvious affection."

"I'm starting to think you're right. But back then I was an angry, confused kid. When my sister couldn't get love and assurances from my father, she turned to me, and I failed her."

"You can't blame yourself." Elena reached out and placed her hand over his. "You were so young. It was just too much."

"But I was the oldest. I should have been there for Annabelle. I should have been her rock."

"And because you couldn't be there for your family after your mother's death, you're trying to make up for it now?"

He shrugged and then nodded. Finding warmth and strength in her touch, he laced his fingers with hers. "Do you think it's too late?"

"No. I think saving your family's business is heroic."

"But I haven't accomplished it yet. The only option I can think of is to gain one of Mirraccino's contracts. They are lucrative and far-reaching with their export business. I talked with Demetrius, but he said that they are experiencing a full audit after what the king's lord-in-waiting did to my mother. There's fear that he was embezzling from the crown. Demetrius said he couldn't do anything for me now, but that we could revisit it in the future. The problem is that will take too long. The creditors will call in their loans before then. The only way to get around Demetrius's decision is to go directly to the king, but I can't get to him."

"And you need my help to get access to him."

Luca nodded.

Now it was up to Elena. And he had no idea how she would feel about pulling strings with her father in order to help him. He hated to put her in this position, but at that moment, he just couldn't think of any other plan.

CHAPTER TWENTY

TALK ABOUT STRESSFUL.

Luca had been in a lot of tense business meetings, but this one was the worst.

He sat on a wing-back chair in the king's suite of rooms. He hadn't been in here since he was a little kid, and to be honest, it was still a bit intimidating as an adult. The room was regally decorated, mostly in maroon, with cream-colored walls. The furniture was all antique and he couldn't even begin to guess their ages, but every item was well maintained.

The king was up and dressed, but he looked to be a shell of the man that Luca once knew. Luca couldn't decide if it was age or stress or a little of both.

Luca had given his uncle an overview of the challenges facing the DiSalvo family. He had brought some projections with him, but he knew not to present them unless invited. As of yet, no invitation had been extended. The king had merely listened and nodded at the appropriate moments. And now that Luca had said everything that he'd come here to say, silence filled the room.

After a few moments, the king said, "Luca, I am sorry I haven't been around, especially as I hear that you and Elena have married. I want to offer you my best wishes."

"Thank you, sir. We appreciate it."

"I hadn't realized that you two were seeing each other. But then again, I haven't exactly been accessible recently. But I thought that Elena's father would have mentioned it."

Luca swallowed hard. "Actually, it was a bit of a whirlwind relationship, and we sort of kept it to ourselves."

"I can understand. Once upon a time I was a young man. Things can happen quickly." The king stared off into the distance as though he was caught up in memories. "I've watched Elena grow up, and there's something very special about her. She'll make you a good wife. You take care of that girl."

"I will, sir." This was his chance to get the conversation back on track. *Please let him agree.* "That's why I'm trying to secure a deal for the lemon grove."

"About that, I am sorry. But my son is right. We cannot grant new contracts right now. The kingdom's records and finances are all under review. Everything is on hold at the moment."

"I understand." He might understand, but that didn't make his situation any better.

"Once every file and account has been audited to make sure that criminal didn't embezzle or sell any national secrets, our security will return to normal and new business will commence. If you could just wait, we will give your proposal due consideration."

Luca couldn't just walk away. Even though the king couldn't help him now, he wanted to do or say something to help his uncle, or to just let him know that he wasn't alone. "Sir, you know that what happened with my mother wasn't your fault. And no one blames you."

The king's tired eyes widened. "How can people not blame me? That murderer worked for me. He was right here in this palace." A sorrowful expression filled his face. "I am so sorry this happened to your mother. I can't express enough my sorrow and regret that this happened."

How exactly did he respond to that? Luca never blamed him. "I appreciate your words, but you don't need to apologize."

"I should have known something was wrong." His fist pounded on the arm of his chair. "What kind of ruler am I if I can miss something so important?"

"You are human like the rest of us. Please believe me that

no one in my family—or in the palace or, for that matter, the nation—blames you. But people do miss you."

"Thank you. I will take that under consideration."

After thanking the king again for seeing him, Luca made his exit. He was in no better position than when he'd arrived. But he was in no worse shape, either.

And yet, he could feel everything he'd strived for slipping away. His childhood home, his legacy—it all now hung in a very precarious position. And should he fail to save it, he imagined that he would lose contact with his father and sister once more. This was why he kept people at a distance. Letting them in just set him up for more pain.

Most important, he would lose all of his savings on this venture and have no way to support Elena and the baby. He raked his fingers through his hair. If this was the best he could do, then perhaps he didn't deserve this family.

As he made his way out of the palace, he knew he would find a way to make this all work. He had to. Everyone was counting on him.

The deed was done.

Elena couldn't believe she'd begged her father to let Luca speak with the king. She knew her father didn't want to do it, but she'd pleaded with him and told him that her entire future was on the line. He'd asked if it was really that important, and she'd promised that it was. She knew that if Luca didn't save his legacy, their marriage didn't stand a chance of surviving—if it ever had.

She sure hoped Luca knew what he was doing. He seemed so certain the king would help that she wondered what would happen if the king's hands were tied just as his son's were. Elena didn't know a lot about how the government worked, but something told her the king would not override the crown prince's decision, not when the king was positioning his son to take over the kingdom—at least, that was what her father had led her to believe.

After stopping by to check on her mother, Elena retrieved her sketch pad and colored pencils. If nothing else, she could get some work done. Now that her modeling contract with Lauren Renard had been dissolved, Elena needed to focus on her new career path—designing her own fashions.

When she arrived back at the cottage, it was empty. Luca still hadn't returned. She'd taken that as a good sign—the king was hearing him out. And though Luca didn't go on and on about his family's business being in danger and what that would mean to his father, she knew it had Luca tied up in knots. If it was possible to get the lemon grove on level financial ground, would Luca be more open about his feelings toward the baby? And her?

But Elena foresaw a problem with his plan. Luca was trying to take on this enormous problem all by himself. Granted, she wasn't that familiar with the business world, but to her it seemed like the more people you had brainstorming ways to solve a problem, the quicker and easier the solution would be derived.

She grabbed her phone and selected Annabelle's number. Elena hesitated before she pressed Send. Sure, Annabelle had invited her to her engagement festivities, but how would she feel about Elena inserting herself into family business? Would she be willing to talk to Elena about something so intrinsic to her family?

There was only one way to find out. Elena pressed the button. The phone rang once, twice…

"Hey, Elena, I was just thinking about you." Annabelle's cheerful voice came over the line.

"You were?"

"Uh-huh. I was wondering how the impromptu honeymoon is going."

Elena paused, not sure what to say.

"Elena, is something wrong?"

This was her opening. She just had to take it. "That's the thing—the honeymoon, it's not going so well."

"I'm so sorry. Is there anything I can do?"

"Actually, there is. I need to talk to you about Luca—"

"Elena, who are you talking to?" Luca's voice boomed across the room.

Elena jumped. She hadn't even heard him enter the cottage. She turned to find a dark look on his face. She wondered just how much he'd overheard.

She held up a finger to get him to wait and then she spoke into the phone. "I've got to go."

"I'm here whenever you need to talk."

"Thanks. I appreciate that." Elena disconnected the call. She turned to Luca. "I didn't hear you come in."

"Obviously." His tone rumbled with agitation. "What exactly were you planning to say before I interrupted?"

Elena felt bad that he'd misinterpreted what he'd overheard. "It was nothing bad."

He crossed his arms and waited.

"I was talking with your sister and I was going to see if she had some ideas of what to do about the lemon grove."

"Why would she have any ideas?" His brows drew together in a formidable line. "This isn't her problem."

"The last time I checked, she was part of your family, and the lemon grove does belong to your family."

"But this is my problem, not hers...and not yours."

His last words stabbed at her heart. Even though they'd gotten married, made mad, passionate love and she was carrying his child, Luca still refused to let her in. What was his problem? When was he going to learn that people weren't out to hurt him?

In this moment, she felt as though she was fighting for the future of her marriage. "This *is* my problem. I'm your wife, remember. And it's your sister and your father's problem. What is wrong with you? Why can't you let people in?"

"I don't need to let people in. I do fine on my own."

She lifted her chin. "If you're so fine, why do you look so miserable?"

"Because I came home to find my wife doesn't believe that I can take care of our family."

"And so you're going to stand on your pride instead of reaching out for help."

"I don't need help. Just leave me alone."

Really? This was how he was going to play it? He'd been pushing her away for too long now. And she wasn't going to put up with it anymore.

"Luca, I love you. I want to help you. What is so wrong with that?"

He shook his head, and his gaze didn't meet hers. "I didn't ask for anyone to take pity on me."

"It's not pity. It's what people do when they love each other." And then she realized that the night they'd spent together might have meant something totally different to him than it had to her. "Luca, do you love me?"

He didn't say anything. And then he walked toward the balcony. If he thought he was getting away and avoiding this, he was wrong. She followed him.

"Luca." When he didn't even acknowledge that he'd heard her, she tried again. "Luca, answer me."

He turned to her. "I can't tell you what you want to hear. I can't be the man you want me to be."

Tears pricked the backs of her eyes, but she refused to give in to her pregnancy hormones. She blinked back the moisture. She refused to let Luca see how much his words hurt her.

"You might not love me, but you can't say the same about your family."

"I don't need them, either. Why do you think I can't be happy alone?"

"Because I believe that everyone needs somebody. I have to believe that, otherwise…" She stopped as her emotions threatened to overtake her.

"Otherwise what?" His intent gaze studied her as though trying to ferret out the truth.

She swallowed hard. "Otherwise you won't be able to love our child."

He didn't say a word. Not one syllable. Instead he turned to stare out at the sea.

That's it! She had tried to be understanding, but she'd had enough of his stubborn attitude. If he couldn't meet her halfway, she was done.

"You know, you don't have to face the world alone." She held back from saying that she would stand by his side through anything. "Your family would rally around you if you'd let them in. That's what families do."

He turned to her. His eyes were dark, and his stance was rigid. "And what makes you think I need their help?"

"A better question is how are you supposed to be a loving parent to our baby if you never let anyone in?"

"Stop saying that." He stared at her as though shocked that she would say these things to him. "I do let people in."

"No, you don't." She didn't know why she bothered. He'd counted on himself for so long now that he didn't know any other way to be. "I give up. I love you, but obviously that's never going to penetrate the wall around your heart."

He looked at her, but he didn't say anything. This was where he should profess his love for her, too. And yet there was nothing but a stony silence.

Though it was breaking her heart, she just couldn't imprison him or herself in a one-sided marriage. She knew he would stay out of obligation, and if she didn't walk out that door right now, he would be miserable for the rest of his life. And she loved him too much to do that to him.

"I can't do this anymore." She turned for the door.

"Where are you going?"

"At last, you speak. If you must know, I'm going to my parents' for dinner. They invited us both, but I can't imagine that you would want to go. I'll give them your regrets." She continued to the door. And then she paused and turned. "I guess this is goodbye."

"Goodbye?"

"Yes. Tomorrow I'm returning to Paris. I'll email you with any important information about the baby. Goodbye, Luca."

She turned and headed out the door while she could still maintain a dignified expression. Because that had been the hardest thing she'd ever done in her life. Her heart felt as though it had been ripped from her chest.

CHAPTER TWENTY-ONE

WHAT HAD JUST HAPPENED?

Luca stared at the closed door as he gathered his thoughts. In the heat of the moment, he decided Elena leaving was for the best.

He paced back and forth in the cottage, feeling like a caged animal. Why did everyone in his life keep telling him that he was doing things the wrong way? All he was trying to do was stand on his own two legs. Was that such a bad thing?

Of course not.

He contemplated walking out the door and not stopping. He needed away from the palace and Mirraccino—away from Elena. But for the first time ever, he couldn't imagine being on his own again. Every time he thought of the future, he saw Elena in it.

The voices of Elena, his father, the king and others echoed in his head. He had to get out of there. He headed for the beach. The sounds of the water, the birds and the breeze were calming. Now he had to unravel this tangled mess, because so much was at stake.

Never before had he had this many people foisting their opinions and advice upon him. All of them wanted him to do this or that, but none asked what he wanted to do.

The last time—the only time—he'd done what he was told, it had been with his mother. He didn't let himself think of her very often, but her memory filled his mind now. He reached for the chain that hung around his neck, a constant reminder of her—a source of comfort in times of trouble. He removed the chain from his neck and clutched the St. Christopher medal in his palm.

When he was a child, his mother was the only one to

guide him—to tell him what needed to be done. His sister had been too little, his father too busy and Elena too awe-struck by the fact that he was a part of the royal family.

In the years since his mother's murder, he'd been doing his best to navigate life on his own. Was it possible that in his efforts to avoid another loss that he'd built these walls around himself that Elena mentioned?

He supposed it was true. He'd never really stopped to think about it. But it was the only way he knew how to be. He didn't even know how to change.

But if he didn't do something, he was going to lose the woman he loved. It was the first time he'd allowed himself to admit his intense feelings for Elena to himself. And in-stead of it being scary, it was freeing. It was like stepping out of the shadows and into the sunlight.

He knew she still had the ability to hurt him, but by de-nying his feelings, he was hurting himself more. But was it too late? Would she give him a second chance?

He had to prove to her that he'd changed—that he was willing to let people into his life. And he knew how to do it. He would start with his father and sister.

He had an idea of how to save the lemon grove, but he couldn't do it by himself. Finally, he was hearing what Elena had been telling him. He wasn't in this battle alone. There were people around who wanted to help, if he'd let them.

First, he would speak to his father, Annabelle and the newest member of the family, Grayson. When Luca went to Elena, he was going to show her that family meant ev-erything to him.

Elena and the baby were his everything.

CHAPTER TWENTY-TWO

ELENA HAD ARRIVED home early for dinner.

She had nowhere else to go and nothing she wanted to do. And since she was leaving in the morning, she thought she would spend the extra time with her mother.

"Dear, you really don't have to help with dinner. I can manage," her mother insisted as she tried to prepare food while balancing on her crutches.

"Mother, why don't you sit at the table and I'll bring you whatever you need?"

"Well, that probably would be easier. Thanks." She moved to the table. "But something tells me you have more on your mind than worrying about me. For a newlywed, you've been spending a lot of time at home. What's going on?"

Elena didn't know how to respond. She just wasn't willing to admit to anyone that her brief marriage was a bust. Every time she thought of vocalizing the words, the backs of her eyes started to sting. She couldn't avoid the subject forever, but for just this moment, she wanted to pretend that her heart wasn't breaking in two.

Elena started slicing cheese. "Can I ask you something?"

"Sure. Does it have to do with sex?"

The knife slipped, barely missing Elena's finger. "Mother!"

"Okay. I was just kidding." Her mother sat at the table cutting orange wedges for the fruit and cheese tray.

Elena kept her gaze on the task at hand, not wanting her mother to read too much in her gaze. "When you first got married, did you— Well, was Father a little distant?"

"Your father? No. He's always been romantic and passionate—"

"Mother, I thought we said we weren't going there."

Her mother laughed. "Passionate about his feelings, daughter. I've always known where I stood with him."

Which just reinforced her decision to end things with Luca. She never knew where she stood with him, and she couldn't live like that.

"I take it you and Luca are having some problems adjusting."

"Something like that." Maybe if she opened up a little more, her mother would be able to give her some helpful advice. After all, her mother knew how to maintain a successful marriage. "It's just that he won't open up and let me in. And now that I'm—"

She stopped. How could she just go and almost blurt out that she was pregnant? Now wasn't the time for that news.

"You really are pregnant, aren't you?" The glee was obvious in her mother's voice. She got to her feet in record time and rushed over to put an arm around Elena. "I'm so happy for you."

When they pulled apart, Elena said, "No one knows."

"Haven't you told your husband?"

"He knows." Since she'd already said more than she intended, she might as well finish confessing. "It's the only reason he married me."

"What?" Her mother sounded shocked. "Surely you don't believe that."

"How can I not believe it? I asked him once if he loved me, and he said no."

"But that can't be right. I've watched you two over the years. It's as plain to me as the nose on my face that you two belong together. I just wondered how long it would take you to figure it out."

Elena sniffled. "I figured it out, but he didn't. And I can't live with someone who doesn't love me back. It's not right for me, and it's not right for our baby."

"Oh, Elena, think hard before you do anything drastic. Sometimes we only get one chance at love."

The sound of footsteps had them both turning. There in the entrance to the kitchen stood Luca. He looked awful. His face was pale and drawn. Elena's first instinct was to go to him, but she held herself back. If this was going to work, he had to make the first move.

"I knocked," he said, "but I don't think anyone heard, so I let myself in. I hope that's all right."

"Of course it is," her mother said, as though there wasn't a thing wrong. "You're family now. You are welcome here anytime."

"Thank you." His gaze met Elena's. "That means a lot."

Her mother smiled. "I hope you brought your appetite. Elena and I have been cooking up a storm. We can eat as soon as my husband arrives."

Elena stood by quietly, wondering what his real reason was for being there. Part of her was frustrated and she didn't want to have the same argument with him again. But another part of her wondered if maybe her words had finally gotten through to him.

"Actually," Luca said, "I was wondering if I could borrow your daughter for a little bit."

"Certainly. She's all done here."

When Elena didn't make any movement to go to him, Luca said, "Elena, there are things I need to say to you. It's important."

He deserved to wait a minute. She wanted him to know that she wasn't going to jump every time he called. Most of all, he had to know that he'd truly hurt her.

"Please," he pleaded.

That was what she needed. She turned to her mother. "Are you sure you've got everything?"

"Positive. Thank you for your help. I appreciate it and our chat. Now go." She shooed them from the kitchen. As they were going out the door, her mother hollered, "And if you don't make it back this evening, we'll have leftovers tomorrow."

Oh, her mother, ever the optimistic one.

Elena wasn't as hopeful. Maybe she was building up her own walls now. But she just couldn't get her hopes up and let her heart get broken all over again.

CHAPTER TWENTY-THREE

LUCA HAD NEVER been more nervous in his life.

Neither said a word as they walked. He didn't have a destination in mind. He just needed time alone with Elena. And now that he was with her, the words inside him twisted up in a knot and clogged his throat.

Their meandering led them to the cliff overlooking the sea. The sun hovered on the horizon, sending magnificent shades of pink and purple streaking through the sky. But nothing could hold a candle to his wife's beauty.

And if he didn't say the right things now, he knew he was going to lose her for good. His chance at having a family would be gone. And he didn't know how he would live with the knowledge that he'd ruined it all.

He swallowed hard. "Elena, please don't do this. Don't leave."

She maintained a considerable distance between them. Her gaze was cool and distant. "I want you to know that I really appreciate all you've done for me. Not many men would have stepped up and proposed marriage to protect their unborn baby from a scandal."

"I did what I needed to do. And I'd do it again."

"But that's the thing—you don't need to do anything else. The crisis has been averted. We can now go back to our lives."

"Elena, please don't do this."

"I can't continue to live a lie. If we can't fully and honestly communicate with each other, we can't have a healthy marriage."

"Listen, I'm sorry about not telling you about my family's financial crisis as soon as I learned about it. But thanks to you, we have a plan in place to get us through this rough patch. I just came from talking to my father, Annabelle and Grayson. We are going to contract with Fo Shizzle Cafés for as much produce as they can take. And we spoke with Demetrius, who was able to give us a date for when the royal family will start taking on new contracts again. He said ours would be the first they considered."

Elena shook her head. "You're still not hearing me. I'm not talking about business."

"But I reached out to my family for help. Isn't that what you wanted?"

"Partly. But you still won't let anyone know how you feel."

He raked his fingers through his hair. "And how do you want me to resolve that?"

"I don't know. I'm not sure it can be resolved. That's why I'm going back to Paris in the morning."

"You mean alone?"

"Yes. It's best for everyone."

Again, there was a coolness to her words. Her voice was almost monotone, and he noticed how her gaze didn't quite meet his. He felt like she was blocking him out—like he was suddenly a stranger to her. And he didn't like it. Not one little bit.

He wanted his Elena back—the person who made him laugh, who was full of emotion and tenderness. This aloofness wasn't like her.

And then it dawned on him that this was how it must have been for Elena to deal with him all this time. It was as if he suddenly truly understood what his efforts to protect himself had done to those around him.

"Elena, I am sorry for blocking you out. I was afraid. Afraid of losing you from my life, whether it be an unexpected death or indifference or something else. I'm not afraid to love you anymore."

She stood there much like a statue. She didn't say anything. In fact, she didn't react at all. Hadn't she heard him? "Elena, I love you."

CHAPTER TWENTY-FOUR

SHE'D HEARD HIM.

She'd tried not to, but his words penetrated her heart.

She didn't react right away, because she was still processing this information. It was a lot to take in. And they had to get this right.

Elena lifted her chin. "Are you saying all this because you now feel that you have something to offer?"

"What?"

"The deal with the lemon grove. Are you willing to take a risk on us because you want your child to grow up on the DiSalvo estate?"

"No. No. No. Didn't you hear me? I love you. I know it took a long time for me to get it all straight, but I'm here now, asking you to forgive me. I've made a lot of mistakes, but I never meant to hurt you."

Her heart fluttered. These were the words she'd been longing to hear for so very long. A tear splashed onto her cheek. She swiped it away.

Luca got down on one knee and took her hand in his. "I did this once and I meant it, but I didn't get it exactly right, so I'd like a do-over. Is that all right?"

She nodded as a smile pulled at her lips. At last, the wall around his heart had crumbled. Her heart pounded with love and joy.

"Elena, I love you. If I am honest with myself, I've always loved you. When something good happens, you're the first person I think of to tell. If something bad happens, you're the one I want to share my troubles. Yours is the last face I want to see at night and the first in the morning. I want to spend the rest of my days showing you just how much I love you. Will you spend the rest of your life with me?"

"Yes. Yes. Yes." She drew him up to his feet. "I love you with all my heart." And then she took his hand and pressed it to her abdomen. "We both do."

Luca stared deep into her eyes. "I'm the luckiest man in the world."

"And I am the luckiest woman. I get to spend the rest of my life with my best friend."

She lifted up on her tiptoes and pressed her lips to his.

EPILOGUE

Eleven months later

ELENA STOOD IN the gardens of the royal palace. Annabelle and Grayson had just been married. Elena and Luca had stood up for them. And the king had attended, now that he was back to being himself.

It was so nice to be back in Mirraccino. She said that every time she and Luca visited, which was often. As much as she loved Halencia, it would never have that special something that Mirraccino did. Maybe it was because this was her childhood home...or maybe it was because it was here that she'd met the man of her dreams, who at that point had been a little boy who didn't mind getting his formal clothes dirty playing with a girl. Elena smiled at the memories. They seemed so long ago now.

While Luca talked with one of his many cousins, Elena excused herself. European football was something that still didn't interest her—no matter how much Luca tried to sway her. Although she had enjoyed playing football with Luca as a kid, it didn't hold her attention in the same way. Now the only thing she recognized about the game was which jersey matched which team. What could she say? Fashion was in her blood. Only in a different way now.

She moved around the vast gardens. The walkways were lit up with torches that gave a soft glow to the fragrant foliage. Their garden in Halencia was just as beautiful, but not nearly as vast. It was where Elena spent a lot of time now that their son, Marco, had been born. Instead of modeling glamorous fashions, she was now doing something she loved—designing. Her debut fashion show was planned for this fall. She couldn't wait.

When fingers wrapped around her shoulders, she jumped.

"Hey, relax. It's just me," Luca murmured very close to her ear. Then he leaned over and pressed his lips to the nape of her neck. "What had you so deep in thought?"

"I was just thinking about the path we took to get here. It's hard to believe that we once played hide-and-seek in these gardens and now your sister is having her wedding reception here."

"I was beginning to wonder if she was ever going to get married—"

"Luca, really. Just because you rushed me down the aisle doesn't mean everyone wants to elope."

"Are you saying you regret our rush to the altar?"

"Of course not." She lifted up on her tiptoes and pressed her lips to his. "I love you, Luca. With all my heart."

"I love you, too." He kissed her again. "Are you sure you don't want a wedding do-over?"

"I'm positive. But I must admit that if I was going to have a wedding, I'd want it to be like this one, even if it took your sister a year to plan."

Luca glanced around. "I guess it isn't too bad."

Elena lightly punched him on the shoulder. "It's gorgeous. I'm so happy for your sister."

"I'm thinking I might have to hire her."

"For what?"

"I want to throw a party."

Elena frowned at her husband. "I told you I don't want to get married again. We got it right the first time, even if it took us a little bit to figure it out."

"Who said anything about getting married again?" He arched a dark brow. "I'm thinking that we have our first anniversary coming up and it deserves a party."

"You really want to go to all that trouble?"

Luca drew her close in his arms. "Mrs. DiSalvo, haven't

you figured out that I would go to the moon and back for you?"

She tilted her chin up. "I wouldn't let you get that far away."

Between his sweet words and the way he stared deeply into her eyes, her heart tap-danced in her chest and her knees became rubbery. She loved the way he could still make her feel as giddy as she had when this whole love affair began.

"Why's that?" he asked.

"Because I couldn't bear to be separated from you for that long."

"Don't worry. I'll always be right here." He pressed his hand to her heart.

She lifted up on her tiptoes and pressed her lips to his. Her heart swelled with love. She didn't know it was possible to love someone this much.

A lifetime together would never be enough.

* * * * *

ONE NIGHT THAT CHANGED HER LIFE

EMILY FORBES

For Felicity.
Thank you for your love and support. It means so
much to me that you read and enjoy my stories!
This one is for you. xx

Wishing you a very Happy Birthday!

With all my love,
your goddaughter,
Emily

CHAPTER ONE

BRIGHDE HID BEHIND a conference banner as she stabbed her finger at the screen of her phone. Her hand was shaking as she tried to end the call and it took her two attempts to press the right spot. She took a deep breath, fighting to remember her yoga breathing as she fought back the tears that threatened to spill from her eyes.

She was happy for Nick, really she was, but her brother's phone call had confirmed her worst fears.

Good news for him could only mean bad news for her.

She struggled with the clasp of her bag, eventually managing to open it, and shoved her phone inside before snapping the clasp shut. She needed a drink. A strong one.

There were plenty of free drinks on offer in the hotel ballroom where one of the major pharmaceutical drug companies was hosting the end of conference party but Brighde didn't feel like going back into the crowd. She needed space almost as much as she needed a drink.

The ballroom was on the hotel's mezzanine floor but on the floor below she knew there was a bar ad-

joining the lobby. She looked at the staircase; the ex-
panse of carpet between her and the stairs looked
immense and she wasn't sure if she'd make it. Her
knees wobbled as she took the first step and she focused on putting one foot in front of the other until
she could reach for the banister. She clutched it tightly,
steadying herself for the descent. The simple task of
negotiating a staircase suddenly seemed to require
enormous effort. Was that a sign? She knew difficulty with motor skills was often one of the first obvious symptoms of the disease, impaired voluntary
movements like gait and balance were hard to ignore,
but surely that would be too much of a coincidence.

Get a hold of yourself, Brighde, she admonished
herself. *You're only twenty-eight—you're not about
to fall apart yet.*

She hoped she was right but it was hard to discount
the feeling of mounting panic. Her chest was tight and
she was finding it hard to breathe. She was surprised
by her reaction to Nick's phone call. She'd always suspected that she would be dealt the bad hand and she
hadn't expected to be so shocked.

This was what she'd always dreaded. It wasn't exactly a surprise but, at the end of the day, it obviously
didn't matter how prepared she thought she was; the
truth of it was no one wanted to know they were going
to an early grave.

Somehow she managed to get down the stairs and
into the bar on her wobbly legs without taking a tumble. She perched on a stool and ordered a vodka Mar-
tini. She had no idea if she liked Martinis—she drank
vodka—but she felt she needed something more po-
tent. Something that would numb the pain and a Mar-

tini sounded like it might do the trick. She didn't want to ask the bartender for suggestions; she just wanted to anaesthetise herself.

She plucked the olive from the toothpick as she drained her glass.

Martinis weren't too bad, she decided as she ordered another.

'Brighde! What are you doing down here?'

Brighde turned at the sound of her name and found Sarah, her best friend, colleague and roommate all rolled into one, making a beeline for her across the room.

'Just collecting my thoughts.'

'Looks like you're collecting more than thoughts,' Sarah said as the bartender put a fresh cocktail on the bar.

Sarah was watching her closely as she pulled out another bar stool and sat down.

'Who was on the phone?' she asked. She'd been standing next to Brighde when she'd taken the call.

'Nick.'

'Is everything okay?'

'He got his test results back.'

'At nine o'clock at night?'

Brighde shook her head. 'No. But it took him a while to figure out how to tell me.'

'Was it bad news?'

'Not for him.' Sarah and Brighde had been friends for ten years since meeting at university, where they'd both studied nursing. Brighde had no secrets from Sarah. 'He had ten repeats.'

'He tested negative?'

Brighde nodded.

'That's great news.'

'Yes. It is,' she said, fighting to speak past the lump in her throat. She still felt like crying, even though nothing she'd heard in the phone call should make any difference. Nothing had really changed. She had her reasons for not getting tested and those reasons hadn't altered. She could go on just as before. Nick's results didn't affect her future plans but she knew they solidified her fears. His results didn't confirm her suspicions but they definitely strengthened them.

'You don't seem happy,' Sarah said.

'We each had a fifty-fifty chance of inheriting a faulty gene. There's only two of us,' Brighde explained. 'What do *you* think the chances are of both of us dodging a bullet?'

'You know the answer to that. It's still fifty-fifty. Just because Nick is clear doesn't mean you won't be. The chance of you inheriting the gene or not hasn't changed. Nick's results have no bearing on you.'

Brighde knew Sarah's facts were correct. The reality was her chances of inheriting the mutated gene hadn't changed but she still felt the odds were not in her favour. She'd always felt that. Which was why she never intended to get tested. Who wanted to know that they were going to die young? Who wanted that fear confirmed?

Not her.

'I know you're right. In theory. But I've always felt that I was going to draw the short straw and knowing Nick is okay just reinforces all those feelings. Huntington's Disease is dominantly inherited and I can't believe we'd both dodge the bullet. I don't think we could both be that lucky.'

'And I don't think there's anything you can do about it tonight,' Sarah said as she shook her head at the bartender, who was clearing Brighde's glass and asking if she wanted another. 'Come and dance, have some fun. The band's playing some good music—dancing will take your mind off it.'

Brighde let Sarah convince her to vacate the bar in favour of the dance floor. She didn't really feel like dancing but she felt less like going back to the hotel room and staring at the walls. She was feeling miserable enough already.

Xavier nursed his beer as he watched the dance floor. It was taking him a little while to get back into beer drinking. He hadn't realised he'd acquired such a taste for whisky in his years of living in Scotland, but when in Rome... Or Edinburgh.

What he was getting accustomed to far more quickly was the plethora of attractive young women at the conference. The band had been playing for some time and the dance floor was full. His eyes were drawn to a petite blonde in a sapphire dress. He'd been watching her for a while now; she'd been late onto the dance floor but even among the crowd she'd stood out. He'd tried to look elsewhere but his gaze continued to return to her. He believed you could tell exactly what a woman was like in bed by the way she moved on the dance floor. The blonde had rhythm and energy. Her dress shimmered under the lights and her hair shone, contrasting brightly against all the black outfits in the room. She was striking to look at. She wasn't smiling, she looked focused, but she danced as if she enjoyed it and he'd put money on her enjoying sex too. She looked fit and flexible and carefree, all admirable traits in his opinion, and he was hooked.

He waited until she left the dance floor. He wasn't going anywhere until he'd spoken to her. He could dance, but he wasn't about to dance in front of hundreds of his fellow medicos. He'd rather dance *à deux* and so he waited.

The band were playing a love song that was impossible to dance to without a partner. She needed pop music. Something she could lose herself in. She gestured to Sarah—she was going to grab a drink—and made her way to the bar at the side of the ballroom.

She had intended to get a water—dancing had taken her mind off the earlier phone call—but once she stopped dancing and reached the bar all her doubts returned. She'd have a water later. She needed another drink to numb the pain.

'Can I buy you a drink?'

Brighde's skin tingled as she felt, rather than saw, someone behind her. His voice was deep and quiet and although she couldn't see him she knew he was addressing her. She closed her eyes, imagining a face to go with the voice, before she turned around, hoping she wasn't going to be disappointed.

She wasn't.

She turned to find the most gorgeous man she'd seen in a long time at her side. How had she not noticed him in the room? Okay, there were hundreds of people at the conference but seriously, he was magnificent. She must have been more distracted than she'd realised.

He watched her as he waited for her answer. His dark eyes studied her, captivating her with his gaze.

'The drinks are free, you know,' she replied.

'In that case, I'll get you two.' He grinned at her, lightening the seriousness of his dark stare, and Brighde lost the last remnants of her composure.

He looked like European royalty. No, he wasn't clean-cut enough for royalty. His dark hair was slightly too long, exploding around his oval face into soft curls that just begged her to reach out and touch them. His jaw was covered in designer stubble, his eyes were dark and his forehead was strong. He was dark and swarthy and sexy as hell. Confidence oozed from him. He was impeccably dressed—his dark navy suit hung from his shoulders and fitted his frame, the pants were slim, encasing powerful thighs. He looked like a European polo player. Something out of a Jilly Cooper novel. He looked rich and successful, although of course she had no idea if that was the case, and he wanted to buy her a drink. If there was a downside to his offer she couldn't think of one.

'What are you having?' he asked. He didn't wait for her to accept his offer. He just assumed she wouldn't refuse. Was that confidence or was it simply an assumption based on the fact it was an open bar? She didn't know but she also didn't care. She wasn't going anywhere. Not now.

She shouldn't mix her drinks but the bar wasn't offering Martinis and she knew she needed more than water if she was going to be brave enough to keep up her side of the conversation with this gorgeous man. 'I'll have a white wine,' she said as she perched on a bar stool. She didn't need to sit down but she needed to take a step back. He was standing close to her; that wasn't a problem but she wanted to get a good second look at him and she needed a bit of distance to do that.

He ordered and handed her a glass. His fingers brushed hers and a spark arced between them, setting her already nervous heart racing. It had been several months since she'd shared a drink with a man but she knew it wasn't the length of time making her react this way.

Was the touch accidental? she wondered as he tapped his beer glass against her wine and made a toast. 'To new experiences.'

He held her gaze a fraction longer than was polite and her stomach flipped and she knew his touch had been deliberate. Her body was responding to him in a way it never had before. She'd never felt such immediate attraction or, if she was honest, such blatant lust before. He made her think of naked bodies and tangled sheets and raw, amazing sex and she knew exactly how this night would end. 'Indeed,' she replied as a sense of delicious anticipation flooded through her. She smiled and added, 'I'm Brighde.'

'Xavier.'

She didn't need to know any more than that.

'Have you enjoyed the conference?' he asked her.

So he was part of the conference and hadn't just snuck in for the free drinks.

'It's been really good,' she said as she put her glass on the bar and crossed her legs, pleased that she'd had a little bit of free time to lie by the hotel pool and work on her tan. 'But I could do with a few days off to recover before I go back to work. I'm heading home tomorrow, back to work on Monday.'

'That's a pity. I'll be here for a few more days.'

'Work or pleasure?' she asked.

'Purely pleasure.' He kept his dark eyes fixed on her as he reached past her shoulder, picking up a napkin from the bar. His arm brushed against her skin and she could feel his words on her cheek, soft little puffs of air. She knew he didn't need the napkin, she knew it had just been an excuse to lean in but she wasn't complaining. She could feel the electricity surging between them. They could power the room with the heat that was being generated between them. She wasn't aware of the music, the dancing, of anything that was going on around them. She was lost in the sensation he was evoking in her. She could feel his charisma wrapping itself around her as his pheromones enveloped her. Her nipples hardened and she squirmed in her seat. She pressed her thighs together as heat pooled low in her belly.

'I've been working in Scotland,' he told her, 'but the conference seemed like a good way to keep the taxman happy and visit my family.'

'Family?'

'My parents live here.'

'You're travelling alone? No partner? No wife?' She played with the ends of her hair, feigning casualness. She had to know the answer. She had rules and standards. She knew she would have sex with this gorgeous stranger—having sex would be a far healthier, and much more entertaining, distraction than drowning her worries with alcohol—but first she needed to establish some ground rules. She didn't want to make any mistakes.

'No wife. No girlfriend. No significant other.'

Now it was her turn to smile. 'Good to know.' She kept her gaze fixed on him now, wanting him to know where she stood. What she wanted. She didn't need to know anything else about him. She knew she wouldn't see him again. He was only visiting; she was leaving tomorrow. She hadn't had sex for ages and a one-night stand with this gorgeous man was a good option all round. No commitment, just a bit of fun and a good way to keep her mind busy. She didn't want time to think about her brother's phone call. She wanted something to take her mind off her situation. This was perfect.

She wanted Xavier.

And she wanted him to know that.

But Xavier was looking to his right.

Sarah had joined them.

Brighde watched her friend looking from her to Xavier and she knew she was taking in the distance, or lack of, between them. She watched as Sarah, quite blatantly, checked him out.

'I'm off,' Sarah said when she'd finished her inspection. 'Are you coming?'

Brighde thought about it for a second—okay, to be honest, a millisecond—she didn't need any longer than that when Xavier was looking at her with his come-to-bed eyes. 'No, I think I'm going to stay here for a bit.'

She knew Sarah's question had been rhetorical. She knew her plans for the rest of the evening were written all over her face but she didn't care. She wasn't even looking at Sarah as she answered; she couldn't make herself tear her eyes away from Xavier. He oozed sex appeal and she knew it was only a matter of time before she would be in his bed. She could feel it. She knew he wanted it too. She could feel the desire coming off him in waves and he was just what she needed. Taking a gorgeous man to bed ticked all the right boxes and it was a habit she had no intention of breaking. Okay, so she didn't do it all that often—she could barely remember the last time she'd even had sex—but a one-night stand was the perfect way to scratch an itch.

She needed sex but she didn't need a relationship. One night was enough. There was no need to go into details, no need to reveal anything personal about herself. She didn't consider sex to be personal—sex with a stranger couldn't hurt her, not as much as revealing her fears. She could happily share her body but not her mind. Her body was going to let her down one day; she owed it nothing.

Sarah nodded and smiled. She lent forwards and kissed Brighde's cheek. 'Have fun,' she whispered into Brighde's ear.

Brighde watched her go and when she turned back to Xavier she found he'd moved closer to her. His thigh pressed against her knee. She shifted forward on the bar stool, sliding her knee against the inside of his thigh. Their intentions were perfectly clear.

She looked up at him to find his dark eyes watching her. Her reaction was immediate and primal and she could feel her nipples jutting against the cool silk of her dress. She saw his gaze drop lower, saw him take in the peak of her nipples against the fabric of her dress. When he looked back at her his gaze was so intense and full of heat she thought she might melt into a pool of desire at his feet.

'Can I offer you a nightcap upstairs?' he asked as he lifted her glass from her hand. He reached across her to put her half-finished drink on the bar and the back of his hand brushed across her chest, grazing her nipple. Brighde felt as if she might climax on the spot.

She swallowed and nodded as she licked her lips. Despite everything she'd had to drink her throat was suddenly dry and she was having difficulty breathing, let alone speaking. She was experienced in the art of seduction but not in relationships. She didn't communicate with words. She sought the comfort of sex when she needed it, emotionally or physically. Tonight she needed it to distract herself. It had worked in the past and, looking at Xavier, she was sure it would work again today.

He took her hand and helped her off the stool. Once again her legs had turned to jelly but she barely noticed this time. She was too aware of the tingling in her belly and the intense weight of expectation and excitement in her groin.

Xavier held the door for her as she stepped into the lift. The lift had four other occupants and Brighde stood slightly apart from Xavier. She needed to keep some distance, otherwise she was in danger of throwing herself at him in front of a crowd. He pushed the button for the sixteenth floor while she leant against the wall of the lift; she needed something solid to keep her upright. She wanted to lean against Xavier but didn't dare while they had company. She didn't trust herself to maintain a sense of decency.

'What floor would you like?' one of the other passengers asked her.

'Sixteen,' she replied as she tried to avoid eye contact with Xavier, the gorgeous stranger.

Over the heads and shoulders of the other people sharing their lift she was totally aware of him. The man exuded sex appeal. Tall, dark, handsome and well-built. His dark hair was thick and just long enough to show the wave through it. There was no grey in his hair but a hint of it lightened the tidy stubble that darkened his jaw. He was well-groomed but definitely all man and he was watching her with his dark chocolate eyes as she studied him. His eyes were slightly hooded; he reminded her of a predatory bird. She felt like a sparrow in the piercing gaze of a falcon and she knew she was firmly in his sights.

The lift stopped several times but it wasn't until the fourteenth floor, when the doors closed, that it was finally just the two of them who remained.

She continued to study him. His hands were large, as were his feet. Even his slightly hooked nose was on the generous side. Brighde was twenty-eight years old and she was a midwife, she knew anatomy, and even though it was purported to be an old wives' tale she knew you could judge the size of a man's appendage by the size of his hands, feet and nose. She swallowed. She wouldn't have to wait long to test her theory.

His eyes hadn't strayed from hers and she knew he was visualising what was under her dress, just as she was imagining what she might find under his clothes. The idea gave her a rush of lust and she stepped a little closer as the lift doors eased shut.

He smelt fantastic. She was tempted to press the emergency stop button but she didn't want to be surprised by a maintenance team coming to rescue them. She could wait two more floors. Maybe.

She was aware of her breathing now. Heavy and laboured.

He reached out one hand and put it on her waist and she could feel the heat of his fingers through the thin silk fabric of her dress. He pulled her closer until she was pressed against him. She could feel his desire now, a thick, hard bulge pressing into her. She tipped her head back and looked up at him as the lift stopped and the doors slid open.

CHAPTER TWO

SHE LEANT AGAINST HIM, not trusting her legs to support her, as he led her to his room. He swiped the electronic key card over the door and held it open for her.

The room was a carbon copy of hers, with the exception of the bed. She was sharing with Sarah so their room had twin beds. Xavier had a room to himself, and a king-size bed that she intended to put to good use dominated the space.

She stepped inside and somehow managed to wait until he stepped in behind her and closed the door. She turned around and his mouth was instantly on hers. His hands at her back.

She wasn't interested in talking. She didn't want to know anything about him. She didn't *need* to know anything about him. His voice was deep and velvety smooth and it did funny things to her insides but she didn't need to hear it.

She parted her lips and his tongue delved deeper, exploring her, tasting her.

She pulled his shirt free from his trousers and undid the buttons, running her hands over his chest. The muscles were firm and warm under her fingers and dark hair covered his skin.

She could feel wetness pooling between her thighs. She pressed against him, wanting to feel the thickness of his erection, knowing she wouldn't be disappointed.

She closed her eyes and the room started to spin. Just a little, just enough for her to recognise she'd had more to drink than she'd realised. Drunk and emotional. That wasn't a good combination. But she wasn't so drunk that she didn't know exactly where she was and what she was doing, she thought as she felt his hand slide up under her dress. She opened her eyes as his hand cupped her buttock. He lifted her off her feet and continued to deepen the kiss as she wrapped her legs around his waist.

He carried her to the bed. She knelt on the edge as he opened the bedside drawer and retrieved a little foil packet. He put it on the bedside table, watching her as he let it go. His intentions were clear and Brighde knew he was asking for her acquiescence. In reply she reached up and slid his jacket and shirt from his shoulders, letting them drop to the floor. She wasn't changing her mind now.

He kicked off his shoes as she fumbled with the buckle of his belt. Finally, the belt came loose and she undid his trousers, letting him step out of them.

She swallowed as she looked at him standing before her. He pushed his boxer shorts off his hips and his erection sprang free.

He was even more impressive than she'd imagined. Thick and proud. He was glorious.

He reached for her again and she lifted her arms above her head as he whipped her dress from her body. She wasn't wearing a bra; she was as naked as he was save for her knickers and heels.

She stood up, brushing her breasts across his chest, and watched in fascination as his chocolate-brown eyes darkened further.

She spun him around, pushing him lightly backwards, making him sit on the edge of the bed. She needed to control this.

She stepped out of her underwear and put her legs either side of his, straddling his thighs.

She pushed him gently again, forcing him to lie back, as she climbed onto the bed and sat across him.

She plucked the foil packet from the bedside table and tore it open, sheathing him and protecting herself.

She was in a hurry now. Foreplay had been dealt with at the bar and in the lift. Silent communication and agreement had got them this far and she was ready and eager for the satisfaction she anticipated.

She put one hand on each side of his head and lifted her hips as he guided himself inside her, filling her. She closed her eyes as she concentrated on the sensations swamping her. The thickness of his shaft, the slight stretch of the muscles in her inner thighs as she spread her legs wider to take him deeper inside her.

She leant forwards as she raised and lowered her hips, sliding up and down his length. She opened her eyes and watched as his lips parted, listened to his sigh of pleasure. His hooded eyes were darker now, even more intense. She felt his hands on her skin and then his breath as he lifted his head and took one breast into his mouth.

Brighde moaned as waves of pleasure consumed her and her body came to life.

His hands were on her bottom and she could feel each individual finger against her skin. He wasn't controlling the pace though; his hands were just following her movements, following her rhythm and pace. She was setting the tone. She was in control.

She sat up and felt her nipple peak as the cool air replaced his warm mouth. She wanted to watch him as they made love. She wanted a chance to commit it all to memory.

She reached behind her back and down between his thighs. Her fingers searching. She cupped his balls in her hand; they were hard and tight and cool in her grasp. She rolled them in her hand before circling his shaft with her fingers, following its movement to feel it disappear inside her. Deep inside her.

Her knees were shaking but the muscles in her buttocks and between her thighs were tight. She was panting quickly now, her breath coming in short, shallow gasps almost as if she were forgetting to breathe. She didn't have enough muscle control spare to focus on breathing.

She couldn't wait much longer. She could feel the waves of an orgasm threatening to break over her.

His hands had moved to her hips now, keeping her in place. Not that she had any plans to go anywhere. Maybe he was just holding her up.

She could barely keep her eyes open. Every cell in her body was focused on pleasure and there was nothing left for the basics. Nothing left to spare on breathing or thinking.

Brighde let herself go, giving in to the burst of light that wanted to explode in her.

'Now,' she begged and she felt him shudder and heard herself cry out as they climaxed together.

She collapsed, exhausted, spent and fulfilled onto his chest.

He wrapped his arms around her and she felt him kiss the top of her head. She closed her eyes and breathed deeply, inhaling his scent. She'd had a few one-night stands—she considered them her only practical option as she wasn't willing to risk having a real relationship—but she couldn't say she'd ever found them terribly satisfying and she definitely couldn't ever remember one as immensely gratifying as tonight.

She wouldn't mind repeating it, but that wasn't in her rule book.

One night only. With single men. And only with men she knew she wouldn't bump into at work or in the supermarket.

But Xavier was on holiday from Scotland. Maybe she could stretch it to twice. But she was leaving tomorrow. Going back to Melbourne and back to work. She only had one night so she'd have to take her second chance tonight and surely twice in one night didn't count.

She lay with her head on his chest and her fingers splayed across his stomach and listened to the rhythm of his heartbeat under her ear. She closed her eyes and let the silence drift over her.

She woke an hour later. The hotel room curtains were open and the city lights lit up the room. Xavier's arm was draped over her shoulder and she slid out from under it, careful not to disturb him. She needed to go.

She ducked, naked, into the bathroom but when she returned to collect her clothes he was awake. He was lying on his back watching her. The covers were off and he made no attempt to hide the fact that he was ready and willing to make love again.

Brighde forgot all about getting dressed as she let him pull her back into bed.

But this time she took care not to fall asleep afterwards. She waited until he drifted off before she dressed and snuck out in the early hours of the morning.

There was no exchange of phone numbers or even last names. She didn't know anything about him and that was the way she wanted it. She would never see him again. She felt a tiny twinge of disappointment but even though he was magnificent she wasn't about to break her own rule.

She didn't do weekends. She didn't do relationships.

One night was enough.

There was no danger of falling in love in only one night.

Brighde changed into scrubs ready for another night shift. Her fifth straight. She was exhausted; the maternity wing had been really busy. That wasn't unusual; Parkville Private Hospital had the largest private maternity service in Melbourne and they were always busy, but the past few shifts had been ridiculous. The nurses were blaming the full moon; there was no scientific evidence to back up their suspicions but years of experience had taught them that a full moon seemed to trigger labour, not only in the women who had reached full term but also for those who were overdue as well as for plenty who were a week or two away from their due dates. The department was bursting at the seams and Brighde was looking forward to a few days off at the end of this shift. Only eight hours to go.

She tied the laces on her sneakers and headed for handover, hoping that tonight would be quiet.

'Brighde, you can take over from Jacqui. She's got delivery room three.' The charge nurse distributed the patients among the new staff.

'I've got Kirsty Jones,' Jacqui told her.

Brighde remembered Kirsty from prenatal appointments. 'First baby, husband is Matt, right?' she clarified.

Jacqui nodded. 'She's been in labour for about twelve hours and in active phase for a few hours now. Seven centimetres dilated, contractions four minutes apart. She probably hasn't got long to go. Do you want me to stay until she delivers?'

It was common for the midwives to extend their shifts if they thought their patients were close to delivering. It made for good continuity of care and the mums appreciated having one midwife throughout. But it wasn't always possible. Lots of babies took far longer than one shift to make their appearance.

'Is there much else happening at the moment?' Brighde asked, meaning, *Are we likely to be run off our feet?*

'No.'

'Go home, then,' she told Jacqui. 'I know Kirsty. I've got this.'

'Thanks. I've called her doctor. He's on his way. Dr Davey is on holidays and Dr O'Donnell, the new OB/GYN is covering for him.' Jacqui was already untying her ponytail, getting ready to leave, as she gave Brighde the final information.

'OK, all good.'

'Kirsty, how are you?' Brighde stepped into delivery room three and greeted Kirsty and her husband. Kirsty looked tired and Matt didn't look as if he was faring much better. 'We've had a shift change, it's my turn now but you won't have any more changes after this. I promise I'll be here when your baby is born.'

'You'd better be,' Kirsty panted. 'Your shifts are eight hours, right? If this baby isn't out by then, I'm leaving.'

Brighde smiled.

'What?' Kirsty asked.

'We hear that a lot at this stage, when you've had enough, that's when we know you're getting close.'

Kirsty grimaced as she was gripped by another contraction.

'How are you doing, Matt?' Brighde asked as she waited for Kirsty's contraction to ease. This stage was hard on the partners; she knew he'd be feeling useless.

'I'm okay but isn't there anything to do to speed this up?' he asked.

'Sorry, not at this point. She's very close. We've just got to let things take their course. Natural is best.'

Jacqui had attached a monitor to Kirsty's abdomen to record the contractions and Brighde checked the readout. The contractions were now two minutes apart, lasting for around sixty seconds and getting stronger.

'I'm just going to take a look to see how your labour is progressing,' Brighde said as she pulled a pair of gloves on.

'Eight centimetres. You're getting there,' she said. 'You're in the transition phase now. It won't be much longer.'

'We haven't even seen the doctor,' Matt said.

'He's on his way. There's nothing for him to do yet. Trust me, you don't want the doctor in early. If things are going well you don't need him until the end.'

Kirsty's labour seemed to be progressing as expected and Brighde thought they wouldn't really need the doctor at all but she also knew that at Parkville Private the patients paid for, and expected to see, the doctor.

Kirsty cried out as another contraction took over. She was getting restless. 'God, it hurts.'

'If you think you can manage to get onto all fours that might ease the pressure on your back,' Brighde told her. 'Matt, you could run a flannel under hot water and give Kirsty's back a rub.' That would hopefully distract Kirsty, ease her discomfort and give Matt something useful to do. 'You'll meet your baby soon.'

Matt had followed her suggestion and returned from the en suite bathroom with a warm flannel. Brighde let him look after Kirsty while she checked the equipment, making sure she had everything she needed for the delivery at arm's reach. As she worked she listened to Matt as he tried to reassure Kirsty. She could hear the love and affection in his voice, along with concern, and it made her wish that she had someone to share her life with. Someone who would love and support her. But she knew that would be asking a lot. She'd vowed long ago that she wouldn't put someone through what she'd been through. She'd made a pact with herself that she would stay single. She wanted to be loved but she wouldn't risk it.

Thinking about being in love led her to thinking about her brother. After all the pledges they'd made, the promise not to get tested, Nick had fallen in love with Imogen and everything had changed. The pact she and Nick had made years before, agreeing not to have genetic testing, had ended when Nick had fallen in love. He wanted to start a family and he needed answers. Brighde couldn't blame him for that. But now she knew her decision to stay single and free was justified. She had watched her mother's life disintegrate and she'd vowed not to put herself or loved ones in that same position. Which meant not allowing herself to fall in love. That was the only way to avoid the heartache. To avoid the risk. She had to stick to her plan. As much as she'd like to share her life with someone, she couldn't commit to anything more than one night.

The last night she'd spent with someone had been with Xavier. She wondered how he was. Whether he was back in Scotland. Whether he ever thought about her. She couldn't deny she'd been thinking about him. A lot. In the maternity suites she'd found herself comparing all the partners to Xavier. Wondering what he would be like in the same situation. Would he be the bossy, know-it-all expectant father who'd read all the books? Or would he be the kind, gentle, supportive partner who was only concerned about his wife. Not that it mattered. Her silent imaginings were a waste of time. Xavier was gone.

She had to stick to her plan and even if she wanted to change her mind Xavier wasn't around. That boat had sailed. That was why she'd let her hormones carry her away that night. Because she'd known she'd never see him again. But she hadn't been able to get him out of her head, despite the fact that the night she'd spent with him was now almost eight weeks ago. She really needed to get him out of her system.

She'd expected the sex to be good—the sparks she'd felt between them had been too huge to ignore—but she hadn't expected it to be the best sex of her life. But that didn't mean she couldn't have better. Xavier might have become her new benchmark but that didn't mean someone else out there couldn't match up or even improve on him.

Maybe that was the answer. Maybe she just needed to have sex with someone else. She needed to erase the memory of him. Something about Xavier had got under her skin but she couldn't afford to get fixated on someone she'd never see again. That had been the whole point. Anonymous sex was the only way to go. She didn't get involved. She didn't do relationships and she really didn't have time to spend thinking about him. She needed to get this baby delivered, and however many others decided to be born tonight, and then she'd go home, get a good eight hours sleep and tomorrow she'd start to wipe all traces of Xavier from her mind. She'd go back to the old, independent Brighde. She didn't need a man; she was fine.

She didn't *want* a man she told herself as she prepared to check Kirsty's progress again.

She was now nine centimetres dilated and Brighde could see the baby's head. She wondered how far away the doctor was. If he wasn't already here he was likely to miss the delivery altogether.

'Almost there, Kirsty. You're doing really well. Not long now.' She stood and pulled off her gloves. 'I'll fetch the doctor.'

Brighde stepped out of the delivery room and was surprised to find Sarah just outside the door. She was working a late shift too but she was working in the nursery. Maybe she was collecting a baby. But she grabbed Brighde's arm.

'Good, I'm glad I found you.'

'What's the matter?'

'There's something I need to tell you,' her friend said as she dragged her towards the nurses' station.

'What is it?' Brighde had no idea what could be so urgent. 'I'm in the middle of a delivery.'

'I know,' Sarah said, 'but this is important. Dr O'Donnell—the doctor covering for Dr Davey—you're looking for him, aren't you?'

Brighde nodded.

'That's him.' Sarah tilted her head to her left a few times in quick succession, nodding towards the nurses' station.

Brighde frowned. 'Who is?'

'Dr O'Donnell. It's him. From the conference.'

Brighde saw the back of a head. Her eyes took in the thick, dark, slightly curly hair. The tall, broad, masculine shoulders. Her stomach flipped as recognition slapped her. He wasn't someone she knew from staff but he wasn't a complete stranger either.

He turned, maybe a sixth sense alerting him to the fact he was being scrutinised, and their eyes locked.

Brighde took a deep breath and held it. The man she'd shared the best sex of her life with was standing six feet away.

CHAPTER THREE

'OH, MY GOD.'

He wasn't supposed to be here.

Brighde turned to Sarah, dragging her eyes away from Xavier's perfect face. Her heart was racing. 'What the hell is *he* doing here?'

Sarah shrugged. 'He's the new OB/GYN.'

'Seriously?'

'Yep.'

She swore under her breath.

Be cool, Brighde, she told herself. *No one needs to know anything.*

But she had to fight the urge to turn on her heel and run out of the door.

She looked back at him. He didn't look nearly as surprised as she felt. Maybe he was just better at hiding his feelings. He nodded in her direction, a half-nod, and smiled and Brighde's heart did a little flip. How the hell was she supposed to handle this? She was always so careful to ensure that she didn't mix her private and professional lives, yet here was the man who had quite literally swept her off her feet, had seen every naked inch of her and given her the time of her life, standing in front of her expecting to work together. She'd never, ever been in this situation before.

Her flight and fight responses were having their own private battle inside her. She was very tempted to go with flight but she knew that wasn't going to give her the answers she wanted or make the problem go away. If he was, as Sarah had said, the new OB/GYN, she had to assume he was here to stay.

Maybe she could just ignore him, she thought as she half turned away, giving herself a moment to try to get her reactions under control. But she knew that was impossible. He was the doctor she was looking for. He was the one she needed to deliver Kirsty's baby. They'd be working together, which meant she wasn't going to be able to ignore him.

And now he was beside her. She knew he was. She could feel him. Ignoring him was definitely not going to be an option. Thankfully, Sarah still stood to her left, giving her moral support. She needed it.

Sarah had heard Brighde's recount of the night spent in Xavier's bed many times over the past eight weeks but Brighde had never expected the two of them to meet. She felt her cheeks redden as she thought about the intimate details she'd shared with her best friend.

'Hello, Brighde. I didn't expect to see you here.'

His deep voice washed over her and she fought the impulse to close her eyes and give in. His tone was seductive. She knew he probably didn't mean it to be but that was the effect it had on her. She glanced at Sarah, wondering if Xavier affected her the same way, but she seemed completely relaxed whereas Brighde felt as if someone had tied her up in knots while she wasn't paying attention.

Was he pleased or disappointed to see her?

She shouldn't care.

But she did.

And she couldn't ignore him. Not while he stood beside her. She turned towards him, lifted her head and willed herself to keep it together as she looked into the depths of his dark eyes.

And there it was. The same seductive come-to-bed expression that had drawn her to him the first time. Different circumstances, same reaction. She was in trouble.

Her eyes drifted lower, away from his carnal gaze, as she fought temptation. She couldn't afford to go to pieces here. She had a job to do.

He was wearing scrubs. Shapeless blue hospital scrubs that did nothing to disguise the width of his shoulders, the length of his legs and the flatness of his stomach. She could still remember how every ridge and groove of his abdominals felt under her hand. She closed her eyes briefly and when she opened them she was looking at his hand. He had his fingers wrapped around a coffee mug. She could remember when those fingers had been cupped around the cheek of her arse.

Her breath caught in her throat.

She couldn't breathe. She needed to breathe.

She looked at Sarah in desperation.

Sarah stuck out her hand. 'Hi, I'm Sarah, one of the midwives. I don't think we were ever properly introduced.'

'Nice to see you again,' Xavier replied as he took her hand.

He was all charm. He even remembered Sarah.

'Brighde is looking after your patient,' Sarah said, obviously figuring she'd given Brighde enough time to gather her wits. 'She'll take you to the delivery room.'

'Lead the way.' He was looking at her again. She was caught, spellbound, by his gaze. *Come on, get yourself together.*

Sarah gave her a gentle push, making Brighde's feet move. She doubted she would have been able to put one foot in front of the other otherwise.

Okay. Focus, Brighde. Just do your job and worry about Dr O'Donnell and his bedroom eyes later. That's the way. Think of him as Dr O'Donnell and not Xavier. Separate him into two parts, professional and private, and just remember to keep them separate. Pretend you've never met him. He's nothing to you. And, whatever you do, don't start a personal conversation.

But she was aware of his body heat as they walked side by side down the corridor. His scent. She even imagined she could hear him breathing. And she had the feeling once again that her cells were straining towards him. She concentrated hard to make sure she kept walking in a straight line. She could feel herself veering towards him. She needed to stay on track.

She breathed deeply as she put her hand on the door to the delivery room.

Focus, Brighde.

'Our mum-to-be is Kirsty, twenty-nine years old and forty-one weeks' gestation with her first baby, so a little overdue. No complications with the pregnancy. She's been in labour for about twelve hours but just reached nine centimetres. Kirsty is tired but the baby is fine, although it's quite large. Around four kilograms. Her husband is Matt.'

Xavier pushed open the door and strode into the room, full of confidence. No one would ever imagine he was new to the hospital. He looked as if he'd been here for ever. He looked completely comfortable. *She* was the one who was unsettled.

Xavier introduced himself to Kirsty and Matt while he washed his hands. He pulled on a pair of gloves while Brighde fastened a gown over his scrubs and resisted the temptation to run her hands down his back. She stepped away as soon as she was done; the further away she could stay the better.

'Let's see what's going on, shall we?' Xavier said as he crossed to the bed.

Kirsty was still kneeling on the bed with Matt supporting her as she rocked. Brighde expected Xavier to reposition Kirsty. She expected him to ask her to lie down, as that would make it easier for him to see what was going on, but she was pleasantly surprised when he pushed a small wheeled stool over to the bed with his foot and sat behind Kirsty.

'Good news,' he said as he finished his examination. 'You're fully dilated and I can see the baby's head. Everything's good. Are you comfortable in that position?' He was calm, relaxed, friendly, engaging. He was perfect.

'No,' Kirsty half laughed as another contraction gripped her.

'Sorry, bad choice of words,' Xavier admitted. 'What I meant was, would you like to stay in this position or did you want to try something else? From my experience this is often the most comfortable position to give birth but it's up to you.'

'I don't think I can move,' Kirsty said.

'All right, stay just like you are. Are you okay, Matt?'

Matt would need to support Kirsty in that position. Kirsty was leaning on his shoulders and he had his arms wrapped around her waist. It was an awkward position for both Matt and Xavier but Xavier didn't seem fazed by it. Brighde didn't know many obstetricians who would happily make their own job more uncomfortable. Most still went for the standard, 'lie on your back, bend your knees and push'.

Brighde had to force herself to focus on the task at hand. She couldn't afford to be distracted by Xavier although it was hard when all she could see was the width of his shoulders, the dark curls on the back of his head and his long fingers as they rested on the bed. His voice alone was enough to distract her without the additional fact that he was sitting mere inches from her. Her fingers itched to reach out and slide through his hair. She stepped away to check that she had a warm blanket ready for the baby. Knowing she did but needing an activity to keep her hands busy.

But she kept one eye on him.

'Your baby is doing fine,' he said as he checked the foetal heart rate monitor before checking Kirsty again. 'When you feel the next contraction I want you to push. It's time to meet your baby.'

Brighde took up her place at Xavier's side, ready for the delivery.

'Okay, here we go. Push!' Xavier instructed. 'Stop

now, breathe. Okay, nearly there, you're doing great, Kirsty. All right, you can push again.'

He delivered the baby's head before letting Kirsty rest again. The baby's shoulders would be next and Xavier had to reach and contort himself for this part due to the position he'd left Kirsty in. 'Okay, one last push. You're almost there.'

The baby slid out into Xavier's waiting hands. 'Congratulations. A healthy boy.'

Kirsty collapsed back onto her haunches and Brighde helped her to lie down. Xavier handed the baby to his mum, laying him on her chest.

The next few minutes were busy but Brighde knew Kirsty and Matt would barely notice as Xavier gave the required injections and Brighde did the Apgar scores. They worked smoothly together and as Xavier got ready to deliver the placenta Brighde took the baby to be weighed, measured and attach the identification bands.

She loved this part of her job. She took any chance she could to hold and cuddle the babies, getting her fix, as she didn't plan to have children of her own.

'He's absolutely perfect,' Brighde said as she handed him back to Kirsty. 'I'll give you some time together,' she said once the new parents looked settled, 'and I'll be back in a little while to help you shower.'

She would attend to the rest of Kirsty's care later. For now, they just needed some time alone to get acquainted with their new arrival.

Xavier followed her out of the room, untying his apron as he walked. They threw their dirty aprons and gloves into the rubbish and stood, side by side, at the sinks to wash their hands.

Brighde's skin tingled with his proximity. She still couldn't quite believe he was here. One part of her wanted to tear off his scrubs, another wanted to scream at him and a third part of her wanted to burst into tears. She had no idea why she felt like crying. She'd been highly emotional lately but she'd been blaming the fact that her brother had found love along with her own inability to stop thinking about Xavier and now he was here, standing beside her, smiling at her, and she had no idea what she was supposed to do.

He wasn't supposed to be here and he *definitely* shouldn't be smiling at her, turning her insides to mush and her legs to jelly.

His pull on her was magnetic. It felt as if all her cells were straining towards him, giving the impression that, if it were possible, they'd leap out of her body and into his. It felt as if he could absorb her, as if she could disappear into him and all that would be left of her would be her empty skin pooled on the floor at his feet. All traces of her gone.

She'd never felt anything like this before.

All her one-night stands had been just that. One night. She'd never seen any of them again and she'd never had to think about how she would feel if she found herself in this exact situation. She certainly hadn't expected to feel such a strong attraction and her reaction frustrated her.

'What the hell are you doing here?' Her voice was quiet but her tone was anything but friendly. She was irritated with herself and annoyed with him. She didn't want to cause a scene but she had to have some answers, otherwise she knew she would go crazy. 'Why aren't you back in Scotland?'

'Because I live here now.'

What? She *never* would have slept with him if she'd known he was going to turn up on her doorstep.

'You live here?'

'Yes.'

'What about Scotland?'

'I said I'd been working in Scotland; I didn't actually say I was going back.'

Her brow creased and he knew she was trying to recall the scant conversation they'd had. They hadn't spent much time talking. She probably knew as little about him as he did about her. Although he could recall every curve of her body, the softness of her skin and the touch of her hand, he didn't know much beyond that. He hadn't needed to at the time. He hadn't even known she was a midwife. He'd assumed she worked in the health profession because she was at the conference but he hadn't given any thought to what she did for a living. He hadn't been interested in that.

But now he praised his good fortune in accepting this job at Parkville Private. Working with Brighde could turn out to be a pleasant surprise, although her tone suggested she wasn't quite as excited about the idea as he was.

'But you're not supposed to be *here*!' she said, confirming his suspicions that she wasn't especially pleased to see him. '*Why* are you here?'

'Have dinner with me and I'll tell you.'

'No, thank you.'

'No?' He wasn't sure that he'd heard right. She was turning down his invitation. 'Really?' He couldn't remember the last time he was knocked back.

'Haven't you ever had anyone say no to you before?' she asked, but she was still frowning as if this was all very serious rather than the pleasant coincidence he saw it to be.

'Not often,' he admitted. And never straight after he'd spent the night with someone. 'So, what's your objection to dinner?'

'I didn't expect to see you again.'

'Nor I you, but that's no reason not to share a meal.'

'And I never would have slept with you if I'd known we'd be working together.'

'It's just dinner, Brighde. You can show me around Melbourne.'

'I don't think so.'

'Why not? Are you seeing someone?' That was a possibility he hadn't thought of until now but it was quite likely. The conference and the one night they'd shared was now months ago. Maybe she wasn't single any more. That wouldn't surprise him but it would definitely be a shame.

'No.' She shook her head and the golden curls that had come loose from her ponytail bobbed around her shoulders.

'Well, in that case, how can I convince you to change your mind?' He wasn't one to give up easily. And, besides, sex with Brighde had been incredible and he was more than willing to get to know her better and see if she could be persuaded to give it another go.

'You can't.'

'There's nothing I can do?'

She shook her head again. 'It's not you. It's me.'

Xavier almost laughed until he realised she wasn't kidding. 'Seriously? That old chestnut.' What could he have done to offend her so terribly that she wouldn't share a meal with him?

'I mean it. I don't date and I don't do dinner.'

'Ever?'

'Never.'

He'd never heard anything so ridiculous. Who didn't date? Even his disastrous last relationship hadn't put him off the idea of dating. If you didn't date you were destined to spend your life alone and who wanted to do that? Not him. 'Why is that?'

'I'm happy on my own.'

'That's a very male attitude. Don't all women want a partner?'

'You don't know much about women, do you?' she countered.

'I actually thought I knew women pretty well. I have four sisters and I work as an OB/GYN. I work with women every day.' Hormonal ones too, but he thought better of mentioning that.

'Maybe so but there are always exceptions. You can't put us all in the one basket.'

So it would seem.

'I don't need a man to complete me,' she continued. 'I might need him for sex but there is more than one way to skin a cat.'

'You're very direct.' Her directness was appealing. Another tick in the box. After playing guessing games with his ex, Brighde's honesty was refreshing. But it wasn't getting him what he wanted.

'I don't see the point in playing games. Life is short; I intend to live my life by my rules. So, why didn't you go back to Scotland?'

She looked as if she'd have him on a plane right then and there if it was up to her.

'I'm Melbourne born and bred. I've come home.'

'So you don't need me to show you around Melbourne, then.'

'No.' He laughed, trying to ease the tension he could feel emanating from her. She was wound up tight. 'Guilty as charged. But I warn you, I will try again. I'd like to have dinner with you. Just dinner; we won't call it a date. No expectations, no strings.' He wasn't looking for a serious relationship but Brighde wasn't even looking at him any more.

'I need to get back to Kirsty,' she said as she dried her hands. And then she was gone. Leaving him alone and completely confused. And naturally intrigued. She'd thrown him a challenge by knocking him back and he wasn't about to retreat.

Anyone listening to her would think she was mad. *He* probably thought she was mad. But she'd prefer to risk being considered crazy than to risk falling in love. That was not on her agenda. She needed to get away. Far away. From his easy charm and his come-to-bed eyes and his to-die-for body before she made any more mistakes. She could totally understand why he wasn't often rejected. He was completely gorgeous and the sex had been fantastic but he wasn't for her. She couldn't afford to relax her rules. She didn't do second dates or dinner or whatever he wanted to call it. She couldn't accept his invitation, no matter how much she was tempted.

So she walked away, even though it was hard to do, and returned to Kirsty and her baby. She had a new mum to care for. A job to do. There was no time to think about what-ifs and to wish things were different.

She helped Kirsty to breastfeed her baby, then shower and dress. She settled her into her room and left Kirsty and Matt alone with their baby. She was due for a tea break but she didn't want to risk having it in the staff kitchen and bumping into Xavier so she escaped to the nursery, looking for Sarah. She needed to debrief.

Brighde offered to take over from the other nurse on duty so she could take a tea break which allowed her to talk to Sarah without interruption. The nursery was quiet. It was three o'clock in the morning and most of the babies were with their mothers. Sarah was feeding a premmie baby and there was another who needed changing. Brighde picked her up, changing her nappy before holding her for a while. She loved the weight of a newborn baby in her arms. Loved the new baby smell. She would love one of her own if things were different.

'Are you going to tell me how it went?' Sarah asked as she settled her charge.

'Fine,' Brighde replied. 'Good, even.' Xavier was a good doctor but Brighde hadn't been able to think straight. She needed a plan. A way of knowing she was going to be able to hold herself together and do her job. She couldn't afford to be distracted.

'And?' Sarah queried. 'You obviously have something on your mind. Spit it out.'

'He asked me out.'

'And you said yes?'

'I don't do second dates. You know that.'

'Technically, it's not a second date. You never really had a first one and a good bonking is not the same thing as a candlelit dinner. And I've never seen you so obsessed.'

'I'm not obsessed,' Brighde objected.

'Fascinated then.'

'Well, there's a lot to be fascinated about,' she admitted.

'There's no harm in going on a date with him. Especially as you can call this a first date.'

'I don't need anyone else in my life. I have you and Nick and now Imogen.'

'Would it be so terrible to have one more?'

'You know I can't afford to let other people close.'

Brighde would love to fall in love but that was a risk she couldn't afford to take. She was worried she wouldn't be able to resist Xavier. She was worried that he'd only have to look at her with those eyes and she'd melt into a pool of desire and do whatever he asked of her. She got all hot and bothered just *thinking* about him.

'Well, say no then. It's as simple as that. You have two choices. Yes or no.'

'It's hard to say no to the best sex of my life.'

'In that case—' Sarah sighed '— maybe you should have another go. Perhaps you're putting him on a pedestal. Perhaps it will be easier to let go if you find out he wasn't so fantastic after all.'

Brighde didn't think that would be the conclusion she'd come to. She couldn't possibly sleep with him again. That would be risking too much. The way her body reacted to him, she knew the fire would burn just as brightly the next time. The heat would be just as intense and she couldn't afford to let her guard down. Something about Xavier made her feel that it would be all too easy to lose control. There was something insanely attractive about him. She *had* to resist. It would be too dangerous not to.

'I can't,' she said. Not sure who she was trying to convince.

She had thought that perhaps more sex was the way to put him out of her mind but she didn't think that more sex with Xavier was the answer.

But it was an answer.

CHAPTER FOUR

BRIGHDE HAD MANAGED to avoid Xavier for the best part of a week but her luck ran out on Wednesday night, when she last expected to see him. She knew he had Wednesday afternoons off—she'd checked—so she was surprised to quite literally bump into him in the hospital corridor.

Just the sight of him set her heart racing. Her palms were sweaty and her throat dry throat as she struggled to form a coherent sentence. 'I thought it was your afternoon off.'

'There was a baby with other ideas,' he told her. 'But I'm finished now. Safely delivered. Are you on your way home too?' he asked and she saw him glance at her bag that was slung over her shoulder.

Brighde nodded.

'Can I walk you to your car?'

'I'm catching a bus.'

'At this time of night?'

'I do it all the time. I only have to get to North Carlton.'

'Let me give you a lift,' he offered as they headed out of the hospital. 'My car is in the doctors' car park.'

That was closer than the bus. Brighde didn't think

it would count if she let him drop her home. She didn't have to ask him in. And she would be home much faster. She could think of a dozen good reasons to accept his offer. So she did. 'Thanks, that would be great.'

She sank gratefully into the leather seat. The car smelt new but in the close confines she could also smell Xavier. She remembered his scent. Part shampoo with traces of pear and honey and part man.

Her stomach growled as he turned the car into Lygon Street. 'Do you want to grab something to eat? Not dinner,' he clarified with a quick glance at her, 'just a snack.' She could see him smiling. In profile the corner of his delicious mouth turned up; he obviously thought he was going to win this round.

But she *was* starving. Surely there was no harm in grabbing a quick bite to eat in a public place? No risk.

'Okay.'

'Really?'

She nodded, pleased that she had surprised him. 'I'm starving,' she admitted, just in case he thought it was his company she couldn't resist.

'Italian?' he asked as he pulled to the kerb.

It was close to midnight and there weren't a lot of restaurants still open but Italian sounded good. They ordered bowls of pasta accompanied by a glass of wine. The pasta smelt fantastic but the wine left a metallic taste in Brighde's mouth. She pushed it to one side and concentrated on her pasta.

They chatted about work and which football teams they supported. Nice, neutral, typically Melbourne conversation and Brighde wondered if this was how normal people felt. Was this what it felt like when you actually wanted to get to know someone? Was this what a proper date felt like? Was this how people behaved when they hoped it might lead to something more? She'd never been out with anyone she'd slept with before. Things always ended after that. She'd never let herself have a second date.

She waited until Xavier was halfway through his dish before asking, 'So is now the time you tell me why you came back to Australia?'

'Was that part of the deal?'

Brighde nodded. 'I think it was.'

'There were lots of reasons. I'd been away for four years and my parents aren't getting any younger. I wanted to spend some time with them.'

'Are you close to your family?'

'I am but it's kind of hard not to be. I'm the middle of five siblings, two older sisters, two younger sisters. It's impossible not to get caught up in all the craziness.'

'Wow! Five!'

'And eight nieces and nephews.'

Hearing that made Brighde wistful. Her family had been torn apart, and then depleted, due to disease. Her father had left when she was only nine. Unable to cope with her mother's illness, he had abandoned his family and Brighde had never come to terms with that. How could someone walk out on the people that supposedly meant the world to them? People they loved? She would never put her faith in love. Happily ever after endings were for other people. Other families.

Her mum had succumbed to the disease and for the past five years it had just been Brighde and her brother. That was all that remained of the Campbells now and she wouldn't be adding to the family tree, although she was looking forward to Nick and Imogen having a family. It was nice to think their family would still grow even if it wasn't going to be her doing.

'Do you want kids?' she asked.

'Definitely.'

He sounded so certain and Brighde knew then that she had to cross him off her list. Her silly fantasies about what might be had to stop. She should get up and walk out right now. There was absolutely no point in getting to know him—their paths were headed in completely different directions—but she couldn't make herself leave. Not yet. She could share a meal with him tonight and tomorrow she'd start again.

'What about you?' Now it was Xavier's turn to ask the questions.

'I'm in no hurry,' she said, using her usual excuse. 'I get my fill at work.' She couldn't answer honestly. She couldn't bring herself to tell him 'no'. She knew that would just open her up to a whole lot of questions that she didn't want to answer.

The waitress cleared their plates and Xavier ordered dessert. One serve of tiramisu with two spoons. Brighde didn't think she could fit another thing in but when it arrived it looked so good she couldn't resist. She wondered what was happening to her willpower. She'd have to watch herself around Xavier.

'So, how come you haven't found the mother of your children yet?' She steered the conversation back to him. 'You didn't fall in love in Scotland?'

A dark expression flashed across his face. It could have been sorrow or pain but it was gone so quickly she wondered if she'd imagined it and she certainly didn't have time to interpret it. Maybe he was just tired or didn't like being questioned. Maybe he really wasn't the talkative type. They certainly hadn't talked much on first meeting.

'No. Scottish girls are not my type.'

'So you've come home to settle down?'

'No. It was always my plan to come back at some stage. Now seemed like a good time but my focus at the moment is work. I'm in no hurry to start a family. I'm going to focus on my work. Build up my practice, get established back here. I don't have time for other distractions.'

Brighde relaxed. It didn't sound as if he was looking for anything more than she could offer at the moment. Maybe they could share one more night without any expectations.

'None?' she teased.

'Well, maybe a couple of distractions would be okay.' The corners of his mouth lifted into a smile. His gorgeous lips were closed; it was only a half-smile but she knew exactly what he was thinking. She could see it in his eyes. They were dark and languid. Just begging her to take him to bed.

Was she prepared to break her own rule? Just this once?

She knew it would be dangerous but she was sorely tempted.

He stood and pulled some cash from his wallet and tucked it under his wineglass before holding her chair for her. He held out his hand to help her up and kept hold of her hand as they left the restaurant. It felt nice, almost as if they were on a real date.

Her house was only a couple of blocks away. They didn't talk as he drove her home. Brighde couldn't think of anything sensible to say. All she could think of was what she should do when they got home. She knew if she invited him in he would accept. It was a big risk but one worth taking. She wanted one more chance. She wanted one more opportunity to commit everything about him to memory.

'It's that house there,' she told him as they drove past a single level terrace house. 'You can drop me out the front if you like,' she offered. Maybe that was one way to resist temptation. The only way.

But Xavier was going to be a complete gentleman. 'No, it's late and it's dark. I'll just find a gap and walk you to your door.'

Sarah was working a night shift and the house was in darkness but Brighde knew the porch light would come on as soon as she opened the front gate.

Xavier parked the car several houses away—parking spaces were hard to find—and followed her through the gate and up the front path. The outside light clicked on and Brighde slid her key into the front door and turned to thank him for the lift.

He was standing centimetres from her. His eyes were dark and serious and she knew exactly what he was thinking.

'Don't look at me like that,' she said.

'Like what?' He grinned and his eyes lightened. 'Like I want to peel off all your clothes and make love to you again?'

Brighde nodded. She was lost for words. That was exactly the look in his come-to-bed eyes.

She couldn't think when he was looking at her like that.

'But that's exactly what I want to do,' he said. 'Are you going to invite me in?'

Brighde's eyes were fastened on his mouth, reading his words as they fell from his lips.

She started to speak, intending to be strong, intending to tell him 'no', but Xavier bent his head and claimed her lips with his, silencing her words and dissolving all her objections.

She lifted her hands, intending to put them on his chest, intending to push him away, but instead she found her arms winding around his neck, holding him closer.

She thought about telling him to stop but as his tongue parted her lips her final resistance crumbled.

She wanted this. She wanted one more night.

Was that really so bad?

His hands were under her buttocks and he scooped her up. She wrapped her legs around his hips as he pushed the unlocked door open with his foot and carried her inside.

'First door on the left,' she managed to tell him.

He didn't let her go until they were in her room. He lowered her to the bed but by now her fingers were tearing at the buttons on his shirt. She pulled his shirt from his trousers before unbuckling his belt and unzipping him. Now that she'd made her decision she wasn't about to change her mind.

Xavier pushed his trousers from his hips, exploding from the confines of his clothing, as he stepped out of his shoes.

The only light in the room came through the curtains from the porch but that was enough to illuminate him in all his glory.

He bent over and slid his hands under her skirt. His fingers were warm and firm as he slipped them beneath the elastic of her underwear and pulled them off. Next his fingers slid the zips down on her boots and he removed them and tossed them to one side as she reached for him.

Her fingers wrapped around his erection. His shaft was thick and hard and he moaned and moved closer.

Brighde was on the edge of her bed, still almost fully clothed but she didn't care. There was no time to get undressed; she was in too much of a hurry.

Xavier knelt on the floor and parted her legs. His fingers slid inside her. She was warm and wet and ready.

She inhaled and let her knees fall further apart. Then his fingers were gone and she was about to beg him not to stop when she saw he was reaching for his trousers. He pulled his wallet out, searching for protection. He rolled the sheath on and she lifted her hips and wrapped her legs behind him as he thrust into her, filling her.

His arms were under her shoulders, controlling her movements, holding them together. Brighde threw her head back but fought to keep her eyes open as waves of pleasure rolled through her. She wanted to watch him. His eyes were fixed on her, taking it all in as he took her.

They were keeping time to the same orchestra, their bodies perfectly in tune. Xavier rolled his thumb over her swollen sweet spot and Brighde thought she was going to burst into a thousand tiny pieces.

'Oh, God, Xavier.'

She heard him hold his breath, felt him start to come and she cried out as he knelt between her thighs and brought them both to a climax.

Xavier collapsed on the bed beside her and wrapped her in his arms.

'Can you stay?' she asked, hating the fact that she was asking but she really didn't want him to leave. She wanted him to stay the night. She wanted to get completely naked and make love again, one final time. She wasn't ready for it to end just yet.

He nodded and kissed her.

She sat up and unzipped her skirt, sliding it from her body. She lifted her arms and Xavier pulled her shirt over her head. He undid her bra with one flick of his fingers and bent his head to her breast. Brighde lay back as Xavier's tongue circled her nipple. Their initial frenzied desire had been sated; she knew that she would have a chance to take it slow this time, to savour every second and commit it all to memory.

She'd broken all her rules for him in just one night. She never spent a second night with a man. She never invited them to her house and she definitely had never slept with someone she worked with. But she was finding him difficult to resist. She'd have to come up with a new plan but that could wait until tomorrow. For tonight she was staying right where she was. She fell asleep in his arms, her head on his chest, lulled to sleep by the rise and fall of his chest and the sound of his breaths.

'Good morning.'

Brighde woke to the sound of his voice. He brushed a strand of hair from her cheek as he leant down to kiss her. He was already out of bed and dressed. 'I need to get home and shower for work,' he said. 'What are your plans for the day?'

Brighde took a moment to remember what day it was. 'I'm having brunch with my brother and his fiancée and then I'm on another afternoon shift.'

'Shall I come and pick you up after work? I could give you a lift home again.'

It was clear he wanted to continue on from last night. Brighde liked the sound of that. She was flattered but she knew she shouldn't accept. She couldn't start something with Xavier. They shouldn't have even had last night.

'I'd like that,' she said, meaning to add *'but I can't'* but the words never made it out.

Xavier grinned and kissed her again. 'I'll see you later then,' he said.

She rolled over in bed and watched him leave. She wondered what it would be like to be like normal people and make real plans for the day or the week or next weekend. She knew she needed to be careful; Xavier was testing the limits of her willpower. She knew she would never make plans for the rest of her life but waking up with someone and knowing she would see him again felt nice.

Was this how it had started for Nick and Imogen? Had Nick's plans crumbled in the face of his feelings for Immy? She'd love to ask him but she didn't want that to lead to questions about what was going on in her life.

Nick and Imogen were waiting for her at the café.

'Are you feeling okay?' Imogen asked her as she gave her a hug.

Brighde knew she looked pale and washed out. Hardly the glow of someone who'd spent a passionate night in bed with the sexiest man alive. She had dark circles under her eyes and really needed to spend more than two minutes on her make-up but she'd run out of time and hadn't wanted to keep Nick and Immy waiting.

'I didn't get a lot of sleep last night.' She knew they'd assume it was because of work and she was happy to let them think that. She wasn't prepared to talk about Xavier. Talking about a man would be completely out of character for her and would only invite questions she wasn't prepared to even think about, let alone answer.

'We've got some good news,' Nick told her as the waitress took their order. This was a regular meeting spot for them and Brighde always ordered the same breakfast. Eggs Benedict with Hollandaise sauce.

'You've picked a date for the wedding?' Brighde guessed.

'No, that's next on our to-do list.' Nick held Imogen's hand. A gesture that looked so tender and sweet that Brighde felt a pang of longing. 'We're having a baby.'

'It's a bit sooner than we planned but we're really excited,' Imogen said.

'A baby! Wow.' Brighde sat back in her seat as she digested the news. 'I'm going to be an auntie.'

She smiled. It was good news. Happy news. Nick's negative test results meant that he and Imogen could start a family without any concerns about passing on the mutated gene. Brighde would love to have a family of her own and while she knew that was a possibility with the assistance of genetic testing she wasn't going to risk putting her own children through what she and Nick had gone through with their mother. Watching their mother deteriorate and eventually die at a young age had been horrific and it was something Brighde had no intention of repeating. But Nick and Imogen didn't need to worry about that. That worry was Brighde's alone now.

Brighde didn't want to think about how alike she and her mother were. Nick and Brighde had the same colouring—they were both blonde and with the same blue-grey eyes—but Nick was tall and lean and his face was longer than hers, not as square, although he still had a very defined jawline. They were similar enough that people recognised them as siblings but Brighde was the spitting image of her mother while Nick had more of their father in him. Because of the similarities in appearance between her and her mother she had always assumed they'd be alike in other ways too. Right down to the faulty DNA.

But Brighde didn't want to think about her mother today. It always made her sad and today she wanted to be happy for Nick. 'Congratulations. I'm really happy for you.' She stood up to hug them both again, determined not to let her dark thoughts ruin their excitement.

'We thought it might take longer to happen, so as soon as we got my test results we started trying.'

'How many weeks are you?' she asked Imogen.

'Only eight, but we couldn't wait to tell someone. We knew you'd understand.'

She did understand the excitement and she was happy for them but it didn't stop her from wishing things were different for her. She'd have to be content with being an auntie—that was almost as good as having a family of her own.

'We'll have to move the wedding forward now,' Nick was saying. 'I'd like to be married before the baby comes. Make an honest woman of you.'

He was looking at his fiancée with such adoration that it made Brighde's heart ache.

'That shouldn't be hard,' Imogen replied. 'There's only a few people we really want to be there with us. You,' she said, looking at Brighde, 'my parents and my sister.'

'What about Dad?' Brighde asked. She knew that Nick had some contact with their father. She had severed all ties with him when he'd walked out on them and their mother but, as an adult, Nick had reconnected with him and they caught up occasionally.

'That's up to you,' he said. 'If having him there would make you uncomfortable then we won't invite him. It's more important to me—to us—' he smiled and picked up Imogen's hand '—that you'll be there. We'd like you to be our witness.'

Brighde smiled. 'I'd be honoured.'

'Thank you,' Imogen said as she stood up. 'I'll be back in a minute.'

'I really am happy for you, Nick. The two of you are going to have a beautiful life.'

'You might be able to have the same. Have you thought any more about getting tested?'

Brighde shook her head. 'Nothing has changed for me. I didn't want to get tested before and I definitely don't want to get tested now. I don't want to know and part of me feels even more certain that it would only be bad news. I'm okay as I am.' She was more convinced than ever that she had inherited her mother's DNA and she really didn't want to know that she'd be going to an early grave. It was far better just to avoid going down the path of marriage and babies.

Imogen returned to the table carrying two glasses of champagne. 'I can't have any but I thought we could toast the baby,' she said as she handed Nick and Brighde each a glass.

'To your family,' Brighde said as she raised her glass. She put it to her lips to take a sip but the yeasty smell turned her stomach. She forced down a sip so she didn't appear rude and then put her glass on the table.

'I might just wait until I've had something to eat,' she said. Drinking on an empty stomach and on top of a limited amount of sleep seemed like a recipe for disaster.

'You sound like how I feel in the morning,' Imogen said. 'I'll be pleased when my morning sickness stops.'

'Well, I don't envy you that.'

Brighde didn't finish her champagne and even her breakfast sat heavily in her stomach as she walked home. She was feeling a little queasy. Perhaps she was coming down with a cold. She'd felt a bit flat for the past few mornings, she realised, but once she'd got to work and was busy she'd been okay.

Her symptoms were mimicking Imogen's morning sickness but Brighde knew she was only thinking that way because of all the baby talk at brunch.

She couldn't be pregnant.

But her last period had been exceptionally light.

Surely that didn't mean anything?

The idea of it made her feel queasy and her legs

were shaky. She stopped walking and rested her hand on a street bench as she waited for the queasiness to pass.

She looked up and saw she was outside a pharmacy.

There was only one way to make sure.

She went inside and bought a pregnancy test kit.

She took it home and went straight to the bathroom.

CHAPTER FIVE

'WHAT ARE YOU doing in here?'

The bathroom door opened and Sarah stepped in. Her hair was dishevelled and Brighde realised she'd just woken up after working a night shift.

Brighde hadn't realised how long she'd been sitting in the bathroom. She hadn't been able to make herself move after taking the test. Waves of nausea had swamped her and she'd vomited a couple of times. But she refused to think the vomiting was symptomatic; she was sure it was stress-related.

'Are you sick?' Sarah asked.

'Not exactly,' Brighde said as she pointed to the stick sitting on the side of the bath.

'Oh, my God.' Sarah was looking at her in shock. 'You're *pregnant*?'

Brighde nodded.

'How the hell did that happen?'

'I don't know.' She was on the Pill and she took it religiously and also practised safe sex. She'd always been afraid that one mistake would mean something like this might happen.

'Didn't you use a condom?'

'I think so.' She honestly couldn't remember. It

was weeks ago. It would have been very unlike her to be so careless but she really couldn't recall. How could she not remember? How could she be so reckless? But what did it matter now? The *how* was irrelevant. She was pregnant and what mattered now was doing something about it and there was only one option in her mind.

'Are you going to tell Xavier?'

She shook her head. 'No. He doesn't need to know. I'm not going to keep it,' she said before bursting into tears. Termination had always been her fallback position and she knew that was her only option, but she wished just for a moment that things could be different.

Sarah hugged her. 'My God, you're freezing.'

Brighde had been sitting in the bathroom for so long the cold had seeped into her bones. She was shaking now with shock and cold.

'You need to go to bed,' Sarah told her. 'There's nothing we can do about this right now. I'll bring you a cup of tea and then I'll call the hospital and cancel your shift.'

'Xavier!' Surprise was written all over Sarah's face when she opened the front door, answering his knock. 'What are you doing here?'

'I heard Brighde was sick,' he said. 'I brought her some of my mum's chicken soup.' He held up the container as evidence of his good intentions.

'That's really sweet but I don't think that's going to help.'

'What's wrong with her?' he asked. She'd been fine that morning so when he'd heard that she'd called in sick he'd figured it couldn't be much more than a gastro bug or something similar.

'She's in bed—do you want to see her?' Sarah asked as she took the soup and stepped back, letting him into the hall.

He followed Sarah to the back of the house, walking past Brighde's room. 'I'll just wash my hands,' he said. He didn't want to expose Brighde to any more germs but as he washed his hands he realised Sarah hadn't answered his question. He dried his hands and returned the towel to the hook that hung over the rubbish bin. A box for a pregnancy test kit poked up out of the bin and caught his eye. He reached for the bin and then hesitated. Was this any of his business?

He dropped his hand to his side, resisting the urge to pick up the kit.

But his heart was beating furiously in his chest and his mouth had gone dry. He needed to see the kit. He needed to see the result.

His hand shook as he picked up the empty box and exposed the little stick that lay in the bin underneath.

He could see two pink lines in the window.

Someone in this house was pregnant.

He lifted the stick from the bin and carried it out of the bathroom.

Sarah was in the kitchen, boiling the kettle. She turned when she heard him enter. 'Would you like…?' The question died on her lips when she saw what he was holding.

'Is this yours?' he asked.

Her eyes were wide with fright but she shook her head and he had his answer.

His heart was hammering in his chest. He could

feel the blood pumping in his neck, flooding his carotid artery. Sarah was biting her lip. Was she wondering what he was going to do next?

He felt dazed, sucker-punched, but he knew he had to talk to Brighde. He had to find out what was going on.

He left the kitchen, still holding the test stick, and knocked on Brighde's door. He didn't wait for permission to enter. He was going in, no matter what she said. They had things to discuss.

'Brighde?' he said as he pushed the door open. Her bedside lamp was on, bathing the room in a soft yellow light. Her blonde hair was tousled and thick. Her face pale and tearstained.

He sat on the edge of her bed and put the stick on her bedside table. He saw her eyes dart to the stick, widen and then look back at him.

'Where did you—?'

'I found it in the bathroom,' he said, cutting her off. 'You're pregnant?'

Her eyes were enormous, grey and frightened, as she nodded.

'Is it mine?'

Brighde wanted to be offended that he'd asked her that but she knew it was a legitimate question.

'Yes. There hasn't been anyone since you and I...' She drifted off, letting him fill in the blanks. Despite the impression he might have of her, she didn't jump in and out of men's beds on a regular basis. Once or twice a year for one night didn't make her promiscuous. Not in her opinion anyway, but she wasn't about to share the finer details of her love life with him.

She sat up in bed. This wasn't the place she'd envisaged having this conversation. If she was going to be brutally honest, she hadn't planned on having this conversation at all. She had thought the best thing to do was not to say anything to him and just deal with it as she thought best. She knew he would want to keep the baby and that was not her plan. The less said the better, in her opinion. But it looked as if that option had been taken away from her.

'Wow.'

He said nothing more for a moment. He just sat and stared into the distance.

Brighde waited. She had no idea what to say so thought it best to stay silent.

'This is huge,' he said eventually. 'We have to work out what we're going to do.'

'There's nothing to work out,' she told him. 'I know what I'm going to do and don't worry, I won't put any pressure on you. I don't intend to keep it.'

'*What?*'

Xavier sat back, reacting as if she'd slapped him, his gorgeous face showing his complete shock. But he shouldn't be so surprised. She'd told him she wasn't ready to have children of her own. Ironic that she'd only mentioned it last night.

'I know you said that you get your fill of babies at work,' he said, clearly remembering the conversation, 'but surely this has changed things?'

She shook her head. 'No, it hasn't.'

'I understand this is unexpected, a shock even, and it may be sooner than you would have planned but you're *pregnant*. That *must* change things?'

'No.'

'Surely you haven't come to that decision so quickly? Surely you'll consider your options?'

'To be honest, I didn't decide overnight not to go ahead with the pregnancy. I decided that a long time ago. I never intended to have children.'

'Never? You must have planned to have children of your own at some point.'

'No.'

'We're not even going to discuss this?'

'There's nothing to discuss. I'm not keeping it.' Brighde took a deep breath. 'I know you want kids but I didn't think you wanted them right now. You told me you wanted to concentrate on your work. I imagine your plan of fatherhood is vastly different to this situation too. I can't imagine you thought you'd have a baby with someone you barely know. You didn't sign up for this and I definitely didn't.'

She was counting on the fact that he wasn't any more prepared to become a parent than she was.

'I realise it's not ideal,' he said, 'and maybe I'm not the man you had in mind to be the father of your children, but can't we discuss this?'

'This isn't about you and what sort of parent you'd be. I've never even *thought* about the type of man I'd look for as a father to my kids. It was a moot point, considering I decided a long time ago that I wasn't ever having children.'

'But that's crazy! That must have been a hypothetical discussion you had with yourself? Surely this situation changes things?'

Brighde shook her head. 'No, it doesn't.'

'How can you say that? I think you should take some time, we both should, and let this sink in.'

'I'm not going to change my mind.'

'How do you know?'

'It's complicated,' she said. Although that was a lie. It wasn't complicated, in her opinion.

'I think you owe me an explanation.'

Brighde sighed. 'I know I do.' It was only fair. To him. Not to her. None of this was fair to her. She'd always tried to ensure she would *never* find herself in this position. Nothing about this was fair. And there was no easy way to start this conversation. She took a deep breath. 'Have you ever had a patient who suffers from Huntington's Disease?'

'Huntington's Chorea?'

She nodded.

'Not that I can recall.'

'Do you remember anything about the disease from your training?'

He frowned. 'A little. It's an inherited condition, right? That causes degeneration in the brain and affects movement. Which is where the term "chorea" comes from.'

'It's a genetic mutation that ultimately kills the nerve cells in the brain. It affects mood, memory and movement and results in premature death. There is no cure.' She hesitated very briefly, dreading the idea that she had to have this conversation but knowing she couldn't avoid it. 'As you said, it's an inherited condition. It runs in families and my mother had it.'

'Had?'

Brighde nodded. 'She died five years ago. She was forty-nine. The mutation is a dominant one. There's a one in two chance of children inheriting the fault and therefore developing the disease. I have one brother; he doesn't have the mutation.'

His face went pale under the dark stubble that lined his jaw. 'Are you telling me you do?'

'There's a strong possibility.'

'Don't you know? You said there's no cure but surely there's a test for it?'

'There is but I've never been tested.'

'So there's a good chance you don't have it?' Xavier's shoulders relaxed as he let out a breath she hadn't noticed him holding.

'I wouldn't say a good chance. My brother tested negative. If there's a fifty-fifty chance of inheriting the gene and he didn't get it, I reckon the odds are not in my favour.'

'But why haven't you been tested to make sure?'

'I don't want to know.'

'How does that work?' He was frowning now. 'How can you not want to know?'

Brighde, like many other people whose lives had been affected by Huntington's, had her reasons and, to her, they sounded logical, sensible and reasonable. But she had to try to explain it in a way that would make Xavier understand. She knew that was vitally important.

'Imagine if you were told today that you were going to be hit by a bus and killed in five years' time. Would you want to know? Would it change the way you live your life?'

'I think it probably would.'

'What if you were told you were going to be hit by a bus at the age of forty and that you'd survive but you wouldn't be able to walk or talk any more? That, more than likely, you'd lose your memories and you wouldn't be able to communicate. Would you want to know that your future looked like that?'

'That doesn't sound appealing.'

'Trust me, it's not. Nick and I watched our mother suffer that exact fate and it's horrible. Knowing your life is heading in that direction might make you determined to pack as much into the days you have left, but what about when your fortieth birthday gets closer? What about when it's a month, a week, a day away—how do you think you'll feel then, knowing what is about to happen? How would your family cope with that scenario? I don't want to know if my life is going to end prematurely. I watched my mother die and I don't want to know if that is my future too. I'm happier not knowing. That's why I haven't been tested.'

'I think I understand but I don't see how this means you want to terminate a pregnancy. You don't know if you have the faulty gene and you don't know if our child does either. We're talking in hypotheticals.'

'There's every chance I have the mutation. Nick and I nursed our mother until we couldn't manage. We had to put her into care and then we watched her deteriorate a little more every day until she died. I'm not going to put anyone I love through that and especially not my own child.'

'But don't you see, you don't know for certain what you're faced with?'

'But what if *I've* passed on the gene? How do you think you would feel watching your child die before you? I can only think of one thing worse than watching my mother die and that is watching my own child suffer and die. I can't do it.'

'But you might not have to. You could get tested and then make a decision.'

Xavier picked up her hand and held it. It was a surprisingly comforting gesture but it didn't change anything.

'You're not listening to me,' she said as she pulled her hand from his grasp. She couldn't think when he was touching her. 'I really don't want to know what my future holds. I don't think Nick and I could both be that lucky and I don't want to live with the knowledge of a premature death and what that looks like. I don't want to pass on this gene. I don't want to be pregnant.'

She was scared. She was terrified. She couldn't do this.

'I think we're probably both in a bit of shock. There's a lot to think about but we don't need to make decisions tonight. We have time. It's what…ten weeks since the conference?'

'Nine and a half.' Which made her eleven and a half weeks pregnant.

'Please. Don't make any hasty decisions. Can we both take some time to think about what this means and talk about it some more?'

He could talk about it all he liked but she wasn't going to change her mind. But she nodded anyway. It was easier to give in for now. It didn't mean she had to change her mind and she was going to go crazy if she had to talk about it any more tonight.

'Do you want company?' he asked.

'No.' She shook her head. 'I want to be alone.' Seeing Xavier would just remind her of the situation she was in. If he wasn't there she could pretend it was all a nightmare.

* * *

Xavier's head was spinning when he left Brighde.

She was pregnant!

He was going to be a father.

He wanted kids, had always wanted them, and he made no secret of the fact to those nearest to him. He'd grown up in a close family, doted on by his sisters and, in turn, he doted on his nieces and nephews but he wanted children of his own. He'd actually thought he'd be a father already—he'd certainly thought he was on the way with his ex until she had ripped his dreams from him. But that hadn't deterred him. To acquaintances he said he was concentrating on his career but that was what people expected a man to say. He'd always intended to have children, a family of his own, and he knew he could do both. Granted, this current situation wasn't exactly what he had in mind but that didn't mean he was prepared to give up his dream. Not again.

He wanted to be a father. He was *going* to be a father, only that wasn't Brighde's plan.

He could understand her anxiety but to him things were black and white. He dealt in facts and figures, not in suppositions. He knew emotions could influence decisions—he saw that every day in his job—but he didn't believe that emotion should be the deciding factor, not without the facts. Brighde was making decisions based on assumptions. He wasn't discounting her experiences but she wasn't being reasonable. In his experience, you gathered the facts and then you dealt with them. You didn't worry about things that hadn't happened yet.

He could acknowledge her fear but he wasn't going

to give in to it. She *had* to get tested. He couldn't let her make such a monumental decision without gathering all the facts. Ultimately, he might not stand in her way but that was a discussion for another day. A day when they had some facts to deal with.

He started his car and pulled into the traffic.

He didn't want to go. He didn't want to leave her alone. She'd said she needed space and he would respect that, but it was hard to leave.

He wanted to comfort her but he realised he probably also needed some time to clear his head. They obviously had differing opinions on this situation and if he was going to convince her to see his point of view he needed time to work out a strategy. There was a lot of information to take in, a lot to think about.

She was scared; he got that. He wanted to erase her fears but he needed information.

She was talking about terminating the pregnancy. He wanted her to keep the baby and he needed to work out how he was going to achieve that.

He needed a plan.

Brighde had three days off work and she managed to avoid any further discussion. She ignored Xavier's phone calls and only replied to his text messages very briefly, telling him she wasn't ready to talk yet. But after three days she was going stir crazy in the house, alone with her thoughts.

She pounced on Sarah when she walked through the door after her shift. 'How was work?' she asked, desperate for news of the outside world. Of Xavier. Not that she would admit it.

'Quiet. No dramatics today.'

'Who were you working with?'

'Paul Davey,' Sarah replied. She paused slightly before she added, 'You could always call him, you know.'

'Who? Paul? What for?'

'You know I don't mean Paul. Xavier.'

'Have you seen him?'

'Yes.'

'Did he ask about me?'

'No.' Sarah shook her head. 'I'm sorry.'

Was it a good thing or a bad thing that Xavier wasn't asking about her? Brighde didn't know. Part of her wanted him to worry about her. She wanted him to tell her everything would be all right, even though she knew that was unlikely. If he was worried about anything it would be about the baby and what her plans were.

'I think you should call him,' Sarah said. 'You need to talk about this. You can't keep avoiding the topic. It's not going to go away on its own.'

Brighde knew that. She knew she would have to make a move. She couldn't delay the inevitable. She had to make plans but she didn't have to discuss them with Xavier, yet she knew that was the decent thing to do. She was going to have to continue to work with him. She couldn't pretend this hadn't happened and she couldn't terminate the pregnancy without another conversation with him. He was no longer an anonymous one-night stand. He was her colleague and she knew more about him than she wanted to. He seemed like a good person; he deserved some consideration. This wasn't all his fault; she had to take some of the blame, and therefore some of the responsibility. She knew she needed to speak to him but it was a daunting task.

She still intended to terminate the pregnancy. She didn't need Xavier's permission but part of her wanted it. In her mind, when she'd thought about what she'd do if she was ever faced with this decision, there was never a father of the baby that needed her consideration. She'd never envisaged this scenario.

But now there was very much a father in the picture. She couldn't deny that but she still wasn't ready to see him. She didn't want to give him an opportunity to try to talk her out of her decision.

But she knew she couldn't avoid him for ever. She was due back at work tomorrow.

She had half hoped he wouldn't be on the ward today but she'd barely finished handover when he found her.

'Hi, how are you?' His voice wrapped around her like a comforting hug and made her want to step into his arms. She could use a hug.

'Good,' she lied, as she fought back tears. She was an emotional wreck and she knew she looked like she'd been through the wringer. She was pale, tired and unhappy. Xavier, by comparison, looked gorgeous. His eyes were bright, his hair was shiny, thick and healthy, his skin lightly tanned.

'Brighde, I have four sisters and I work with women all day. I can tell when a woman is lying.'

'Okay. Since you asked, I've been throwing up constantly—' morning sickness had arrived with a vengeance '—I'm exhausted, physically, emotionally and mentally. I've barely slept. The whole thing is a nightmare. Is there anything else you want to know?' She had a slight sense that she was being cruel but she couldn't help it. This situation was partly his fault. Why should he get off scot-free? If he pulled her up for being harsh she could always blame a lack of sleep and an excess of hormones.

'I need to ask you something.' He put his hand on her elbow and steered her towards a quiet spot in the corridor.

'Oh, God, Xavier, not now.' He couldn't possibly want to have the conversation she'd been trying to avoid, here at work? She felt her eyes widen with panic and her heart was racing. Was she going to throw up again? Early shifts were perhaps not the best for her in her state and if he was going to put her under the pump she didn't think she would cope with that *and* morning sickness.

'What do you take me for?' he said and she could hear the offence in his voice. 'It's a work question.'

'Oh. Sorry.' Perhaps she wasn't giving him enough credit. He hadn't really done anything wrong.

Except get her pregnant.

'You're taking over Amelia's patient in labour, correct?'

'Yes.'

'I'm the obstetrician. There's a slight problem and I told Amelia I would discuss it with you.'

'With labour?' Brighde frowned. It was unusual for the doctors to seek out the midwives in order to discuss their patients. Usually any issues were raised during handover.

'Not exactly.'

'Don't you want to work with me?' Maybe that was

what this was about. Nothing to do with the patient and everything to do with trust?

'No, it's nothing like that. I have no issue working with you.'

Did he have other issues with her? She supposed it was highly likely but she was happy to avoid that topic as he continued. 'Labour is going well but this delivery isn't totally straightforward and I wanted to talk to you about it in private.' He paused and took a deep breath, giving Brighde the impression that he was steeling himself for something. 'The baby has Down Syndrome.'

'Do the parents know?' Brighde asked before she held her breath, waiting for his answer. She hated those deliveries where the parents were expecting a normal, straightforward delivery of a healthy baby and things didn't quite go to plan.

'They do.'

Brighde breathed out. That was good. No surprises was a good thing.

'And they are looking forward to a normal delivery and to welcoming this child into their family. They want the experience to be joyful and they have specifically requested that the staff are aware of their wishes and that the staff will respect the fact that this baby is loved and wanted. I need to know how you feel about that. Whether you can give them what they want or if you want to swap patients with one of the other midwives?'

'You think I can't do my job?'

'I don't know.' He was watching her carefully. Perhaps he was worried she was going to lose the plot completely. 'Given our last conversation, I wasn't sure how you would cope with this. I need to know that you can give the parents the support and attention they want and need and deserve.'

'Of course,' she replied. The parents had made their decision and she would respect that. Just because she would choose differently didn't mean she would treat them differently or without respect. 'I am not going to judge people for their decisions, just like I hope I'm not judged for mine.'

Let him think about that!

Brighde managed to hold herself together through the delivery and while she settled the new parents and their baby. The baby was beautiful, ten fingers and ten toes and big blue eyes, and Brighde felt the usual pang of longing. But it wasn't enough to convince her to change her mind about her own pregnancy. If anything, despite what she'd told Xavier, she was more adamant now than ever about termination. This family had chosen to welcome their child into the world but there was a difference. This child had Down Syndrome and would lead a normal life within those parameters. In all likelihood, he would lead a long life and wouldn't experience any dramatic changes in quality of life once into adulthood. In Brighde's opinion, one couldn't compare Down Syndrome to Huntington's Disease but when it came down to it the real issue was with her. Bottom line, she didn't think she was strong enough to go through the trauma of suffering from Huntington's herself or watching her child suffer.

But what if she didn't have the mutation? She knew that was a possibility.

Could she be that lucky?

Was she strong enough to risk finding out?

She let the tears that she'd been holding back flow as she washed her hands in the sluice room, hoping for some privacy. She was super emotional at the moment and every emotion—happiness, sadness, fear—all seemed to be magnified. Especially fear.

'Are you okay?'

His voice made her jump. Was he going to follow her around, constantly checking on her?

'I don't know. I don't even know why I'm crying.' She rinsed her face as she tried to work out how she was feeling. *What* she was feeling. Confused. Guilty. Sad. In equal parts.

'Why don't you come for a walk with me? Get some fresh air and clear your head. You're on your lunch break now, aren't you?'

Xavier needed to talk to her. He'd done some research and he wanted—needed—to talk about their options. He had some suggestions to make and a walk in the garden next to the hospital might be the perfect place to have a neutral discussion. If they walked and talked Brighde wouldn't need to maintain eye contact and then she might feel less like he was pressuring or interrogating her.

'Yes, but surely you don't have time?' she replied.

'I do,' he said. 'Unless another expectant mum goes into labour, I'm good. I want you to know that I'm here to support you and that starts now.'

He waited until they were out in the autumn sunshine before he began. 'I've been doing some research. I was surprised I'd never come across Huntington's Disease, except in theory, but when I found out there are only sixteen hundred Huntington's sufferers in Australia it made more sense.'

'Only sixteen hundred that we know of,' Brighde said.

'But, with the genetic testing that's available now, in a few more generations there could be none. The disease could be eradicated.' He thought this was incredible.

'If people choose to get tested.'

'That's my point. Why wouldn't you get tested if you've got the option?'

'Would *you* want to know that you're going to die a premature death?' she asked again.

Xavier had thought about this since she'd first posed the question days ago. 'I think I would. I'd like time to prepare.'

'You can't prepare for something like Huntington's Disease. It's not like getting killed in a plane crash,' she said. 'It's not sudden. It's a horrible, debilitating disease. It takes your life slowly over several years. There's no cure. I don't want to know if that's what my future holds.'

'So instead you want to terminate what could potentially be a perfectly healthy pregnancy?' Xavier knew he needed to stay calm and in control but he was really struggling to follow Brighde's logic.

'I know you want children, Xavier. I know that's in your plans for the future but I'm not the one to give them to you. I'm pregnant but it wasn't planned and I don't have to stay pregnant. It's my prerogative.'

'We can do this together.'

'There is no *together*. There is no *we*. We don't have a relationship. And even if we did, this disease

destroys lives. My own father walked out when I was
nine. He promised to love my mother through sickness and in health and that didn't last. It wasn't enough
to make him stick around when the going got tough.
How could I expect you to stay and support me if we
start out with nothing substantial between us in the
first place? I've made my decision. I'm not having this
baby. I've made an appointment to see Julie Stewart
to discuss a termination.'

Xavier felt as if she'd punched him. His stomach
lurched and he had a pain in his chest. If he didn't
know better he'd think he was having a cardiac epi-
sode but he knew the pain was caused by Brighde's
words. He couldn't comprehend that she could so
blithely announce that she was going to deprive him of
his child. He'd lost a child once before and he couldn't
bear to think of it happening again and he would do
anything to ensure it didn't. He needed to have some
control this time. He knew that would be difficult but
he refused to back down quietly. This was his child
and he would do everything in his power to make sure
he would meet this one.

'Brighde, please. I'm begging you. Can't we discuss this some more?'

She shook her head. 'You're an obstetrician. Surely
you've had patients who have had terminations arranged by you? There must be some instances where
you agree that it's the right thing to do?'

'Yes,' he admitted. On a couple of occasions where
it had been best for the baby or for the mother's health,
physically or emotionally, he'd been involved but that
was different.

'So what's the difference now?'

'Now it's *my* child we're talking about.' It couldn't be *more* different, in his opinion. But he knew Brighde could do as she pleased. 'But I guess it doesn't matter what I think or what I want. You hold all the cards.'

A termination wasn't necessarily what Brighde wanted either. She would love to be a mother but this was what was best. She didn't need, or even want, Xavier's permission but she did want him to understand her decision. And, hopefully, support it. She didn't want him to think she was being selfish or unemotional. She wanted him to like her. She thought he was fabulous and she wanted him to think the same of her. But she knew that was unlikely, especially given these circumstances, and she wasn't willing to trade her decision for his approval.

Xavier stopped walking and turned to her as he said, 'I know I don't legally have any say in this decision, I understand that, but there's something I'd like to tell you.'

'What is it?' she asked, even as she wondered if she should warn him that there was nothing he could say or do that would convince her to change her mind. She should warn him he was wasting his breath but he looked so desperate to be heard that she couldn't refuse to listen.

He sat on a park bench and Brighde sat with him.

'I wasn't totally upfront with you,' he told her. 'Remember you asked me if I'd fallen in love in Scotland?'

Brighde nodded. 'You said Scottish girls weren't your type.'

'I did. Which wasn't quite true. Three months before I came back home I broke up with my girlfriend.'

'Oh.' Brighde thought about that for a moment, wondering what that had to do with their situation.

'We'd been together for two and a half years.'

Again, Brighde wondered what relevance that had. Then she remembered the expression on his face when she'd asked about his girlfriends. That look she hadn't been able to decipher. Sorrow or pain. Maybe it had been both. 'Were you in love with her?'

'At the time I thought so. And I thought she loved me.'

'You couldn't work things out?'

'No. Things got complicated.'

'What happened?' Surely things couldn't have been more complicated than the circumstances he found himself in now?

'She was pregnant.'

He'd been in this situation before? And last time he'd been in a relationship and things still hadn't worked out, yet he seemed to think they would be able to muddle their way through this. As if things weren't difficult enough.

Was. He'd said *was.* Something must have happened. Something must have gone wrong because she knew Xavier didn't have children. 'Did she lose the baby?' she asked. That might explain Xavier's expression, might explain the pain and sorrow she'd seen in his eyes, but it didn't necessarily explain the break-up.

'No. We hadn't planned it, hadn't even talked about it really, but I was over the moon. Until she told me that she'd been having an affair. She told me it had started because I spent too much time working. I was doing my speciality training so I figured that it went without saying that I would be doing ridiculous hours, but she figured that seeing I was studying OB/GYN my hours were always going to be ridiculous and she felt she was never going to be my first priority. And then she told me there was a chance the baby wasn't mine.'

No wonder he'd asked if Brighde's baby was his when he'd discovered the positive pregnancy test.

'Anyway, it turned out she was right: the baby wasn't mine.'

'She's had it?'

He nodded.

'And you're sure it's not yours? You're not going back to Scotland to check? To have tests?'

'No. We did the tests while she was pregnant. We did a prenatal paternity test at fourteen weeks. You know the one, a blood sample from her and mouth swabs from the possible fathers. I was excluded as a potential father based on the DNA testing. The baby wasn't mine. And that's when I decided to come home. I needed to come home. I needed a break, to take some time out. Once I got here I realised how much I'd missed Australia and I decided to stay.'

'Are you asking me to have the same test? Is that why you're telling me this?' Was that why he'd told her this story?

'No. You've told me the baby is mine and I believe you. You didn't have to tell me that. You're probably regretting the fact that you did, given what your plans are, but it seems to me that you're making some big decisions, huge decisions, without all the facts. And these decisions affect me too. And our baby. Won't you at least get the baby tested? Then we'll know what we're dealing with.'

'But that's just it,' she replied. 'I don't *want* to know what we're dealing with. I made the decision long ago *not* to get tested and if I test the baby and the result comes back positive then I will know my fate too. I'm not ready for this.'

Xavier was nodding but he wasn't finished. 'Can I ask you one favour then?'

'What is it?'

'Before you make any further plans would you please have an ultrasound? I'd like a chance to at least see my baby.'

CHAPTER SIX

BRIGHDE LAY ON the exam table and pulled the shirt of her scrubs up and eased the waistband of her pants down, exposing her midriff.

She was a lot quieter than he was used to. She wasn't even giving him any grief and she definitely wasn't making eye contact. He expected she'd agreed to the ultrasound out of a sense of obligation but he didn't care. He was desperate for a glimpse of his baby. He was amazed at how important this was to him. He'd made no secret of the fact that he wanted to be a father, that it was in his plans for the future, but he'd anticipated that, like a lot of other fathers he'd spoken to, the sense of responsibility and love for his offspring wouldn't eventuate until he held his child in his arms. But he already felt an overwhelming sense of responsibility and an urge to protect his unborn child. And that was his second reason for asking Brighde to let him do an ultrasound. He hoped that once she saw the image of her baby—*their* baby—on the screen, she might be more willing to discuss alternatives.

This baby was a gift he hadn't expected and one he would do everything in his power to keep. Despite what had transpired with his ex, or maybe because of it, his dreams of fatherhood were strong. He would have to wait and see how he and Brighde would get through this together but he was determined that they would. Their relationship might not be a traditional one but he wasn't going to let go of his dream. He wasn't going to give up his child without a fight and he was pinning all his hopes and dreams on this scan.

But the procedure wasn't going quite as he'd anticipated. Brighde had given him clear instructions as to how this was going to work. She had agreed to an ultrasound but only an abdominal one. She'd said no to a pelvic one, claiming that seemed far too personal, which was ridiculous considering they'd had sex, but she'd been adamant—he could do the ultrasound abdominally or not at all. But that was okay and it was definitely better than nothing. She was twelve weeks pregnant; an abdominal ultrasound should give him a clear picture.

Her face was stony, expressionless, set, as if she was deliberately blocking all thoughts on what was about to happen. She'd told him she didn't want to look at the monitor. She didn't want to see the baby.

He knew she'd prefer not to be pregnant and he assumed that she didn't want to see the image because that would make it real. He wished she would change her mind but he wasn't about to argue with her now. He was grateful that she'd agreed to the ultrasound at all and he wasn't going to jeopardise this opportunity. She might not want to see their baby but he sure as hell did.

Had she suspected that his motivations for the ultrasound were not completely altruistic? He should have thought about the chance that she would refuse to look at the images. She was a midwife; she'd seen plenty of scans before. She would know what to expect and she would prepare for it. This was obviously her way of preparing—by denying it all. It seemed to be her way of coping.

But this pregnancy was really happening and he just wanted time to convince her not to end it prematurely. He was counting on this ultrasound, but she was playing tough.

Her head was turned away from the monitor. It looked as if she was going to stick to her decision. While he was all for a woman knowing her own mind, Brighde's stubbornness was infuriating. He knew he was only irritated because she was refusing to agree with him or listen to his point of view and he had enough grace to admit that that was part of the problem, but he was also terrified that he would either run out of time to convince her that he was right or that she was going to go ahead and make a decision without him. He knew she was perfectly entitled to do that but he'd be damned if he was going to make it easy for her.

He looked at her exposed stomach. Her skin was pale and soft. Her stomach flat. She was only twelve weeks along but it was incredible to think that his baby was in there.

His hand shook as he picked up the ultrasound head. He was unbelievably nervous. He'd done hundreds of ultrasounds for all sorts of reasons but he'd never done one where he'd be looking at an image of his own child. It was an incredible moment.

He squeezed the gel onto the machine, flicked the switch and pressed the transducer into Brighde's abdomen. The picture came onto the screen—white stripy muscle fibres, a black womb.

Brighde's head remained turned away from him although he'd angled the screen so she couldn't have seen even if she wanted to. He moved the ultrasound around as he searched for the baby.

There! He felt a goofy smile spread across his face. That was his child. His trained eye took in the details. At twelve weeks the shape of a little person was easily identifiable. The foetus was about two inches long and he could see the head and body as well as four limbs. It looked perfect.

He moved the head of the ultrasound lower, trying to see if he could change the angle and see the baby in profile. He lost the picture and had to search again. The baby had changed position. Flipping itself around to face the opposite direction. Or had it?

He frowned and moved the transducer head higher again. It took him a moment to figure out what he was seeing.

Brighde could feel Xavier moving the ultrasound over her belly. He was stopping and starting as if he was having trouble getting a clear view. Or looking for something. She started to worry. She'd seen hundreds of ultrasounds. She knew the routine and he seemed to be having trouble making sense of things. Was he having trouble getting a good view? Was something the matter? She was getting nervous.

She turned her head to look at him. 'What is it? What's wrong?'

'Nothing.'

She still couldn't see the screen but she could see Xavier's face. He was smiling. He didn't look worried.

'What is it?' she asked. 'What are you looking at?'

He was looking at her now and she could see tears in his eyes.

Brighde's heart was in her throat. Why was he crying? What was wrong with her baby? 'Tell me,' she insisted. 'What's the matter?'

Xavier shook his head but the wide grin remained. 'It's twins,' he said.

'*Twins?* Are you sure?'

'Absolutely. I can see two sacs and two heartbeats.'

'I want to see,' Brighde said. She couldn't resist looking now. She'd been hoping that the ultrasound would show nothing, that it would tell her the pregnancy test had been a false positive. She'd known that was a long shot—she'd done three pregnancy tests now and all three had returned a positive result—but she had still held on to that hope. But now that the ultrasound had confirmed the pregnancy she had to see for herself.

'You do?'

She nodded and Xavier turned the screen to face her. The screen was black. He moved the transducer head around, pressing on her stomach.

'There. Twin A.'

Brighde caught her breath. She was tiny and perfect.

Xavier pressed a couple of buttons and Brighde could hear the printer spitting out a picture. She wanted to ask him for one for her as well but she couldn't bring herself to ask the question. If she wasn't going to keep the baby did she really want a reminder of her decision?

Xavier was moving the transducer head again and the image disappeared briefly before another one took its place.

'There's Twin B.'

A carbon copy of the first appeared on the screen.

She could hear Xavier clicking buttons again as the printer whirred in the background but she couldn't take her eyes from the screen. She could see the little flicker of a tiny heart beating.

'Can I hear the heartbeats?' she asked.

Xavier turned on the speakers and the thump-thump of two little hearts echoed in the room. It was the most beautiful sound she'd ever heard.

She blinked back tears.

She was pregnant with twins.

'They look perfect,' Xavier said.

She nodded. They did. But she knew looks could be deceiving. The babies might look perfect on the outside but that was no guarantee. There were no physical signs of Huntington's Disease until much later in life. Who knew what terrible gift she might have passed on to her babies? How was she going to fix this? Now that she'd seen her babies—both of them—the decision to terminate was going to be almost impossible but she was still afraid.

She was afraid to ask the questions. Did she have the gene? Did her babies?

She was scared of the answers and of what the answers might mean.

Being in a state of denial was preferable but was it too late for that now? This was *exactly* why she didn't want to know her status. She didn't want to deal with her own mortality or make tough decisions. It was better not to know. Ignorance was bliss.

She couldn't stay in that state any longer. She knew that.

But what were the chances that she would have escaped inheriting the mutated gene? Surely either she or Nick must have it. They couldn't both be lucky enough to escape.

It was better when they'd both been oblivious. If she hadn't escaped she didn't want to be talked out of the termination. But she knew she had until twenty-four weeks. She had some time. Maybe she could hold on a little longer. Pretend everything was normal, live in denial and enjoy being pregnant.

But she worried that the longer she took the harder the decision would become.

Brighde hesitated at the door to the hospital nursery. She needed to collect a baby to take to her mother but through the glass she could see Xavier. He was standing by a crib, holding a newborn, and Brighde was certain it was the one she was coming for.

She'd avoided him for twenty-four hours. Since the ultrasound. They hadn't discussed it. She needed time to work out what she was going to do and she suspected that Xavier hoped the ultrasound would make her change her mind. She hadn't changed it yet but she was wavering. And she couldn't handle any increased pressure, however subtle, from him. She was barely holding things together without throwing additional emotion into the mix.

She took a minute to watch him holding the baby.

He hadn't seen her; he was too caught up in the moment. The baby was clutching his finger and looking up at him, no doubt transfixed by his mesmerising eyes. Seemed like he had the same effect on females of all ages. His lips were moving as he held a one-sided conversation with the baby. He cradled the baby like an expert and she could just imagine him with his own child. He looked utterly gorgeous.

God, she wished things were different.

She shook her head as she punched in the access code and pushed open the door. There wasn't really any room in her head for what-ifs.

'What are you doing in here?' she asked him. There was normally no reason for him to be in the nursery and she hadn't seen him there before.

'Just a quick visit to see how my deliveries are faring. I know they're not my responsibility any more but I like to know how they're going and Shadow here was a bit grizzly so I thought I'd see if I could quieten her down.'

'I've come to take her to her mum,' Brighde said.

'Can you ask her what they were thinking, naming her Shadow?' he asked. 'I can't say I've heard that one before.' He smiled and her heart pounded in her chest, beating frantically like it always seemed to whenever he was near.

'It's not the worst name we've heard,' she replied. She'd seen or heard of many more ridiculous names than Shadow. 'And at least people will be able to spell it,' she added. She'd always hated the fact that no one could spell her name.

Xavier bent over and put his lips to her ear. Brighde's skin tingled as he started to whisper. 'I think we should stick to something simple for our children, like Mary and James.'

Brighde hadn't changed her mind about the fate of her pregnancy but she liked the way 'our children' sounded on Xavier's lips, though she wasn't about to admit that to him.

She knew he wanted kids. Could she really deprive him?

As long as the risks were still there, she knew she could and would. She would much rather deprive him than have him suffer the agony of watching his child die before him.

She locked her gaze onto his. 'Xavier, nothing has changed. Not the risk and not my mind. I can't give you what you want.'

She could work with him professionally—at the moment she didn't have a choice—but there could never be anything personal between them. He wanted things she couldn't give him. It would never work.

She reached out and took the baby from his arms, using Shadow as a shield to separate them in distance while she willed herself to stay strong and reasonable. 'I'm sorry, Xavier, but this would never work.'

She needed to leave now. She needed to get away from the pain she could see in his eyes. She hated knowing that she was hurting him. That she was potentially taking away something he cherished, but the pain now would be nothing compared to the pain later if his children had inherited the mutated gene.

She turned around, leaving him standing there empty-handed. She felt as if she was taking his dream away as she left the nursery but she had no other option. He didn't realise how easily his dream could become a nightmare. She was doing this to protect him. To protect them both.

Her way was still the best way.

The only way.

'Brighde Campbell?'

Brighde glanced at Sarah as the receptionist called her name. Xavier had offered to accompany her to her obstetrics appointment but Brighde didn't want him there. She deliberately hadn't told him when it was. She didn't need someone with a different opinion or agenda to her clouding the issue. She was confused enough already. It was important to her to retain control of the situation but she'd needed some moral support and, besides her brother, Sarah understood what she was going through better than anyone.

She had made an appointment with Julie Stewart. She'd worked with Julie many times and liked her skills and manner. She needed someone calm and unflappable who she hoped would listen to her concerns and help her through this difficult and confusing time.

'Do you want me to come in with you?' Sarah asked.

Brighde shook her head. 'No, I'll be okay. It was the waiting part I was worried about.' Brighde hadn't trusted herself to go through with the appointment, but having Sarah to keep her company had stopped her from fretting or fleeing. The rest she needed to do on her own. The rest was up to her, completely her decision, and she needed to be strong and independent and take responsibility for her decision.

'Brighde, congratulations. Fourteen weeks, I see, from Xavier's referral,' Julie said as she welcomed her into her office. 'You don't want to see him for your antenatal care?'

Brighde shook her head. Xavier had written the referral for her but that was the last thing she was going to ask of him. 'No,' she replied. 'He's done enough already. He's the father.'

'I see. He didn't want to come to the appointment today?'

'I didn't ask him to. He knows about the pregnancy,' Brighde added quickly when she saw Julie's expression. She knew that was the next question. 'I just didn't want him here today.'

'I don't need to ask if you've had the pregnancy confirmed.'

'Xavier did an ultrasound. It's twins. Two placentas so we're not sure if they're identical or not.'

'Twins is exciting but, as you know, that can be a little more complicated. However, the first appointment is routine either way.'

'It's not quite as routine as you might hope. There's some family history I need to talk to you about. A genetic abnormality.'

'What are we talking about here? Cystic fibrosis? Down Syndrome?'

'No.' Brighde shook her head. 'My mum had Huntington's Disease.'

'Your mum?'

Brighde nodded.

'But not you?'

'I don't know,' she admitted. 'I haven't been tested.'

'Do you want to get tested? I would need to refer you to a genetic counsellor.'

'I want to discuss a termination.' Brighde tried

to stay strong. And focused. But she could hear the slight waver in her voice as she tried not to think of the two tiny life-forms growing inside her. She hoped Julie didn't pick up on it. Her hand itched to rest on her belly. A protective gesture and one she resisted. Her body was at war with her mind but she needed to stay resolute.

'Have you discussed this with Xavier?'

'I have. He knows about the Huntington's and he knows my thoughts but, as I understand it, I don't need his permission.'

'That is correct.'

'I don't want to take a chance that either my children or I could develop Huntington's. I've seen what it does. I've lived through it with my mum and I know I couldn't go through it again. I don't plan on letting it take my life if the worst comes to the worst and I don't want to put my family through that, nor do I want to see my family suffer the same fate.'

'Well, the simple answer is yes, I can arrange a termination. We'll need to do an ultrasound scan so I can confirm your dates but we have until twenty-four weeks' gestation. It's better to do these things as early as possible. After that you would need to get a second specialist to support my recommendation. It's a big decision and I want to know that you've considered all options. I'd like you to have an appointment with a psychologist prior to scheduling a termination, if that is what you decide on. I insist on that for all my patients. You have some time so I'd like you to think about it and call me after you've seen the psychologist to schedule a time, if that's still what you want to do. But if you change your mind and want me to organise a referral to the genetic counsellor that's fine too. The other alternative is testing the foetuses. I can do an amniocentesis if you choose.'

'No. I don't want that. If one of the babies tests positive then I'll know my prognosis too.'

'Fair enough,' Julie replied as she handed her a card with the psychologist's details on it. 'Call me or schedule another appointment once you've seen the psychologist, okay?'

Brighde took the card as she agreed with Julie's conditions. She needed to get out of there. She needed to think.

'How did it go?' Sarah asked when Brighde reappeared.

'I'm not sure.'

She waited until they had left the rooms. This was not a conversation she wanted to have within earshot of any other mothers or pregnant women.

'Julie will perform the termination if I want her to but she insists on an appointment with a psychologist first.'

'That makes sense.'

'Am I doing the right thing? What if the babies are perfectly fine?'

'Only you can make that decision, Brighde.'

'I spoke to Nick and Imogen about testing the other day.'

'Are you thinking about it too?'

'I still don't know but the fact that I even want to talk about it worries me. I'm second-guessing myself now. I was always so sure, so convinced that I would never have children and everything has changed overnight. Nick and I spent so many years being adamant that we wouldn't get tested. I understand why Nick changed his mind but I wanted to know what they would have done if he'd tested positive. I wanted to know if Nick would still marry Imogen, knowing what we went through with Mum. Whether he would have been prepared to put Immy through that.'

'And what did he say?'

'He said no. Which was what we always thought, and that's effectively where I stand too, but Imogen said yes. She said they would still get married but they would have done pre-implantation genetic testing done on any embryos to make sure they didn't inherit the mutation. I can see her point of view but I don't have that option. I'm already pregnant.'

'But you could test the babies. An amnio would tell you what you need to know, right?'

'Yes. But it might also tell me my fate, one way or the other, and I'm not sure if I'm ready to know that.'

'Brighde, if I'm honest, this is about more than just you now. I understood your reasons for not getting tested but this isn't just about you any more. I know you're battling with this decision and you need to ask yourself why. I know you're scared but I also know you want these babies. You have to find out what you're dealing with. You need some answers so you can make decisions with a clear conscience. I know it's hard but we will support you, Nick, Imogen and me.'

She noticed that Sarah hadn't mentioned Xavier. Did she presume he wouldn't support her decision?

But Sarah was right. She couldn't in good conscience go through with a termination without all the facts. She put the psychologist's business card in her pocket. She would save that number for later. She had another decision to make first. Who should she test? Herself or her babies?

Brighde switched her phone on as handover finished and her shift officially ended and saw two missed calls from the same number. The number wasn't programmed into her phone but she recognised it instantly. It was the genetic counsellor's number.

It had been three weeks since she'd called her obstetrician and asked for a referral to the genetic counsellor and two weeks since she'd had blood taken for the test. The counsellor had promised to get the results rushed through. The results must be in. This was it.

She saw Xavier walking along the corridor and felt the blood rush from her head. She wasn't ready for this.

She was vaguely aware of darkness swirling at the edges of her vision and she could feel the floor rising up to meet her as the room started to spin. She reached for the desk, trying to steady the room, to steady herself, but her hand found only thin air.

'Brighde!' She heard Xavier's voice. He sounded miles away.

'Brighde?'

She opened her eyes to find herself in Xavier's arms, pressed against his chest, as he carried her along the corridor.

How did she get there? 'What happened? What are you doing?'

'You fainted.'

'Fainted?' She wasn't a fainter. 'Where are we

going?' she asked as he pushed open a door to an examination room.

'To check you out,' he said as he laid her on the bed and reached for the blood pressure cuff. He wrapped it around her arm and she watched his long fingers fix it in place.

She wanted to sit up. She felt perfectly fine but something must have happened. Something must have triggered the fainting spell. She lay still and tried to remember what had happened. The counsellor!

The blood pressure machine beeped and the monitor showed one-ten over seventy. 'That's a little low.'

'It's normal for me,' she told him.

'Is fainting normal too?'

'No.'

'Then we should find out what caused it.'

'I know what caused it,' she said as she patted her pocket. 'Where's my phone?'

'Here.' He pulled it from the pocket of his trousers and handed it to her. 'What's so important?'

Brighde's hand shook as she took her phone from him. 'I saw a genetic counsellor a couple of weeks ago. I had blood tests done.' She swiped the screen as she spoke; she couldn't bring herself to look at him.

'Why didn't you tell me?' She could hear the hurt and confusion in his voice. The one thing he'd been asking her to do and she'd done it behind his back.

'I didn't tell anyone,' she explained. 'I thought it would make the wait worse if other people were also expecting news.' And she didn't think she was strong enough to handle the weight of expectation. If no one else knew, she could pretend for a little longer. And she didn't want to answer questions until she had the results. 'I didn't want to make any promises I couldn't keep. I just got a message on my phone. The test results must be back.'

'What did the message say?'

'I don't know. I haven't listened to it yet. That's what I was doing when I fainted.' She hit voicemail and held the phone to her ear.

'Do you want me to wait outside?'

She shook her head. She thought she might chicken out if left on her own. Xavier's presence was the catalyst she needed to listen to the message. His calm demeanour and physical size gave her a sense of strength she didn't have if left to her own devices.

'He wants me to go in to his office,' she said as she ended the call. 'He's there until six o'clock today.'

'Is that all he said?'

She nodded, knowing what Xavier was asking. 'He won't open the results until I'm there.'

'Where is his office?'

'South Melbourne.'

'I suppose you want to catch the tram,' Xavier said but his tone was teasing and there was warmth in his dark brown eyes. 'Would you like me to drive you?'

'I don't know if I'm going to go yet. I'm not sure I'm ready to hear what he has to say.'

'Brighde, I know this must be daunting for you. Just making the decision to get tested must have been difficult and I understand if you need more time but you don't have to go alone. I imagine the suggestion was made to bring someone with you?' He waited while she nodded. 'I can do that for you. No pressure. Just a friendly face. Someone to hold your hand.'

She didn't want to go on her own. She knew she wouldn't cope. She could ask Sarah to go with her but she wanted Xavier. She felt safe with him. She wanted to be back in his arms. She wished she could stay there for ever and she wished she could make everything else go away. She wished she could be normal. They might not have a future together but she needed him with her just for now.

And besides, if Xavier heard the results it might be easier to persuade him that she was right. She felt bad that she couldn't give him what he wanted but maybe letting him accompany her would make up for that somehow.

Xavier noted that Brighde introduced him to the counsellor only as a friend, not as the father of her twins. It seemed she was determined to keep him at arm's length. He supposed he should be thankful that she'd allowed him to accompany her for this meeting even if he obviously still wasn't going to be asked for his opinion. He wondered what it would take to get her to let him into her life properly. He was determined to be a part of it; she had got him thinking about the future, imagining a life with his children and with her. Very definitely with her. She was stubborn but fragile, independent but wounded and he wanted to take care of her. He wanted to give her peace and security, even though he knew that might be out of his control. She brought out all his protective instincts and he wanted her to feel protected and cherished. But he knew he had some work to do if he was going to convince her that he should be part of her life. She was so set on shutting him out.

'How much has Brighde explained to you about testing?' Tuan asked after the introductions had been made.

'Not a lot,' Xavier replied. Although the honest answer would have been 'nothing'. If he'd known Brighde was being tested he would have done his research. He hated being unprepared. He'd done a bit of background reading on the disease early on, trying to get inside Brighde's head, trying to understand her thought processes, but he hadn't spent a lot of time on the science of the testing procedure. 'I am an obstetrician so I'll understand the facts, but Huntington's Disease is not something I've had first-hand experience with.'

'All right then. I'll just explain what we are looking for in the testing process. Huntington's Disease is caused by a mutation in the HTT gene which is instrumental in making the Huntingtin protein. The faulty gene produces an oversized version of the protein which builds up in the brain and attacks the neurons, causing the symptoms we see in Huntington's Disease. We still don't know why the faulty gene only attacks the nerves in the brain but that's what happens. In order to determine whether an individual is likely to develop Huntington's Disease we need to count the number of CAG trinucleotide repeats. Normally a CAG segment is repeated between ten and thirty-five times within the Huntingtin gene. In people who are going to develop Huntington's Disease the number of repeats will be anything in the range of forty to more than one hundred and twenty. Thirty-six to thirty-nine repeats is considered the grey area where individuals *may* develop the disease.'

Tuan's desk was clear except for a single white envelope. He reached for the envelope and picked it up, looking at Brighde. 'These are your test results. Do you have any questions before we open it?'

'We're hoping for a number less than thirty-six?' she checked. She knew that her brother's tests had shown ten repeats and that had been good news but she had never bothered to investigate further than that. She was still of the opinion that ignorance was bliss.

'For you to test negative, that's right. Have you thought about what you will do if the test is positive?'

Brighde nodded. 'If I have Huntington's Disease I will terminate the pregnancy.'

'You understand that even if you test positive the babies could still be fine? They may both have inherited the healthy gene.'

Brighde understood exactly what Tuan was telling her. Which was that if she tested positive but didn't test the babies she wouldn't know their fate for certain; therefore, she could be terminating perfectly healthy foetuses. She got that, but this wasn't something she was prepared to negotiate. Huntington's was a genetically dominant disease. If Brighde tested positive the chances of both babies escaping the mutation was not impossible but it was improbable. 'Yes. But I watched my mother die and it was the worst thing imaginable. If I have the disease I don't want to put my own children through that. And I won't.'

'All right,' Tuan continued. 'It's not my job to tell you what to do; it's my job to give you the facts. Are you ready?'

Brighde looked at Xavier. She was terrified but it was time to find out.

He squeezed her hand and she looked back at Tuan and nodded. He slit open the envelope and pulled out a single piece of paper.

The piece of paper that would determine her future and possibly that of her unborn children too. It didn't look important enough to Brighde.

She held her breath.

'You have twenty-nine repeats.'

Brighde breathed a sigh of relief. Tears came to her eyes. She couldn't believe it. 'I'm going to be okay?' She and Nick had *both* had a win in the genetic lottery? She was safe. She'd dodged a bullet. It was hard to comprehend; she'd been so certain her test would be positive. She hadn't dared let herself believe her result could be anything else. How could they both be so lucky?

Her hands and her knees were shaking. Adrenalin coursed through her. Fear was replaced with relief, leaving her light-headed. She took a deep breath. 'So I won't develop HD?'

'That's right.' Brighde felt like bursting into tears of relief. '*You* won't develop HD…'

She could hear a *but* in Tuan's voice. Why was there a *but*? She'd tested negative. She was going to be okay. She frowned. 'Is there more?' she questioned him. 'What aren't you telling me?'

'Fewer than thirty-six repeats means that you won't develop the disease but there's a range termed the unstable range.'

'Which is what?' Her voice shook. Fear was back.

'Between twenty-seven and thirty-five repeats.'

'And I'm in there? The unstable range?'

Tuan nodded.

'And what does that mean?' Xavier asked.

'It means things can be a little ambiguous.'

Brighde didn't like the sound of that at all. What did Tuan know that she didn't? She could feel herself starting to panic. Xavier was still holding her hand and she was squeezing his fingers so hard she feared she would cut off his circulation but he wasn't flinching.

'It means you won't develop HD,' Tuan continued. Brighde watched his lips carefully. He sounded as though he was speaking underwater; she knew it was because her brain was fuzzy, and she had to concentrate hard to make sense of what he was telling her. 'But there's a possibility that the CAG gene could expand when passed from a parent to a child.'

Her fainting spell had passed but she now thought she might vomit as Tuan's explanation sunk in. 'Are you telling me I won't develop HD but my children might?'

CHAPTER SEVEN

BRIGHDE STARED AT TUAN. 'So, I'm safe but the babies might not be? I might still have passed on a faulty gene?'

'It's more likely that the gene could continue to expand when the gene is passed through the father's side. We're not certain about the mother.'

'But you don't know for sure?'

Brighde fought back tears. The test results hadn't helped at all. They had made things worse, not better, and given her more questions than answers.

Tuan was shaking his head. 'No. I'm sorry.'

Xavier started to speak but Brighde held up her hand. 'Stop.' She couldn't look at him. She was seconds away from bursting into tears, from losing her composure completely and she knew that if she looked at Xavier and saw compassion or concern in his eyes she wouldn't be able to maintain her composure. She needed to think. She couldn't afford to go to pieces. 'I need a moment.'

She wasn't coping. Not at all. This was even worse than she'd imagined. She'd been prepared to hear that she had the mutation but to learn that she would be okay but she might have condemned her unborn babies was devastating. She'd chosen not to test the babies since it might have given her an insight into her own future anyway. If one of the babies had tested positive it would have confirmed that she carried the gene. But to find out she might have passed on the gene *without* testing positive herself—that she hadn't expected and she wasn't sure how to deal with it.

She took a deep breath and kept her eyes fixed on Tuan. 'What do I do now?' In her mind, it was still a question of her options. The decisions were still all hers. This was her family's legacy; Xavier was just a bystander.

'That's up to you,' Tuan replied. 'You can test the foetuses or terminate the pregnancy. The only way to know for sure is to have an amniocentesis but the choice is yours. You've got time. You have got until twenty-four weeks before a termination gets complicated but you need to make sure you're okay with whatever decision you make.' Tuan stood up from behind his desk. 'You'll need some time to process this. You're welcome to stay in here for as long as you need and if you want any more information or would like to discuss anything further, today or in the future, I'm available. I really am sorry.'

He left them alone. Brighde knew she was in shock. Xavier was silent too; she supposed the shock was just as great for him. Worse, maybe. She'd always expected that she would have the repeat so she should have anticipated bad news. But to hear what she thought was good news and then to have it tainted by premonitions of disaster was almost more than she could bear.

'Are you okay?' he asked.

'No. I'm definitely not okay.'

'You didn't know the significance in the different numbers of repeats?'

'No. I knew nothing about unstable ranges or grey areas.' She'd never researched testing as she'd never intended to get tested. She'd preferred to live in a state of denial.

What had she done to her babies?

Her hand was resting on her stomach. An unconscious, protective gesture she'd found herself making more and more often.

She dropped her head, imagining for a moment that she'd be able to see her babies. What would she tell them?

I'm so sorry. I never meant to hurt you.

I never meant to have you.

But now that she was pregnant she knew she couldn't terminate the pregnancy without knowing what hand she'd dealt them.

Everything had changed yet again. If the twins had escaped the mutation then everything was good. She would be around to see her children grow up. But if they hadn't she would have to go ahead with a termination. She couldn't stand the thought of passing on the faulty gene. She couldn't do that to her own children.

She felt Xavier's fingers under her chin. He lifted her head and she could see the worry in his dark eyes. Was it her worry reflecting back at her or was he just as concerned?

His thumb brushed across her cheek and she could feel dampness on her skin. She hadn't been aware that she was crying but now she could feel the tears gathering on her bottom lashes and spilling over onto her cheeks.

'I'll take you home,' Xavier said.

She nodded mutely. She just wanted to curl up in a ball in her bed in the darkness and wait for this all to go away. She hadn't prepared herself for this news at all and it was overwhelming. She didn't know if she was strong enough to cope with the decisions that she still faced.

Xavier's phone rang just as he pulled up in front of her house. He'd been silent on the drive home and Brighde was grateful. She didn't feel like talking. She didn't think she was capable of holding a conversation. Her brain wasn't holding any thoughts at all. It kept jumping from one thought to another. She was completely unsettled.

She climbed out of the car and walked up the path. Xavier followed her up the path, talking on his phone.

'Is Sarah home?' he asked as she unlocked the front door.

'No. She's working a late. Why?'

'That was the hospital. One of my patients is in labour. I should go but if you like I can call someone to cover me so I can stay with you.'

'No. I'm fine,' she lied. She wasn't fine but she didn't know if she wanted company. She just wanted to be left alone with the consequences of her actions and her grief.

She wanted everything to go back to normal.

'Is there someone else who can come and stay with you? I don't think you should be alone. What about your brother?'

Brighde shook her head. 'No. I'm okay.' She still hadn't told Nick she was pregnant and she wasn't about to tell him today. Definitely not today. 'It's all right. Go.'

Brighde had a restless night's sleep. She dreamt in vivid Technicolor. Disturbing dreams. She finally fell asleep again as Saturday dawned, only to be woken later by a knock on the front door. She waited to see if Sarah would answer before remembering that she'd been doing a late/early and would already be back at work.

She stumbled out of bed and pulled her curtains back at the corner, craning her head to see who was disturbing her.

Xavier.

'What are you doing here?' she asked as she opened the door. Was he checking on her or the babies? Worried about her or only about them?

'I came to see how you are. Whether there's anything you need.'

She shook her head as she stepped aside to let him in. She couldn't stand in the doorway dressed in nothing but an old T-shirt. 'I'm fine.'

The expression on Xavier's face told her he didn't believe her but he didn't argue.

'In that case I have a suggestion.'

'What is it?'

'How would you like to get away for the weekend?'

'Why?'

'Why not? I know Sarah is working this weekend. Which means you'll be home alone. I don't want you staring at the walls and worrying.'

'Maybe I want to be alone,' she grumbled.

'If you won't listen to me, would you listen to my sister? I've learnt that in order to live a stress-free life it's wise to listen to her. She suggested that a change of scenery might be good therapy. Please, won't you give it a shot? Twenty-four hours, that's all I'm asking for.'

What else had she planned for the next twenty-four hours? Nothing at all. He was right. She would just sit and fret. She sighed. 'What do I need?'

Xavier grinned and her spirits lifted instantly. She could think of worse ways to spend the next day than in his company. 'Walking shoes, a warm coat. Something a little smart for dinner and a smile.'

'Where are we going?'

'That's a surprise.'

'Brighde? We're here.'

Xavier's voice roused her from sleep. She hadn't been able to keep her eyes open once they'd hit the highway out of Melbourne; the steady thrum of the car engine had lulled her to sleep and she still had no idea where Xavier had taken her.

'Welcome to Daylesford.'

'Spa country?'

Daylesford was famous for its mineral springs, spa retreats, restaurants and natural beauty and it was putting on a magnificent display today, Brighde thought as Xavier drove through the picturesque country town. She'd heard about the area but never visited. It looked spectacular. The myriad trees showed off their autumn colours. Gold, fiery red, burnt orange, a touch of green against a crisp, clean blue sky. It was one of those beautiful Victorian days when the weather was being kind and anything seemed possible.

Xavier turned off the road into their accommodation that sat on the edge of the lake. Brighde had heard about this five-star restaurant and hotel. 'Are we staying here?'

'As long as you've got no objections,' Xavier said as he switched off the engine. He smiled at her and Brighde's stomach flipped.

He jumped out of the car while Brighde sat for a moment to gather her thoughts. This wasn't a romantic couple's weekend away; this was Xavier's version of R&R. He'd promised to give her time and space to rest and recover but she couldn't afford to let her guard down. She needed to keep her wits about her and remember what was at stake. She still had some decisions to make. Big decisions. And she couldn't get too comfortable with Xavier as it was more than likely that her decisions would destroy any chance they might have had at any sort of relationship.

'Are you hungry?' Xavier opened Brighde's door and reached for her hand. She took his hand without thinking; it was warm and large and reassuring and his touch sent her stomach tumbling again.

She wasn't hungry or tired. She was restless. She had to move. Had to get busy. Had to get her mind off Xavier and his smile, his come-to-bed eyes and his warm hands and how he made her feel. Maybe it was the pregnancy hormones but she was feeling very much like ripping his clothes off.

'Not really.' She was dying to see their room—she wondered if he'd booked one or two—but she could see the lake from the car park and it looked so peaceful and serene and it called to her. 'After we check in I might go for a walk.'

Xavier checked them in—just the one room, she noted—and they followed the porter.

The door swung open to reveal a light-filled space with views of the lake through expansive windows set either side of a pair of French windows. The king-size bed had a plush bedhead upholstered in a black and white fabric, the bathroom was as big as her kitchen with a bath the size of her dining table and a couch was positioned in front of the window to catch the view but also angled towards a gas fire. The black and white theme continued in the soft furnishings of the room and into the bathroom with hints of gold. Brighde had never seen anything as luxurious as this suite.

She spun around slowly, taking it all in. 'Wow! This is gorgeous.'

'You like it?' Xavier asked as he tipped the porter.

'It's amazing.'

'I didn't intend to book just one room—it was all they had left at short notice but I thought you could have the bed and I'll take the couch.'

Brighde looked at the couch. It looked comfortable but not nearly long enough to accommodate Xavier's six-feet, two-inch frame. She would offer him the bed but she'd leave that discussion for later; she knew he wouldn't accept now. 'Are you sure?'

'Positive. This weekend is all about giving you a chance to recharge. I want you to have a good night's sleep.'

Sleep was the last thing on Brighde's mind. The

first thing wasn't wise though so she went for option two.

'I think I'll go for a walk around the lake while the weather holds,' she said. The Victorian weather was notoriously fickle and locals learnt to take advantage of clear skies whenever possible. The weather could change in an instant. 'Would you like to come?'

They were able to step out through the French windows onto a small deck from where stairs led down onto the lakeside path. The gardens were planted with Australian natives and Brighde could hear frogs croaking in the reeds and a kookaburra laughing in the distance. She wasn't watching where she was walking, mesmerised by her surroundings, and she missed the bottom step, stumbling slightly. Xavier grabbed her hand, preventing her from falling, and he didn't let go even as she recovered her feet. Brighde wondered if she should pull her hand away but it felt so good she decided not to make a fuss. Her body was flooded with pregnancy hormones, which made it difficult to think straight. Her brain felt like complete mush at times while at other times she was so sexually charged she couldn't think about anything else. But it was strange how those times only occurred whenever Xavier was near.

They walked in silence and Brighde savoured the peace and the sensation of having her hand in Xavier's. Her situation could be so perfect if it wasn't built on mistakes and haunted by her fears.

'Was this really your sister's idea?'

She was curious to know what Xavier had told her family about her. She liked the idea that they knew about her. It meant she existed in his life.

Did she want that?

She did but she doubted she'd get what she wanted. That would be too much to ask for and she'd learned not to ask for, or expect, too much.

For the moment, it was enough to know that she was free of the possibility of inheriting HD. That was good news and she needed to remember to cherish that outcome. Could she dare to hope that both her babies had also been spared? If they hadn't then she and Xavier didn't stand a chance.

'She suggested the change of scenery. I chose the location.'

'You've done well,' Brighde said as she watched a pair of black swans glide serenely past them on the lake. 'Which sister was it?'

'Mary. She's the eldest and the bossiest. It's good to let her get her way occasionally and I think she got it right today.'

'What about the others?' Brighde was enjoying the chance to talk about someone else's family for a change. Hearing about his life meant she didn't have to think about hers.

'Eve is number two. She's not quite as serious as Mary. A bit more of a free spirit. She's pregnant with her third child; Mary has four. Then, Angie and Gabby, the twins, are younger than me.'

'You have twin sisters?' Brighde was surprised that he hadn't mentioned that before.

He nodded.

'Why haven't you told me about them?'

'Would it make any difference?'

'I guess not.' It was irrelevant to her situation, she supposed, but it felt like another connection to his family and she liked that idea. 'But what was it like having twins in the family?'

'Awful,' he said but he was grinning. He really was irresistible when he smiled. 'I was four when they were born and they made my life hell.'

'Did they really?'

'Of course. But I adore them. Now. But I imagine they were hard work to begin with. I'm sure my mum would happily pass on any words of advice about raising twins if you're interested.'

Brighde wasn't sure she was ready to go there. Either to meet his mum or to talk about raising twins. That would be admitting that she was going ahead with the pregnancy.

When she didn't reply he continued. 'I just remember a lot of bottles and nappies and crying. I can't say I'm an expert on raising kids but I'm getting plenty of practice with my sisters' tribes.'

'You've got eight nieces and nephews, you said?'

'Yep, plus one on the way and a couple of godchildren as well.'

'That sounds busy,' she said as she wrapped her scarf around her neck a little more tightly. They had reached the far side of the lake and the wind was blowing more steadily on this side and there was a bit of a chill in the autumn air.

'It is,' he said as they approached a picturesque red-roofed weatherboard kiosk. 'Shall I get us both something hot to drink?' he asked, leading her onto the deck of the kiosk that extended out over the lake. 'Would you like to sit inside or out?'

A row of brightly coloured paddleboats was tied to the bank and several had been rented and were drifting on the water. Despite the wind, the views were pretty. 'Outside, I think.'

Xavier found a table and chairs on the deck that was partly sheltered from the elements. Brighde sat and thought about his large family as she waited for him to return with their drinks. His family sounded close and she tried to imagine her babies with a heap of cousins. She and Nick only had each other. Their parents had both been only children but her babies would have cousins on both sides *and* of similar age. She wondered what her family would think about this whole situation. What would her mum have thought of Xavier? What she would have said if she'd known Nick and Brighde were both going to give her grandchildren.

Xavier put Brighde's hot chocolate on the table but she didn't acknowledge his return. She was gazing across the lake, lost in her thoughts. But she didn't look relaxed. She looked like she had the weight of the world on her shoulders. He'd brought her here hoping to give her a chance to relax, rest and replenish her reserves. He knew she wouldn't be able to make sensible decisions if she was exhausted and emotional. He knew she hadn't been sleeping well. Sarah had mentioned it but he could see it in her face. She'd lost weight and had dark circles under her eyes. Her energy seemed to have been extinguished and she'd lost some of her spark. Seeing her like this made him feel terrible. He'd done this to her. He'd put her in this position.

But there was some good news in all of this. She had tested negative. She was going to be okay.

That should be one less concern for her but he knew

she was still stressed about what she might have inflicted on their children. He'd hoped that bringing her to Daylesford would help to get her mind off that. It had to be better than leaving her home alone, with only her thoughts for company. He didn't want to put any pressure on her but he'd hoped a change of environment might allow her to forget her worries and fears. Even a temporary reprieve had to be a good thing, but it didn't look as though his plan was working.

'Is everything okay?'

She jumped in her chair. 'Sorry, what did you say?'

'I asked if you were okay.'

'Yes, I'm fine.'

'If you want to talk I'm a good listener. My sisters have taught me that as well. Whether by accident or design, I'm not sure, but they talked so much it was always hard to get a word in so I learnt to listen.'

He was rewarded with a smile. Her smile was fantastic. Wide and sincere. Although this one didn't quite reach her eyes. What was on her mind?

'I was just thinking about my mum. Wondering what she would think of my situation. And what she would do.'

'What do you think she would do?'

'I don't know. I guess her situation was completely different to mine. Things have changed so much since I was born. Not in terms of any treatment for HD but in terms of the genetic testing. Almost all the worthwhile discoveries about the disease and all the useful advances that have been made have happened since I was born, but none of it is going to help me.'

He begged to differ. The tests that were available

today gave them a lot more information than ever before. Information that could be used to make informed decisions. And he was all for that. He still couldn't understand how testing could be a bad idea. Or an idea that wasn't on the table for consideration. But he'd promised that he wouldn't pressure her. This weekend was all about peace.

'The Huntingtin gene wasn't identified until 1983 and genetic testing wasn't an option until 1994, five years after I was born, so by the time Mum could have learned that she was going to develop HD Nick and I were already born. And pre-implantation testing has only been possible since 2003 so Mum didn't have any of the options that are available today, but I still wonder what she would have done if she'd had access to testing. Would she have taken a chance and had a family?'

'You never asked her?'

Brighde shook her head. 'No. We never really spoke about the future. We were too busy trying to survive in the present. I wish I had though—not that it would have changed anything, really. Her only option would have been not to have kids. But it's too late to know now and it's a regret I'll have to live with. I guess I just wonder what advice she'd have had for me.'

'Have you spoken to your brother?'

'No,' she said as she picked up her hot chocolate.

'Why not?' He was curious to know why she hadn't said anything to her family.

'We've had enough bad news in our life. He's happy now. He's getting married and they're expecting their first child. I don't want to take the gloss off their news with my troubles.'

Xavier finished his drink and checked his watch. 'I made a massage appointment for you,' he said. 'I wasn't sure if you'd like it but there weren't many spots available so I took the liberty. If you'd like it we'd better head back.'

'That sounds fabulous—thank you.' She drained her hot chocolate, leaving a dusting of chocolate powder on her top lip.

He reached across the table and wiped the chocolate from her lip with his thumb. Brighde's blue-grey eyes widened and her pupils dilated and he fought the urge to lean across the table and kiss her soundly.

He wished things were different. Less complicated. He was still prepared to try to work things out but so many of the decisions were Brighde's alone to make. He really didn't have much influence over how things were going to turn out. There was nothing much he could do except to try to show her that he was there to support her and hope for the best. He knew there were no guarantees in life but he didn't doubt that, if Brighde was willing to give him a go, they could have a future together. But it was all up to her.

He stood and held her chair for her and kept her company as they walked back around the lake.

Brighde stretched out on the couch in front of the fire. Housekeeping had been to their room while they were at dinner and had turned down the bed and turned on the fire. The room was lit by lamps and by firelight, casting a warm glow.

Xavier picked up a chocolate that had been left on the pillow by Housekeeping.

'After-dinner chocolate?' he offered.

Brighde groaned. 'I couldn't eat another thing.' Dinner had been divine. Poached pheasant with autumn vegetables, followed by a pear and rhubarb tart. She couldn't remember when she'd had a nicer meal. 'I should go to bed but I don't think I can move.'

'That's my bed, don't forget; you'll have to move at some stage.'

'Come and sit with me.'

Xavier sat on the floor at her feet, leaning his back against the couch. That wasn't what she'd intended. 'That doesn't look very comfortable,' she said as she sat up and shuffled to one side to make some room. 'You can sit up here.'

He sat in the corner of the couch, his long legs stretched out in front of him towards the fire, and pulled Brighde down again so she could lie with her head in his lap. She closed her eyes and breathed out slowly as he stroked her hair.

'Have you had a good day?'

Brighde sighed. 'I've had a great day. Thank you.'

'How are you feeling? Apart from full?'

She felt safe but she wasn't about to share that with him. She wasn't used to revealing her innermost thoughts. 'I'm feeling relieved.'

'About testing negative?'

She rolled onto her back, opened her eyes and looked up at him as she nodded.

'I kind of ignored that yesterday. I was so worried about what still might be that I sort of forgot that Tuan told me I'd be okay. I'd always been so certain that I would test positive so it didn't sink in that the tests were negative. But it's a double-edged sword. On one hand I'm relieved, but if I wasn't pregnant I'd be absolutely ecstatic, not just relieved. But knowing that I still might have inadvertently affected my babies is hard to come to terms with. In a way I think it would have been easier to deal with if I *had* tested positive. But it's ironic, isn't it? If I wasn't pregnant I never would have got tested and I wouldn't have this sense of relief. I've got one answer from the test results but more questions.'

'About the babies?'

'Yes.'

'I know I said I would just listen,' he told her. 'That all decisions were yours, but from a purely medical point of view the sooner you make decisions the better. Particularly regarding a termination.'

'You do agree that a termination is okay in certain cases?' she asked. 'I've been thinking about the ramifications a lot, particularly since delivering the baby with Down Syndrome. There's a difference between that and HD. That child will grow up with the syndrome; they won't know any different, their life will be constant. A child who has the mutated HTT gene will lead a completely normal life for thirty or forty years and that means that when the symptoms start it will be a massive blow. They will lose all normality. That's what worries me. That seems cruel. It *is* cruel. I lived through it with my mother and I can't do it again. I need to know how you feel about that.'

She'd been avoiding asking him direct questions. She'd been making assumptions about what he would say but maybe he had changed his mind. She hadn't asked. But now she was struggling with the decision-making. She didn't want him to feel excluded but she also didn't want to make all the decisions. He'd shown her his support and she felt she needed to show him some consideration.

'I need to know for certain one way or another before I would be happy with a termination,' he replied. 'The babies might be fine and then we're worrying for no good reason. Will you have an amnio to find out?'

She'd been thinking about this. A lot. Her babies might be fine and part of her would love her own happily ever after—a husband, children, a family of her own—but she was still scared. When Xavier was around it was easy to forget all the bad things that could happen and she found herself thinking ahead to the future, daydreaming about falling in love and living a long and happy life. But if she was ever going to get a chance at that she needed to make some decisions and she knew she didn't really have a choice. It wasn't the testing she had to consider now—she knew that was inevitable—it was what would happen next. Whether Xavier would agree with her decisions once they got the results or whether he'd still want her to continue with the pregnancy.

'Would you agree to a termination if the tests came back positive?' she asked. She had to know. She couldn't go ahead with the tests if he would give her grief over her decisions if the tests *were* positive. Legally she didn't need his consent but she wanted his support. They might not agree on everything but he was entitled to his opinion, although, in this case, she was going to do what she believed was best.

'Can I have some time to think about my answer?

It's a big decision and I'm just not sure how I feel about the termination when, regardless of the genetic make-up, our babies will be perfectly healthy well into adulthood.'

'Have you ever seen, with your own eyes, someone with late stage Huntington's? Not read about it or watched videos but actually seen for yourself what it does?' she asked.

He shook his head. 'No, I haven't.'

'Then you have no idea what this disease does to someone. Not just the person who has the disease but the entire family. It destroyed ours.' She sat up on the couch and turned to face him, sitting cross-legged on the cushions. She didn't know how to make him understand the horror of this disease. 'You can spend thirty or forty years of your life being perfectly fine and then, one day, your world starts to crumble. Just little things at first, a slight change in your personality or moods, some forgetfulness—things that you probably won't even notice but your family will. And then depression might be the next thing or your motor functions will deteriorate. You'll start to stumble or have trouble holding your knife and fork. Over the next fifteen or twenty years your body and your brain decay and there's nothing you can do.

'Nick and I watched our mother suffer through this. Our father left us to do that alone. I was nine years old when her symptoms started. We did what we could until we couldn't cope any more. When I was twenty we had to put her into full-time care. She was forty-nine when she died. That is too young. Way too young. And the only reason she lived that long was because of us. I think she would have given up long before if it wasn't for us.

'That is why I didn't want to know if I carried the gene. I've seen what it does and it scares me. It terrifies me. But now I know. And that should be good news but now I'm frightened of what it means for my children. You need to understand what this could mean. I know how much you want children and, believe me, this isn't an easy decision. I would love children too but not if I have passed on a faulty gene.' She shook her head. 'Not Huntington's. It's too awful and I could never forgive myself. You need to understand what it is like.'

'What are you saying?'

'I want you to go and see someone who is suffering with late stage HD and then tell me if you could imagine seeing your own children suffer the same fate. Once you've done that I will agree to an amnio but *only* if you agree, in writing, that the pregnancy should be terminated if the tests are positive. If we don't get them tested while they are in utero then we have no control over anything and I can't have these babies without knowing their fate. And I can't have these babies if the test is positive either. If we don't get the tests done now then once the children are born they would have to wait until they turn eighteen before they could request testing and then, at this stage, if the test is positive there is *still* nothing that can be done. I want you to see what this disease looks like and I need you to remember that, right now, there is no cure. There is no way to stop the suffering.'

CHAPTER EIGHT

XAVIER STOOD IN the car park. He wasn't sure about this. He had agreed to Brighde's request as he couldn't imagine her terminating the pregnancy without doing an amniocentesis. And if he had to visit the care facility in order to meet her terms then he would.

She hadn't offered to accompany him and he hadn't asked her to. He knew she would refuse. She wouldn't want to see the patients here—he'd learnt that denial was her preferred way of coping—but she had given him the address. He wondered if this was where her mum had spent her last days or months or years. He didn't know. There was so much he didn't know. She didn't volunteer a lot and he was reluctant to ask her. He had no idea where he stood within the framework of her life. Did she trust him? Would she want to confide in him? How did she view him? Did she see him as the enemy? Someone who had gotten her into this position in the first place? Someone who wanted a different outcome from her? Was there a chance she could see him as someone permanent in her life or was she eager to cut him out of her life as quickly as possible? Would seeing him always remind her of this situation she was in? This awkward, unwanted situation? How did she feel about him? How did he feel about her?

There were far too many questions to tackle at the moment. He'd take one step at a time and the first step, before it was too late, was to try to convince Brighde to find out exactly what they were dealing with. To find out exactly what situation they were in. He didn't want to play guessing games and if he needed answers he needed to go inside the building. From the outside it looked harmless enough, ordinary even—a two-storey brick building, surrounded by gum trees. He could hear birds chattering and water flowing.

He was nervous but he couldn't stand outside all day. He headed for the front entrance. A fountain bubbled in front of the building. From the outside everything seemed calm and peaceful. In complete contrast to how he was feeling.

An elderly woman staffed the reception desk. Xavier hadn't really thought of how he was going to explain his visit here but he'd been hoping for a younger staff member. In his experience they were less likely to question his motives once they knew he was a doctor and, if he was honest, a young female employee wouldn't hesitate to let him have his way when it came to work.

'Good morning.' He flashed his best smile, deciding against the full charm offensive. He needed to present himself as a professional. That was the angle he was going to use. He pulled his identification from his wallet, his driver's licence and business card, and slid them onto the desk. 'My name is Dr O'Donnell; I was wondering if there was someone I could speak to regarding Huntington's Disease.'

The woman, who according to her badge was named Joyce, studied his ID before returning it to him. She looked up. 'What is it you want to know?'

'I'm an obstetrician and I have a patient who is pregnant and the baby has tested positive for Huntington's Disease.' He'd stretched the truth marginally but refused to feel guilty about a slight exaggeration of the facts. They were mostly accurate. 'She is considering a termination and I really don't have much idea about the disease and what she's dealing with. I'd like to get a better understanding of the condition.'

'You need to see Dr Baird,' came the reply, 'but she's not here at the moment. We don't have doctors on site. Would you like me to take your details and pass them on to her?'

Did he? He really wanted to see some of the patients. That was the task Brighde had set him. 'Is there someone else I could talk to while I'm here, one of the nursing staff maybe?'

Joyce frowned. 'I'm not sure,' she said. 'I'd have to check with the manager.'

'If you could, I'd really appreciate it.'

Joyce made a call. 'If you go up to the first floor, to the east wing, Steve, one of our RNs, will meet you there. But you'll need to sign the visitors' book first,' she told him as she handed him a visitor badge.

Xavier did as he was instructed; he signed in and then made his way to the east wing, where Steve was waiting for him.

He was a big burly man in his early thirties. His hair had a buzz cut and he was heavily tattooed but his uniform was neatly ironed, his shoes were polished and his nails clean. He looked like ex-defence force and Xavier wondered what made him work here. His look was unexpected but he must have chosen to work here and if he was here because he wanted to be, not just for the pay cheque, then Xavier had learned from experience that would make him an excellent nurse. It was a vocation, not just a job.

'Dr O'Donnell?'

'Xavier, please.'

'You want some information on HD?'

Xavier nodded and repeated his reason for the visit.

'We are one of the only care facilities in Australia to have a specialised HD unit. We can accommodate twenty sufferers at a time,' Steve told him as they walked along a corridor. 'Most people are cared for at home initially, until it gets too much for the families, either physically or emotionally. The majority of our HD patients need twenty-four-hour care, which becomes virtually impossible in a home environment.' Steve punched a code into an electronic keypad at the end of the corridor and pushed open the door. 'This is our day room.'

Steve stopped just inside the room and his voice was low and quiet as he explained the situation further to Xavier. 'The majority of our patients are late stage and many have lost the power of speech so you won't be able to talk to them. Many sufferers choose not to get to this stage; some choose to find another way out. Huntington's is hard on the sufferer and on the families. There's no cure. No hope. It's a waiting game; the end is just a matter of time.' Steve paused as Xavier looked around the room.

He saw several wheelchair-bound residents. Some were being fed but many had naso-gastric tubes, obviously no longer able to swallow. The room was large and light with pretty views out to the gardens and the gum trees but Xavier knew these patients would never walk out there and might not even remember what it was like to be mobile.

'You're wanting to know more about the impact on a family rather than the symptoms and progress of the disease, correct?' Steve asked. When Xavier nodded Steve added, 'Give me a minute, would you?'

He left Xavier and went to speak to an elderly woman who was spoon-feeding a younger woman. Xavier watched the interaction.

'Merilyn is happy to talk to you,' Steve said when he returned. 'She can give you her perspective if you like. Why don't you grab a coffee and take her outside?' he suggested. 'She could do with a change of scenery. She spends a lot of time with her daughter.'

Xavier bought sandwiches and coffee from the café on the ground floor and followed Merilyn to a wooden bench.

'You want to know what it's like living with Huntington's?' Merilyn asked as she sat down.

Xavier nodded. 'My partner—' he really had no idea how to describe Brighde and he suspected she'd have a fit if she could hear him but she wasn't there; this was all up to him and he was determined to find out everything he needed today; he didn't plan on coming back '—is pregnant. HD runs in her family and she is understandably concerned about the risk. She nursed her mother through the disease but I have no experience with it whatsoever and I'm trying to get an idea of what she went through. Of what we might be facing in the future.'

'You didn't use pre-implantation testing? That's been an option for years now.'

'We didn't plan the pregnancy,' Xavier admitted.

He could see the look of surprise on Merilyn's face but it was only there briefly before her expression went blank. She obviously had an opinion about their recklessness that she had decided to keep to herself.

'Are you going to test now? Before the baby is born?' she asked.

Xavier was appreciative of the fact that Merilyn had agreed to talk to him and he wanted to be honest even though he had no idea how she might interpret his candidness. 'I want to do the test but my partner wants to terminate. I'm not sure that I agree with her and that's why I'm here—to try to see things from her point of view.'

'Well, I can't speak for her but I can speak on behalf of the families of sufferers. I love my daughter and I would never wish that she hadn't been born but I *do* wish that she hadn't been born with HD. I wish that every day. It is a horrible disease.'

'But you chose to have a family.'

'The disease runs in my husband's family. Elise is forty-nine now and things were different fifty years ago. The disease was never talked about, never discussed, in his family and it was like that in many families who suffered the same fate. Because of the shortened life expectancy of sufferers, most die somewhere between their forties to sixties; many of us had already had children before we learned that there was a family history. It was brushed under the carpet and not spoken of, certainly never by its correct name, and a lot of sufferers were diagnosed with other afflictions—dementia, alcoholism and the like. Not a lot was known about HD when Norm and I got married—the gene was only identified in 1986—and even less could be done. Testing wasn't available when I had my children and pre-implantation testing wasn't available until Elise was nearly thirty-four. By then my husband had died from the disease. Elise and her sister had watched their father succumb to the disease.' She paused before asking, 'Are you sure you want to hear all this?'

Xavier nodded. 'As long as you don't mind talking about it.'

'My husband became aggressive and mean,' Merilyn continued. 'We had to keep reminding ourselves that this was a result of the disease, that he couldn't control it, but every day was a struggle to keep our family together. Elise was profoundly affected by the changes in her father and she decided early on that she wouldn't have children. She became a kindergarten teacher and those kids became her surrogate children.'

Brighde's choice of career sprang to Xavier's mind. She'd told him she'd never planned to have children, that she got her fill of babies at work. Had she chosen her career because of her family history?

Was he being unfair? Was he putting undue pressure on her? He hoped that if the babies were okay that she would be happy. But maybe she still wouldn't be. How did she really feel? She had told him she would love children of her own providing she hadn't passed on the gene but he had no idea if that was true. Maybe she really didn't want children, no matter what, and was using HD as an excuse. He really wasn't sure of the answers.

'I have two daughters and they both chose to get tested as soon as that was an option. Sometimes I wish they hadn't.'

'Why is that?'

'Carmel tested negative, Elise obviously didn't and that put a terrible strain on their relationship. They'd always been close until then. After the diagnosis, Elise got depression—it's a very common outcome—and that changed her long before her symptoms became apparent. Sometimes I think the diagnosis was the beginning of the end. She had no symptoms yet but everything changed from that day.'

Again, Xavier was able to see the similarities between Merilyn's family and Brighde's. Brighde and her brother had made a pact not to get tested for HD but what effect had Nick's change of mind had on Brighde? Would she be even more worried now, not only about her test results, but how that might affect her relationship with her brother? There were so many things to consider. So much more than just the physical aspects of the disease. He was beginning to understand just how complicated this all was and the stress that Brighde would be under.

'Elise's physical symptoms started about nine years ago but, by then, we had battled with her depression for six years already. Her balance was one of the first things affected. She had been a competitive swimmer but gymnastics might have been a better option to counteract the decline in her balance. At this stage the disease has affected her ability to walk, talk and think. Next to go will be her ability to swallow and she will end up being tube fed. I am seventy-four years old. It's taken forty years of my life and people would say I'm the lucky one, that I don't have the disease. But I've lived it twice over.'

Merilyn had nursed her husband and now her daughter. Xavier knew she'd been beaten down by the disease; he could hear it in her voice and see it in her face. Listening to Merilyn, he could hear how difficult her life had been. Not only had her husband and daughter been afflicted but even Merilyn's memories of them were being replaced by more recent, devastating memories. Her story was heartbreaking and he suspected it was very similar to Brighde's story.

He was so relieved that he hadn't asked Brighde to accompany him today—he hadn't really had any idea how emotional this would be—but, talking to Merilyn, he felt like he could be talking to a future Brighde. Her mother had died at forty-nine, the same age as Merilyn's daughter was now. That surely would have brought Brighde's memories to the fore and he was glad he hadn't subjected her to that.

He knew Brighde had watched her mother suffer, had nursed her through the early stages of the disease and was now facing the possibility of doing it all over again with her own child. *Their* child. And, potentially, both babies could be affected. Xavier knew he couldn't put her through that. It wasn't only the person with the faulty gene who suffered; it was the entire family.

'Do you have any words of advice for me?' he asked.

Merilyn shook her head. 'I'm not going to tell you what is right or wrong. I'm not going to give you any advice except to say that everyone has their choice to make and don't judge someone for what they choose to do or not to do. Not before you've walked a mile in their shoes.'

Xavier nodded and stood up. 'Thank you for talking to me; I really appreciate it.' And now he needed to talk to Brighde.

Sarah answered his knock on the door.

'Hi. Is Brighde home?'

'She's just gone down to the shops. Are you okay? You don't look well.'

He felt awful. Merilyn's insight had been an eye-opener for him. He'd done his research and thought he had been prepared for the visual side but he hadn't been prepared for the emotional side. Listening to Merilyn had been confronting. An awakening. An emotional punch in the face—there had been so many parallels between Brighde's life and Merilyn's. He wasn't surprised to hear he looked terrible. It had been a lot to absorb. 'I've just been to see some HD patients.'

'Oh.' Sarah stepped aside, holding the door open. 'I think you'd better come in. Brighde won't be long. Can I get you something to drink? You look like you could use a whisky.'

He would love a drink to take the edge off the pain he was feeling but he knew that was nothing compared to what Brighde had been through. 'No. Thank you, but I need to keep a clear head.'

'So, how did it go?' Sarah asked as he followed her inside. 'It's pretty confronting, isn't it?'

Xavier nodded. 'It was one of the worst things I've ever experienced and, considering I've been a doctor for ten years, that's quite a statement.'

'So you see why Brighde feels the way she does?'

'Yes, I can.'

'What are you going to do?'

'I'm going to speak to her again about having an amnio.'

If he wanted her to have the test he knew he had to agree with her conditions. If he didn't she could terminate the pregnancy without his consent *and* without getting tested. The amniocentesis was the only chance he had of convincing her to have the babies; therefore he had no choice but to agree to her decision regarding the pregnancy if the babies had a positive score on their CAG repeats. He knew that was the only way.

'If she agrees to the amnio you can't ask her to go through with the pregnancy if the test comes back positive. It would destroy her,' Sarah said. 'No matter what happens, she's already a victim of the disease. She lost her mother and lost contact with her father because of it. She's scared. You need to understand and respect that.'

Brighde held all the cards. He knew that. She'd lost both her parents because of the disease and he couldn't ask her to go through it again with her own child. She might not have the symptoms but if she had passed on the mutated gene she wouldn't escape the suffering or the guilt and he couldn't ask her to spend half a lifetime with her child only to then watch that life disappear in a terrible fashion. But he also couldn't agree to take a life now without knowing the future. If Brighde would agree to an amniocentesis, he would agree with her subsequent decision.

'I do. I get it. She's agreed to having an amnio on certain conditions. Having seen what I did today, I'm prepared to agree to her terms,' he said as they heard the sound of Brighde's key unlocking the front door.

Brighde was surprised to see Xavier sitting in her kitchen. She didn't think they'd made plans but she couldn't be one hundred per cent sure. She'd been extremely forgetful of late. She didn't think it was pregnancy brain, more likely a symptom of everything that was on her mind. There was no room for the little day-to-day things when her head was so full of big decisions that needed to be made.

'Hi. Sorry, have I forgotten something?'

'No,' he said as he stood up.

He looked uncomfortable. Uncertain. It was the first time she could remember seeing him ill at ease.

'Is something wrong?' she asked. He didn't look his usual robust self. He was still gorgeous—she doubted he could look anything else—but he looked exhausted, drained.

'You were right,' was all he said.

'About what?'

'Huntington's Disease and what it does.'

'You went to the care facility?'

He nodded.

'Are you okay?'

'Not really,' he admitted as they sat at the kitchen table. 'But this isn't about me. I spoke to a woman there. A mother. She was visiting her daughter. She'd nursed her husband and then her daughter. She was strong but you could tell it has destroyed her. You were right; I didn't understand what it was like. I'm not sure I really do, even now, but it's a lot clearer. The pain, the helplessness. I'm sorry I've made this difficult for you.' He picked up her hand. 'If you will have the amnio I will be guided by you when we get the results. It's all up to you.'

'Are you saying that if the result is positive you won't fight a termination?'

Xavier nodded. 'That's what I'm saying. But I need to ask: if the tests are negative what are your plans then? Would a negative test result change your mind about having a family of your own? Would you have the babies?'

'Of course.'

'You're happy about the pregnancy?'

'Not completely,' she admitted. 'Not yet. I never thought I would have children—you know I never planned to—but *if* the test is negative, if everything is okay, then yes, I will be happy. But I can't allow myself to think like that yet. I'm scared I might still be disappointed, that it will all come crashing down and that would be devastating.'

'There's something else,' he said. Brighde expected him to look pleased that she would be prepared to give him the children he was so desperate for but there was still a crease of concern running between his brows. 'Have you thought about what would happen if only one twin tested negative? What would you do then?'

Brighde frowned. It was a possibility, given that they suspected the babies were non-identical, but, once again, it was another thing she hadn't thought through. 'I'm not sure. Would selective reduction be an option, do you think?' She knew it was possible to abort one twin but she didn't know the details.

'Yes. But the further along the pregnancy is, the

more difficult that becomes. And there's also the risk of losing both. The longer you wait, the harder it is.'

'Even if Julie can do the amnio this week it will take a couple of weeks to get the results back. I'll be twenty weeks by then.' Her voice was laced with worry; she could hear it.

'That's okay, but it's something you need to think about over the next fortnight. I know you'd rather not have to deal with it but, if it comes to that, time will be of the essence. It's better to think about that scenario now so you're prepared.'

Brighde could see Xavier's point. She had to get all her facts straight. She needed to get her ducks in a row and then she'd be able to make informed decisions. That *had* to be better than making decisions based on guesswork.

She would make an appointment with Julie for an amniocentesis.

'Are you okay?' he asked as she sat on the edge of the examination bed. She'd asked him to accompany her this time. He was calm, unflappable and knew what to expect. She wouldn't have to explain anything to him or worry about him coping with the procedure. Sarah would have accompanied her but having Xavier there was the right thing to do. And she wanted him there.

She had never gotten over her father leaving her and Nick to cope with their mother's disease on their own and she was terrified of having to face more tragedy without support. 'I'm scared.'

It felt as if she was permanently afraid of late. This pregnancy was very real to her now. Her body was changing: her boobs were bigger, her stomach a little rounder. Her morning sickness had almost resolved and this morning she'd felt flutterings in her stomach that she knew was the babies moving. She would have loved to share that information with Xavier but she still didn't want to invest too much emotion into this pregnancy. It would destroy her if she got too attached, only to find out she had to terminate.

Her whole attitude had changed and now she was praying that her babies would be okay. She couldn't imagine the alternative. Not any more.

Xavier held her hand. 'I'm right here. You don't have to do this alone,' he said as Julie came into the room.

'Good morning. How are you feeling, Brighde?'

'I'm really nervous,' she admitted. 'And apprehensive.'

'About the test itself or the result?'

'Both.'

'The amnio may be a little uncomfortable—'

Brighde shook her head and interrupted. 'It's not the discomfort that's bothering me. It's the risk.'

'There's a small risk of miscarriage associated with amniocentesis,' Julie told her, 'The risk decreases after fifteen weeks' gestation so that's good news for you at eighteen weeks. There's no clear reason as to the cause of miscarriage; it may be due to infection or trauma to the amniotic sac. Here in Victoria it's about one in two hundred into the second trimester and my statistics are a bit better than that. In theory, about one in twenty women miscarry before twelve weeks but you do already have an increased risk because of a twin pregnancy. But, with regard to the amnio, because your twins are fraternal I need to take two separate samples. So the risk is the same but the likelihood of a miscarriage is slightly higher because you are having two needle aspirations. That's the facts. I'm not sure if that will help to put your mind at ease but you do need to know the risks before we go ahead. Do you still want to do this?'

Brighde knew she didn't really have a choice. As frightened as she was of having the procedure, she was more afraid of passing on the gene. This was the only way to know for sure. She nodded and squeezed Xavier's hand a little more tightly.

'I'll do the amnio under ultrasound guidance,' Julie said as she switched on the machine, 'so let's have a look at your babies.'

Brighde lifted her shirt and turned her eyes to the screen as Julie moved the transducer head over her abdomen.

'There's Twin A,' Julie said as the image of one tiny baby came onto the screen.

'He's a little footballer. Look at him kicking,' Xavier said. If Brighde hadn't been so nervous she would have smiled at the note of pride in his voice.

'Girls can play football too,' she said. With the way the baby was positioned she couldn't see anything to suggest the sex and she knew Xavier was just using a figure of speech but she was convinced both babies were girls.

Julie paused the image and clicked buttons, measuring the foetus. 'Fourteen centimetres. Just what we hope for at this stage.' She printed a picture and then moved the machine onto Twin B.

'She's sucking her thumb!' Brighde exclaimed.

'Do you want me to take the measurements for

foetal anomalies?' Julie asked as she measured Twin B's length.

'Can you do the amnio first?' Brighde asked. 'I want to get that over and done with.' She really was nervous about the test and wanted it out of the way as soon as possible.

'Of course,' Julie replied. 'Now, the results are about ninety-nine per cent accurate. Do either of you have any questions before I begin?'

Xavier and Brighde both shook their heads.

'I'll just put a bit of local anaesthetic on your tummy, Brighde, and call the technician to monitor the ultrasound.'

Julie gave the anaesthetic time to work but when she pulled out the long, thin biopsy needle Brighde turned her head. She didn't want to watch the procedure. She held on tight to Xavier's hand and kept her eyes focused on his gorgeous face. He smiled at her and kissed her. The kiss was unexpected and Brighde's heartbeat picked up its pace. If his intention was to distract her it was working.

Xavier had been so gentle and considerate recently. He was thoughtful and gorgeous and just what she'd imagined she'd look for in a boyfriend if she'd ever let herself have one. But even though they were spending time together she hadn't slept with him again. She was trying hard to keep some distance between them. She didn't want things to become messy or awkward so, no matter how much she longed to share physical intimacy, she knew she couldn't risk it. Her heart was conflicted enough with the idea of a pregnancy; she couldn't afford to throw an intimate relationship with Xavier into the mix. She would love to be able to say he was her partner or boyfriend but that would be taking things further than she could handle at the moment.

'Do you want to know the sex of the babies?' Julie asked. 'The test will be definitive on that too.'

'I'm not sure,' Brighde replied. Even though she felt they were girls she hadn't actually thought about finding out. She hadn't dared to think too far ahead.

'Do you want to know what I think?' Xavier said.

'What?'

'I think we're having a pigeon pair. A boy and a girl.'

He sounded so certain that Brighde wondered if he'd glimpsed something on the ultrasound that she'd missed. 'Did you see something?'

'No—' he grinned and Brighde's heart did a little flip in her chest '—did you?'

She shook her head.

'What do you think they are?'

'Two girls.'

'Why?'

'I have no idea.'

'Shall we have a bet on it?'

'I am *not* betting on the sex of our children.'

'Why not?'

'I don't trust you. I think you saw something.'

'Cross my heart. Shall we find out officially?'

'No.' She didn't want to know for sure until they had the results and she'd made a decision about what would happen next. She felt knowing the babies' sex might strengthen the attachment she was beginning to feel and that would only make things more difficult if the results came back positive. She couldn't afford to get too attached. Just in case.

'Okay, I'm all done,' Julie said.

'Thank you,' Brighde said to Xavier.

'What for?'

'For distracting me.'

'Did it work?'

'Yep.'

'All right, next question,' Julie said. 'The anomaly scan?'

'I'm not sure,' Brighde said as she looked at Xavier. This test would check for other more common anomalies like Down Syndrome. Brighde didn't think she would terminate a pregnancy in that case but, like many other things, she and Xavier hadn't actually discussed this.

'It's not just for Down syndrome,' Julie said when Brighde posed the question. 'There are a whole host of things we look for. You know that. I will check the heart, kidneys, spine, palate and stomach plus take some further measurements of the head, abdomen and thigh and also check your placenta.'

Xavier was nodding. Of course he'd want the tests done. He liked to be prepared.

'Okay,' Brighde agreed.

It took another hour to scan both babies, by which time Brighde thought her bladder would burst, but Julie hadn't finished with her yet.

'Miscarriage will usually occur in the first seventy-two hours after testing so I recommend that you take it easy for the next few days,' she said as she helped Brighde to sit up. 'You don't need bed rest but you have got time off work, right?'

Brighde nodded. 'Three days.'

'Good. Tell me if I'm singing to the choir, won't you, but I know from when I was pregnant myself that being on the other side of the fence is a very different experience. So much of your medical knowledge seems to disappear into the ether when it's your own children. So, don't forget about what can be perfectly normal happenings after an amnio. Things like mild, period-like cramping abdominal pains with some light spotting. You can take paracetamol to help ease the pain. The results will take a couple of weeks. I'll call you to schedule an appointment when the results are back.'

'You know,' Xavier said once Julie had left the room, 'during the amnio you said "our children". That's the first time you've said that.'

Brighde frowned. 'No, it isn't.'

'Yes, it is. You've said "my children" and "your children" but never "our children". Does that mean you've been thinking that we might be able to make a go of this? That maybe we could have a future. Not just co-parenting but the two of us, together.'

'What do you mean? Together?'

'I think we should get married.'

'What? Why on earth would you want to get married?'

'It's not about getting married. It's about showing you my commitment. To you and the babies. Showing you that, whatever happens, you can rely on me. That I'll be there to support you.'

'Marriage is no guarantee of that. Trust me, I know. And I'm still no closer to knowing what I'm going to do yet, Xavier. I'm not making any more decisions until we get the results of the amnio back. I'm not doing anything until I know my children's future.'

'Our children.'

'Our children.' She did like the sound of that phrase and she couldn't disagree—he'd been very considerate and supportive of her so far—but marriage was no guarantee of commitment. She'd seen evidence of that first-hand with her own parents.

'Would you think about it at least?' he asked. 'If not from your point of view, how about from the babies'? Surely having parents who are married gives them that stability and surely that is best for them?'

She couldn't help but wonder if his suggestion was only tied in to his desire to be a father. Was it his way of making sure she couldn't leave him out?

'Don't be ridiculous. The babies won't know and won't care if we're married. Having two parents who love each other is best for children. Having parents who are going to live a long, healthy, happy life is best for the children. As a matter of fact, having a parent who would not choose an early death sentence for a child is best for the child. Marriage isn't the answer.'

'But it's my promise. My way of showing you that I will be there for you and our children,' he argued.

'You can't promise that. And I've told you, I'm not going to inflict this disease on my children—that's why we're doing these tests—and if they have escaped the mutation there is still no reason to get married. Any promises you made would only be false ones if there's no relationship between us to begin with.' Xavier wasn't in love with her. How could she trust him to stick around and support her if they started out with nothing substantial between them in the first place? 'I don't *want* to get married.'

'Why not?'

'Because relationships don't last. Marriages don't last. Not even love is enough to get people through the tough times and there is no way I can trust a marriage that is based on a misguided sense of duty to survive.'

'It's more than duty,' he said. 'We have plenty of chemistry. That's something. I know marriages that have started with less.'

'Chemistry isn't enough to get us past our first wedding anniversary, let alone all the obstacles we could be facing. Neither of us should expect everlasting married happiness, given what we've seen. Your girlfriend cheated on you and my father walked out on us.'

'We are not those people. What they did doesn't define us.'

But Brighde had spent too many years avoiding relationships to change her mind that easily now. There was a reason she didn't date. She didn't want to fall in love. To fall in love was to risk everything.

And while knowing she wasn't going to develop HD had unlocked an alternative door to her future, she still couldn't afford to think about marriage yet—no matter how much she wanted to. She had to wait for the results of the amniocentesis now before she could think ahead and, regardless of those results, she couldn't have it all. Xavier wasn't offering his love and she refused to be married to someone out of an obligation.

She shook her head. 'I can't marry you.'

* * *

'I don't know what to do.'

Xavier sat at his sister's kitchen table, nursing a whisky. Mary's husband was putting the kids to bed and Xavier was picking Mary's brains. Her suggestion to get Brighde out of Melbourne and into a fresh environment had prompted their trip to Daylesford and he hoped she'd have more good advice this time. 'I know Brighde's stressed about the amnio results but she's barely speaking to me.'

'You can't blame her for being stressed. From what you've told me, it's a terrible disease and she must be worried sick that one or both of the twins might have it. She must be terrified and I can't imagine that she's got the energy to worry about you too. I know what it's like. Sometimes there's a limit to what you can focus on. Give her time.'

'But we need to think about the future.'

'That's a bit difficult at the moment. The future might change in the blink of an eye, depending on the amnio results. If you want my advice, I'm telling you to just be patient. I know it's not always your forte. I know you don't like to wait, but there's nothing you can do about the test results and I don't think you can expect Brighde to move forwards until she has those.'

'I promised her that if the test results came back positive I wouldn't oppose a termination, but I don't think I can give the babies up.' Xavier could see Brighde's point of view about a termination but he still couldn't imagine ending the life of a child—his child. But he was fast running out of ideas of ways to get around her concerns.

'So what are your options?'

'I don't really have any. It's all up to Brighde.'

'As long as she knows you're there for her. That's what she needs at the moment.'

'I'm not sure that she wants that either. I asked her to marry me. She said no.'

'Why?'

'Why what? Why did I ask her to marry me or why did she say no?'

'Both, I guess.'

'I wanted her to know she has my support and I thought getting married would show her I meant to stick around. I thought she'd appreciate it after her father walked out on them when she was very young. That's really messed her up and I thought I was doing the right thing.'

'Her parents were married, weren't they?'

'Yes.'

'And her father still left. In Brighde's mind, marriage probably isn't the promise you think it is.'

'But marriage makes sense.'

'Getting married only makes sense if you love each other. Do you love her?'

Did he?

'She's going to be the mother of my children,' he replied, not sure he was ready to give an answer. He thought he'd been in love with his ex-girlfriend but that was nothing compared to the way he felt about Brighde. Brighde was different—she lit up his life and he couldn't picture his future without her in it. He thought he could be falling in love with her but she kept pushing him away.

'That's not necessarily love. Would you marry her if she wasn't pregnant? I know you love the idea of settling down, getting married, having a family of your own, but there are lots of ways to do that. Marriage may not be your only future. Brighde can still be in your future without marriage. There's nothing wrong with choosing to co-parent. Plenty of people opt for that and do it successfully. Marriage isn't for everyone.'

'But it is for me.'

'I know that but maybe it's not for Brighde. Give her some space. Don't crowd her but don't desert her either.'

'How do I do both?'

'You're a smart man. You'll figure it out. She *will* need you. She might not need a husband but she will need your support, no matter what happens. And if everything goes well she will need a father for her children—your children. Don't muck this up. Give her what she needs.'

She needed him.

No, she didn't.

But she did need someone to love her. And that someone was him.

He would tell her how he felt. He would give this one last shot. All or nothing, he decided. Go hard or go home.

Brighde opened her eyes and checked her alarm. Something had woken her but it was still half an hour before she needed to get up. She had taken three days off after the amniocentesis but she was due back at work today.

As she lay in bed she felt a fluttering in her belly. Maybe the babies had woken her. She smiled and put her hand on her stomach. She was scared to admit it but she had bonded with her babies and with every breath she took she hoped that they would be all right. That maybe they would all get through this. But she knew she wouldn't relax until the test results came back. There was still too much at stake.

She rolled onto her side. She would stay in bed for a little longer; there was no hurry to get up. She would lie still and see if she could feel any more tiny movements. She liked to think of the twins communicating with each other as they wriggled and kicked.

She waited until her alarm rang before getting out of bed but she had only taken four steps into the hallway when she felt a sharp pain in her side. That wasn't a fluttering; it was a strong cramp. She clutched her side and put her other hand on the wall to steady herself as she took a deep breath and waited for the cramp to pass. It subsided but, before she could move, she felt something warm running down the inside of her thigh. She put her hand between her legs. It came out red.

CHAPTER NINE

'SARAH!'

Brighde's voice echoed in the hallway, bouncing off the floorboards and the walls, and Sarah burst out of her room, spurred on by Brighde's cries. She took one look at Brighde, who was leaning against the hallway wall, her hand and legs smeared with blood.

Sarah's eyes were wide. 'We need to get you to the hospital.'

Brighde nodded mutely. Her heart was racing and her knees shook. She didn't want to lose her babies.

Sarah grabbed a cardigan and wrapped it around Brighde's shoulders. She yanked a towel from the linen cupboard, picked up her keys and both of their phones from the hall table and bundled Brighde into her car. 'Is Xavier's number in your phone?' she asked as she put her seat belt on.

Brighde nodded again and Sarah called the number. She heard her leave a message.

'Xavier, Brighde is bleeding. I'm taking her to Parkville.'

Sarah ended the call and pulled the car into the traffic as Brighde sobbed quietly in her seat. She had her hands resting on her stomach, willing these babies to stay put. These babies she'd never dreamed she would have were now the most important things in her life. She couldn't bear to lose them.

Sarah drove her car into the turning circle at the front entrance to the hospital and Xavier was the first thing Brighde noticed. He was pacing up and down the driveway, an empty wheelchair abandoned to one side. The moment he saw Sarah's car he was by the door, opening it almost before Sarah had stopped completely. He scooped Brighde into his arms and carried her to the wheelchair.

'I'll take her upstairs,' he said over his shoulder to Sarah.

He pushed Brighde into the foyer; avoiding the emergency department, he wheeled her to the lifts. 'I've called Julie. She'll meet us in Maternity,' he told Brighde as they waited. He didn't tell her everything would be okay. She knew he couldn't but she longed to hear those words anyway.

He wheeled her into an exam room and lifted her onto the bed.

She curled herself into a ball and faced the wall. She couldn't bear to look at him.

She wondered if it was something she'd done. Maybe she'd strained something? But she couldn't imagine how; she'd barely done anything for the past three days but that didn't stop her from worrying. From feeling guilty. She'd never forgive herself if she had caused this and she couldn't bear to look at Xavier. She couldn't bear to see any recrimination in his dark eyes.

She didn't need anyone else questioning her actions or wondering what had gone wrong. Because in her heart she knew that something was wrong. Something was *very* wrong.

There was way too much blood.

She heard the door open, heard Xavier greeting Julie.

She turned her head as she listened to Xavier telling Julie the little he knew.

Someone had to help her. Someone had to do something.

'I think I might be losing the babies,' she said as she burst into another flood of tears.

Xavier was by her side. He pulled a chair closer to the bed as he grabbed some tissues from the dispenser on the wall and pressed them into her hand. He sat beside her and stroked the hair back from her face.

'When did the bleeding start?' Julie asked as she snapped on a pair of surgical gloves.

'Maybe an hour ago,' Brighde told her. She wasn't really sure what the time was. Everything was a blur since she'd started to bleed.

'Are you in pain?' Julie asked as she attached monitors to Brighde to record her blood pressure, heart rate and oxygen saturation.

She was scared and anxious and felt as though her heart was breaking but she knew that wasn't what Julie was asking. 'No.' She'd only had the one cramp and, while it had been painful, it didn't come close to the pain in her heart.

Maybe it was nothing. Maybe it was just a bit of spotting. But in her heart she knew that wasn't the case.

Something had gone wrong. She could feel it.

'Any temperature?'

'I don't think so,' Brighde replied as Julie picked up the thermometer and popped it into her ear.

'That's normal,' she said as the thermometer beeped. 'Let's have a look, shall we?'

Brighde had come to hospital in the old T-shirt she'd worn to bed. She had Sarah's cardigan wrapped around her and a towel between her thighs. Her underwear was soaked in blood. Julie lifted Brighde's shirt and removed the towel. Brighde saw the look that Julie and Xavier exchanged as they examined the towel.

It was stained with dark red blood.

'I'll need to do a scan,' Julie said. 'That will show us what's going on.'

Brighde waited in silence while Julie got the machine ready and ran it over her abdomen. She couldn't speak. She couldn't think straight. All she wanted was to hear that her babies were fine.

Julie kept the screen turned away from Brighde and she didn't think she could bear the suspense. 'What can you see?'

'Twin B is fine. I can see a heartbeat and the rate is perfectly normal,' Julie said, keeping her eyes on the monitor.

'And Twin A? What about Twin A?' Brighde could hear a trace of hysteria creeping into her voice as Xavier picked up her hand and held it. Tight.

Julie was shaking her head. 'I'm sorry, Brighde; there's only one heartbeat.'

'No!'

'Let me see.'

'Brighde—'

She heard the note of warning in Xavier's voice

but she knew she wouldn't believe it until she'd seen it with her own eyes.

She turned to face him. His eyes were brimming with unshed tears. Shiny and bright.

'I need to see.'

He nodded slowly as Julie turned the screen to face her and moved the ultrasound head around, capturing the picture.

Two sacs, two tiny babies, but only one heartbeat.

Tears streamed down Brighde's cheeks. The front of her T-shirt was soaking wet. 'No! Why? What happened?'

'Often we don't know why these things happen,' Julie said as she lifted the transducer head from Brighde's stomach and the image disappeared.

Brighde lifted one hand, reaching for the screen, trying to bring her babies back. 'But they were both fine three days ago.'

'You had a viable pregnancy three days ago, but that's all we know.'

'Was it the amnio?'

'It could have been but I think it's more likely to be unrelated. The amniotic sacs are both intact and you don't have a temperature so I don't think there's an infection but I'll take a blood sample and we'll check that. As you know, there is a much higher rate of miscarriage with twin pregnancies. I'm sorry.'

'What happens now?' Brighde felt like she should know but her brain seemed to have completely shut down. Nothing made sense.

'I'm going to admit you. I want you to have bed rest for a few days.'

'I have to stay here?'

'I think it's the best place for you. We can keep an eye on you here. We need to make sure the bleeding stops and I need to monitor the other twin.'

'You think I might lose the other baby?'

'I couldn't say for certain. The twins were dizygotic and dichorionic—two sacs and two placentas—and being non-identical reduces the risk of both miscarrying. Plus your general health is good. These things are all in your favour, which lessens the likelihood of a second miscarriage, but I can't make any promises. So, for now we wait. There's nothing you can do. I'll take some blood and you rest and I'll see if I can get the amnio results through a little faster.'

'Once the bleeding has stopped, what then?' Brighde asked as Julie took a blood sample. 'What happens to the babies?'

'If you don't have any cramping and the blood tests are normal, so no sign of infection, then once the bleeding stops I will discharge you. We shouldn't need to do anything more except closely monitor Twin B.'

'And the other baby? What happens to the other baby?'

'The sac is intact. Both babies can stay in there for as long as possible. Given the chorionicity, your gestational age and your health, letting your pregnancy continue is low-risk. I don't want to do any unnecessary procedures.'

'Can you tell me if Twin A was a boy or a girl? I'd like to know.' She didn't ask Xavier. She had to know now.

'A boy.'

Brighde closed her eyes. She'd lost their son.

She opened her eyes. 'And the other one?'

'A girl.'

Xavier had been right. She turned to look at him. He had tears in his eyes but he hadn't said a word.

Did he blame her? Did he think this was her fault? She knew how much he wanted these babies; he'd made that perfectly clear on many occasions. Would he think this was her fault?

She didn't dare ask what he was thinking; she was too scared of the answer.

'We'll get you cleaned up and admitted,' Julie said, interrupting her thoughts. 'I'll be back to see you later.'

Brighde was in a private room, attached to a drip and various other electrodes, lying in bed while Xavier hovered. There was nothing for him to do; there was nothing he *could* do and his presence was irritating her. She still didn't want to look at him, still couldn't bear it. She didn't want to see her loss and despair reflected back at her from the depths of his eyes. She was feeling terrible enough already.

'Don't you have patients to see?' she asked.

'I've rescheduled or postponed them,' he replied. 'I can stay as long as you need me.'

'I don't need you. I think you should go.'

'What? Why?' She could see the confusion in his eyes. But that was better than accusations.

'Don't you see? I shouldn't even *be* pregnant. I've just lost one baby and I might lose the other one too. I shouldn't *be* in this position and I wouldn't be if it wasn't for you. Every time I look at you I'm reminded of what I've lost or might still lose. I don't want to see you. I just want to be alone.'

'Brighde, you don't have to be alone. I'm here for you.' He'd stopped pacing and was standing by her bed, a worried expression on his gorgeous face. He reached out one hand towards her but when she folded her arms across her chest, blocking him out, his hand dropped to his side. 'I'm hurting too, Brighde.'

'It's not the same. You've never lost anyone.'

'This baby was ours. Yours and mine. I've lost just as much as you have. Don't shut me out. I want this baby more than anything.'

Was that part of the problem? She knew it was. Xavier wanted the baby but he wasn't talking about wanting her any more. Had his suggestion of marriage been his way of making sure he was in his children's lives? Making sure she couldn't cut him out? She had never intended to do that but, right now, she just didn't want to see him. She needed some space. 'I don't want you here,' she said bluntly and she could see she'd hurt him but she was hurting more.

He stood, watching her silently, for what seemed like hours before, eventually, he nodded. 'I will go now but I'm not walking out of your life. You can keep sending me away but I'll keep coming back. I can be just as stubborn as you.'

Brighde closed her eyes and turned her head away, waiting until she heard him leave, until she heard the door close.

She was better off alone.

That was what she'd always thought but meeting Xavier had made her believe, just for a short while, that maybe she could have a happily ever after. But it seemed she'd been wrong.

This was all his fault. If she'd never met him she

wouldn't be pregnant. If she'd never met him she wouldn't be grieving for a child she'd never expected to have.

How could it hurt so much?

She just wanted to be loved. For her life to have a happy ending. But that was a foolish dream. Everything was unravelling. Everything was out of her control. She never should have let her guard down.

She'd always believed nothing good would ever come of letting someone into her life, into her heart. Well, now she had the proof.

If she'd had any tears left to cry she knew they would be falling. She didn't think her heart could take any more.

CHAPTER TEN

XAVIER LEFT THE room but he wasn't about to leave the hospital. He had nowhere else to go. He'd cancelled his lists so unless someone went into labour he had nowhere to go *and* nothing to do. He didn't think he could face delivering someone else's baby today. His heart was bruised, aching.

He'd lost his child. His son.

Brighde had said he'd never lost anyone before but that wasn't true. He'd lost once before. He remembered when he'd found out that his ex was expecting another man's child, that she wasn't pregnant with his baby. He remembered the day she'd taken that dream from him. He'd thought he could never feel worse than he had that day but to physically lose his own child, his own flesh and blood, was devastating. Heartbreaking.

These babies were real to him and he couldn't bear to think about potentially losing them both or not being allowed to have anything to do with the surviving twin. His daughter. If she made it.

He had to convince Brighde to let him back into her life. He wasn't prepared to lose another child or his chance of fatherhood.

He needed a plan. Another one. And this time it

would have to be the perfect plan. Flawless. Because he was in love with a woman who couldn't bear to look at him.

He hadn't had a chance to tell her that he loved her. Or maybe he just hadn't taken the chance. He'd been caught up with other priorities. Had his ex been right? Had he, once again, put too many other things before the important people in his life? Had he not given Brighde the priority she deserved?

He'd have to make things right. He had to let her know how he felt.

He gave her as much time as he could. He tried catching up on paperwork but found he couldn't concentrate. He tried catching up on journal articles—that was even worse—so eventually he gave up and returned to Brighde's room. She'd have to see him. There were some things that couldn't wait.

He was several rooms away from hers when he saw a couple knock on her door and enter. He couldn't see their faces but the woman was petite and dark and the man was tall and slim with hair the colour of Brighde's with the same thick wave. Was that her brother and sister-in-law? He hesitated. There were some things that couldn't wait but there were also some things that could only be said in private and this was certainly not a discussion he wanted to share with Brighde's brother on their first meeting.

He pulled a chair along the corridor and positioned it outside her room. He'd wait.

He sank into the chair. The adrenalin that had been pumping through him at the thought of declaring his feelings continued to surge through his body but, with no release, the energy it had created left him feeling exhausted. He stretched his legs out and leant back against the wall.

He could hear voices, snippets of conversation, coming from Brighde's room. He didn't mean to eavesdrop but he didn't have the energy to stand and walk away.

He was done walking away.

'You're pregnant?'

A female voice. The sister-in-law?

'Why didn't you tell us?'

Brighde's brother.

Xavier strained to hear her reply. He was interested—very interested—in the answer. He hadn't realised she'd kept her pregnancy a secret. Had she kept *him* a secret?

'Lots of reasons. But mostly because I didn't know what I was going to do about the pregnancy. I didn't know if I would go through with it. I didn't know if I *could.* I was worried about telling you—especially when Immy is pregnant too. I was worried about HD and how you would react if I chose *not* to be pregnant. This wasn't planned. Not at all.'

'What are you going to do?'

'I still don't know. I'm waiting on test results.'

'And the father? Who is he?'

'No one important.'

Pain pierced Xavier's chest. A pain so sharp it made him catch his breath. Was that really how she felt about him? He was imagining a life with her and yet she could dismiss him so easily? Her words cut him to the core. Surely she didn't mean them?

'Does he know about the baby?'

'He knows.'

'And what does he think?'

'That doesn't matter. This was all a mistake. A big mistake.'

Xavier had heard enough. He summoned his energy and stood and walked away. He would retreat but he would return.

His problems were multiplying. He was in love with a woman who wanted nothing to do with him. That presented a challenge but he wasn't defeated. Not yet.

It had been forty-eight hours since their loss and Brighde was still refusing to see him. Sarah had given him some brief reports but nothing she said eased his concerns. Brighde was barely talking to Sarah either and Sarah suspected she wasn't eating properly. Xavier was concerned she was in real danger of sinking into a depressed state of mind.

He had snuck in late at night to watch her sleeping. She'd been curled into a tight little ball, elbows flexed, hands tucked under her chin. A defensive position. She hadn't looked relaxed even though she was asleep and his heart ached and his arms longed to hold her.

He had finished his morning visits and was hovering near Brighde's room, hoping to catch Julie as she finished her rounds. He saw her walking towards him, a frown between her eyebrows.

'What's going on?' she asked him as she approached.

'What do you mean?'

'I've just seen Brighde to give her the results of her second blood test.'

'Her *second* test?' His heart hammered in his chest. What was wrong now?

'Yes. I asked if she wanted to wait for you. She implied you weren't here.'

'I'm here. I've barely left the hospital for the past few days. What did the blood work show?'

'You know I can't give you Brighde's results,' Julie said as she shook her head. 'You'll have to ask her.'

He hated the rules. The fact that Brighde was the only one with a say. That the father had no rights. 'She's not talking to me,' he admitted. 'She doesn't want me anywhere near her and, from what I hear, she's not doing too well. I'm worried about her but she's not telling me anything.'

Julie considered him carefully before she spoke and he could almost see the wheels turning in her mind. 'Can I ask your professional opinion about one of my patients?'

'Sure.'

'She's a first-time mum who has just lost a baby, a twin. All her blood work has come back clear, no sign of infection, and she's generally healthy.'

'No infection, you said?'

'That's right. I think the miscarriage was probably related to the twin pregnancy. Maybe there was something wrong with the baby but everything seems okay now and she's recovering well, physically, from the loss and I could discharge her but I'm worried about her mental health. We are still waiting on some other test results so I'm considering keeping her here for a couple more days until those results come back. It's not really necessary but I'd feel better if I could keep a close eye on her. What would you do if she was your patient?'

'I'd definitely keep her in.'

'I thought so. Right. Thanks.'

Imogen had been in several times over the past four days, bringing with her pictures of wedding dresses, wedding cakes and bouquets. Brighde knew she was trying to distract her but she wasn't able to get enthused about anything at the moment. Her concentration was shot and she just wasn't interested in what was going on in other people's lives. It was very unlike her but she couldn't shake herself out of the despondency that had settled over her. She wasn't sleeping or eating properly either, which she knew was only making things worse, but her appetite had deserted her along with her sense of humour.

Now it seemed it was Sarah's turn to try to jolly her out of her slump. Although she'd chosen a strange topic to try to cheer Brighde up.

'So, have you seen Xavier?' Sarah asked as she rearranged a bunch of flowers on the bedside table, pulling out a few sad, droopy stems in an effort to revitalise the display.

Brighde wished she could do the same to her. Pull out the sad pieces of her heart and plump it up with some fresh water. She wished it was that easy to bring her back to life.

'No.' She still wasn't ready to see him. To see the sadness in his eyes. She didn't have the energy to deal with his grief as well as her own.

'You can't put it off for ever. He is still going to be the father of your child.'

'I know.' But there was still a possibility that she could lose this baby too and then there would be no need to see Xavier. There would be no need to have anything to do with him. She was convinced he was only interested in their child and where did that leave her? 'But I could lose this one too. There's no point in speaking to him until I know for certain what's going on. I haven't even got the amnio results back yet.' The lack of information was hanging over her head like a big black cloud.

'You are nineteen weeks pregnant. This baby looks perfectly happy; there's no reason to think anything untoward will happen. If everything comes back clear, which I'm sure it will, then I think you two need to have a serious conversation.'

'About what?'

'Life, the universe and everything in between. You are going to have to find a way to work things out. You'll be tied together for ever through this baby. If you wanted to you might even get to live happily ever after.'

'I don't think so,' Brighde said with a shake of her head. 'He doesn't love me.'

'Has he told you that?'

'He hasn't told me he does. Everything he's done has been about the baby,' she replied just as her OB/GYN entered the room.

'Good morning, Brighde,' Julie said as she breezed in. Everyone's spirits seemed high today, Brighde thought. Everyone, that was, except for her.

'Please, can I wait just a bit for another ultrasound?' Brighde asked, assuming that Julie was planning another scan. She'd been checking the baby regularly and Brighde knew her little girl was developing well. Julie would show her the images on the screen but Brighde always had to battle to avoid thinking about the baby Julie *wasn't* showing her. Her little boy. Where there had been two babies to keep an eye on, now there was only one. Where there had been two heartbeats there was now only one and Brighde wasn't feeling up to coping with that today. Not straight after her conversation with Sarah, which had filled her head with thoughts of Xavier.

'I'm not here to do an ultrasound,' Julie replied, pulling a letter from the pocket of her white hospital coat. 'I have the results of your amniocentesis.'

'Oh.' Brighde could feel sweat gathering on her upper lip.

This was it. She would no longer be able to put things off. No longer be able to hide behind the excuse that she didn't have all the facts. She was about to find out, once and for all, just exactly what she was dealing with.

'Do you want me to look at the results first or would you like to do it?' Julie asked.

Brighde shook her head. 'You do it,' she replied. She knew she wouldn't be able to even open the envelope. Her hands were shaking and she was terrified of what she might find. No, it was much better to be told the results. She couldn't bear to have to read it for herself.

'Do you want to wait for Xavier?' Julie asked.

Did she? She wasn't sure.

No. It was better to get this over and done with quickly, like pulling off a sticking plaster. She didn't want to delay the inevitable and this way there would be time then for her to digest the information before she would have to share it with anyone else.

She shook her head. 'No. I'll tell him later.' Once she'd had time to compose herself, if necessary.

She reached for Sarah's hand and held it tight as she closed her eyes. 'Okay.'

She could hear the rustle of paper as Julie opened the envelope and pulled out the contents. Brighde held her breath and kept her eyes closed.

'Two tests,' she heard Julie say. 'Both negative.'

She hadn't passed on the defective gene. She felt the tears well up as reality took hold. Both her babies would have been fine. If they'd both survived. But she'd already lost one.

Sarah was by her side before the sadness could overcome her. She wrapped her arms around Brighde, providing comfort. 'It's okay. You'll have a healthy child who will have every chance of living a long life,' she said, understanding what was going through Brighde's mind while reminding her of what was important.

Everything she'd been worried about hadn't come to pass. She had much to be grateful for. She would have a healthy baby. She needed to be strong and focused now. She could still mourn her loss but her daughter deserved all her attention now.

It was hard to believe. She was going to be a mother and Xavier would get the child he wanted. Their daughter.

Xavier.

'Shall I get him?' Sarah asked.

'Get who?'

'Xavier,' came Sarah's reply and Brighde realised that she'd spoken his name out loud.

She nodded. He deserved to know the outcome.

She had no reason to delay. They would have to work out their arrangements. They needed to have a discussion about what would happen next.

Brighde caught her breath when Xavier walked into the room. She hadn't seen him for four days but it felt like weeks and she'd almost forgotten how gorgeous he was. His familiar scent of honey and pear followed him in, wrapping around her. God, she'd missed him.

He looked divine but he also looked miserable.

She'd done that to him and she felt terrible. This separation had all been her fault. She knew she had been unfair. She couldn't put all the blame on him but it had been easier to shut him out than to see him. Seeing him just reminded her of what she'd lost.

But she hadn't lost everything—she was going to have a healthy baby—but her behaviour meant that she had lost more than she needed to. She'd lost one baby and pushed Xavier away. Xavier who, just possibly, might have been the love of her life.

But she was too proud to admit that.

'Sarah said you wanted to see me?' He looked utterly dejected. She wanted to put a smile back on his face and she hoped her news would do that. She hoped she hadn't made such a mess of things that she couldn't fix it. She hoped she hadn't left it too late.

She nodded. All the anger she'd felt had dissipated and now she was just sad that that things hadn't worked out. Tears welled in her eyes but she fought them back. This wasn't a time for tears. Crying would be self-indulgent. She owed Xavier an explanation. She owed him the truth. There would be time for tears later.

He took a step closer. 'What's happened?' he asked. Had he seen the tears in her eyes?

'Nothing,' she replied as the tears spilled from her lashes; triggered by the concern in his voice, she couldn't hold them back.

'Shh.' He was by the bed now. He sat down and took her in his arms. She closed her eyes and leant against him as he stroked her hair. 'It's okay. I'm here.'

He kissed her forehead and waited for her to calm down. Waited for her tears to subside. She sniffed as she got her emotions under control.

'Are you sure everything's okay?' he asked as he passed her a tissue.

She nodded again and took the tissue from him, aware that she was still clutching the piece of paper that Julie had left with her.

'I'm glad you asked for me,' he said as she blew her nose. 'There are some things I need to tell you.'

Brighde steeled herself for bad news. She couldn't believe that today could only bring good news. That wasn't how her life worked. Good news was always followed by bad.

'I need to talk to you,' he continued. 'I've had some time to think since you banished me.' He put a finger on her lips as she opened her mouth to protest. 'It's okay, I probably deserved it. I realise that I might have made too much of an issue about your pregnancy and the babies and not enough about you. This isn't just about the baby. I want the whole deal. The baby and you.'

'Xavier, we've discussed this. You don't have to make promises just to ensure you see your daughter. I'm not going to cut you out of her life.'

'That's not what I'm doing. I know I didn't give your feelings, your needs priority. I didn't give *you* priority. I was doing exactly what my ex-girlfriend accused me of, putting everything else ahead of a relationship. My work, the decisions about our children, and forgetting about you and what you need. I made a mistake. One I'd like to rectify if you'll give me a chance. I don't want to lose you. You're too important to me. I want you in my life, not because you are the mother of my child but because I love you.'

'You love me?'

'I love you and I want to share my life with you. Not co-parenting. I want it all. I want us to have a future together, a family together.

'You know, you were right, this wasn't how I would have planned to have a family, but I'm glad it's you. You captivated me from the moment I first saw you and when I learned you were pregnant I could imagine us as a family, but now, even more than that, I can imagine us as a couple. You are strong, brave, honest and beautiful and I don't want to think of my life without you in it. Things happen for a reason and I think we were supposed to meet.

'You challenge me, you can be stubborn and opinionated but, according to my sisters, I need that, and according to me I need you. And I'd like you to give me a chance. To see if there's any way you could love me too. We've got four months to ourselves. To spend some time together. You might even decide you like dating me. And then we can work out what is best for us as well as for the baby. I promise not to mention marriage again, not until you're ready, but I want us to do this together. What do you think?'

'I like the sound of that.' Brighde smiled, almost afraid to believe this was really happening. 'I'm sorry I shut you out.'

'It's okay. I know you were scared. There were so many things we couldn't control but I meant it when I told you I had no intention of going anywhere. I know you felt alone and I was trying to make sure you knew I would be there for you, but I should have told you sooner how I felt. I'm not about to walk away from the best thing that's ever happened to me. And, just to be clear, I'm talking about you. Our baby is the icing on the cake. I know you are reluctant to make any commitments until you have the test results back but I wanted you to know how I feel *before* then. I can be patient, despite what my sisters might tell you. I can give you the time and space you need, but it was important to me to tell you how I feel. I love you and I want to be a part of your life. Regardless of what happens with this pregnancy.'

'We need to talk about that. That's why I needed to see you. I need to speak to you about the baby.' She held up the piece of paper. 'I got the amnio results back just now.'

'Oh.' That worried look was back in his eyes but this time Brighde knew she could erase it. He loved her and she had a chance of getting everything she wanted. They both did. 'And?' he asked.

Brighde grinned. 'She's fine. She tested negative.'

'Everything is okay?'

She nodded.

'Really? You're certain?'

She handed him the results and waited while he scanned the page.

His answering smile was enough for her. More than enough. But he followed it with a kiss. A lingering kiss on her lips that brought her back to life. He loved her. His kiss was the water for her damaged heart and it swelled with love for him as his kiss nourished her.

'So, what do you think?'

'Do you really love me?'

'I do.'

She didn't think she would ever get tired of hearing that. 'I find it hard to believe I can get good news and to have two lots in one day, it's almost too much.'

'Every day can be a good day if we are together.'

'I can't believe I almost blew my one chance at my own happily ever after.'

'You didn't blow it. I'm right here and here I intend to stay, if you'll have me. Do you think there's room for me in your life?'

'Yes,' she said as her smile threatened to split her face in two. 'Definitely.'

'What do you think of this one?' Xavier asked as he pushed a pram back and forth on the shop floor. 'We can add a toddler seat to it later.'

Brighde didn't mind which pram they got; she just wished he'd hurry up and choose one. Her back was aching and she wanted to get home and put her feet up. She knew they had to choose a pram, and a bassinette of some description, as they were running out of time to get organised. She was booked in for a Caesarean section next week, but she was having trouble concentrating. She rubbed her stomach as a ripple of pain ran across her abdomen.

'Are you okay?'

'I think I need to sit down,' she replied as a second spasm gripped her, hard and fast and low in her belly. She gasped as the pain made her catch her breath. That was way too close to the first one.

'Was that a contraction?' She could hear the concern in Xavier's voice. She didn't want him to worry. She needed him to keep her calm.

'I'm not sure,' she said, but what she really meant was, *It's too soon. I'm not ready to have a baby.*

And then Xavier was beside her. Right where she needed him to be. He took charge, took control, took care of her and she felt her panic ease. As long as he was beside her she would be okay.

'Congratulations. She is perfect,' Julie said as she handed Brighde her daughter.

She was early and tiny but she was perfect. Ten fingers, ten toes and downy blonde hair. She grasped Brighde's finger and looked up at her with blue-grey eyes.

'Hello, Bessie.' She and Xavier had agreed to name her after Brighde's mum. It was the perfect name; she was a miniature version of her grandmother.

'You did it.' Xavier leant over and kissed her forehead.

Brighde lifted her face, meeting his lips with hers. 'We did it.' She smiled. 'Together.'

'Xavier?' Julie interrupted. Xavier straightened

up and Brighde held her breath as Julie passed her husband a second blanket-wrapped baby. Their son.

'Can I hold him?' she asked.

The midwife took Bess. 'I'll clean her and do her name tags,' she said as Xavier laid their baby boy on Brighde's chest.

'Hello, my darling.' He was exceptionally small, still the size he had been at eighteen weeks, but he was recognisable as a tiny person. Brighde's eyes filled with tears but she refused to be sad. Not today.

She held him for a long time but her arms longed to hold Bess too.

'There's a cuddle cot in here,' Xavier told her. 'Would you like to use that and then you can say goodbye when you are ready?' Had he seen the longing in her eyes? The dilemma she was facing? She wasn't ready to say goodbye but she needed to cuddle Bess. Her arms needed to hold her daughter.

She nodded. The refrigerated bassinette was the perfect solution. She could keep her son with her until they were ready to let go.

Xavier lifted him from her arms and the midwife returned Bess to her.

'Are you okay?' he asked.

'Yes.' She had Xavier beside her and their daughter. She had more than she'd ever thought possible. 'I am.' She smiled at the father of her children. 'I have everything I need.'

'There's one more thing I need,' Xavier told her as he put their son into the chilled bassinette and wheeled it closer to Brighde. 'I need us to be a proper family.

I love you and I want to be your husband. I want to give you commitment and security and love. I want the world to know we are a family. Will you marry me?'

EPILOGUE

BRIGHDE STOOD AT the end of the aisle and took a minute or two to savour the moment. She'd never dared to dream that she would have this day—a wedding of her own—and she wanted to be able to remember every second. She only intended to do this once.

'Are you ready?'

She turned to her brother. He stood beside her, strong and steady, waiting patiently to walk her down the aisle. For so long it had been just the two of them but now Nick had a wife and baby of his own and today it was her turn to extend the family just a little more.

She nodded and tucked her arm through Nick's as the organist started to play. She was vaguely aware of the guests swivelling in their seats as they turned to watch her make her entrance but she only had eyes for Xavier.

He was waiting for her at the altar. Her stomach did a little flip as he met her gaze with his come-to-bed eyes. She hoped she never got used to the effect he had on her whenever she saw him.

She kept her eyes on him as she walked down the aisle. He was wearing the dark navy suit he'd worn on the night they'd met. His hair was a little shorter but still had the wildness in the curl and his thighs were just as lean and powerful under the fabric, his shoulders just as broad. The suit wasn't necessarily traditional wedding attire but Brighde suspected she'd fallen in love with Xavier on that very first night and she wanted a little reminder of that evening. Although, she conceded, the suit was probably unnecessary as Xavier held another, far more precious reminder in his arms. Their four-month-old daughter, Bess.

Nick put Brighde's hand into Xavier's and took his niece, leaving Brighde and Xavier alone at the front of the church.

Xavier squeezed her hand and smiled. 'You look beautiful.'

Brighde got lost in his eyes and, despite her plan of memorising every minute, she scarcely heard a word the priest said. All she could focus on was Xavier, the love of her life, and the fact that they were about to officially become a family.

'I now pronounce you husband and wife.'

Brighde tuned back in as the priest said the words she'd been waiting to hear.

'You may kiss the bride.'

Xavier turned to her. He was grinning from ear to ear as he cupped her face in one hand and tilted her head towards him before bending to kiss her.

She closed her eyes as his lips found hers. She reached for him, her fingers curling around the back of his neck, holding him to her, never wanting to let him go as they sealed their commitment to each other.

'And now, if the godparents could bring Bess up

to join us,' the priest invited as Xavier and Brighde finally broke their kiss.

Today was going to be a double celebration. While family and friends were already gathered, Brighde felt it was the perfect time to christen Bess as well. Sarah carried Bess to the baptismal font, her maid of honour duties temporarily suspended as she, along with Xavier's sister Mary and her husband, took on their responsibilities as godparents.

'Brighde and Xavier, what name have you given your child?'

'Elizabeth Marie O'Donnell.'

Bess had been named after both her grandmothers, although she remained the spitting image of Brighde's mum. Brighde thought about the son they'd lost. He was a constant presence in her subconscious and she knew she'd never forget him. Each milestone Bess marked would be another reminder but the pain and sorrow Brighde felt was lessening with time. She had a lot to be thankful for and plenty to look forward to.

Mary held Bess above the font as the priest continued the proceedings. 'Elizabeth Marie, I baptise you in the name of the Father,' he said as he poured warm water over her blonde curls, 'and of the Son—' Brighde waited for the tears to start but Bess was quiet until the second wetting '—and of the Holy Spirit.'

She started crying in earnest now, reaching her chubby little hands out to her father as Mary lifted her from the font. She settled the moment she was in Xavier's arms. She was such a daddy's girl but Brighde could understand why. She loved him just as fiercely and felt just as safe and secure when she was in his arms.

She smiled as she looked at her family. It was a perfect day, surrounded by everyone she loved, and she couldn't ask for anything more.

* * * * *

LET'S TALK
Romance

For exclusive extracts, competitions
and special offers, find us online:

 facebook.com/millsandboon

 @MillsandBoon

@MillsandBoonUK

Get in touch on 01413 063232

For all the latest titles coming soon, visit
millsandboon.co.uk/nextmonth

MILLS & BOON

THE HEART OF ROMANCE

A ROMANCE FOR EVERY READER

MODERN

Prepare to be swept off your feet by sophisticated, sexy and seductive heroes, in some of the world's most glamourous and romantic locations, where power and passion collide.

HISTORICAL

Escape with historical heroes from time gone by. Whether your passion is for wicked Regency Rakes, muscled Vikings or rugged Highlanders, awaken the romance of the past.

MEDICAL

Set your pulse racing with dedicated, delectable doctors in the high-pressure world of medicine, where emotions run high and passion, comfort and love are the best medicine.

True Love

Celebrate true love with tender stories of heartfelt romance, from the rush of falling in love to the joy a new baby can bring, and a focus on the emotional heart of a relationship.

Desire

Indulge in secrets and scandal, intense drama and plenty of sizzling hot action with powerful and passionate heroes who have it all: wealth, status, good looks…everything but the right woman.

HEROES

Experience all the excitement of a gripping thriller, with an intense romance at its heart. Resourceful, true-to-life women and strong, fearless men face danger and desire - a killer combination!

To see which titles are coming soon, please visit

millsandboon.co.uk/nextmonth